THE
CHILL

THE
CHILL

SCOTT CARSON

W

WELBECK

Published in 2020 by Welbeck Fiction Limited, part of Welbeck Publishing Group
20 Mortimer Street London W1T 3JW

First published in the United States by Emily Bestler Books/Atria Books,
an imprint of Simon & Schuster, in 2020

A CIP catalogue record for this book is available from the British Library

ISBN: 978-1-78739-513-8

Printed and bound by CPI Group (UK) Ltd., Croydon, CR0 4YY

10 9 8 7 6 5 4 3 2 1

Thinking of Thad Beaumont and George Stark

"Sometimes I feel that the stories were written by them to me, asking me to communicate their sorrows and explain their dreams."

—Kenneth Millar

Presque vu:
"The phenomena and events in the visual field point in a certain direction; that is, they suggest an end which is not quite reached, or they lack proper completion . . ."

—Heinrich Klüver

"He also added, somewhat apocalyptically, that the dam would represent a perpetual menace to towns downstream."

—Bob Steuding, *The Last of the Handmade Dams: The Story of the Ashokan Reservoir*

PART ONE

1

Molly packed a black silk bag that could be worn as a hood, because she did not want her eyes to open again until she was back in Galesburg.

The bag was soft and lovely but it was also thick and dark, a stronger shield than the burlap sack or simple white pillowcase that she'd considered. And a kinder shield than the black garbage bag.

She put the silk bag inside her purse beside the spools of heavy saltwater fishing line and the long stainless steel hooks. The iron chains and padlock were already hidden on the bluff above the lake.

The sight of the hooks quickened her pulse, but she didn't pause, simply folded the silk bag on top of them and closed the purse. She was a stoic woman and took pride in it. *Unflappable*, her father had called her once when she was a girl, and she'd taken pride in that, too. That was back when the town was emptying out, fewer families left each day, and each night her father took to his chair on the front porch and sat with his shotgun across his lap, prepared for the looters. He was wary of them but not enraged by them. He insisted the real looters had come from the state, and that the dam across Cresap Creek was the real theft.

The rest of this, he said, all rippled out from that first crime. Condemn a town and what did you expect to happen? Sin would flow downhill then, and the town would be left lawless and ungoverned after the ribbon-cutting was held.

She didn't know if he slept at all those nights. In the mornings, he kept the gun in hand while he walked Molly to school. They would pass the ancient one-room wooden structure where he'd been educated, and he would nod at it or gesture with the barrel of the 12-gauge and tell her how much better it had been back then. Less greed, he always said. Less greed and more principles. Back then, Galesburg was a community rather than a place.

Then he would walk her to the top of the concrete steps in front of the new but already condemned brick school, watch her open the door, and give her a smile and wave, the shotgun held in his free hand.

She would smile back, refusing to show fear, not even in the final days when she was the only pupil in the school, when she sat alone at her desk in the two-story brick building with all of its strange sounds. Or, stranger still, its absence of sounds.

She was Molly Mathers, and she was unflappable. Stoic.

Decades had passed since then, but her temperament hadn't changed. When she left her bedroom, she was tempted to pause and look in the mirror, to stare at her own image as if it were another person and offer that woman a farewell. That was overly dramatic, though. Unnecessary. She passed by the mirror, knowing that the only face she needed to see today was her granddaughter's. Of course, that meant a stop by the school. Molly dreaded setting foot in the school, but it had to be done.

She walked out of the bedroom, shut the door behind her, and went down the narrow hall with its antiquated floral wallpaper and then down the creaking stairs to the foyer. To her left was the dining room and, to her right, the library. A formal, stuffy room, a heightened version of the rest of the house, more museum than home. She'd always liked the walls lined with bookshelves, though.

She passed through it now, crossing to the far wall, where a weathered wooden sign read THE GALESBURG SCHOOL. Her father had pried it off the original one-room schoolhouse before the building burned.

Molly hooked her fingers under the molding of the shelf below the sign and pulled. The wall swung inward on oiled hinges, the only door in the house that was always silent. She could smell the smoke and dampness on the other side before she could see the room.

She paused to let her eyes adjust to the darkness before stepping inside. It was too dark in here despite the numerous lanterns that hung from hooks embedded in the center beam. In all directions of the room, in every corner, the walls were lined with old photographs. Mostly photographs, at least. Some of the oldest were sketches. She was aware of each photo or sketch, knew precisely where and when it had been taken. It had been years since she'd allowed herself to study them closely, and she still knew them by heart.

She saw her granddaughter beneath the lantern light. Gillian sat at the desk, facing the chalkboard. Once it had been Molly's desk.

Gillian didn't notice her. She was immersed in a book. Brunette head down, blue eyes flicking left to right, nibbled fingernails—her one unbreakable bad habit—drumming off the empty inkwell at the front edge of the desk. Its emptiness was a tribute to Molly, symbolic of one of the few battles she had won with her own mother. Molly had promised she would attend to the lessons of the Galesburg School, but she'd also insisted that her knowledge of the contemporary world wouldn't be denied. Respect the past but don't live in it. The Pentel gel pen that rested near Gillian's hand was a monument to Molly's victory, relegating the old school desk's inkwell to pointless status.

Looking at the desk now, though, Molly wasn't so sure she'd won. Yes, the inkwell had been rendered pointless, but still it was present. The past was always present. It lived in antiques and memories, war stories and warnings, but it was never gone.

And never passive.

Molly left the bookshelf door ajar, casting a thin beam of gray light into the schoolhouse, and walked to her granddaughter's side. As she walked, she glanced at the ceiling uneasily. The worn poplar planks above were always dark with char marks. Back when Molly sat beneath them as a student, they'd dripped as they slowly dried out, the water coming down in fat, chilled drops. She remembered when her own mother had first hauled them up from beneath the lake, working in a johnboat and using a grappling hook. Molly had been sure the terrible old planks would dry out eventually. They never seemed to, though. Even now, after the driest summer and early autumn in years.

Gillian turned a page in the book and read on. She still hadn't looked up. She was through the portal now, transported to a fictional world. Molly loved to watch her when she was like this. Loved to know that she'd been carried away so completely.

"Do you like this story?" Molly whispered.

Gillian nodded without speaking. "*Gill*-ian, *Gill* like the ones on a fish," her granddaughter would say indignantly when anyone softened the *G* and called her Jillian. Her right hand crept toward her mouth, a fingernail aiming for the edge of her teeth, that nail-biting habit that she couldn't seem to outgrow. As if anticipating Molly's correction, she stilled her hand and used it to turn the page instead.

The book was a battered paperback from Molly's own childhood, *The House with the Clock in Its Walls* by John Bellairs, a lovely story that her mother had proclaimed an endorsement of witchcraft. That statement was made shortly before the family took the old homemade tincture to ward off flu season. What was the tincture if not witchcraft? Molly asked.

Tradition, her mother had said. *Tradition and common sense. The world will forget them both until the world is reminded. Now take your medicine.*

Now the book rested in her granddaughter's hands, beside the empty inkwell.

The past was never passive.

Beneath the book were the worksheets that Gillian was supposed to be focused on. Molly could see some of the questions—Galesburg history, with multiple choice options, filled with old names and dates, people and places long forgotten to the world outside of this room. Then there were the math and science assignments. The formulas were advanced for a student of Gillian's age, asking a lot of her, yes, but Galesburg had unique demands.

$$F = P \times A$$

Beneath the formula, Gillian had sketched a picture of water pressing up against a wall. Beside the sketch, she'd written *force on the dam = pressure of the water (x) area.*

Molly tapped the worksheet with her index finger.

"Remember to think of this one as if you're swimming underwater," she said. "You know how your ears feel like they're going to pop the deeper you go? That's pressure. It's the weight of the water above you."

"Okay," Gillian said, her attention still on the book.

"Which means," Molly said patiently, determined to refresh this last lesson, "that the pressure increases when . . . Gillian? When does the pressure increase?"

Gillian finally looked up from the book. "When the depth increases."

"Excellent," Molly said, and leaned down and kissed the top of her granddaughter's head. She wanted to linger, wanted to hold the touch, but knew she could not. She had rehearsed for this moment, had cried behind closed doors for years simply imagining this moment, and thanks to the pain of that preparation her eyes were dry now, and they would remain dry.

So long the planning, and so difficult the action.

"I'll be gone for a while," she whispered, giving Gillian's left shoulder a squeeze.

"The store?" Gillian asked without looking up. Who could blame her for not looking up? As far as she knew, Molly was running nothing more than a mundane errand on a mundane day, and meanwhile Gillian had a great story in front of her, albeit an imaginary one.

Oh, how Molly wished her granddaughter might live forever in those imaginary stories. The real world waited, and the real world had sharp teeth. Each day apart from it was a treasure.

But the past wasn't passive, and the past wasn't patient.

Yes, the store, Molly thought, but in the end she could not lie.

"The lake," she said.

Gillian looked up then. Turned up her earnest nine-year-old's face, which had the dark complexion of her black father but the blue eyes of her mother's Dutch roots, and looked into Molly's eyes with the first of the questions rising, raindrops ahead of the flood, and only then did Molly succeed in recovering the focus of her long-rehearsed mission.

"I need to take a walk," she said, managing a smile. "I need to take a walk by the lake."

And so her last words to her granddaughter were honest ones.

She kissed Gillian once on the forehead. It could be only once, because Molly feared that any lingering show of affection would attract Gillian's attention and then more questions.

When Molly stepped back, though, Gillian merely nodded and turned her face to the book once more.

Molly left the schoolhouse then, walking beneath the lanterns and the charred and water-stained ceiling. You could smell the water. It wasn't a cellar odor, damp and musty, but the scent of a wild brook or spring, fresh and clean.

Fresh, at least. Hardly clean, though. Hardly that.

She made it out of the house before she began to cry, and even then it wasn't bad. She let the tears fall but there were not many of them. Stoic.

She walked northeast through the woods, shunning the road and following the ridgeline, shortening the trip to the lake. The ground was blanketed in fallen leaves, so dry from weeks of drought that they crackled beneath her feet like kindling in a fire. The day was dull and gray but the leaves were a brilliant assortment of orange, yellow, and red. A long, lovely summer with its throat cut.

She came out of the trees on a high bluff overlooking the lake's tailwaters, just below the dam. At the edge of the bluff a fist of bluestone jutted out of the earth. She sat on the stone, took her cell phone out of her purse, and made the call she had to make.

The dispatcher with the Torrance County Sheriff's Department was both confused and concerned when Molly made her request for a welfare check and provided the address of her home.

"Why do you think something is wrong, ma'am?"

"It's not what I think," Molly said. "It's what I know. Please send someone to that house right away. But I wouldn't use the lights and sirens if you can help it. The little girl in there doesn't need to be scared any worse than she will be already."

The dispatcher pressed with more questions, but Molly disconnected. She made her second call then, and no one answered this one, which was not a surprise. Gillian's father would be somewhere deep underground at this hour, somewhere beneath the sidewalks of New York City. He would understand the message she left for him, though. Molly didn't know much about the man, but she knew that he would understand the message.

She knew that he would come quickly.

When she was through with her calls, she tossed the cell phone into the water below, then emptied her purse onto the rocks and threw the purse in after the phone. The purse stayed on the surface for a moment, and she watched as it was swept downstream, pulled hurriedly, hungrily, by the current before it sank.

She wrapped the fifty-pound-test monofilament fishing line around her belt, tied off the large hooks to the free ends, and let them dangle. They were probably unnecessary, but she was a thorough woman. There were plenty of timber snags in the water below, and between those and the weight of the chains there was little risk of being swept too far downstream, but she had to be sure. Go too far, too fast, and it might all be for naught.

Who really knew, though? There was no ritual for this moment. She'd created one because she wanted rules to support the promise. All she really had was the promise. The one made to her as a child. Galesburg waited for her.

Galesburg needed her.

When the hooks and lines were tied, she leaned forward, scraped leaves away from stone, and found the chains where she had hidden them. She wrapped these around her ankles, moving swiftly now, her breath beginning to tighten, her pulse accelerating. When the padlock snapped closed she felt her lungs loosen, as if this last step had been the relief of a burden. She felt better now. Not fearless, but not fearful, either. Just brave enough. That was all she had to be.

She stayed seated on the rock while she slipped the black silk bag over her head. The fabric was soft and smooth against her cheek. She secured it with a cinch and twist of the twine, a fast motion because she did not want to feel the trapped warmth of her own breaths while she could still rip the hood away. Her eyes were closed now, although it would not have mattered either way once the hood was on. She could feel the silk against her eyelashes like dust, something that could be blinked away.

Four steps to the edge of the bluff. The chains would keep her from taking full strides, of course, so she expected it would require eight steps, shuffling forward. Ten at the most.

She sat perfectly still for one long moment, feeling the cool hardness of the rock beneath her and listening to the rippling water below, and she reminded herself that she'd been grateful for each day of grace in this world and steadfast against each horror.

That was the job of living.

Molly Mathers had worked hard at it.

When she moved, it was in a single, fluid motion, rising and taking the first shuffling step forward. She counted the steps, curious about this final question: How many were ahead of her?

The answer was seven.

Then she was falling, the weight of the chains spinning her as she tumbled, a whirling pirouette of motion, like a leaf blown free.

The water was a savage shock, but it didn't rip the black silk bag from her head.

2

Deshawn Ryan came out of one hole in the ground and walked thirteen blocks through the rain to reach the next.

Around him, the city of eight million people was a chaotic but soothing serenade of engines and exhaust, voices and shouts, horns and machinery. For thirteen blocks he would enjoy the sounds of the city, and then he would disappear from it once more.

This was the rhythm of his days. Descend into the subway, ride through the tunnels below the city to reach his stop, climb back into the daylight, walk the thirteen blocks, and descend again into different tunnels.

Usually he enjoyed the walk. Today, though, he hustled with his head down as cold rain fell from a washed-out sky that had hung above the city for a week at least, it seemed. Bleak. The rain came and went, but for the most part Deshawn wasn't aware of it: he was six hundred feet belowground. A hurricane could blow through and he might not know. The twin towers had crumbled and he hadn't known until he and the rest of the sandhog crew were rushed to the surface, birthed into the chaos and terror of that day.

Life could pass you by down in the tunnels, that was for sure. The tunnels kept life going up above, but up above, people didn't give much pause to consider all that lay beneath. So long as things worked. When the lights went out or the water stopped flowing or the gas cut off, that was when they'd remember what went on down below.

Once out of the subway tunnel and down his thirteen blocks of crowded sidewalks, everyone jostling with heads down or umbrellas held close, taxi tires spraying water on people with outstretched hands at the curb, he made a right turn and walked another half block to a place that looked like any of a hundred other construction sites in the city. Tall aluminum fences, CAUTION and KEEP OUT signs, orange cones and reflective tape.

And cameras. Some easy to spot, others concealed.

A security guard let him through the gates. Inside were earth-moving machines, monstrous stacks of pallets, piled rebar, and wooden spools that stood taller than Deshawn and were lined with cable thicker than his forearm. There was so much crap stacked just inside the gates that the northwest corner of the lot didn't draw your eye until you were almost up to the hole.

The hole was twenty-two feet in diameter and looked both innocuous and dangerous, like an oversized manhole missing its cover. That was how it seemed, at least, until you stepped into the cage.

The cage of green metal bars always made Deshawn think of the suet feeders he'd seen up in the Catskills, the ones that drew woodpeckers and nuthatches and ambitious squirrels. It was suspended by a steel cable that ran through a crane and down to a winch.

His morning commute ended, like it did for so many other New Yorkers, with an elevator ride. His just went down instead of up.

There were three men already inside, and about fifteen crates of dynamite. Josh Dunham was manning the controls of the winch, and he saw Deshawn and waited for him.

"Good day to go belowground," Josh said as the rain sheeted down.

"Yeah, but that means I can't keep a nice suntan like you."

Josh laughed. He was an Irish kid who was so pale, he looked translucent. Forget sunburn; Dunham could get moonburn.

A lot of the guys were Irish. Plenty were Italian. Deshawn, the son of a black father and a Caucasian and Cuban mother, didn't really fit the mold of the crew. The Irish guys and the Italian guys were mostly second-generation sandhogs. Some of them were third, and Matty Silvers was a *fourth*-generation sandhog. A lot of the old timers had turned it into a family affair. You were either born to go underground or you weren't. You either appreciated the engineering majesty that was New York City's Water Tunnel Number 3, or you didn't.

Actually, you probably either appreciated it or didn't really know that it existed. You just turned the tap and counted on the water to flow. Didn't know that it was flowing down out of the mountains upstate, that nineteen reservoirs satiated the city's thirst by funneling water through two tunnels that were tall enough to drive a bus through in some places.

Two tunnels for now. Three tunnels soon. That mattered, too, because the first tunnel had been completed in 1917, and the second in 1935, and those old boys needed some maintenance. Water Tunnel Number 3 would allow for the old tunnels to be shut off, inspected, and repaired, with many areas being seen for the first time since their construction. Water Tunnel Number 3 would allow for a crucial supply of fresh water in the event of any collapse of one of the others. Water Tunnel Number 3 had also been under construction for almost fifty years now, and more than twenty men had already died building it.

It was almost finished, though. Almost.

Deshawn would be glad to be done. As he stepped into the cage, heard the door clang shut behind him, and listened to Josh Dunham holler "Headed down!" he felt a pang of apprehension that was coming to him more and more frequently these days. He didn't understand it. He'd worked in these tunnels for thirty years, and for twenty-nine of them he'd never been nervous on the descent.

Lately, though . . .

The sound of the rain faded to a faint patter drowned out by the mechanical hum and groan as the winch lowered them. The crew fell silent.

At one hundred feet belowground, the gray daylight was dimming rapidly above them, like a flashlight on dying batteries giving you one last memory of brightness. At two hundred it was full dark. The cable creaked, water dripped. Matty Silvers ripped a fart that echoed. Brian Bell told him to keep that pointed away from the dynamite. A few chuckles, then silence.

Four hundred feet. Five hundred. Cold air and moisture all around in the blackness. Deshawn's hand on his flashlight but not triggering the light. Not yet.

Six hundred. The cable groaned, the cage shivered, and then they settled onto solid ground once more. The cage door opened, and everyone filed out. You moved fast leaving the cage, because lingering at the base of the shaft was one of many good ways to die down here. If anything tumbled into the hole, it was at killing velocity by the time it landed. Once a sandhog had been killed by an icicle. Thing broke off, fell noiselessly through the blackness, and impaled him like a sword.

Electric lights were strung ahead, but not many of them. That was why you always carried your own flashlight and headlamp. You relied on yourself for light when you needed it. At least, you did if you wanted to last.

Deshawn had lasted for three decades. He could retire now and he knew it. His muscled-up body, which had once sliced through high school defensive lines, was a constant chorus of aches. He was tired. He had savings, had a pension. He didn't need to keep at the job.

But he wanted to see it through. Wanted to say he'd been here when it ended, when they finally opened up the valves and ran billions of gallons of cool Catskill water through these massive tunnels, and a half century of work was done. Lives had been lost down here, and too many limbs to count. Yeah, Deshawn wanted to say he'd been here when they opened it up and the whole damn job was done.

Lately, though . . . lately he was in a hurry. Not because of the fatigue or even the pain. No, it was his mind. His focus. He'd get to thinking about his daughter, who was with the city's Department of Environmental Protection Police but stationed a hundred miles outside of it, guarding the reservoirs upstate, and then his mind would drift. Take him back to that strange weekend when he'd made the trip to see for the first time where, exactly, the water for his labors came from.

He would remember Gillian's mother then. Kelly Mathers. Skin almost as pale as Josh Dunham's, but with a glow. Eyes so blue they seemed like ice over water. But she had a shine about her, too. A pulse of energy, fully charged. And the passion? *Damn*, how he could still remember that. *Passion* wasn't even the right word, maybe. Intensity. Her body lean and firm, powering against his, the way she'd swell with heat and the muscles in her thighs and ass would start trembling under his hands...

There'd been something different about that girl, no doubt. He'd known it from the first, but hadn't understood the depth of the difference until too late. For twenty years now, he'd been wondering if he got his daughter out of the house in time. She never should have been left in that place, but that was exactly what Deshawn had done, overwhelmed by the sheer terror of responsibility that her tiny presence carried into his world. The need in her eyes. The scrutiny in them, like she knew he'd disappoint her.

I took her back, he thought, defensive and defiant, the same thought he'd had every day for two decades. Yeah, he took her back. As if the first nine years of Gillian's life hadn't mattered. Even after her mother died in the car wreck, he'd left his daughter in that strange house in that strange town. Entrusted her to her grandmother, making excuses that it would be temporary. If the grandmother hadn't vanished, though, would he have ever come for his daughter?

You did. That's what matters now.

He had gotten her the hell out of that madness, and she'd turned out so well. He was so damned proud of her. An accomplished young police officer; how could you not be proud of raising a woman like that? He'd found her the right tutors, the right schools, the right path.

As he walked through the cool concrete tunnel toward his day of blasting and hauling bedrock stone, the only thing he wasn't sure of was that last part. Maybe he'd helped *too* much. Urging her to join the DEP police had made sense once, because it was the only department where Deshawn had contacts. She'd be guarding the city's water supply, just like her old man. They'd both liked that idea.

At least he had until she'd requested the assignment upstate.

The academy was in Kingston, but he expected she'd be sent back to the city. The relocation to the Ashokan Precinct in the Catskills was unanticipated. The notion that she'd requested it was concerning. Did she have some desire to explore her old hometown, to remember old stories? He hoped not. He hoped he was the only one who'd—

"Deshawn?"

The voice came from over his left shoulder, back in the dim light of the bare bulbs that were hung along the concrete walls. Soft but not a whisper. Just low.

He stopped and turned toward the sound, expecting it was Matty Silvers back there, warming up to rip on Deshawn's beloved New York Jets or share some dumbass joke or another.

It wasn't Matty, though. The man who'd called his name was sitting astride a massive timber beam that held back the threatening press of loose dirt. He was at least fifteen feet in the air, way up above Deshawn's head, and water dripped from his old leather boots and plinked off the timbers below. He was dressed in worn dungarees. A crushed-down, filthy felt hat rested on his head. He was young, no more than twenty-five, maybe not even twenty yet. Nearly a boy. Serious eyes, though, and they were locked on Deshawn's.

"You gotta listen," the kid said. "We keep tellin' you things, and you gotta start listening to them."

Deshawn was about to respond when he remembered that all the walls here were concrete, that no wooden timbers had ever been hauled down into or up out of this stretch of Water Tunnel Number 3. Then he hit the switch on his SureFire flashlight and sent two hundred lumens in the strange kid's eyes.

The kid was gone. The light bounced harshly off the bare concrete walls, not a wooden timber in sight, and Matty Silvers lifted a hand and swore.

"The hell you doing, Deshawn? Tryin' to blind me?"

The others stopped and looked back. Deshawn lowered the light, feeling their eyes on him but also feeling the prickle of fear along the back of his neck, something between a premonition and a memory, a tingle that reminded him of the weekend fling he'd had nearly thirty years ago in a quiet Catskills village, when a blue-eyed beauty traced his flesh with her fingertip.

"Yeah," he said. "Figured I'd blind you, give you a chance to play quarterback for the Giants. Seems to be their only requirement."

Matty snorted and raised a middle finger and someone else gave a chuckle, which was more than the line deserved, and then they were all in motion again, just a group of men walking along to work, six hundred feet below a city that was famous for all of its crowded buildings reaching to touch the sky.

Nobody else aware that Deshawn Ryan, who had more experience than any of them, was hearing voices that weren't there, seeing things that couldn't exist.

Maybe I shouldn't stick it out. Maybe I should start pulling my pension. They'll finish this thing with or without me down here, and the way my mind's been drifting, it could be time to go.

Deshawn kept the flashlight beam pointed at his feet and walked on beneath the city.

3

Steve Ellsworth's grandfather had always feared the rain.

There was a time when Steve had found that funny. Back when the confidence of youth allowed him to laugh at the way his grandfather would pace the porch and stare at the western sky when thunderheads formed. In those days, when Steve asked what was so worrisome about a little rain, Ed Ellsworth would cast an aggravated glance his way and then nod at the massive old birch that stood a dozen paces from the house.

"That big bastard will come down in one of these winds."

He referenced only the wind, but it was the rain that scared him. He might face into a howling gust for an hour without complaint, but when the first fat drops of a summer storm or the sleeting shards of a winter shower blew in, he'd hustle for the door.

As Steve drove through a late-autumn storm with his windshield wipers slashing, he couldn't fathom why his mind was on the past. All that mattered today was his son. Why his mind kept drifting back, he didn't know.

Just focus on Aaron.

Aaron, yes, *Aaron*—waiting on a $500 cash bond against a $5,000 surety. You paid that whether you were the county sheriff or not. In Steve Ellsworth's county, you paid it whether you were the president or the pope. The fact that it was his own son didn't matter. And the fact that his own son had been arrested in his own county once more should have mattered a lot. That should occupy his full attention, demand every emotion and every jangling nerve, and instead he was thinking of old times, remembering his grandfather's uneasiness with the rain, and thinking of how much this flood season would have distressed the old man.

Relentless rain for days upon days.

Steve tried futilely to accelerate the wiper speed, which was already on high. It was pouring down in a torrent, the type of storm that had troubled his grandfather the worst, one of those car-wash rains.

His grandfather had been in the ground for thirty years now. And, truth be told, Steve was relieved. Ed Ellsworth was a good, God-fearing man, and if he'd ever seen the day that his grandson drove to the jail not on duty but to bond out Ellsworth family, it would have crushed him with shame.

Outside of the jail, Steve's parking space was open, of course; the sheriff of Torrance County had a reserved space. He was embarrassed to pull into that for business such as this, so he passed by and parked on the street, where he had to walk through the rain like any other parent coming to post bail for their wayward child.

He was soaked by the time he hit the booking room, entering in a rush of wind and water, and Gretchen, the booking officer, looked at him with surprise. Then her lean black face filled with sorrow behind the bulletproof glass. She hit the lock button without a word and there was a hum and then a metallic crack as the bolts in the steel door ratcheted back. Steve took off his wide-brimmed hat and shook it, shedding water onto the tile floor as he crossed the room and pulled the door open. The sheriff's star on his hat glistened.

"Morning, Gretchen. I've come for—"

"I know, Sheriff. We'd have let him out earlier, but they told me you didn't want that."

"They told you right."

Gretchen had been working at the jail for nearly twenty years, and she'd watched Aaron Ellsworth pass through first in a stroller, then riding astride his father's shoulders, and now, three times in these last ten months, in handcuffs.

"He was with the Riggins boy again," she said in a low voice. "If you could keep him away from that boy, Sheriff, I wouldn't see Aaron in here again. The Riggins family has been—"

"Trust me, I know the family. But, Gretchen? So does Aaron. He's making his own choices."

She looked away. "You wanna go back and get him?"

"No. And I want him brought out in cuffs."

She tugged on one carefully twined braid and chewed her lip as if she wanted to object, but finally she turned, hit the intercom button, and told the jailer who answered to bring out Aaron Ellsworth and to keep him in cuffs.

"The sher— uh, his father is here," she said. "It's what he wanted."

It wasn't so long ago that Gretchen had put together a care package for Aaron during his days in boot camp with the Coast Guard. Steve had been so proud of him then. How had it unraveled so fast? The dishonorable discharge, the return home, the drugs, and the fights. What had Steve failed to do that might have stopped it?

Gretchen didn't speak while Steve paid her the five hundred cash bond against the five-grand surety and filled out the paperwork. The charges were possession of stolen goods, and possession of paraphernalia. That it was only paraphernalia told Steve this time Aaron had been smart enough to dump the drugs.

The boy could still learn, after all.

The door at the far end of the hall opened with a clang, and Steve looked down to see a jailer named Mike leading Aaron out in handcuffs. Aaron was long and lean, still with the deceptive muscles of the world-class swimmer he might have been, broad shoulders and disproportionally thick traps and triceps offsetting a greyhound's build.

Of course, you had to look past all the tattoos to notice the muscles. How many of those had he added in the last ten months? Steve hadn't minded the first few—what business was it of his?—but when the ink crept out onto Aaron's forearms and the backs of his hands he began to worry. Was he hiding track marks? No evidence of that, and yet in a strange way Steve would have been relieved if he'd found them. If he had something new to blame for his son's spiral.

Mike kept his eyes downcast as he walked down the hall. Aaron didn't bother with that, regarding Steve with slouching amusement.

What did I do wrong? Steve wondered. *If his mother had lived, would this have still happened?*

"Okay, Mr. Ellsworth. Let me get your hands," the jailer said. Aaron stopped walking and offered the handcuffs with a practiced under-standing that made Steve's mouth go dry. It wasn't just that his boy knew the routine; it was that he seemed indifferent to it.

"Tell the officer thank you," Steve said, his voice tight.

"Thanks, yo," Aaron said, and Steve's hands clenched the wet leather brim of his hat. He couldn't lose his temper. Not here. Not in front of Mike and Gretchen.

"I'll see you both in a bit," he said, and they nodded in silence as Gretchen buzzed the locks again and Steve opened the outer door and watched his son swagger by and back to freedom. Twenty-three years old and walking like some jackass kid in a locker room, thinking he was hard, thinking it was all a game.

They went out into the blowing rain and Aaron turned toward the police parking lot.

"Wrong way." Steve headed toward the street.

"The hell did you park all the way out there for?" Aaron said.

Steve's foot wavered as he brought it down, the simple act of find-ing solid ground suddenly difficult. He took a breath and tried to tell himself that it was the drugs speaking and not his son, and also that it wasn't his fault. Mostly he tried to tell himself that it wasn't hopeless.

"Because I'm not here on police business," he said, and then he walked to the car without another word, his hand clenched so tightly around the keys in his pocket that the edges bit into his skin.

They didn't speak on the drive home. It was nine miles from the jail to the house. They drove through the heart of Torrance and wound up into the Catskills, Maiden Mountain looming in the fog, and below it the

Chill—or, technically, the Chilewaukee Reservoir. Nobody in Torrance County called it anything but the Chill. Steve lived above the reservoir, well outside of town.

The rain had lessened, but a low gray mist hung around the brick ranch house that Steve had bought twenty-four years earlier with his wife. The yard looked bleak in the autumn mist, the grass browning, the woods long past full leaf. The basketball hoop where he'd spent so many hours with Aaron, games of H-O-R-S-E and around-the-world and free-throw contests, still stood in the driveway, but the old net was rotting, just a few filthy threads dangling from a rusted rim. Steve kept meaning to tear the whole thing down. It was nothing but an eyesore, and drive-way basketball games were not coming back to the Ellsworth house. He could never bring himself to do it, though.

He pulled his cruiser into the drive and parked beneath the ancient hoop. Cut the engine and spoke without looking at his son.

"I've got to get back to work and catch up on the time I wasted on you this morning."

"Sure thing," Aaron said, popping the door and starting to step out. Steve grabbed him by his collar and slammed him back into the seat with force that seemed to startle—scare?—them both.

"The fuck are you doing?" Aaron said, and his voice cracked, the hard-guy act fading. He looked like a child once more, and there was a hint of fear in his eyes that both disturbed Steve and pleased him. You didn't want your own child to be scared of you, but when you needed him to care, wasn't fear better than *nothing*?

"I will be at work, so that gives you the rest of the day," Steve said, forcing himself to stare into his son's eyes, "to pack your things. What-ever you want to take from this place, go on and take it."

"What are you talking about?"

"I'm evicting you," Steve said, and suddenly he understood the rea-son those old stories had been floating through his mind on the drive to the jail. It wasn't the rain; it was the knowledge of what he had to do, and knowledge of the way those things intersected. Once, his grandfather had been forced to evict an entire town in the interest of greater responsibilities.

"*Evicting* me?" Aaron echoed in disbelief. "I'm your *son*!"

"Yes, you are, Aaron. You're my son, and I love you. But I do not know how to get through to you anymore."

"Oh, come on." Aaron rolled his eyes. If you could get paid for rolling your eyes, the boy would already be retired.

"You're my son," Steve said, "and you're also supposed to be a grown man. Been back here nearly a year after you washed out of the Coast Guard, and you've got no job, you aren't taking any classes, you aren't doing a damn thing except getting arrested and bringing shame down on this family. And you don't care. I can't be the only one who cares. I *can't.*"

"You're throwing me out? You're serious? You are throwing me out of my own house?"

"Your mother and I bought that house. Your name isn't on the deed. But I am giving you an option if you want to stay. There's paperwork on the kitchen table about Peaceful Passages."

"Oh, you gotta be kidding me." Aaron lifted one tattooed hand to his face. "I'm not going to rehab. I don't *need* to go to—"

"If you're willing to go there, I'll pay for it, and I'll welcome you back here when you're done. I'll also pay for a lawyer to argue that you don't need to take up residence in my jail. I'll put my name and your mother's name on the line for you again, in the courtroom and as a job reference. If you go that route, I'm in your corner against all comers, son. Do you understand that?" Steve was talking fast now, and his voice was thickening. "That's where I want to be, but you gotta meet me halfway, Aaron. You *have* to."

"It was just a bad night, and you haven't even bothered to ask a single question about what actually happened!"

"Peaceful Passages for three weeks," Steve said. "You come out of there, and then you come home. But if you're not going there, then you're not staying here. You figure out where you want to lay your head down tonight. If you want it to be on Tyler Riggins's couch with ten beers in your bloodstream and whatever you put in your lungs or up your nose, you can go that way. Your next bed will be in a cell. We both know that. And, Aaron? This morning was the last time I'll put up bail. Believe me on that."

"This is bullshit."

"Sure. So was the arrest, I know. So was the dishonorable discharge. So was everything in life that hasn't gone your way. It's all bullshit, isn't it, son? Never your fault."

Aaron smirked. It was an expression he'd patented in the past few months, one that said, *Old man, you just don't get it, you don't begin to understand, you're so damn dense that all I can do is laugh about it.*

"You used to work so hard," Steve said. "You'd go down to the lake and swim in the cold, swim in the dark, it didn't matter, you worked your ass off because you knew what you wanted in life and you *cared.* Look at yourself now. I bet if you went out to the Chill and tried today, you wouldn't be able to keep your head above water."

"Like hell I couldn't."

"Well, you can't do it in any other aspect of your life!" Steve shouted.

For a moment they sat there staring each other down, Aaron's face filled with hate, Steve dearly hoping his own was conveying both love and resolve. They were intertwined, always. When Aaron had headed off to basic, Lily sent him a photograph of a rescue swimmer in high, turbulent seas off the Alaskan coast, and beneath it she'd written *You can't spell* resolve *without* love. Steve had told her not to send that. *It's corny,* he'd said. *Moms are allowed to be corny,* she'd told him with a smile, both of them happy and proud that day, both of them blissfully unaware that a clot was slipping toward her brain.

"I want you to think about your mother today," Steve said, and, damn it, now his voice was shaking and he was close to tears. He could not allow that—not today. Today he had to be hard.

"Get out of my car, Aaron," he said. This time, he got the hardness.

Aaron hesitated, bristling, and Steve thought first that he was going to speak, and then that he was going to throw a punch. Instead he simply climbed out of the cruiser and slammed the door.

Steve watched him stride toward the house, head down, shoulders hunched.

The rain had started again.

4

After he finished burning the paperwork from Peaceful Passages Recovery Center, Aaron Ellsworth found the spare key to his father's Silverado and then jogged through the rain to the truck, thinking that he'd head to a bar before remembering that it wasn't yet ten in the morning.

He wasn't sure if Tyler Riggins was out of his cell yet. Probably not. Tyler's family wouldn't jump quite as fast as the good sheriff.

For the last time.

What an asshole. Never even asking Aaron for his version of how the night had gone, just doing that bullshit routine of Big Cop Man, setting him straight. No questions from Sheriff Ellsworth, because he always knew the truth.

Somehow the most aggravating, bone-deep-insulting thing was the accusation that Aaron couldn't still keep his head above water. Never mind that his father had meant it to matter in the figurative sense; he'd offered it in the literal sense, too, and that was the only thing that had stuck.

Of course I can still do the old swims. Every one of them.

But could he?

After thirty minutes of aimless driving, Aaron found himself pulling into the parking lot beside the dam at the Chill. Once he would've run here from the house, following three miles of ridgetop trails that led down toward the lake. He'd swim, then run again, chasing those ridge trails away from the looming peak of Maiden Mountain.

Today he drove into the parking lot. There would be no running. He just needed to prove he could conquer the tailwaters below the dam at the Chill. Shove that in his father's face.

The big reservoir was an important spot to his family—they'd had the job of evicting a handful of weird-ass hillbillies who'd refused their eminent domain money back when the reservoir was created. Aaron knew those stories, and he'd heard others as a boy, as everyone in Torrance had.

Most of the stories concerned the Dead Waters. It wasn't even part of the lake itself but the flood control system built downstream. There was a place below the dam called a stilling basin, a sort of pond below the churning tailwaters, an area for the water to spread out in during flood season, to calm itself before it roared toward town. It was known as the Dead Waters because it was one of the few places where you could still see the remnants of the gutted, burned-out foundations of old Galesburg, which had been torched before the reservoir filled. Most of the area beneath the lake had been farm fields and isolated homesteads, but below the Dead Waters were the remains of an old town hall, two churches, and a school.

In a dry year, when the water was low and the sunlight slanted at the perfect angle, you could see the silhouettes of the ancient structures below, particularly one tenacious church steeple that reached for the reservoir's surface like it was trying to gasp a last breath.

Or grasp someone from above and pull them down below.

His grandfather, a man who'd known Galesburg when it was a town and not an artificial reef, had forbidden him from fishing in the Dead Waters. Aaron had been happy enough to stay away, lunker walleye be damned. There was something undeniably strange about that area, particularly in the twilight, when the fish were active but the dimming sun also seemed to expose more of the buildings below than it ever could at high noon on a warm summer day.

Strange, how that worked.

Naturally, the place bred superstitions, and superstitions drew crazies. Aaron remembered at least a dozen times when his father had responded to some weird-shit trouble out there. A murder-suicide one year. A group of overdosed junkies another. The wife of a local doctor who'd been found standing on the ice, stark naked, in February. She'd gone into a psych ward and, to the best of Aaron's knowledge, never come back out.

The area between the dam and the Dead Waters was a magnet for madness.

Or, if you were a swimmer, it was a first-class test course.

Down where the tailwaters thundered like a Rocky Mountain river between the dam and the stilling basin, Aaron Ellsworth had become the best swimmer Torrance County had ever produced. Night swims and cold-weather swims—those had been his secret.

He'd trained that way since boyhood, and when he shattered every Torrance County record and several state marks, it had been those swims in the dark and in the cold that gave him the edge.

The swims his asshole father didn't believe he could still achieve.

Let's see about that, Pop. Let's see about that.

He parked the Silverado directly in front of a sign that banned everyone except for authorized personnel. Beyond the small parking lot was an eight-foot-high fence with razor wire coiled over the top, and beyond that a stark and dismal-looking stone tower that seemed like it should have been part of a Depression-era prison. That was where the dam operators worked, staring at computers and opening gates to allow water to flow through the spillway, or sealing them to keep the water in. Maybe there weren't even computers inside; Aaron had no idea. He just knew it looked like an awful place to work. He'd never set foot in the gatehouse, just walked by it on his way to swim in the restricted area below, the only place in Torrance County that had any current.

Everything in Torrance was stagnant.

The tailwaters, though, could get intense. When the reservoir was high, the tailwaters could get downright mean, in fact, and that was how a kid from the backwaters of the Catskills had become the best in his Coast Guard rescue swimmer class.

Until they booted him from it.

There was only one car parked below the gatehouse tower, and Aaron recognized it as belonging to Arthur Brady, the dam operations supervisor since time immemorial and a friend of Aaron's father. Old Arthur had spent years looking the other way when Aaron came down here to train. He was always edgy about it, making Aaron swear not to bring down friends, to keep it secret, but he'd allowed it. That probably had more to do with Aaron being the sheriff's son than anything else, though.

There had to be cameras somewhere on the property, or at least a motion sensor, because you couldn't pull into the lot without someone stepping outside pretty quickly. If an operator other than Arthur was working, Aaron had learned to park up on the shoulder of the road and walk through the trees. Today, though, it was just Arthur.

Aaron had barely gotten out of the truck before Arthur appeared, walking out onto the iron staircase that led to that single door and peering through the rain.

"Mr. Fleming?" Arthur hollered. "Is that you?"

"No. It's Aaron."

"Huh?"

"Aaron Ellsworth."

"*Aaron!*" Arthur Brady put a hand on the railing and leaned out, and for the first time that day Aaron felt a pang of shame, wondering if the old man knew that he'd just bonded out of jail. He'd hated growing up the sheriff's son, feeling exposed and disliked, but somehow Arthur Brady didn't fall in with those memories of the town. He'd taken risks to give Aaron the best shot possible at getting out of this place.

"I sure didn't expect to see you," Arthur said, climbing down the stairs, boots clanging. "What're you doing back in town, kid?"

I guess Arthur doesn't read the paper. Or at least not the jail bookings.

"Just passing through," Aaron said, not wanting any dialogue, not wanting anything except the press of cold, angry water. "I'm gonna take a swim. Old times' sake."

"Oh, not today, Aaron. You kidding me? Water's runnin' too high."

"Not for me."

Arthur gave him a forlorn look and nodded. "Sure, *you'll* be fine, but I got a pain-in-the-ass inspector comin' down here from Albany, lookin' over my shoulder, all on account of the rain, you know? Last thing I need is for him to see somebody in the water."

"I'll be fast. Gone before he gets here."

"He's already late! I can't risk it, Aaron."

Aaron felt like he could hear a ticking in the back of his skull. "Arthur? Mr. Brady? I'm going to get in the water now."

"Damn it, boy, this is not the day to screw with me. You can't go—"

"Call my dad if you've got a problem with it," Aaron said, and he turned and walked away, somehow feeling cocky and feeling like shit at the same time. Like throwing a punch or crying.

"If you see that inspector, you best stay out of sight, or I *will* call your dad!" Arthur shouted.

Aaron gave him a thumbs-up without turning.

He walked out of the parking lot and followed a footpath through the weeds and the small trees and then he came out alongside the spillway below the dam, where the water thundered and churned. There, in front of fencing and chains and signs that shrieked about trespassing penalties, he peeled off his hooded jacket, T-shirt, and jeans, until he was standing in his underwear in the rain. He rolled his socks and jammed them inside his shoes and left it all in a pile under the jacket as rain beaded on his bare skin. Already he felt better, stronger and cleaner. Meaner.

This place could do that to him.

He still wasn't sure why he'd come here. Proving a point to his father? It was the wrong point, he knew that.

I'll move out of the house and out of the town and find success, but first I'll show him that I'm strong as I ever was. I'll show him that much before I leave.

His father didn't really care whether he could still make the swim or not, of course. He didn't care about that at all. Neither did Aaron— not anymore. But this was the place where he'd long turned fear and doubt and fury into something productive, and some child's impulse whispered that if he could do it once more, he could reverse course. He could become the man he'd once been destined to be. The man that he alone, apparently, still believed he actually *was*.

He ignored the pain of jagged rocks against his bare feet as he walked across the slick, treacherous riprap and down to the shore. Generations earlier this area had been home to the camps where construction workers lived in temporary housing, building the dam that would flood out the village of Galesburg. He'd heard stories of terrible fights between the Galesburg residents and the workers, but he wasn't sure he believed them. After all, the workers had finished their task, packed up, and moved on. Who was left to tell the legend but the ones left behind? They tended to be a pissed-off bunch, too.

Aaron knew a bit about that.

But I'm leaving again, and this time I'm not coming back, he promised himself as he neared the water's edge. *One last swim to show the old man he's wrong about me, on this count and all the others, and then I'm out of here. I'll keep silent for a few months, make him rue the day he threw me out, and then, once I'm in good shape somewhere else, and he's had time to chew on the loss of his own son, then and only then will I call him. I'll invite him out to . . . to wherever the hell I've ended up—doesn't matter where, because it will be better than here—and I'll have him down for a nice dinner and I won't say "I told you so"; I'll just let him soak it all in. I'll let him see how wrong he was.*

He hesitated at the water's edge. The current was really pulling today.

"Let's go," he said softly, unsure of the reason for his own pause and unsettled by it. Used to be, he'd hit the water without so much as a glance upstream.

If not for the hesitation, he might never have seen the photographer.

Had he just slipped into the water, as he'd planned, his eyes would have been down and he'd have had almost no chance to catch sight of the man in the gray vest standing against the gray-and-white backdrop of birches and oaks. Because he hesitated, though, he spotted motion— or maybe it was the flash of light reflected off the camera lens—and so he looked downstream and saw the photographer.

The man was wearing jeans and a dark green shirt with the gray vest on top, the wrong clothes to wear in the woods during hunting season. He had a thick shock of jet-black hair and a goatee that was every bit as unnaturally dark, as if inked on rather than grown. He was kneeling on a flat rock just downstream and had a camera on a tripod, pointed up at the dam.

Pointing at Aaron.

"Hey! What the hell you doing, man?" Aaron shouted, both embarrassed about being caught out here in his underwear and angry about it, as if the stranger had popped out of his bedroom closet and not a public forest.

The photographer looked up as if seeing him for the first time. He looked Aaron up and down and cocked his head like he was studying him as a potential subject, and now Aaron was less embarrassed and angrier.

"Yo, pervert. I asked you—"

"The name is actually not 'Pervert' but Curtis B. Haupring," the man said brightly. "Photographer." He chuckled. "As you might have guessed."

"Terrific. Point that thing away from me, all right?" Aaron stepped into the water. *Damn*, was it cold. He felt his testicles shrivel and his cock duck for cover and looked back at the photographer like a shamed boy. *The water's cold! It's the water!*

The photographer was smiling at him as if reading Aaron's thoughts, and this was even more infuriating.

"I'm not kidding. Turn the camera off."

"I'm documenting the dam," the man said softly. "Not you, sir."

Autumn in the Catskills seemed to bloom morons with cameras. Out-of-staters or down-staters.

"Any interest in it?" the photographer asked.

"In the dam? No. I have zero interest in the dam."

The photographer stared at him.

"No desire to help tell the story of Galesburg?"

The story of Galesburg? What in the hell is wrong with this guy?

"That town drowned about seventy-five years ago," Aaron said, "and, no, I have no desire to help you." He took another step into the water, now turning his body self-consciously to avoid the camera lens. There was something strange about the way the light reflected off it, glaring and harsh, when the day was so overcast. "I also don't need any pervert pics, and this area is closed, so why don't you move on down the road?"

"If it's closed, then we're both trespassing, correct? Or do you have some official capacity? If so, I apologize. I'm just not sure where your badge is kept."

Where my badge is . . . Aaron took a deep breath, lifted his middle finger, and said, "Got your badge right here."

The man studied him with that smile again, a wan, mocking smile, and said, "I don't think you're what I'm looking for, unfortunately. Enjoy your swim. Careful out there. Current's strong."

"No," Aaron said, "it's not."

He took a breath and dove. He relished the frigid shock, the way his chest tightened and his lungs clenched.

Almost immediately, the current snatched him, and he allowed himself to be pulled down, down, down, before he finally began to move. He swam underwater for the first thirty meters and then broke the surface in a smooth ripple, arms stretched out, hands curved, legs driving, every motion a fine-tuned feat of perfect unison, the human body turned to engine. He waited until his lungs were begging for air before he surfaced, and when he finally did, the water was still beating on him, and it was hard to get a full, dry breath.

It took him a few moments before he realized that some of the pounding water was coming from above. The rain was really pouring down now.

He rolled onto his back and looked upstream. The photographer was gone.

5

The drive to the Chilewaukee Reservoir should have been two hours from Mick Fleming's house outside of Albany, but it took him nearly three because of the rain.

It fell unremittingly, and Mick missed an exit sign, which took him twenty miles off course. By the time he finally reached the reservoir he was late and frustrated, and that wasn't good, because all of his preliminary calculations told him he was going to need full focus today.

If his math was right, and rains like this one kept falling, the Chilewaukee Dam could be in big trouble very soon. Mick badly wanted his math to be wrong.

His math rarely was, though.

His initial assessments were bad: the dam's age and the rapidly rising water levels combined to make demands on the spillway intense, and the spillway had been on Mick's critically endangered list for years now. If it kept raining? What was left on the scale of concern then? Dire? Catastrophic?

He was concerned when he left for Torrance County, annoyed by the drive in the rain and the time he wasted getting lost, then further disgusted to discover two vehicles parked in the lot when he finally arrived. He'd been promised that only the dam supervisor, Arthur Brady, would be on hand for this visit. If Mick's inspection necessitated a more formal review with more parties present, that would happen soon, but for the first visit he was to be alone.

That was his only rule, and he was entitled to make it. As the section chief for inspections with the state's division of dam safety of the department of environmental protection—try fitting all that on a business card—Mick was the front man, the reconnaissance scout. It was a position that he'd earned from years of hard work, yes, but also one that suited him. Many engineers liked a full team for inspections, wanting to engage in debate and hear alternate ideas, relevant memories, and obscure observations. Mick needed to be alone first, though. He'd learned that the hard way over the years. From childhood through college and on into the workforce, communicating with others had always felt like he was talking underwater while everyone else was on the surface. For all of his unique knowledge of structural engineering and a nearly encyclopedic recall of dam disasters and dam fixes the whole world over, Mick struggled to hold focus in a group with people talking all around him, and he struggled even more to communicate his own process. Any crucial discovery that Mick Fleming made was likely to occur in privacy, and thus his initial reviews were to be done solo. Arthur Brady certainly knew that, because Mick had spoken to him just yesterday.

Why the two cars, then? Who else was here?

He was flustered as he got out of the car, forgot his pencil in the cupholder, and then dropped his iPad when he reached back for the pencil. He was cursing and brushing water and gravel from the case when he looked up and saw the photographer.

The man was standing on a wide, flat rock just above the turbid, churning tailwaters. He had a camera on a tripod pointed at the spillway. Despite the pouring rain, he wore no jacket, just a soaked gray vest. No hat, either, his thick, dark hair streaming water, as if he'd just emerged from a swim. If the rain bothered him in the slightest, he didn't show it. Just raised a polite hand in greeting.

"Beautiful, isn't it?" he said. No trace of sarcasm. Mick looked from the photographer up to the dam and felt inclined to agree. It *was* beautiful. The massive stone blocks laid like steps, the gatehouse looming like something from another age. It was nowhere near as bland as the modern structures, with their blank faces of concrete.

It was also nowhere near as safe.

"Beautiful until it bursts," Mick said.

This seemed to intrigue the photographer. "You think it will?"

Mick didn't want to get into this conversation—any conversation, really—with a tourist who was apparently happy to trade pneumonia for photographs.

"It will if I don't do my job," he said curtly. "And I'm afraid part of my job will be asking you to leave. This is a closed area. The signs are very clear."

"Apologies. I must have missed them."

Mick waved at the Silverado. "You drove right past them."

The photographer shook his head. Water sprayed from his hair and beard. "I didn't drive in. I walked. Out of the woods."

Out hiking, dressed like that? He really will get pneumonia.

"Nevertheless," Mick said, "it's a closed area."

The man frowned, but it was the look of someone who was about to break bad news rather than someone who'd received it.

"Do you have some sort of official capacity? Or are we not both in the same trespassing boat?"

"We certainly are not," Mick snapped. "My *official capacity* is that I'm the chief dam engineer down from Albany. Is that sufficient for you?"

The man's eyes seemed to brighten. He tilted his head and looked at Mick with real interest for the first time.

"Chief dam engineer. I didn't know there was such a thing."

Mick was getting good and tired of him now.

"There is, and I'm it," he said.

"I'm documenting the story of Galesburg," the photographer said. "Do you have any interest in helping me tell it?"

"Galesburg?" Mick almost laughed. "What I have an interest in is helping keep Torrance from ending up in the same place."

The man's eyes seemed to brighten. "You know of Galesburg, then?"

"Of course. It was destroyed for the reservoir. Big news in a small town, long, long ago. My grandfather designed the dam, actually."

"Your *grandfather* was Jeremiah Fleming?" The man seemed fascinated by this, and Mick was astonished that he'd ever heard the name.

"You've done your research," Mick said.

The photographer smiled, tilted his head, and said, "I can see it now, yes. The jawline, mostly. And about the eyes. Yes, I should have recognized you."

Mick felt unsettled by the scrutiny, this stranger talking about his resemblance to a man he'd never even met, a relative who'd been dead decades before Mick's birth.

"If you say so. Listen, I really do not have the time to—"

"You know it's important that the story of the place be remembered, then. Excellent. You're one of the few with a personal connection."

Mick took a deep breath. "Sure. But the way I'll remember that story is by making certain it's not repeated. We don't need any more flooded-out towns in the Catskills. Now, please—"

"Of course." The photographer lifted a placating hand. "I understand. You've got important work to do."

"That's right."

The man looked from Mick to the spillway with a speculative gaze. "Crucial work, in this weather. So many days of rain."

"Yes," Mick said. "Crucial." He was taking a breath to offer one last demand that the photographer hit the road, when the man spoke again.

"I'll get out of your way, then, and with my apologies, but is there any chance I could take just one picture? Would you mind?"

"Of me?"

The man nodded. "It's a striking background. And with your family connection and your own current role . . . it's just very dramatic. You standing in front of all that water, and in the rain . . . Please, it will only take two seconds."

Mick didn't have many seconds to wait, but when he glanced back at the spillway he had to admit that it *did* look impressive. And while he wasn't an egotistical man, he could imagine that the image of the chief engineer out of Albany standing in front of the Chilewaukee Reservoir spillway would be a dramatic photograph. You couldn't blame the stranger for wanting that shot.

"One photo," Mick said, "and then you're gone. Deal?"

The man's smile broke wide and white across his dark goatee.

"Deal," he said, and then he lowered his eye to the camera. Mick faced it, standing a little straighter and sucking in his stomach. He had to squint; the lens was reflecting some trapped light that was otherwise missing in the lead-sky day.

There was a shutter click and a popping flash that turned into squares of brightness, disorienting orbs that floated through Mick's field of vision. Then they were gone, and the photographer was already standing up with his camera in one hand and his tripod under his arm. Mick blinked at him, puzzled. How had he moved so fast?

"Thank you, sir," the photographer said. "I appreciate it, and I wish you luck in the flood."

"Sure." It wasn't a flood, just rain, but he seemed to be a dramatic fellow.

"Would you mind telling me your name? For my caption."

"Mick Fleming."

"Mick Fleming." He spoke as if tasting the words. "Excellent. Chief engineer, you said? Grandson of Jeremiah Fleming?"

"That's right. But I really do have to ask you—"

"I'm already leaving."

And he was. He was walking right back into the woods, angled toward Maiden Mountain, which was very rough climbing.

"You ought to get a jacket," Mick called out.

The photographer just laughed. Mick watched him go, frowning, and then said, "Hey!"

The photographer turned back. He was barely visible now, obscured by the birch saplings and the sheeting rain.

"What publication?" Mick said. He was thinking that he wouldn't mind a copy of that shot. If he told Lori, his wife, she might even frame it. That would give him an excuse to put it up in the office and pretend that it wasn't his own idea.

"No publication just yet," the photographer called back. "I'm free-lance."

Mick nodded, trying not to show any disappointment. "Even free-lancers can use a raincoat," he said.

The laugh came once more, and then the photographer was gone, and Mick could finally get to work.

6

The current was ferocious, just as Aaron hoped.

This was the test, see, this was what separated your average swimmer from Aaron Ellsworth. Anyone could swim in an indoor pool or off a Florida beach or in a summer lake. Give them a strong current and a chill that spread through every nerve and engulfed the heart and lungs, and then see what they could do.

It had been these lonely cold swims under a coal-black sky that convinced him that he wanted to be a Coast Guard rescue swimmer.

He'd been dominant in Coast Guard training, too. He ate it for lunch. It was supposed to leave you begging for a respite. He begged for more.

"Natural talent," the same sergeant who would later kick him out had said on the day Aaron completed his first dark water search and rescue simulation.

Aaron had been annoyed by that. There was nothing *natural* about something hard earned, and too often the word *talent* suggested a gift that had been handed to you rather than a skill extracted from burning muscles and scorched lungs on miserable nights in frigid waters. He understood that a compliment was intended, but didn't anyone know how damn hard it was to achieve *natural talent* status, how hard you had to work and how deeply you had to care?

Natural talent. Sure.

To say that he was the best swimmer in his class of twelve was a joke. He was better than the other eleven put together. Faster, yes, better endurance, yes, but what separated him was his ability not to panic. Nothing they threw at him in the water scared him, and everything was designed to. It wasn't long before his instructors and fellow trainees alike realized one thing: Aaron Ellsworth had no fear of death in the water.

Still they'd sent him home.

It was panic training that got him, ironically. The drill was simple enough: one recruit would play the role of a hysterical victim, thrashing in the water, and the other would restrain and retrieve him, bringing him toward a basket in the center of the pool that was supposed to simulate a helicopter drop basket.

The guy they put in the water with Aaron was one of those hoorah, chest-thumping assholes who was always trying to be the group's unofficial leader and morale booster, telling them they had to dig deep, telling them pain was weakness leaving the body, like a walking, talking Nike ad.

Johnny—that was the guy, a grown man who called himself Johnny—outweighed Aaron by probably thirty pounds, and when he went into victim mode, he went all out. Even if Aaron hadn't caught him getting whispered instructions, he would have known what was coming. Johnny Brass Balls was going to give Aaron a real tussle, try to show him up.

Into the pool they went, and Johnny immediately took his panicked-victim role toward Oscar-nominee territory. He was thrashing like there was a downed electric line in the water, knees and elbows flying, hunting for Aaron's groin, stomach, kidneys.

With the training officer barking at him incessantly from the pool deck, Aaron had gotten the prick secured with a rear-approach hold and was towing him back toward the rescue basket. It was then, just as they neared the basket, that Johnny decided enough was not enough, and he made a massive shake-and-roll, trying to shed Aaron, but instead dragging them both back underwater.

Aaron choked as he went under. They slid halfway down to the bottom of the pool, and now their roles had been reversed: it was Johnny securing Aaron in his grasp now, only Johnny was supposed to be playing the victim role, fighting for the surface, not holding Aaron beneath it.

Aaron's lungs were scorching by then, the need for a breath urgent. He leaned forward, just enough so that he could see the other man's eyes. For one instant, one fraction of a second, the communication between them was as complete as if they'd been at the surface and engaged in conversation.

Help, Aaron's blue eyes screamed, *I'm not faking anymore, I need air, HELP!*

And Johnny's eyes, dark as a lonely Catskill creek at night, answered: *No.*

Something snapped in Aaron then, something born out of fear and grown into rage. Fight or flight had merged and all that remained was a primal desire to be the last one left.

When Johnny Brass Balls began to turn into Johnny Blue Face, he pushed for the surface, satisfied that he'd won. Aaron didn't let him go. Instead, he tugged him back down, and now it was Johnny's panicked eyes looking into his, predator turned to prey.

Thought it was your show, didn't you, Johnny? Thought you were in control. They remained on the bottom, arms and legs tangled together, eye to eye, linked in this pissing match gone terribly wrong.

Then Johnny blacked out.

Aaron felt the moment that consciousness left the man in his arms. A final tensioning, then a slackening of every muscle as his lips parted and a stream of bubbles emerged. Aaron, whose own lungs were at their limit, his chest spasming, braced his feet on the bottom of the pool and pushed hard. He shot up, flutter kicking and using his left arm to stroke, his right wrapped around Johnny's deadweight body. For an instant, as the overhead fluorescent lamps turned the surface into a sheet of gray light, he wasn't sure that he'd make it. For an instant it seemed he probably would not.

Then he broke the water and found air and sucked in a gasping breath, taking care not to show desperation, not to cry out in relief. He breathed again, spit water, and then saw that chaos had broken out: everyone was trying to save Johnny.

"He tried too hard," Aaron said between gasps. "He wouldn't stop. He knew what he was doing, and he wouldn't stop."

They'd saved the prick easily enough. Damn well should have been able to; it was a course taught by rescue experts, after all, so what was a little CPR? They got him breathing, and then they took him out, and while Aaron tried to explain the situation, he got the clear sense that from the surface it hadn't looked the same. Meanwhile, Johnny's brass balls turned to tinfoil in the ambulance, and he told a different narrative.

Aaron did it intentionally, he said, had grabbed him and pulled him back under and held him there. Aaron Ellsworth had tried to kill him down in that pool.

They believed him.

It was about four hours later that they came for Aaron. He would withdraw, they explained, and be grateful that nobody was pressing charges.

He looked them all in the eyes one at a time, nodded, got to his feet, and left the room with a salute, an utter absence of future plans, and a brand-new fuck-you attitude.

Now, ten months and two thousand miles removed from his Coast Guard training pool, he stopped his crawl stroke below the reservoir dam and rolled onto his back as the current clutched him, sweeping him back toward the town that he'd intended to leave forever.

7

Mick was studying the spillway when Arthur Brady began hollering his name from the gatehouse.

"Mr. Fleming? I was beginnin' to wonder what had happened to you!"

I got distracted because I was wondering how much longer your dam has, Mr. Brady, and I missed an exit.

But all Mick said was "Bad drive. Bad weather."

"Sure it is. Come on in, come on in. Let's get outta the rain, get warmed up."

Mick had no interest in the gatehouse. The potential problems weren't there, they were out here in the spillway, which was too old and, frankly, had been a flawed design from the start.

That wasn't Arthur Brady's fault, though. He was a smart man and he was hardworking, but he had no imagination. That was fine for him; he didn't need to have it. The sad reality was that his job would belong to a robot soon enough. Then again, Mick's might, too. It stood to reason that at some point robots would design the future generations of them-selves, didn't it? The simple laws of progress seemed to dictate that the definition of rote tasks would shift as technology became—

"Mr. Fleming?"

Mick blinked at Arthur. "Yes. Sorry. Lost in my head there for a min-ute. It happens sometimes."

It happened a lot, actually.

"No problem," Arthur Brady said with a chuckle as he came down the steps, his bald head bowed against the rain, glistening. They shook hands—Mick just managed to avoid dropping the iPad again—and then he nodded at the two vehicles parked beside his own.

"I thought operations here were solo shifts?" he said.

Solo shifts at a critical piece of infrastructure were surprising to many people, but the reality was that even the Hoover Dam might be manned by shifts of as few as six. Smaller reservoirs simply didn't have the need for much manpower, particularly if they didn't have shipping traffic or hydroelectric generators. The Chilewaukee had neither, but it held one hell of a lot of water back from the residents in the floodplain below. It was also man-made, and anything made by man had the potential to be laughed at by nature.

"That's right, just me," Arthur Brady said.

"I saw the two cars, and I wondered." Mick nodded again at the pickup truck beside him. There was a sheriff's star on the license plate. Arthur followed his eyes to it, put his big hands in his pockets, and pursed his lips.

"Sheriff's truck. Probably looking for meth heads or something. You wouldn't believe the shit that people try to dump down here, Mr. Fleming. I mean to tell you, people treat this place like it's their own private—"

"Sure, sure, I don't need to hear about all that," Mick said, nonplussed because Arthur was crowding him and some of the numbers that had been dancing through Mick's head on the long drive were shuffling back into the shadows. He couldn't listen to this droning talk. He needed to see, needed to *think*, and you couldn't do that and talk at the same time.

At least, he couldn't.

"Right," Arthur said, rain beading on his glistening scalp. "Of course you don't."

His voice was calm, but his eyes looked wounded. Mick tried to recover by asking him a question he could answer that *did* matter. Oh, how it mattered.

"What's your intake level today?"

"Hair under seventy thousand."

The reservoir was filling at seventy thousand cubic feet per second. Mick took a sharp breath, and Arthur Brady nodded grimly.

"Record's eighty-two thousand," he said.

The record, Mick knew, had also occurred twenty years ago, which meant that it had been endured by newer equipment. The infrastructure at Chilewaukee had received far more trust than investment over the years. This didn't set it apart from many of the nation's dams, but in the state of New York the Chill always lagged behind. It was the bastard son of the grand Catskill Aqueduct. The Catskill and Delaware Aqueducts had been more than just remarkable feats of engineering; they'd been massive public works projects, bringing jobs to the mountains, and water to the city.

The problem with the Chilewaukee was that they'd never really seen it home. Sometime after World War II the money once slated for tunnels tying the Chilewaukee to the massive Ashokan Reservoir and linking it into the city's water supply was instead allocated toward other reservoirs and then to Water Tunnel Number 3, a billion-dollar project that was still not completed decades after it had begun. When it was finally finished, though, it would assure New York of an almost peerless water supply—and one that didn't need, and never really had needed, the Chilewaukee Reservoir.

They'd spent an enormous amount of money constructing it and destroyed the entire village of Galesburg and the tiny hamlet of Grubb's Landing on Cresap Creek. Along the way, they discovered that the Chilewaukee was determined not to cooperate. Preliminary engineering on nearly everything proved wrong, especially the logistics of boring tunnels through Maiden Mountain to connect the Chilewaukee to the Ashokan. There'd been better sites from the beginning, and the city moved on to them, coming up with a clever new term to explain that their expensive abortion in Torrance County wasn't actually a mistake at all.

The Chilewaukee, they said, was a *surplus reservoir*: not part of the system yet but available to it in the future. The tunnels connecting it to the rest of the supply could be completed if necessary. In reality, that was never going to happen, and because it wasn't actually linked into the city water supply, the Chill received far less attention—and funding—than the rest of the reservoirs in the system.

It had also been the death of Jeremiah Fleming, Mick's grandfather. Fleming had been murdered on a site visit to the Chilewaukee, killed by furious locals who'd refused to leave, who simply could not accept the idea of eminent domain.

He'd been dead long before Mick's birth, but his professional legacy lingered both through a family of engineers and a majestic, if largely forgotten, dam.

Mick didn't think about him often, but on visits to the Chilewaukee, it was hard not to. Maybe that was why he took these inspections a little more personally.

I won't let it burst on my watch, Mick thought, and then he asked Arthur Brady what the current release level was.

"Twelve-five," Arthur Brady said.

So the flooded western fork of Cresap Creek that had been dammed to create the reservoir was spewing into the reservoir at 70,000 cubic feet per second, and the Chilewaukee gatehouse was siphoning that off at a rate of 12,500 cubic feet per second. Enough to limit the lake level rise, but not enough to hold balance with it for the long haul.

This October was beginning to turn into a long haul. Days and days of rain stacked atop each other like something biblical.

"I'm going to get to work," Mick said. "I'll come up to see you when I'm through. I might have some questions."

"Sure." Arthur Brady chewed on the corner of his lip and shot a fretful glance down toward the churning waters in the spillway. "You hear the rumble?"

"Pardon?"

"It's different. The sound. It's not like it should be."

Mick listened to the cascading water pounding down the stone face of the spillway. It hadn't changed since he got here, but that didn't mean Brady was wrong. In fact, Brady was the man most likely to notice a change in timbre.

"Deeper?" Mick asked.

"Yup. Like it's coming more from the chest. Not a head cold anymore."

It was, Mick thought, both an apt analogy and a frightening one. Arthur Brady was humanizing the structure—and its ailments.

"How many years have you worked out here?"

"Twenty-eight. Said I'd be gone at twenty-five, but I couldn't do it. I keep hoping to see her repaired before I'm done." Brady cocked his head and lifted a finger. "Hear it? Right there. The sound is deeper, and not just because there's more water." He pivoted to Mick, grim-faced. "It's like you've been sayin' for years now: that spillway needs to be relined and aerated."

"Yes. We will discuss it all. First, I've got to make my visual inspection, please."

"Right, we can do that." Arthur started out of the parking lot and toward the trail that wound alongside the spillway.

"I'll do it on my own," Mick said. "It's about my thought process, do you understand?"

Arthur, clearly stung, turned and walked back to the gatehouse. "You know where to find me."

Mick sighed, unzipped his rain jacket, then took off his glasses and dried the lenses on his shirt. He hadn't wanted to insult the man, but he couldn't afford the distraction, either. Strangers did not understand this dilemma. For that matter, not many people other than his wife, Lori, understood him at all.

That was fine, though. It wasn't his job to win friends and influence people. It was his job to make sure houses weren't swept off their foundations downstream.

He turned back to the spillway.

The massiveness of a dam made its engineering seem complicated, but the basic principles were simple enough: you built an impediment to the natural flow of water, the water backed up, and, *ta-da!*—a creek became a lake. You managed the stress by allowing water to breach the dam in a controlled fashion. If you couldn't release it, the water had only two options: crest the dam or burst it. Over time, it would do one or the other.

There was no force on earth so determined and patient as water.

With spillways and gates, though, humans could help the water make its choice. That worked well, provided the equipment could keep up with nature.

It wasn't all that easy. Each year dams around the world failed and people were killed. Mick had devoted a lot of years to studying how those tragedies had come to pass and how they might have been averted. The closest partner he saw to the Chilewaukee was Lake Oroville, in California, which had forced the evacuation of 200,000 people. Both the Chilewaukee and Oroville were reservoirs made from rivers, lakes emerging within an existing flow, like a bubble in the blood. They shared two other similarities, and Mick didn't like either of them: requested maintenance on the spillways had been deferred for years, and people lived in the floodplain.

And why not? People trusted dams.

As he strolled down the path, studying the water thundering and growling through the spillway, his glasses misted again and he wiped them clear and replaced them, then stopped and stared and felt his breath catch.

Were those bubbles rising up from below the surface?

He stepped closer, squinted, cleaned his glasses again, cocked his head.

Bubbles. Yes? No? Were they bubbles? It was so hard to tell. With the water roaring this way, the surface current created a dizzying distortion of everything below. It was like driving through a downpour without windshield wipers. Still, he was almost certain . . .

Yes, there they are.

Streams of small bubbles were rising and bursting on the surface, swept away by the current and concealed by the rain, as if the elements were working in tandem to hide evidence of a crime, one diversion and one getaway driver.

In contrast to the showboating power of the cascade upstream, the bubbles looked tiny, innocuous, and innocent.

They were the far more terrible threat, though.

The big water could be managed. That was all the product of design, of careful anticipation. But those bubbles suggested the opposite of anticipation: willful ignorance.

The concrete that lined the spillway was old and in need of repair, as had been noted in inspection report after inspection report, then dismissed as something that could wait for the next budget. Always the next budget.

But those bubbles were an indication of a process called cavitation, which meant that the water was striking a rough surface with such speed and turbulence that tiny vapor bubbles were forming and collapsing, forming and collapsing. It sounded harmless until you watched it work away at stone like a million miniature jackhammers.

Those tiny bubbles had nearly toppled the 710-foot-tall Glen Canyon Dam in 1983. Troubling sounds led dam operators to shut off the spillway, and once the water drained away, they discovered that a crater 32 feet deep and 180 feet long had opened up, threatening to tear a hole in the side of the dam.

Maybe I'm wrong, Mick thought.

But he didn't think he was.

He decided to walk farther downstream, chasing the tailwaters into the valley. As the force of the water diminished, maybe the bubbles would become clearer, and then he would know for sure.

While he pushed through the saplings that lined the bank, his shoes growing slick and clotted with damp mud, he realized this walk was little more than an excuse to keep thinking and delay the trek back up to the gatehouse, where he would have to ask Arthur Brady to begin primary steps on the dam's emergency plan. The only way to be sure of the cavitation risks was shutting off the spillway and sealing in the rising waters behind the dam.

His glasses misted over once more, and as he wiped them dry, he looked up at the gunmetal sky and swollen clouds. Fat raindrops splattered off his face.

Yes, he thought, things could get very bad here.

8

Aaron had been swept farther downstream than he'd expected, and rather than follow his old tradition and swim back up, knifing through the current in a feat of physicality and willpower, he decided to come ashore and walk back.

Rather than push himself to the brink, he gave up—no, he *decided to quit*—several hundred yards downstream. He let the water carry him into a shallow eddy near a gravel bar and then pulled himself out, dripping and gasping and stunned at how little he'd achieved for his efforts. Then again, he'd spent the night in jail and had a hangover. No surprise that he wasn't himself today.

Then why'd you come here? If you weren't going to swim it and beat it, why'd you come at all?

He stepped farther up onto the bank, wincing as rocks bit into the soles of his feet. It was a nasty walk from here. He'd forgotten just how bad.

He paused and looked back at the water, which was dyed deep brown with all the sediment of the recent floods, the swift current giving it a thin white glaze. He considered getting back in, then shook his head, turned, and started ahead on foot. He felt ridiculous walking in the rain in nothing but his soaked boxers. If his father saw this performance, he'd think that he'd won his argument. Not only had Aaron failed to make the swim, but he looked like a drugged-out lunatic.

Screw him and Peaceful Passages. There is no chance that I will check into a rehab clinic. I'll get out of the house, I'll dial back on the booze and the smoking, and I'll stop the pills completely. When I'm making good money somewhere, I'll give the old prick a call and have him visit, have him see just how wrong he was. Give him *a check, maybe.*

A check from doing what, though? What job, and where would he find it? He'd burned his bridges in Torrance County without caring because he didn't want to be here, but . . . where else was he going to go?

Any damn place. Pick a spot and—

He never saw the glass waiting in the rain-soaked weeds. Just brought his bare foot down on it squarely, all of his weight driving the curved base of a fractured Miller Lite bottle into his instep.

"Son of a *bitch!*" he shouted, falling onto his ass in the mud and the weeds, grasping his wounded foot with both hands as blood spurted warm and red between his clenched fingers. The base of the bottle never moved, the bottom of it sunk nearly an inch deep into the mud, the edges glistening, as menacing as a rattlesnake's fangs. He could see the bottle's neck resting in the grass, the wet label peeling away in strips. It had broken neatly in half, neither side shattering the way a discarded beer bottle should but separating, each end bearing a wicked crescent of razor-edged glass.

The blood was pouring out of his foot, splattering the rocks with crimson, and the pressure from his grasp seemed to have no effect at all. The pain rose through his body and into his brain, a high, shrieking chord of agony.

I bet I severed a nerve, he thought as he rocked back and forth, pressing his hands to the wound. He had nothing to use to staunch the blood flow. Not unless he took his underwear off. His phone was in the truck; his clothes were up the trail. It was going to be a long, painful hobble to get anywhere, and he'd be spurting blood with each step.

He screamed then, a howl of rage and pain, and the shout was still echoing when he heard another voice chasing on its heels.

"Who's down there? Hey! Who is down there?"

The photographer, Aaron thought. The photographer was still within earshot. Once Aaron had wanted him gone; now he was grateful that the man was still in the woods.

"Here! I need help!" Aaron tried to stand but fell sideways when the pain lanced through him. With the pressure of his hands removed from the wound, his foot began to leak blood rapidly, coating his toes and heel. He fought upright, all of his weight on his left leg, and then stared in the direction of the voice. It had come from up the trail, and now he could hear footsteps and snapping branches and see the brush shake as someone rushed toward him.

Lucky, he thought, because you could go a long time down here without encountering a soul, even on a sunny summer day. In the middle of an autumn rain, though? This was fortunate indeed.

A man broke out of the trees and into view on the rise just above Aaron. It wasn't the photographer. This was a slender middle-aged man with glasses and a high widow's peak of receding sandy hair, his hands occupied by an iPad and a notebook. A mechanical pencil was tucked behind his ear. He blinked at Aaron and took a step back, and Aaron realized just how he must look, hobbling around in his underwear in the rain, blood on his hands.

"I was swimming," he began, and the stranger blinked again and interrupted before Aaron could get any further.

"That's not allowed. No one is allowed here. There's a fence and signs." His voice was high and prissy, as if Aaron's injury was a personal offense to him.

Aaron gritted his teeth, wiped his bloody palms on his soaking underwear, and said, "The point is I was swimming and I cut my foot."

The stranger frowned and said, "I think the sheriff is looking for you."

Aaron's vision seemed to gray around the edges, and for a moment all he could hear was the thunder of the water up at the dam and all he could smell was his own blood.

"Is that so?" he said.

"Yes. I believe he is looking for you."

So his father had come down here. Maybe old Arthur Brady had called him after all.

"Well," Aaron said in a nearly cheerful tone, "the sheriff can go fuck himself."

The man shifted uneasily and wet his lips. He had a strange, wandering stare; he was looking at Aaron but seeming unable to focus on him.

"Can you come down here and give me a hand?" Aaron asked, taking one hobbling step sideways, the pain reaching excruciating levels and bringing dizziness.

The man looked at him but didn't move.

"Come on!" Aaron shouted. His right foot was painted with blood now. "Help me!"

The man turned away.

"Don't leave!" Aaron called, but the man didn't look back and didn't respond, just started to pick his way carefully over the wet rocks and back toward the trail.

Aaron tried to chase after him, but his first awkward step cost him his balance, and then he fell into the rocks on his knees, landing with a jarring pain.

"Help me, damn you!"

The man didn't so much as turn. He was simply going to leave Aaron here in his own blood, was that it?

Aaron threw the first rock half out of anger and half because he really needed help, he needed this asshole to at least help get the bleeding stopped before he left. The rock sailed high and wide and clattered into the trees, and it didn't seem the man even noticed. He kept shuffling up the bank toward the trail, moving slowly and awkwardly because of all the crap in his hands.

The rest happened almost too fast to register.

Aaron grabbed the neck of the beer bottle simply because it was handy and it was going to make some noise when it broke. He whipped it into the trees in the exact same way he'd thrown the rock, and the rock hadn't come close. He figured the bottle would bust in the trees high above the stranger's head and maybe that would finally get his attention.

It went low, though. It went low and fast, spinning and glittering through the rain, and just as Aaron threw it, the man turned back to him and spoke in a clipped but not unfriendly voice.

"In my car, I've got a first-aid—"

The neck of the bottle hit him in the face.

It burst on impact and knocked his glasses half off, turning one side of them upright but leaving the other in place, so that one eye was covered, like he was wearing a monocle. For an instant he stood there with his lips parted and the glasses hanging sideways on his face, and then a red line opened below his left eye socket and blood sheeted down his cheek.

Only then did he try to move, and when he did, he fell almost immediately, a cloud of papers blowing free from his hands as he went down on the bank, sliding into the shallows before he finally came to a stop.

He didn't get back up.

Aaron looked at him and then down at his own bloody palm and said, "Oh, shit, oh, shit."

His voice cracked like a child's, and he fell silent and looked back up at where the man lay slumped on the rocks. He wasn't far away, but Aaron still couldn't tell how bad the bleeding was.

It was raining too hard to make out anything clearly now.

Whatever he couldn't see about the wound was rendered swiftly irrelevant when the man's body began to shift—and not from his own efforts. The high, swift waters were tugging at him, pulling his body farther down the slick bank.

It was as if the place was hungry for him.

Aaron struggled to his feet, pushing through the cloud of pain as hot blood flowed, stumbling toward the injured man. He could make it. Had to make it, because if the man went into the water . . .

The current had the man's legs now, and it spun him sideways and the rain seemed to fall harder as if in assistance, adding a final layer of slickness to the mud and the rocks, and then he was off the bank and into the current, motionless and facedown as he floated by Aaron, swept downstream with astonishing speed.

Aaron's first step toward the water cost him his balance again, and he landed hard but kept going. He was on his hands and knees when he reentered the water. He lowered his head and swam hard through the pain, leaving a streamer of blood behind him.

9

He'd never saved anyone in the water, and yet he knew that he would. *So that others might live,* said the rescue swimmer credo, and Aaron had taped that slogan to the mirror on the back of his bedroom door when he was a rail-thin thirteen-year-old. His parents had never taken that old sign down. It was faded and frayed now, but it was still there.

He was sure that his moment had finally come. There would be plenty of pain waiting behind it—stitches in the hospital, then a return to jail, maybe for a long stay this time—but those things seemed trivial right now. What mattered was destiny, fate, a *promise*. One he'd made to his mother before her death; one he'd made to himself years ago in this very spot.

I will save a life. I may give my own, but I will save another's. Somewhere, on some unknown night in some distant sea, water will threaten a life, and I'll be in that water. I will make myself whole in that water. So that others might live.

He was so sure of that. Where and when, those were the only questions. He'd certainly never considered it might be the Chill. Or that he'd cause the threat himself.

Doesn't matter, he told himself as he turned his head to the left, sucked in a breath, and swam on. *Nothing matters but the water and the task. It's just you versus the current and the cold, same as you always knew it would be.*

Ahead of him, he saw his victim—who would now become his rescue—float to the surface briefly before being sucked back underneath, pulled down in the stretch where the tailwaters pounded over a ledge and down into a deep pool.

Aaron would reach him. The man wasn't far ahead now, Aaron was gaining fast, and his purpose was clear. As clear, in fact, as anything had been for him in a long, long time. The unknowns were answered now—when and who and how—and he no longer felt guilt or even fear. He was himself again.

This is why I'm here. Why I had to come back. For this moment and this man.

He saw blood in the water ahead of him. It was boiling along in a cloud of bubbles at the surface, tinging the water red. Somewhere behind them, Aaron's blood would be doing the same, pouring from his foot. He was only dimly aware of the torture that each kick caused. Adrenaline was sealing the pain away, holding the full flood of agony back just like the dam itself.

You've got to be nearly to him now. Maybe just above him. It's time to dive, and the water here is dark, so dive left and then swim right, cover ground, scan for him.

Old lessons coming back under duress. He was pleased by that. In those first months of rescue swimmer training, he'd been so damned happy. Each lesson a new chance to perfect the skills that he'd always known as something more than a passion. It was his identity.

Prove it, he thought as the water hammered him past a fallen tree whose branches raked his back, drawing fresh blood. *Prove the promise.*

The current had slowed, because he was in the stilling basin now, down in the Dead Waters. The current wouldn't have pulled his man farther downstream. He'd been sinking, and the stilling basin would have caught him.

Aaron made a head turn, an inhalation, and a dive. Down and to the left, scanning the bottom.

Nothing. The withered limbs of forgotten trees reached for him, and deeper there was a cluster of weeds, but no sign of the wounded man.

Pivot then. Dive deeper and keep turning, scan left to right, not too fast, because if you miss him, you'll miss your chance.

His lungs were beginning to throb, and the pain from his foot was nearing a crescendo that would drown out the numbing adrenaline, but he fought deeper, closing in on the bottom as he scanned left to right. Stumps. A tire. A beer can, a single tennis shoe, an anchor with the rope still knotted to it. The old stone foundation of some forgotten house. All of these things plainly visible despite his searing eyes, and yet nowhere was his man.

He reached out and gripped the anchor with his left hand and used it to hold himself in place while he turned his head back and forth and back again, searching, searching, searching.

Nothing.

Just stumps, rocks, water, and . . .

Got him!

The human figure was undeniable even in the dark water. A pale form pinned between two withered, rotting birches that had come to rest against the old stone foundation.

He swam down, deeper, deeper, hands extended, reaching for the first part of the man that he could grasp.

His hand met something invisible but strong, a thin cord that tangled in his fingers. Fishing line. He tried to brush it away, but when he moved his hand, the man beneath him moved, too, caught in the line.

Aaron almost parted his lips and breathed in water then.

The body he'd been intent on pulling to the surface wasn't the same body he'd been reaching for.

It was a skeleton. The skull turned toward him. Gleaming bone, blackened eye sockets. The face was all he could see, because the rest of the skull was surrounded by a hood or a shroud. Black cloth, picked to pieces by time and fish and crawdads that darted in and out, seeking whatever flesh had once covered the face.

His hand was still tangled, and his oxygen almost gone. He brought his hand up to his eyes, looking for a way to untangle the line, and when he did that, the corpse shifted again, sliding down against the birches, into an area lit dimly but brighter than the rest.

The fishing line was hooked in the tree but seemed secured to the corpse at what should have been the free end. There were multiple lines, too. Aaron looked down in horror, and this time, in the shaft of faint light, he saw the chains.

They were coiled about ankle bones that rested in boots that were now not much more than rubber soles and metal grommets, the leather or fabric that had once been there eaten away. The chains remained, though. And the padlock.

Aaron's vision went gray-black at the edges and he felt his lips start to part against his will. To breathe or to scream, he wasn't sure. He sealed them tight, knowing that he was about to die down here, joined by a length of fishing line to a corpse who'd come before him.

Surface. If your fingers tear out of the sockets and stay in that fishing line, that's fine, but surface now, or you're never going to draw another breath.

His upward motion was explosive, driven by panic and survival, his fear of the corpse and desire to live intermingling. Fight *and* flight.

The monofilament line bit hard at his fingers, but they passed through it, leaving some skin behind. He made a powerful upward stroke and thought, *I will be so close,* just before he broke the surface with a gasp that drew in both water and air.

He choked and sank, then rose and gasped in another breath. Rolled onto his back and leaned his head back, trying to clear his nose and mouth.

He floated to a downed tree near the shore and managed to grab it with a weak hand. Hung there, so exhausted that the simple act of breathing required all of his focus.

He looked upstream and down. No sign of anyone on the surface. His victim had vanished, but he'd found another.

Chains and fishhooks. No accident. And what was that cloth covering the skull?

The rain fell all around him.

He was still hanging on the limb, too exhausted to move, when Arthur Brady began hollering his name. Or maybe it wasn't his name.

There was something else in there. Fleming? Yes, he was calling for a man named Fleming.

That must have been him, Aaron thought, stupefied by fatigue. *That must have been the man I killed. Fleming.*

He wanted to call out for Arthur but couldn't find the strength. He just hung there on the branch, watching the rain hammer off the water's surface and wondering how he'd been so wrong about so much.

He was still there when Arthur arrived. Then and only then did he manage to find his voice.

"Call my father," he said. He finally forced himself upright, forced his head around so he could look Arthur Brady in the eye. "Mr. Brady? Please."

Arthur Brady stared back at him in the rain, blinking in fearful confusion. The rain beaded on his bald head.

"There was another fella down here," he said. "I've been looking for him."

"I know." Aaron's vision blurred again, and he squinted to clear his eyes. "I killed him. You can tell my father that, too."

10

When the call came, Steve was in a meeting with a county councilman who was concerned about the department's lack of aggression in policing the homeless. Two days earlier Steve had met with another councilman who was concerned that the policing was *too* aggressive.

This was the fun of being sheriff—you heard out all of the citizens' concerns and then in your spare time you attempted to see that they were actually being protected and served. Steve's approach to politicking was straight from his father, which came straight from his grandfather. Listen to everyone, ask good questions, and don't say anything in private that you wouldn't want to see quoted in the paper.

"You shouldn't have to search for reasons to be an honest man," his father had once told him, "but I'll give you one anyhow. When you're not hiding anything, you're at a level of peace that most people can't match. It seems simple until you watch the way other folks go about it. An honest man is never worried about being trapped by the thing he said yesterday or last week or last year."

It wasn't so damned hard. Just be an honest broker and do what you promised—which meant that you learned fast not to promise too much. That was good. That had gotten Ellsworths elected for many years in Torrance County, and Torrance County was a safer place to live because of them.

This was the notion in Steve's head—under-promise, and over-deliver—when a deputy summoned him with the news that Aaron was on the phone and that it was urgent. All thoughts of local politicking vanished then.

"Apologies," Steve told the councilman, pushing back from the table. "I'll need just a moment of privacy and then we'll be right back to it, sir."

Already, though, he was unsure about that. If Aaron was calling with something urgent, then it wouldn't be a quick fix. What fresh trouble was this? If it was jail, then he'd let Aaron sit there for a week.

At least a week, he told himself as he picked up the phone and punched the button to accept the call. *Maybe a month.*

"Yes, sir?" he said, the way he always answered the phone when his son called. He'd started that back when the boy wasn't much more than seven or eight and it gave Aaron a thrill to be acknowledged as a man. He'd been worthier of it back then. What in the hell had happened to him?

"Dad? I need you."

His tone gave Steve pause. It wasn't the insolence he was used to hearing from Aaron of late, and it also wasn't the wheedling tone, the *I got screwed by somebody and now I need help against this big bad world that's out to get me* tone. His voice was calm and collected yet underscored with fear.

"What's going on, Aaron? I'm in the middle of a meeting, and—"

"I'm going to need you to leave it. I'm sorry. But I am going to need you to leave and come get me, please."

He'd said *sorry* and *please*? It was almost implausible, a prank call.

He's made the right choice, Steve thought with sudden certainty. *He's read the rehab paperwork, he's thought about last night, and he has made the right choice.*

"Of course," Steve said, hunching forward over his desk, his eyes closing involuntarily with gratitude. "I'll come get you. I can be at the house in—"

"I'm at the dam."

Steve opened his eyes. "Excuse me?"

"I'm not at the house, Dad. I'm down at the Chill. Right here at the dam, with Mr. Brady. You need to hurry."

The steadiness in his voice scared Steve now. There were only two things that could chase the smart-ass out of his boy: maturity or fear. Real fear.

"What's happened?" Steve asked. "Aaron? Are you okay?"

"No," Aaron said. "No, I am not." Each word carefully and slowly spoken, as if they took an effort to find. "I am not okay, and I am sorry."

"I know you are," Steve said, for an instant rekindling the hope that this was all about rehabbing old troubles away and not introducing a new one.

Then his son said, "I killed a man, Dad. I didn't mean to, but I did it, and I . . ." The steady voice finally broke. "I need you to come down here and take me in. Don't send someone else, though. Please. I need it to be you."

Questions rose and faded in Steve's mind like waves on an endless sea, individually powerful but irrelevant because the sum of them was so vast.

When he finally spoke, all he said was "I'm on my way."

Later, he would realize that he didn't remember the drive at all. Couldn't even recall which route he'd taken from the station to the reservoir. He knew only that he drove with the lights on but the siren off, drove through the rain and down to the waters where his son waited, drove with Aaron's words echoing in his mind—*I killed a man, Dad . . . Don't send someone else . . . I need it to be you*—and then those were replaced with his own words from the morning, his own snarling and snapping words. *I'm evicting you . . . I want you to think about your mother today . . . Get out of my car, Aaron . . .*

Why hadn't he just let the boy sleep it off? Why had he come at him so hard, challenging him, pushing him, pushing him, until . . .

I killed a man, Dad.

There were three cars in the parking lot beside the dam. He recognized his own truck and Arthur Brady's old Toyota SUV, but he didn't know the third, a white Honda Pilot. The rain was still sheeting down, but he saw that Aaron was out in it, sitting on a flat rock and staring into the tailwaters, blank-faced. He had a wet towel wrapped around his shoulders, and one of his shoes had been replaced by a gauze wrapping as thick as a boxing glove.

What in the hell had happened down here?

Arthur Brady was at the window before Steve had even cut the engine. The old dam supervisor's face was ashen beneath the hood of his rain poncho.

"I can't find him," Arthur said when Steve opened the door.

"He's sitting right down there." Steve pointed at Aaron, who still hadn't turned.

"No, no. The man he hit with the bottle. Mick Fleming. I've been up and down the tailwaters, Sheriff, but I don't see a sign of him. I knew I should've called for more help sooner, but he was insisting—"

"Arthur." Steve held up a hand. "Slow down. Mick Flemish doesn't mean anything to me."

"Fleming. Mick Fleming. He's the engineer they sent to look at the dam."

Steve tried to process this. His mind was working too slowly. Aaron called out, his voice soft against the clatter of the rain on the car.

"I'll tell him, Mr. Brady. I'll explain it."

"I told him not to swim," Arthur muttered, pacing in a circle beside the hood of Steve's cruiser. "If he says anything else, he's lying. I told him—"

"Arthur?"

"Yes, sir?"

"Stay here and keep quiet. For just a minute." Steve turned and walked to his son.

Aaron was soaked, the mass of gauze on his right foot saturated with blood and water that left it a pale pink mess. His face and arms were lined with scratches, and his complexion matched the sky, a washed-out gray that offered no hope of change anytime soon.

Steve sat beside him on the rock, the rain soaking through his duty trousers, and said, "What happened?"

There had been many occasions over the years when Steve had looked at his son and wondered when he might see the face of a man looking back at him. He'd wondered how it had felt for his own father. When did your boy go from child to man, or did it never feel that way? Steve had wondered if the moment with Aaron might come on the other side of rescue swimmer school. It hadn't. Lately, he'd thought it was unlikely to come at all.

When Aaron looked him dead in the eyes and said, "I killed him. The evidence might not show it—the evidence might show a drowning—but I murdered him," Steve finally saw the man in him.

And, dear Lord, how he wanted to see the boy instead right then.

11

Steve didn't speak while Aaron told it. He sat in the rain and listened to the story of the swim that had gone from bad to worse with the misstep on a broken bottle in the weeds, the throw that had been aimed high but landed low, the desperate but fruitless effort to recover the man in the water. He listened to the report of the second corpse, the one with chains and fishing lines hooked into downed trees, and although he knew this was important, he could scarcely register it. An old corpse, an old murder—these things he'd encountered before.

His own son, a killer?

No.

He listened to it all without uttering a word, and while he tried to stay focused, he couldn't. His mind was stuck on the knowledge that he'd put the whole thing into motion. This one would go on his son's scorecard according to the rule of law, but it belonged on Steve's.

I wanted to show you that I could still do it, Aaron had said. *I wanted to show you how wrong you were. But you weren't wrong. I couldn't make the swim anymore.*

Their dueling failures laid bare: Steve's testosterone-laced taunt had sent his son down here, Aaron had been unable to rise to the challenge, and the resulting frustration had brought disaster. The key in the ignition belonged to Steve. He knew already that he would say something to this effect in the courtroom, and he knew already that the judge and the jury would not care. Oh, they'd sympathize with him, maybe, or blame him, maybe, but they would not be able to hold Steve's guilt up against

Aaron's, not with the family of the dead man also sitting in the courtroom.

The rain fell, and the water flowed by the rocks, and his son's fate drifted away with similar inevitably.

It was a cold world ruled by gravity. This much Steve had known for many years, and still he'd nursed a foolish faith that the world might do better by his child than it had by so many others. Now the fruits of both their sins lay somewhere down there in the depths.

A drowning, Steve thought, watching the leaden water flow by, hammered by the rain. *A drowning is all the coroner will see. The bump on the man's head, well, that was surely from a rock, right, Doc? Of course it was. The man slipped and fell in, maybe knocked himself unconscious—who's to say?—but what's done is done, dead is dead, now go write your report.*

Steve could make that happen. Steve had a lot of capital in this county. The only person who could so much as spread a rumor about anything that had happened down here with Aaron was Arthur Brady, and Arthur could be handled. Hell, he hadn't even seen anything. He'd just heard Aaron's version. Once he learned that the boy was on drugs and hours removed from a jail cell, he'd begin to understand the truth. Steve could make sure that he did. He could make damn sure that the death certificate had one crucial word on it: *accidental.*

And why not? It *had* been accidental, hadn't it? Aaron hadn't intended to hit the man with that bottle, and he surely hadn't intended for him to fall into the water. How in the world could a sane man consider that anything but a tragic accident?

"Do you read me my rights now, or do you need to get somebody else to do it?" the man who had once been Steve's boy asked.

Steve turned and faced him. Aaron looked back with sorrow and resignation. Waiting. Steve put an unsteady hand on his shoulder and squeezed. He realized that he was crying, but out here in the rain, maybe nobody could tell.

It was an accident, Aaron. We both know that, and I'll make sure the rest of the world does, too. It was an . . .

"Can't be me," Steve said, and the words left him like they'd been torn free with a gutting knife. He wasn't sure that it was even him speaking. It was his dead father, maybe, and a grandfather who stood behind him. His wife was with them, and his mother. Also crowding into the mix were the faces of dozens of people he'd visited in the middle of the night to share news that shattered lives. All of them watching him now.

"It can't be me," he repeated. "I've got a . . . conflict." He cleared his throat, wondering who to call, thinking of the state police, and then finally his cop brain caught up with his father brain and he remembered where they were. The Chilewaukee was more than a hundred miles from New York City, but it was still the property of that city's water supply. The water supply had its own police department, too, most deployed in the city, but some scattered in the rural precincts where the reservoirs held the sacred supply. The Chill was in the Ashokan Precinct, and Steve knew who to call: Gillian Mathers, a woman who was scarcely older than Aaron but who was a kind and competent police officer. She was from the city, but her family was from Torrance County. Steve thought she'd be compassionate, because once, long ago, he'd been compassionate with her.

"It's actually the DEP police jurisdiction," Steve said. "That's the right place to start."

His son accepted the news with a single nod.

"I guess we should call them, then," Aaron said. His voice thickened and he nodded once more and then said, "He's down there in the Dead Waters, I know he is. I was sure I could get to him in time, but . . ." He took a shuddering breath, passed his palm over his face, and said, "I'm so sorry, Dad."

Steve had buried his parents and his wife. He had heard all manner of devastating news and endured more than his share of loss, but he had never felt as shattered, as completely drained of hope, as he did listening to those four words from his son.

"Me too," he said, and his voice broke and it took him a few tries before he managed to say, "I love you, Aaron."

His son leaned his face into Steve's shoulder then, and Steve put a hand on his broad but trembling back and thought that they'd sit here together in the rain until someone came to get them.

Then Aaron pulled back and said, "Call them."

Steve rose on weak legs and found his cell phone and dialed. Words left his mouth but he had scant awareness of them. Words came back, and he tried to pay attention to those, but again they proved elusive. He got the location out, though. He knew that because he heard them say it back twice, and he answered each time: "Yes, at the Chill . . . Yes, right down by the dam at the Chill."

Then the call was done, and a car was en route, and Steve sat on the rock with his son once more and they waited in silence and in the rain for the arrival of the arresting officer.

PART TWO

12

Gillian Mathers made her dispatcher repeat the news, as if he'd made a mistake the first time.

"Steve Ellsworth's son killed someone. Steve told me himself. They're down there at the dam, waiting on someone to come arrest him. Steve doesn't think it should be his people. He wants it to be us. You."

Of course he would. Steve Ellsworth was so by-the-book he seemed positively boring—right up until you needed courtroom-ready product. Then you appreciated him. No cases were going to be thrown out for police misconduct when Steve was involved.

He wants it to be me, she thought, and she wondered if that was about police procedure or something deeper. She wondered if Steve Ellsworth even remembered the day he'd come to the house and found her there alone. If he remembered bringing her back to his office and waiting on her father to arrive from the city. If he remembered the letters she'd sent him afterward, asking for updates on the search for her missing grandmother.

He'd responded to every letter.

"You got it?" the dispatcher asked.

"I got it. En route."

She headed east, toward the Chill.

Aaron Ellsworth? Waiting on me to cuff him, with Steve looking on?

She'd known it would be a bad-luck day. The rain seemed to promise that. Even in the early hours of the morning she'd felt trouble on the way, but she had not imagined this. Truth be told, she often felt troubled by the weather in the Catskills, where each storm seemed to carry a more primal intensity than anything she'd known in the city. A city where she was supposed to be working. The dream was NYPD or FBI antiterrorism, and the dream had been rerouted thanks to a series of record flood seasons in the Catskills and memories that Gillian couldn't shake.

Flooding in the upstate reservoirs was dangerous. Maybe more dangerous than people appreciated.

Don't think like that.

How often did she chastise herself for such fleeting notions? The internal lectures didn't take, though. Instead of working in her beloved New York City, she was up here in the rural mountains at her own request, policing the reservoirs. She told herself that it was because she had a chip on her shoulder when it came to the Catskills. Coming back was a middle finger to her family, to the dead. And some of the dead deserved that.

The stay here was supposed to be brief, though. Anyone who held her middle finger in the air for too long began to feel the absurdity of it after a while. You were no longer making a point; you were making a fool of yourself.

Gillian was beginning to think the joke was on her. She was a mere hundred miles away from the greatest city on earth and yet felt like she was on another planet.

She'd gotten to detective sergeant in a hurry, though, and there were opportunities here: a full-time aviation unit, marine patrol, K-9 unit, and detective bureau, all in the tiny force that policed the city's watershed. Still, most of Gillian's cases involved illegal dumping or, in one high point of the past year, investigating the concealment of a series of septic tank failures. It was hard to imagine why they didn't have any franchise movie star playing the role of a DEP detective sergeant. Where was Angelina Jolie when you needed her?

Today, though, Gillian had a murder.

We will need divers, she thought, but she wanted to have a few minutes of a lead on them. She wanted to have Aaron in custody before things got chaotic down there, before anybody showed up with a camera. She wanted to do that much for Steve.

When she turned onto the lonely road that cut through the woods to the reservoir, she had the first of the dark memories that sometimes rose out here, a vision of the old schoolhouse and its lantern-lit room, the chalkboard in front of her, the empty inkwell near her hand. As usual, she was able to push the vision away, will it gone. It had been twenty years since she'd lived near this place, and memories of her time here were both distant and actively resisted. The combination left her feeling as if the memories she did have belonged to another person entirely. It was not her childhood. It couldn't possibly have been.

I need to take a walk by the lake, her grandmother had said the last time Gillian ever saw her.

Soon after that, Gillian was gone from Torrance and off to the city, reunited with a father who'd been a nonexistent presence in her life until her grandmother went missing. Then he came for her, and he took her away. Neither of them had expected her to make a return.

The dam came into sight. A long, bleak stone structure that seemed to match the color of the sky today. She pulled into the parking lot and saw no flashing lights or sign of police presence, let alone any indication that it was a murder scene.

They'd seen her pull in and met her halfway, standing in the gravel that was pooling with rainwater. Steve looked worse than his son, almost. He was a big man, several inches over six feet, with wide shoulders and thick hips. Aaron had the height but not the bulk. He was pale, his pallor contrasted by the dark tattoos on his arms and the bright bloodstain on his heavily bandaged foot.

Steve stood next to Aaron with his arm protectively around his son's shoulders, and Gillian looked at the water dripping off the brim of his hat and wondered how long they'd been out here in the rain.

"I don't know the details yet," she said, "but should we be calling for a search-and-rescue—or is it absolutely too late for that?"

"Too late," Aaron said. His voice was low and empty, but he kept his eyes up, his square jaw held level, his shoulders back. "I had the chance of saving him, and I . . . failed. But I can show you where to find . . ." He cleared his throat, blinked, and faced her through the rain. ". . . where to find his body." He blinked again. "Both bodies. They'll be close together."

Gillian felt a spider-crawl sensation along her spine. She almost lowered her hand to her gun.

"What do you mean, two bodies?"

"An old one," Steve said, lifting a hand as if to placate her. "He found an old one."

He found an old one. Like they were talking about lost golf clubs or something. Gillian looked from Steve to Aaron, struggling to catch up. "You found another corpse?"

Aaron started to nod, then hesitated. "I only found one corpse. But there have to be two now, because the man I hit drowned in the same spot, or close to it. The person I *thought* was him was actually . . . someone else. Someone who's been down there a long time, I think. Chains on their feet, and fishhooks . . . a hood over the head, it looked like." He gave an involuntary shudder, as if trying to push the memory away, and when he spoke again, his voice was softer. "It confused me. It made me waste time. I was trying to save a skeleton because I thought it was . . . the person I'd hit."

Gillian hadn't been prepared for this. Suddenly she had an active case and a cold case? She took a breath and tried to refocus. "You're sure the man you hit went under?"

"I'm positive. I threw a bottle, aiming for the tree above him, but it went low. Caught him in the head and he fell into the rocks and the water got him and he was facedown in it. I could see him when I went in. I just couldn't get to him."

Fifteen years in prison, Gillian thought. *Maybe he's out in ten. Maybe.*

"Any witnesses?" she asked. "Anyone down here who saw or heard what happened?"

"No. Mr. Brady saw me arrive, but he wasn't there when it . . ." His voice trailed off, his eyes went distant, and then he said, "The photographer saw me, too. I don't know where he went, but he saw me go into the water. When the other man came out of the woods, I thought it was going to be the photographer."

Steve Ellsworth stared at his son. "What photographer?"

"I don't know. Just some guy taking pictures of the dam. He was right down there." Aaron nodded toward the water. "I didn't see him until I waded in, but then we had a . . . a bit of a back-and-forth, and then I swam off and I didn't see him again."

"Was he with a newspaper or something, or just a guy on his own?"

Aaron shook his head. "I didn't ask. I didn't recognize him, and I don't think he was local. For some reason I picked him for being from someplace else. He said his name was . . . Hallbright, I think? Curtis Hallbright?"

Gillian's nerves sparked with cold fire.

"Haupring?" she said, and they both turned to her, and she wished she hadn't spoken. She knew better than to speak of these things; she had known that and honored that for nearly twenty years now, ever since the day Steve Ellsworth had visited her house on a welfare check, following her grandmother's instructions.

"Maybe," Aaron said. "Haupring . . . yeah, maybe."

"You know him?" Steve asked her.

"No."

Both of them frowned. Steve was the first to voice the obvious question. "Then why are you asking?"

"Because it's my job," Gillian said, flustered. "When I write up the incident report, Steve, I'll need to get the names right, you know?"

He stared at her, puzzled, and she felt a hot flush in her face.

"I wasn't sure if I'd heard him right." She took a notepad out of her pocket, opened it, and fumbled for a pen while the pages promptly soaked with rain. "So Hall-bright . . . like that?"

"Maybe," Aaron said. "Or what you said. Haup-ring, like with a *p*? *H-a-u-p*?" He thought it over and nodded once. "I think that's it. The one you said."

"But you don't know him?" Steve asked, speaking to Gillian.

"Never met anyone with that name," she said, and she was glad she could say this honestly. "But I'll try to find him if he was down here for the crime."

When she said the last word, Steve winced, his interest in the photographer's name sinking beneath his fear for his son.

She turned back to Aaron. "Looks like you need medical."

"I can show you where they are first." He took a step toward her, pulling away from Steve's protective arm. "I know right where he went in. I was sure I'd make it to him. There was a moment when I thought this was all . . . *supposed* to happen. You know?" His blue eyes seemed aflame in his pale face. "I mean, it all unraveled in just a few seconds, but each step needed to happen, right? I've got to fail the swim. That's first, because if I make it all the way back up, then I never step on the bottle. And then I step on the bottle just as he comes down here, and when I threw it, I couldn't have hit him if I'd been trying. But I did hit him, because it was supposed to happen. When he fell, he landed close enough that the current caught him. The water is higher than ever, too. Any other day he falls there and he stays dry. But today the water is high and it's pulling, and then it tugged him in like it *wanted* him, and he was facedown and I knew exactly what I had to do, and it all felt like—"

Steve snapped, "Aaron."

"Something that was supposed to happen," Aaron pressed on, ignoring his father. He took another hobbling step toward Gillian, and she almost backed up. His words and his eyes were that intense. "I came back here, I was full circle today, and I had just one job left to do, and it was him. He was there in the water, and I was the only one who could get him, right? It was all up to me, and that's the way it was supposed to—"

"*Aaron!*" Steve thundered. "Enough. Don't talk like that. Just answer her questions, show her what she needs to be shown—that's all."

"But it was supposed to be me," Aaron said, wild now, almost enthusiastic. "It was exactly what I was supposed to do. Maybe I *did* aim the bottle at him, maybe—"

"Shut up!" Steve shouted, and Gillian lifted her hands.

"Enough," she snapped. "Enough. Steve, you need to stop interrupting him. Let him say what he's got to say."

Steve Ellsworth stared at her with sadness and an impotent rage, and then in a low voice said, "It's been a long day for my child, Gillian. Just understand that."

A long day for my child. Yes, Steve remembered that welfare check. He remembered the letters, too. She was sure of it then.

"I get that," Gillian said. The wind had shifted and was now blowing the rain into her face. Her dark hair was plastered to her cheek. She ducked her head and pushed her hair back, and she saw that the gauze wrap on Aaron's foot was turning brighter red. He needed medical attention, and she needed to get him calmed down. Get both of them calmed down, actually.

"I just need to know where to send the divers," she said.

"I'm not sure where he ended up, but the one I thought was him is pinned up against trees and an old house foundation or something. There were chains around the feet and it looked like a black hood or a bag over the head. Some kind of cloth hood."

Time seemed to stop again. It was just like when he'd said the photographer's name—the present was gone, and the past was reaching for Gillian with cold hands.

She was afraid that they could see her reaction but then realized they were both looking past her. Aaron's cheeks had drained of color and his eyes had gone wide and white, his lips parting wordlessly as he stared into the woods. She turned to follow his horrified gaze and saw a man approaching through the trees.

He was of average height, slender, and not much of his face was visible except for his glasses. The rest was shadowed by the hood of his rain jacket. He was hugging a notebook and a tablet computer to his chest as if to shield them from the rain.

When Gillian said, "Who is this?" she wasn't expecting an answer. She didn't think either Steve or Aaron Ellsworth had any more idea than she did.

It was the sound of Aaron falling that made her turn back to him.

He seemed to melt, sliding down slowly, until his ass was planted in a puddle, and his bloody foot was stretched out in front of him. His eyes were wide and white.

"That's the man I killed."

13

The stranger walked on up the bank, close enough that Gillian could see his expression. He was looking at them with friendly but quizzical eyes. As was warranted—two cops and a wounded man in the rain. But he didn't seem to understand a bit of it.

Something is very wrong here, Gillian thought.

But hadn't she already known that? Hadn't she known that since Aaron Ellsworth had spoken of the photographer named—

Stop it, Gillian, damn you. Stop thinking of the name. It's not the right name, you put it into his head, and now you need it out of your own head. Fast.

"Sir?" she called out. "Can you come here for a moment?"

The stranger approached without hesitation and offered one damp palm.

"Mick Fleming," he said. "I have authority to trespass."

He gave a nervous smile, his eyes darting from Gillian to Steve and then to Aaron. They lingered on Aaron the longest but showed no recognition, just confusion. As Gillian shook his hand, she realized just how drenched he was. He'd been out here a long time.

Steve Ellsworth said, "What . . . where have you been?"

"All over the place. It's my job to inspect the dam. Mr. Brady can vouch for me."

"I hit you," Aaron said. His voice shook. He was staring up at Mick Fleming as if he couldn't fathom the man's existence. "I hit you with the bottle. I wasn't trying to, but I did."

"Excuse me?" Fleming looked Aaron's way uneasily, a side-eyed glance. Watching him, Gillian thought of the way strange dogs would stand warily and sniff one another, that tense moment that could lead to play or aggression.

"He believes he hit someone with a bottle, and they fell into the water," she said. "We mistakenly thought that someone was you, Mr. Fleming. But can I ask how long you've—"

"There's no mistake: I hit *him*!" Aaron shouted. "*He* went into the water. The bottle broke on the side of *his* head, *he* was bleeding, and I damn near drowned trying to pull *him* back out!"

Mick Fleming took two steps back. His face had gone from bewildered to frightened. Steve put a hand on Aaron's shoulder.

"Easy," he said.

"How long have you been here?" Gillian asked Fleming.

"Most of the afternoon." He passed his hand over his soaked clothing like a wand. "As you can see."

"Did you see him here?" she asked, nodding at Aaron.

"Um, I didn't . . . I can't say I *saw* him."

"You saw me! You saw me bleeding and you wouldn't help!" Aaron's shout had a tremble to it, and he seemed as scared of Fleming as Fleming was of him.

"Let me talk," Gillian said, and when Aaron fell silent, she turned back to Fleming. "So you had no encounter with him?"

"Absolutely not."

"He's told us a story that someone is in the water, and—"

"It's not a *story*, it's what happened, and it was *him*!"

"Aaron!" Steve snapped, tightening his grip and giving his son a shake, as if he could rattle sanity back into him.

"I didn't have any encounter with him," Mick Fleming said. "I heard him, that was all. Or I heard *someone*."

"Heard him doing what?"

"Um . . ." He took a step away from Aaron. "I suppose the word is *raving*? I heard someone sort of . . . shouting to himself. Or I thought it was to himself. I mean, I only heard one person. He sounded, um . . . I would say drunk? A little slurred. But I did not see him."

Aaron tried to rise and Steve had to use some strength to hold him back. The bandage on Aaron's foot darkened with fresh blood.

"You left for a first-aid kit, and I threw the bottle. Why are you lying about that? Do you think this is helping me? Show them your face. Take the damned hood off!"

Mick Fleming pulled his hood down. He seemed less frightened now, more fascinated.

His face was unblemished. No trace of an injury.

"I'm sorry," he said softly, addressing Aaron directly. "I truly don't want to upset you, but"—he spread his arms—"as you can see, I'm quite all right."

"You didn't see anyone else?" Gillian asked. "Hear anyone else?"

Fleming shook his head.

"He said there was a photographer down here," she said.

"I guess I've missed a lot," Fleming said. "But I've been down here for hours and I didn't see any of this. I'm sorry."

It went silent then, the four of them standing in the rain, staring at one another. Gillian said, "Steve, I don't know what to do here."

Steve's voice was low when he said, "I've got it, Gillian. I'll get him home."

"Get him to a doctor," she said, and then, too quickly, "For his foot, I mean."

"Right," Steve said, but she could see in his eyes that he knew exactly what kind of doctor she was thinking of.

"I'll send the divers in," she said. "We'll check it out and—"

"I don't think you need to send any divers in."

"But he said there were . . ." She stopped before saying *two bodies*. She understood what he was thinking: If Aaron had hallucinated his violent encounter with Mick Fleming, why believe the other body was real?

"I'll get him help," Steve said. "I'm sorry. I really am."

Aaron was watching his father. "It's him," he whispered. "I saw *him*. I hit *him*." He pointed at Fleming, who regarded him with a pitying look and then spoke in a gentle tone.

"It's good news that you didn't really, though. Right? That's good news. There was some confusion, but I'm fine. I'm just fine."

It was the way you'd talk to a child who'd awoken from a nightmare, and Gillian saw Steve Ellsworth stiffen. Not from anger but shame.

"I'll get him home and I'll get him help," he said. "I'm sorry. To both of you."

Gillian didn't answer. She looked downstream. For reasons that she didn't want to voice, she still wanted this water searched.

A hood, Aaron had said of the body in the water. The old body, the skeleton.

"We can give it a look at least," she said. "Just in case."

"Don't waste anyone else's time," Steve said. "I've done enough of that."

He helped Aaron upright. Aaron obliged, but his attention was still on Mick Fleming. He couldn't take his eyes off the man.

Gillian considered helping but she didn't want to touch Aaron. The way he looked right now, wild-eyed and wounded, she thought he might lash out at anyone who came near, like an animal with its foot caught in a trap. That was, in fact, precisely what he looked like— caught, hurting, and deeply confused by it all. No, more than confused. Terrified.

"I'm sorry," Steve said again.

"No need to apologize," Mick Fleming said, and then he gave a high, nervous laugh. "Weather like this makes us all a little crazy."

Wrong word, Gillian thought, and Fleming seemed to realize it, too, because he rushed out another sentence as if to distract from calling Aaron crazy.

"The good news is the dam's plenty strong," he said. "All this rain isn't going to give you any trouble at the Chilewaukee. That much I can promise you."

"Terrific," Steve muttered. He had Aaron upright now. Gillian could see the humiliation in Steve's eyes. He didn't say anything, just turned and guided Aaron away, helping him toward the parking lot. Aaron was talking to him in a frantic whisper, but Steve didn't respond.

"Do you need me to stay?" Mick Fleming asked her in a low voice. "I'm happy to, but . . . nothing happened."

"No," she said, "I don't need you to stay. I'm glad you showed up when you did, before I arrested him and sent divers in looking for you."

"He was quite upset."

"Yes." Gillian had to laugh. "I can't imagine what it felt like to hear him insisting that he'd killed you."

"It was a new experience, certainly. Who was that with him? The other officer seems to know the, um, excitable young man quite well."

"He's his father." She hesitated, then said, "Things haven't been trending well for Aaron, but I still can't imagine that his father was prepared for something like this."

Fleming made a soft sound of sympathy and looked skyward. The rain drove into his face.

"Full moon tonight," he said. "Maybe that's what got to him. I don't know. I won't pretend to understand the human mind. All I understand is dams. And that"—he pointed at the vast concrete fortification that held back the reservoir—"is one beautiful structure." He looked back at her. "My grandfather designed it, you know."

Gillian felt very cold, looking at him. He watched her with almost amused eyes.

"Jeremiah Fleming," she said.

"Excellent. There aren't many left who know the name."

Gillian knew the name all too well. Suddenly, though, she did not want to admit that.

"It's on a plaque in the office," she said. "All of the old engineers are."

"Oh, I see. Well, he was a marvelous engineer. Things didn't work out for him as he'd planned up here, but sometimes fate takes success out of your hands. Reshapes it." He smiled at her. "Good luck with your work. I think it's about time to get out of this rain."

With that, he turned from her and walked to the gatehouse.

14

They blasted and hauled, hauled and blasted. Rock crumbled and dust rose. Above them, the city carried on, dependent on the workers below, but unaware of them.

This was the story of Deshawn Ryan's days, but also the story of three, four, even five generations before him. The men who'd dug the first of the tunnels had worked with shovels and picks. Then came dynamite. Then drill-and-blast systems. And now the Mole.

The Mole was a tunnel-boring machine that looked like a giant torpedo. Its payload was made up of massive steel blades, each of them mounted on a circular head. Lasers in the Mole took rock readings; men adjusted computerized controls; the hydraulic-powered blades whirled; granite vanished. A conveyor belt carried the crushed rock from front to back. There, Deshawn and the rest of the crew loaded the rock onto muck cars. Car by car, foot by foot, inch by inch, New York City's third water tunnel moved forward.

Up above, eight million people turned on faucets oblivious to the men below them, relying on the billion gallons a day that already surged through the existing aqueducts, running out of the dark valleys and rugged mountains.

It was a hell of a thing, really, an authentic engineering marvel, and yet a lot of the sandhogs who worked in the city never ventured to see the source. Deshawn had been in the tunnels for two years himself before he got the urge to go there, and then it had been for the silliest of reasons: someone came out to take a photograph of the crew.

Sandhogs intrigued people in the way any dirty job did. Film crews would come and go, and newspaper reporters, and people writing books. Before security tightened down after 9/11, visitors were more common.

The man who came to take the picture of the crew that day was a quiet guy with dark hair and a bearded face that would light up now and then with an odd, private smile. He was particularly interested in taking pictures of Teddy Biddle, for reasons no one understood but everyone found funny, because Teddy was a surly son of a bitch. He didn't like distractions even among his own crew, and he damn sure didn't like outsiders or interlopers. He tolerated a few photographs and when he'd had enough of it, he got into the cage and vanished below the earth, with the photographer standing above, snapping photos of him the whole way down.

For a few hours after they'd all joked about it, calling him Centerfold Teddy. That was before the accident.

Deshawn never caught who the photographer worked for or what the project was. He just lined up beside the others with his hard hat on and gave the camera the flat eyes that said, *This is serious business,* because that's what the photographers always wanted—smiling sandhogs need not apply for photos—and then it was done and he was ready to get back to work, when the photographer approached and asked for his name, age, and hometown.

Deshawn spelled his name, told his age, twenty-three, and answered that, yes, he was a New York native: Queens, to be exact.

"Do you ever think about where it comes from?" the photographer asked.

"Excuse me?"

"The water. Have you seen the place?"

Deshawn shook his head, and the man withdrew a photograph from his bag. It was a black-and-white picture of a two-lane road running straight for the center of a forested mountain in the distance, fences on either side, fields beyond them, fading into more mountains on the photograph's edges. There were shadows across the road that made it seem

like the place was down in a valley somewhere. There was not a building in sight. Just the road. Everything looked parched. Even the weeds
alongside the road were withered.

"That's the source," the photographer told him.

"Looks dry to me," Deshawn said, and laughed, because he didn't
know what else to do . . . and because something about the picture
bothered him. He wasn't sure what. The shadows, maybe? The perfectly
straight road that faded from light to dark? The emptiness? Something
about the place just felt wrong.

The photographer was looking at him hard, like he was hoping for
more, so Deshawn said, "Well, where is it?"

This seemed to please the man. He gave the faintest of smiles and
said. "Galesburg."

Deshawn said, "Looks like a pretty spot," although in truth he didn't
like the picture.

"Gorgeous," the photographer told him. "You should take a drive up
there sometime. See where it all begins. Mr. Biddle has visited. It seems
he's about the only one."

Deshawn agreed that he'd have to do that, but he was just being polite. He had no intention of borrowing his brother's car and driving out
of the city on a hot May weekend to see the reservoirs upstate.

Then the accident happened.

It was a few days after the photographer left. One of the muck cars
went off the rails, and they were winching it back onto the track, Teddy
Biddle guiding the process, standing in the center of the track and mo-
tioning with his hands, beckoning, *A little more, little more,* and then
there was a whip-snap sound and Deshawn looked up just in time to
watch the steel cable boomerang back and cleave through the center of
Teddy's face and his throat.

Teddy stood for an instant in the same posture he'd been in, feet
spread, elbows bent, hands curling inward, asking for a little more tension, just a little more.

Then the blood poured and Teddy fell.

Deshawn was the first one to him, upset but not truly worried. They'd had injuries before; he'd seen plenty of blood stain the stone in these tunnels. Teddy Biddle was going to need some surgery, but he'd be fine.

There was too much blood, though. Deshawn noticed that right away. There was a neat line of blood down Teddy's face, which was split open from crown of the skull to the chin, but the real problem was down near his collarbone, where blood squirted hot against Deshawn's hands.

The cable had severed his carotid artery. Cut it clean.

He was dead before they got him back aboveground.

None of the crew said much about it. That was the way it went with sandhogs. Nobody wanted to relive the horror shows. Not when you knew that a man had died for every mile of water tunnel. They all showed up for the funeral, of course, and Deshawn pressed a note into the tear-dampened palm of Teddy's widow, a few scribbled sentences in which he'd tried to capture the sense of a man's life and the weight of his death and failed miserably. Afterward some of the guys went out drinking, but Deshawn didn't feel like that. He wanted to get out of the city. Felt the concrete pressing in on him, the day too damn hot for May, the whole place too damn loud. After the funeral he wanted to find someplace quiet to just sit and think. A quiet place where the wind was clean.

He didn't know much about Teddy outside of work. It struck him that one of the only things he did know had been imparted by the photographer who told him that Teddy had gone to visit Galesburg.

He headed upstate, too, driving in search of Galesburg.

He didn't realize the joke was on him until he reached Torrance County. There was no Galesburg. Not anymore. He found the lake, though, and then he found the town of Torrance. An idyllic village with the smell of pines and everything so still and quiet.

He liked that. It felt right for Teddy.

Felt damn strange to Deshawn, though. He hadn't been out of the city much in his life and had spent almost no time in the woods. The one time his family had gone on a vacation to New Hampshire, they'd gotten lost and his father had been irate and everyone had needed to pee but didn't want to say it and soon the winding roads and the dark hills had seemed frightening and foreboding to Deshawn. He wasn't able to appreciate the quiet then, and he didn't sleep well in the shotgun-style motel where they stayed with the windows open and the pine-scented breezes blowing cool even on a summer night. He was glad to get back to the city.

He'd been a child then, of course. It was different as an adult.

On that hot day when he left the city to find the long-gone town of Galesburg and ended up in Torrance, he appreciated the forested mountains and their cool shadows and silence. He liked the way you could hear small sounds from far off and always tell which direction the wind was coming from. He liked how far you could see from a ridgetop, and the way the lake whipped up into tiny whitecaps when the breeze built into a gust.

He was at the lake when he saw the girl swimming. Pale above the water; paler still underwater. Lean and graceful, though. Small breasts and a tapered waist and flat stomach. He continued glancing back when she came out of the water, glistening, pine needles sticking to her feet, and toweled off. She caught him looking and smiled and he laughed and lifted his hands in apology. She dried off and pulled on a sweatshirt and loose white cotton pants that showed the still-damp black swimsuit bottom beneath and walked over to say hello.

His daughter's mother.

The next week his body was back in the city, but his mind was in the mountains, wondering when he could get up there again, wondering if it would be the same with her.

He'd asked around about the photographer, trying to see if anyone else remembered him, or where he'd come from, what he was working on. Nobody did. That disappointed him, because he wanted to see the picture again. He wanted to show it to the girl he'd met upstate, because she knew so much about the place. Galesburg. She talked like it was living and breathing instead of submerged. He thought she'd enjoy the picture. Thought maybe she'd know right where it had been and where the road led.

He never found it.

That summer, though, everything was about the girl. Kelly Mathers.

He was back in Torrance the next weekend, and he stayed in a hotel that reminded him of the one in New Hampshire, a long, low building, single-story, with tall pines overhead and only eighteen rooms in the whole thing. He took Kelly to dinner, walked with her around the town square and out past a park with cannons and signs about the French and Indian War. She didn't come back to the motel with him that night, but she did the next.

That was the first day of June. Not quite summer but feeling like it.

Deshawn returned to Torrance four of the next five weekends. When he was with Kelly it always started wonderful and then turned strange. Friday nights were perfect, and Saturdays were good. By Sunday morning, though, he'd be ready to leave, looking for an excuse to slip away without being able to put his finger on what was wrong, and then he'd drive south telling himself that it had been fun while it lasted but now it needed to end. There would be no more trips to Torrance County.

Then it would be Monday, back in the noisy city, and he would find himself needing her in a deeper way than lust. Like a thirst.

She liked to make love in the lake. She'd guide him along narrow paths paved with pine needles that would open up on beautiful but isolated stretches of dark water. Deshawn grew to associate the first shock of cold water with an increased desire.

Her legs were so pale in the water. His own seemed to vanish, so that it was the two of them together at the surface, but just one body below. Her fingernails biting into his back and her breath hot in his ear and all around them the soft sounds of water in motion. Sometimes they'd stay until after dark, and then the stars reflected off the surface in a liquid blackness that felt like its own universe, the stars seeming to belong within the water rather than in the sky above.

It had been a hauntingly beautiful place.

Once, shivering against him, her damp arms hugging tight to his neck, she'd whispered that she wanted to pull him under and stay there, just the two of them, alone in their own world, and he'd never have to go back to the city. He could stay in Galesburg, with her. Wouldn't he like that?

It had been merely whispered passion, but it had chilled him. Such strange wording. But he'd told her yes, yes, of course, he wanted that. He wanted her and only her and he would stay wherever she wanted him to stay.

There were moments when he meant it.

On the last trip she took him to her house. A real pretty place out in the woods, not like anything Deshawn had seen before, no neighbors in sight, no street sounds, nothing but trees in all directions. He thought she was taking him to meet her parents, and he was uneasy about that idea, but when they got there she told him they had the house to themselves, and her hand was resting high on his thigh, and he became immediately more pleased with the idea of seeing her home.

"Come on," she said, taking him by the hand, her fingertips trailing across his palm before they hooked his own. "I'm gonna take you to school."

He thought he knew exactly what she meant, what kind of education he was in for. He was watching the swing of her hips as she led him up the porch, and he felt himself swell and stiffen and he thought he was going to like being taken to school just fine. Learn a few new things indeed.

Then they were inside the house and she was opening the door that was hidden behind the bookcase, swinging it open to show the strange dark room beyond. The single student's desk and the larger teacher's desk across from it. The chalkboard covered in scrawled equations. The walls lined with framed photographs. Old faces, sepia tints, black-and-whites, no color. Almost all men, it seemed. White men with suits and smiles, and then black men and white men in coveralls, with dirty faces and hard eyes. Picks and shovels in some hands, quill pens and ornate documents in others.

"The hell is all this?" he'd asked.

"The school, fool." Light, teasing. "Didn't I tell you?"

"I mean, like . . . for real, what the hell is all this?"

She laughed and closed the door. He wanted her to leave the door open but felt foolish asking, so he kept silent when she lit the lantern and closed them in with that faint flickering light.

"So, seriously? What's with the museum?"

"It's my school."

"I'm being sincere. Like, sincerely freaked out. Who put all this old shit here?"

"The principal. The teacher."

"C'mon."

She kept answering his questions poker-faced. Talking about classes and her teacher—singular: teacher—and how they'd had *an emphasis on history* and all the while he was feeling more and more certain that he should have stayed in the city.

Finally, she ignored one of his questions, took him by the hand, and led him up to the front of the room, like a teacher guiding a student, walking them up to the chalkboard and the big desk. He wanted to leave, but she was smiling at him, the teasing smile again. Then her lips were on his and her hands were on his belt buckle and suddenly he was braced against the desk, his ass resting against it until she'd pulled him toward her and into her.

It was then, when she leaned her head back and moaned, that he looked up and saw the old wooden planks nailed across the ceiling. They were singed and charred, like wood left in a cold stove, but there was a dampness to them, too.

She kept her eyes to the ceiling the whole time, fingernails biting into his back, legs wrapped tight, hips working rhythmically. He closed his own eyes, trying to lose himself in the sensation. When he did that, though, he thought he could hear water. Drips and splashes, the soft popping echoes of puddles in caves. He opened his eyes again, and she was still looking up, and the planks were darker in the lantern light, water shimmering on them.

He shut his eyes again. Kept them closed after that. When he finished, it was with a shudder and a gasp that seemed loud in the room. She swung herself up against him and held him tight, her legs still wrapped around his hips. Nipped his shoulder and collarbone with her teeth, breathing hard. She didn't say a word, just stroked the back of his neck and sighed softly, acting like everything was normal.

He was in a hurry to dress and get out of there. He made a joke about her parents coming home and finding them, and ten minutes later they were back in daylight, and he was making excuses for why he needed to drive home that night.

The next Monday he volunteered for an overtime shift on the weekend. The Monday after that, he bought Yankees tickets for the weekend and invited his brother. He kept planting obstacles in front of himself so he couldn't talk himself into the drive on a Friday afternoon. He did not want to return.

Ten weeks passed before she left the message telling him she was pregnant.

He drove back up then, and that was the first time he met her family. Molly Mathers had sat with him on the front porch of the house and talked as kindly as one could in that situation. She was a trim, handsome woman with a generous smile and a low voice and eyes that felt like interrogation lamps. She didn't attack him or accuse him of anything, though; didn't say a single harsh word. Just watched him. It was only after a long stretch of silence, the two of them listening to the cicadas and watching the fireflies glow and then darken in the woods, that she told him he probably would not like it around there.

An observation, not a suggestion. No hard edge to it, as if he wasn't wanted and he'd be wise to take the hint, but more like a question she was afraid she knew the answer to.

"You probably will not like it around here."

Deshawn protested, assuring her otherwise, telling her how much he liked the town of Torrance, how much he liked the mountains and the streams and the lake, the quiet and the beauty and the people. How much he liked her daughter.

Then he left and made a prophet out of her.

Molly Mathers was damn good and right with her simple statement: Deshawn Ryan didn't like it around there at all.

He went back to Torrance a few times each year. Was there when Gillian was born, and for her birthdays, although usually he pressed for them to meet somewhere in the middle. He sent checks each month, but he never went back to the house. Not until the day he came to take his daughter away from it.

He didn't like thinking about that house, and for years now it had been easy enough not to. Once Gillian was with him in the city, once their days became a shared thing, it was strangely easy to forget about that odd house in the hills, in fact. Or it had been.

Lately, though, the memories were coming in quietly but constantly, seeping like groundwater through the tunnel walls. As he rode the man car down the rattling rail system that took him away from the Mole and back toward the shaft, another day done, Water Tunnel Number 3 another forty-eight feet toward completion, he couldn't stop thinking of his daughter up there in Torrance County. Maybe he should visit. He was always letting—making?—her do the drive, believing her stories about missing the city and wanting the time back home.

But shouldn't a man visit his daughter? Of course he should. See her world, ask her some questions. Maybe tell her some things, too.

Hon, he might tell her, *my mind's been drifting lately. I don't want you to worry, but I'm seeing things, and maybe worse than that, I'm remembering things.*

Not quite yet, he decided as another explosive charge blew down the tunnel and the rock walls shuddered and the dust rose. Because she *would* worry, and that wasn't right.

It was his job to do the worrying for the both of them.

15

"He's lying," Aaron said. "I don't know why, but he was lying. Obviously, I didn't kill him, but I hurt him bad. He's lying about that."

He watched his father drive silently through the rain, refusing to engage. Somehow this was worse than the terrible moment they'd shared while Aaron confessed to the killing. Once again, his father's face was wracked with grief—not anger, not disappointment, but *grief,* which somehow was worse than the others.

He's lying.

No one would lie in that situation, though. And then there was the minor matter of his healing. Aaron had watched the blood run down the man's face, had seen him slip into the water and sink . . . but there'd been no evidence of that. So Mick Fleming hadn't only lied, he'd healed. Impossible. Obviously and utterly impossible.

It was him, though. I should know; I'm the one who killed him!

But he hadn't killed him. The man was alive and well.

I confused him for someone else, maybe.

No, he had not. He'd seen him clearly; he'd *spoken* to him.

Then what in the hell had happened?

The only answer was the very one Aaron knew his father was considering.

I'm insane. I almost have to be, because nothing else makes sense.

The fear he felt then was worse than any he'd ever known.

"You should have let that cop check for the other body," he said. "I saw the skull. There was fishing line and hooks and some sort of hood, and when I moved it, the skeleton slid and I saw—"

"Stop," his father said, and his voice broke with a barely suppressed sob.

Aaron looked over at him and saw with astonishment that his father had started to cry.

"Please, stop," he said, voice pleading, desperate.

Aaron turned and faced ahead. The windshield shimmered with ribbons of water, the wipers slashed, and otherwise the car was silent.

They didn't speak again until they reached the emergency room, and by then his father's eyes were dry. When he came around to help Aaron out of the car, Aaron could feel a reluctance to his touch, as if insanity were contagious.

I didn't imagine it. I watched that bottle break on the side of his head, watched the blood begin to spill, watched him fall . . . and then, down in the Dead Waters, there was the body. I saw the skeleton face, dark eyes under that decaying black hood. I saw it all.

He shook his head as if to refuse the memory.

He kept his eyes down as he limped into the ER, kept his eyes on the blood-soaked bandage and tried to put more weight on his wounded foot to drive the pain up, to give him focus on what was real.

But is it real? If the rest of it wasn't real, how do you know this is?

No, no, no. He could not begin to think like that. Couldn't question everything and anything, that would drive him—

Insane.

They were at the reception desk now, and his father was telling the man behind it that Aaron had stepped on broken glass and would need stitches, probably a lot of them, because it was a bad cut.

It *had* been a bad cut. The glass had razored right through the ball of his foot, into the nerves, an awful, electric pain.

"That's what did it," he whispered, and his father looked back at him. He seemed nervous, as if afraid of what Aaron might give voice to.

"Shock," Aaron said. "It cut so deep, probably into the nerves, and I was exhausted from the swim . . . and I . . . I imagined some things. Because of the shock. Pain and blood loss and shock."

His father stared at him, nodded slowly, and said, "Sure. That was it."

They both knew he didn't believe it, though.

They avoided each other's eyes as a nurse came around with a wheelchair and told Aaron to sit.

Maybe Peaceful Passages is not that bad an idea, Aaron thought as they wheeled him away. *I need to get my mind right.*

You went to rehab to get off drugs and drink. They could help you with those problems. What could they do, though, for a man who'd hallucinated a killing?

16

Long after Steve and Aaron Ellsworth were gone, Gillian remained at the dam. The rain fell and night came on, but still she paced the rocks alongside the Dead Waters, the eerily calm basin below the frothing tailwaters, the deep basin where old foundations still stood. There would be scorch marks on the drowned stones, she knew. She'd never seen them, but she knew they were there.

She knew all there was to know about Galesburg, New York, the forgotten village, the sunken town.

Foolish old stories. Terrible stories, told to a child. An isolated child whose mother had died when the child was only three, leaving her alone with a grandmother who told terrible stories, who asked for horrible promises.

"I don't care if it is her down there," Gillian whispered aloud. "I don't give a damn if it is."

She fought to keep her hand from drifting to her radio. Fought to stop herself from summoning divers to search for a corpse that had been the product of a drug addict's hallucination.

Or maybe it wasn't. Addicts can see real things. A lunatic can be a witness. You never know. Just have the divers take a quick look. Steve Ellsworth can't make that call. It's not his jurisdiction, and he's not thinking like a cop today.

But what was Gillian thinking like? A cop, or a child with bad memories?

It looked like a black hood or a bag over the head, Aaron Ellsworth had said. *Some kind of cloth hood.*

Gillian could see the black silk bag from her grandmother's nightstand, the one that held her Bible and her private journal. The Bible remained on the nightstand but the journal and the bag vanished with Molly Mathers.

Haupring, Aaron had said. *Curtis Haupring.*

She'd fed it to him, though. Projected it onto him.

Maybe you did. But you didn't feed Mick Fleming his own family name.

Jeremiah Fleming's grandson. The old engineer had died in Galesburg before seeing his project to completion. His name had been in Gillian's early history lessons, on quizzes that her grandmother prepared. His name, Haupring's name, and even the Ellsworth name. Edward J. Ellsworth had been the sheriff in charge of evicting the families of Galesburg. One year he'd been elected by them, and the next, he was being told to clear them out.

Galesburg had at least a modicum of sympathy for Sheriff Ellsworth. None for the city that came for their water, though.

She paced the wet rocks, peering into the dark water as if she might spot the corpse Aaron had described. Down along a stone foundation, he'd said. The flooded-out remains of an old house, or maybe a store, one of the buildings of . . .

Galesburg.

The name sent a shiver through Gillian that had nothing to do with the cold rain. She stopped walking, put her hands to her temples, and squeezed her eyes shut. She felt a sudden, intense urge to call her father. To have the conversation that they'd avoided all these years. Talk about the school, about her grandmother, her mother, and what exactly had scared Deshawn Ryan so badly about the place that he refused to visit. Ask why he would meet them only in a public place and never the house when it was clear that a standing invitation to the house remained. There'd been no ill will between her mother and her father. In retrospect, that seemed bizarre. The man had left a pregnant woman and fled like a coward, and who cared if he sent checks and wrote letters? Yet nobody in the house had ever said a harsh word about him.

She remembered the ride back to the city with him after her day of waiting in Steve Ellsworth's office while people came and went and talked in hushed voices. She'd been with a counselor or a social worker of some sort, a woman with bleach-blond hair and a cultivated soothing voice who asked a lot of questions that Gillian didn't want to answer. Gillian had preferred being with Steve Ellsworth, who would make a silly face now and then or tell a silly joke and otherwise just let her sit in silence. He brought her a bag of M&M's and asked her to save the purple ones for him. There were no purple ones. She told him that, perplexed, and he told her to keep looking, because you never knew.

He didn't ask any of the personal questions in the false voice like the social worker did.

Then her father arrived, and then they'd been gone from Torrance. No stopping by the house, just driving south, driving as if they were pursued. She could see his stubby-fingered, over-muscled hand gripping the steering wheel as if he intended to crush it. His jaw clenching as rapidly and steadily as a heartbeat. His eyes were directed straight ahead on the dark highway when she asked him if she was Gillian Ryan now. His voice was thick when he said no, not now and not ever, because a man who wasn't there for his child didn't deserve to have her take his name, and he hadn't been there for her. She remembered so vividly the fear in his eyes when he finally looked back over at her and said, "I'll make up for it. I promise. I'll make up for all those years, baby."

Gillian felt like a monster, something that scared him.

She'd understood something crucial in that moment. *Intuited it,* as her grandmother would have said. She'd intuited that she needed to take her cues from him and learn what he feared about her and then bury those things deep. Never let them out.

It looked like a black hood or a bag over the head, Aaron Ellsworth had said. *Some kind of cloth hood.*

Gillian opened her eyes, lowered her hands, and turned away from the water.

It was time to go home. Whatever sunken tree or old trash bag Aaron Ellsworth had hallucinated into a human corpse could stay right where it was, submerged in the dark, where Gillian's old memories needed to stay.

Where all of Galesburg needed to stay. Underwater and forgotten.

17

The emergency room doctor put twenty-seven stitches in Aaron's foot after cleansing it and then she proclaimed Aaron lucky while Steve looked on.

"It went deep," she told him, "but not deep enough for nerve damage."

Steve was pacing at the edge of the room, unable to still himself. The doc didn't know what had played out down by the tailwaters, of course, but still it was evident that she sensed the tension in the room. She'd chosen not to address it, dealing strictly with her patient, never acknowledging Steve.

"I'm going to prescribe antibiotics for the risk of infection," the doctor said. "A good amount of time passed between the wound and treatment. In that circumstance, I'd always like to give the body a little healing help."

"Sure," Aaron mumbled, and then "Thank you. I appreciate that."

Steve glanced at him with surprise. When was the last time he'd heard Aaron offer politeness? Only a few hours earlier Steve had watched him smirk his way out of jail.

Maybe it was good, he thought wildly, desperately. *Maybe the swim did him some good. Not in the way I wanted it to, but he's . . . he's different now.*

Yes, different. That was the word.

"And for the pain," the doctor continued, "I recommend a mild opioid-based painkiller. It should do the trick, but you need to be careful with it. Be mindful of the doses, of the times, and—"

"No," Aaron said.

"Pardon?" The doctor was surprised; Steve was shocked.

"I do not want that strong of a painkiller, please."

The doctor glanced from Aaron to Steve, then back.

"I understand the caution," she said, "and I appreciate it. But trust me, I'm not handing out refills, either. It would be just enough to get you through the short term with the most tolerable amount of pain."

"I understand that," Aaron said. "But do you have a T3, maybe?"

A T3 was prescription-strength Tylenol, and it didn't carry the abuse potential of the opioid-based options.

"We can do that," she said. "But it may not be enough. You're smart to be wary of the opioids, but it's also important to be aware of the pain level."

"I can take the pain," Aaron said, "better than I can take the wrong drug."

She seemed to get it then. She gave a single brisk nod and said, "Understood. Antibiotics and Tylenol, then. Crutches if you need them, though you likely won't. Just keep the weight off the foot as much as possible. And next time"—she patted his leg—"keep your shoes on when you go wading in the rocks."

"Right."

Two hours earlier Steve thought his son had killed a man, and now Aaron was being chastised for reckless wading. It was a better option, obviously, but it presented fresh problems.

Where do I take him? Who can help whatever is wrong in his brain?

A nurse brought in crutches, and Steve held the door open as Aaron hobbled out. They didn't speak until they were out of the hospital and back in the car. Then Steve turned to him and said, "Proud of you for turning down the pills back there."

"Right." Aaron's mind was elsewhere, his eyes unfocused. Or, rather, deeply focused but not on Steve.

What in the hell is going on in his head? Steve wondered. *Is it worse than I imagined? And if it is worse, what do I do?*

He just had to get through the night and then deal with it in the morning. He needed to get them both far away from the scene at the dam, and only then ...

Shit. The dam. His truck—the truck Aaron had stolen—was still parked there.

"Can you drive?"

Aaron looked at him as if Steve had asked if he could flap his arms and fly.

"My truck is still down at the dam," Steve said. "But if your foot is hurting too bad to—"

"Not in the dark," Aaron blurted. Then he gathered himself and tried again. "I mean, the pills might mess with my vision. I know it was just Tylenol, but ..."

"Right," Steve said, eager to agree, because he hadn't liked the fear in Aaron's voice. "Let's get you home." He desperately wanted to be back in his own house, where the spirit of his wife hung heavy. He needed the reassurances that Lily's memory could bring to him. "And then in the morning, whenever you're rested up and feeling better, we're gonna have to talk about—"

"I'm ready to go."

Aaron said it with the same quiet firmness with which he'd once announced his swimming goals. Pure determination. No doubt.

"Ready to go ... ?"

"To Peaceful Passages. Tomorrow. Actually, tonight if you want me to. Because ..." His voice wavered, and he swallowed and pushed on. "... because, Dad, what happened down there today ... I hadn't been drugging, and I hadn't been drinking, and I believed what I saw was real. I was *sure* it was real."

Steve was imagining all the worst clichés: hospital beds with restraints, padded rooms with guards on the outside, electric currents being fired into his son's brain.

"Shock," he said. "You might've been right about that. It was a bad wound, son. It was a bad shock."

Aaron had been staring out the windshield and into the darkness, but now he turned and faced Steve.

"Nobody's ever had a wound that explains what I saw," he said. His face was very pale in the dim glow of the dashboard lights. "Dad, I saw that man—I saw *him*—and I . . ." He made a slow-motion throwing gesture to mime tossing the bottle, and it seemed he was reliving it all again.

"I killed him," he whispered. "I killed him, and then I found a corpse in the water, one that wasn't him. So I don't know what Peaceful Passages has to help someone who can imagine something like *that*, but . . ." His voice caught, and he was close to tears when he said, "I need help. I need some serious help."

"We'll get it for you," Steve said.

He'd never loved his son more, or feared for him worse.

18

Mick arrived back at the reservoir without making any choice about the destination. He just ended up there as if claimed by gravity.

It was dark now, and the parking area below the dam was empty except for the truck that had been there when he arrived that morning. The one the sheriff's son had driven.

My murderer. Mick tried to smile but didn't succeed.

He drove on past, thinking that the empty parking lot meant there was no night operator. They had cameras and sensors, though. More and more infrastructure security was being entrusted to technology. Mick doubted that anyone was watching the camera feed, but you never knew, and he didn't want to have to explain why he'd returned to the Chilewaukee in the middle of the night.

He drove on, into the protective shelter of the pines and birches that lined the road above the tailwaters, looking for a place to pull over. The trees grew almost up to the asphalt in most places here. He finally found a gap across the road and pulled into it. The Honda was close to the road and facing the wrong way now, but it was a lonely place, and Mick didn't intend to stay long.

Why are you here at all? What are you hoping to see?

He cut the engine. Sat there in the dark while he called his wife, Lori, and told her that he was going to have to spend the night in Torrance. Too much work to be done in a day, he explained, and too little left to make the drive back and forth worth it. If he just stayed the night, he could wrap up quickly in the morning and then be back to Albany by noon.

"How bad does it look?" Lori asked. She knew his worries about this one. The Chilewaukee had been high on his list of *Why can't they budget for this?* bitching for years.

"I don't know," he said. Those were the first honest words he'd offered in hours.

He didn't know how bad the dam looked. He didn't know much at all—not anymore. Some of the things he didn't know were terrifying.

Such as: What happened today?

Mick was a man who liked his facts, liked to see the numbers, to make sense of the world with math. Math made the unknown known, gave you a sense of control over things you hadn't even yet seen.

Mick badly needed some math right now.

He told Lori that he loved her and then hung up and stared at himself in the rearview mirror. Touched the side of his head. Traced his cheek. Felt a hint of five-o'clock shadow stubble but no bruise, let alone a cut. His face looked familiarly boyish in the mirror in the way he'd always hated, a bit too round for someone of a slight build, as if announcing to the world that he was even softer than his size.

The bottle broke on the side of his head, he was bleeding, and I damn near drowned trying to pull him back out!

That's what the kid had shouted. The sheriff's son. But the kid was crazy, of course. A straitjacket psychotic. No question about it.

Then why was the day gone and Mick's memory a blank?

Let's take a look. Let's walk down there and take one more look at the dam. You'll be alone.

Yes, he would be. As he climbed out of the Honda, he felt a familiar anger stirring. The reservoir was vital infrastructure, and the reservoir was also a threat. Every election year, every candidate spoke about infrastructure. Party didn't matter; everyone agreed infrastructure improvement was important.

But they never got it done. You didn't win reelection by fixing out-of-sight, out-of-mind problems. The constituents wanted something new, not repairs to something old. They certainly didn't want to spend money on the bastard-child lake of the great New York City water supply, either, the only real blemish on its remarkable reputation, the reservoir that had been built yet never tapped.

While Ashokan had just received nearly a billion dollars of retro-fitting and improvements, and Gilboa hundreds of millions, and while Water Tunnel Number 3 trudged toward a completion that would offer New York the best water supply of any major city in the world, the Chile-waukee had been forgotten, both its dream scenarios and its nightmare scenarios lost to time.

He walked down the road, tracing above the tailwaters, which offered a soft but powerful soundtrack to his otherwise silent tour. The water was roaring out at . . . how many gallons per second? He remembered Arthur Brady telling him that, but he couldn't remember the exact figure. Couldn't remember much at all.

I'll see a doctor before I tell Lori, he thought. *She'll be terrified if I tell her I spent a full day in a blackout, and that's not fair to her. Get some facts before scaring her. Even if the facts are awful, even if it was a stroke or if there's a tumor growing in my brain, she deserves to be presented with facts. The unknown is worse.*

A break in the trees loomed to his left, and he followed it, stepping off the asphalt and starting through the woods, the damp leaves slick underfoot. He moved quickly, wanting to be hidden from the road. He didn't expect traffic out here at this hour, but he also didn't want to have to explain himself. *You see, I'm the engineer trusted with inspecting this dam, and I spent the day in a waking blackout, so I've come back in the night to sneak onto the property and do the job right. You're welcome, Torrance County. Sleep well!*

The slope was steep. Mick was physically fit, but he'd never been an athlete, never had the coordination or grace. As a kid, he'd always been chosen early in pickup basketball games if the captains were strangers. Once they got to know him, though, he plummeted down the list. He could shoot well, but so many times he bungled things before the shot. Missed a pass, dribbled off his foot, fumbled the ball before he could get into motion.

It didn't take him long tonight to prove that the old gracelessness still lurked. He misjudged a step, missed the grab at a tree, and then stumbled and fell and skidded down the hill on his knees, plowing furrows into the mud.

Clumsy. Once he'd have been irritated by this, but tonight it didn't register. Clumsy wasn't a concern when crazy was in the mix. He fought to get back to his feet and stumbled on, remembering now, only after falling, to turn his body sideways and lean back, which prevented gravity from taking every advantage it could. If you gave gravity a chance, it brought you down. There was something admirable about the totality of its rule on earth. Even when it knocked him on his ass or sent him skidding through the mud on his knees, Mick appreciated the consistency of gravity's dominance. It could be trusted.

As he approached the rushing water below, he considered using the flashlight app on his phone but decided against it. For reasons he couldn't fully articulate, he wanted his presence to be as unobtrusive as possible.

He recalled his drive down to Torrance in the morning's rain, getting lost, and arriving late. He recalled his exchange with Arthur Brady, and he knew that he'd been short with the man because he was in a hurry to focus on the job. He recalled telling the man to put on a raincoat.

No, wait. That hadn't been Brady. Had it? Was it the kid? Had he actually spoken with the sheriff's son?

Damn it. Here was where the blackness slipped in. There was a vague memory of fear, more like a general anxiety than a specific problem. He knew that he'd looked into the water and seen something that bothered him.

But what?

He came to the bottom of the slope. Here the night air was redolent with damp earth and pine needles and filled with the sounds of the relentless water whispering along the banks and gurgling past the rocks. The rain had stopped and it was cool and peaceful and should have felt quite wonderful.

The hairs on his arms and neck had risen, though, and there was a spider-crawl sensation along the base of his skull.

He stared at the dark water, and suddenly he was very afraid.

Bubbles, he thought. *I saw bubbles, and I knew—*

Something flashed to his left, a pale glow within the moonlit water, and when he looked that way he saw for the first time that there was a column of stacked stone winding up out of the water and into the shadows. It was ancient rock, hand-laid and hand-split. Brutal, backbreaking work.

He stepped closer. It was an old retaining wall. The wall extended out into the tailwaters with a slight right-to-left curl, and each span was slightly higher than the next. The spans ran in seven- or eight-foot increments, and then the height rose by one block, creating a graceful stair-stepped wall of bluestone. Those thin but strong sheets stacked atop one another were pure Catskill Mountain product. They'd once paved the sidewalks of New York with Catskill bluestone, that particular rock being preferred because of its natural sheen and the way it handled water—bluestone was coarse enough to provide traction even in the worst rains.

They'd quarried it out of here for years, millions of tons of the stuff, Boss Tweed himself part of the great excavation game, plundering the mountains to pave his city. That was before concrete came along, of course, and then Catskill bluestone went from a boom business to a cottage industry, artisan work for rich people's patios.

How haven't I noticed this old wall before? he wondered. *All of these visits, and I missed this beautiful old wall?*

He'd always approached from the other side, of course. That must be it.

He stepped out onto the wall. The first few blocks were clear enough in the moonlight for him to place his feet with confidence. The rock was firm underfoot. He couldn't see the end of the wall. It seemed to run out there forever. There was no way that it spanned the tailwaters completely. That was impossible. That would make another dam, in fact. A floodplain disaster.

How is the water getting around it, then?

He paused in the dark and listened. All around him was the sound of moving water, but the water on either side of the wall was as placid as a pond. Was there a drain below? No, he'd have seen that before. It would be on the maps and old blueprints. Really, it should be, anyhow. The wall was enough of an obstacle to warrant mention. He couldn't believe that he'd missed it until now.

He took another step. Now he was at the end of the first segment, and his next step would require moving higher. A treacherous choice for a clumsy man in the dark above a churning current.

There is no current. How is there no current?

He didn't feel so clumsy now, either. That ancient bluestone gripped the soles of his shoes as if determined not to let go.

He stepped up.

He was higher above the water now and could hear the current but still couldn't see it. The moonlight showed the next three blocks of stone, and the rest faded into darkness. Funny, the way the moonlight showed only enough to keep moving ahead but not enough to illuminate the destination.

Two more steps.

He knew this was dangerous, but it didn't *feel* dangerous. He felt secure, and he was curious how far this thing extended. He stepped onto the next level, and even while he knew that the old wall should have been blasted away decades ago, Mick could understand the desire to preserve it. It was beautiful, built so carefully and so efficiently. He could only imagine the man-hours that had gone into it, cracking rock, hauling it, cutting it, then stacking and mortaring . . . What a feat. How easily people took modern construction methods for granted—took modern *everything* for granted, with their heads down and their phones in front of their faces. Tech was a remarkable achievement, yes, but the world was, too, and why couldn't they just look up and appreciate it! Why didn't they care how much effort had gone into—

"Water, sir?"

The voice came from his right side, so close that it seemed to be spoken into his ear, and Mick screamed and staggered away and then fell from the wall.

He braced for the splash and shock of cold, rushing water.

There was none. He landed on his ass in high, dry weeds. He felt as if he'd fallen from a great height, and yet there was no jarring pain of impact.

He was facing a boy who couldn't have been more than ten years old, clothed in coveralls and an old-fashioned watch cap. In his left hand was a metal pail; in his right, a dipper with a long handle. He gave Mick a smile that was torn between sympathy and embarrassment.

"Apologies, sir. I didn't mean to startle you."

Mick pushed backward. The dry weeds crackled beneath his hands. Where was the water? The wall? He wanted to look back, but he couldn't take his eyes off the boy, who was still regarding him with pitying curiosity.

"Sir?"

"What . . . what are you doing?" Mick whispered.

"My job," the boy said. "You've toiled all day, haven't you?"

Mick gave a small nod. The boy smiled, as if pleased that he was finally getting through.

"Well, you can't do that without developing a thirst. Water?" He lowered the dipper into the pail, the sound of metal on metal loud in the silent night, and then he removed the filled dipper and advanced on Mick, extending it toward him.

Not real, Mick thought wildly. *He is not real, and you made a very bad mistake coming back here. You needed to go home. Home to Lori and then to the doctor, because you are not just forgetting things now, you're seeing things. This is very bad, Mick, very, very bad.*

Then the dipper was at his mouth. The metal cold against his lips. The water glistening in the moonlight.

"Go on and drink, sir. I've got to be moving along for the others."

The others? For some reason those words chilled him more than the sight of the boy. Who were the others?

Mick closed his eyes. The boy vanished from sight, but the cold press of the metal dipper didn't leave his lips.

I will call Lori, he thought numbly. *First Lori and then an ambulance.*

He opened his eyes when the water splashed over his lips. The boy's grimy face was blank and indifferent, like some zombie version of Oliver Twist. He'd tilted the dipper so the water ran into Mick's mouth. The water was cool and delicious even as Mick tried to spit it out, choking and sputtering.

"Get away," Mick whispered. "Please, get away."

"You'll want me back when the thirst comes," the boy said, and then he sank the dipper into the pail and walked on, passing Mick without a look back. Mick turned to watch him go, and that was when he saw the road.

The tailwaters were gone and in their place a road carved through the valley.

"No," Mick said, almost reasonably. He knew that his fear should be accelerating, knew that he should run or scream—no, run *and* scream . . . and yet he did not. *Could* not.

The next voice he heard was deep and authoritative.

"Shall we have a look at the work, Mr. Fleming?"

He turned slowly, and a man stood before him in an old-fashioned black suit and black overcoat, a white shirt gleaming beneath, and on his head was a black hat with a white hatband that glowed silver in the moonlight.

"Who are you?" Mick asked softly.

"Anders Wallace, sir. I'm the foreman."

"The foreman," Mick echoed. "Of what?"

Anders Wallace looked disappointed in the question. "Time's wasting, Mr. Fleming," he said. "Shall we begin our walk?"

No. I must run, not walk. I must run and I must scream, I must do those things until someone hears, until someone finds me, saves me.

"The crew has been busy," Anders Wallace said, "but there's much yet to be done. They need a surface engineer, sir."

Mick parted his lips, and although he remembered that he needed to scream, it no longer seemed an option.

"I am an engineer," Mick said.

"That was my understanding. We've been waiting."

"But my expertise is in dams."

"Indeed."

"You said a . . . surface engineer? I don't know what that means."

Anders Wallace's chest rose and fell as he took a deep breath, as if searching for patience.

"I think you do, sir. You came here for a reason, did you not?"

"To have a look," Mick said weakly. "To have a look and . . ."

"And?"

"Remember what I forgot."

"Precisely, sir. Let's get to it now."

Mick rose and walked to meet him, his feet crunching through the dry, wilted weeds. Ahead of them, the boy with his dipper and pail was receding into the shadows along the road. A horse whinnied somewhere in the distance, and a dog barked as if in answer.

"It's quite a dilemma we're facing," Anders Wallace told him. "The task is not easy. You'll see. It's a matter of getting the math right. We've got to balance the pressure or the whole system will fail."

And with that, the fear was gone entirely. For many frightened hours, Mick Fleming had needed a problem that could be solved with a clear head and clear numbers.

"I'll figure it out," he told Anders Wallace, and the man smiled.

"That's what we're counting on, Mr. Fleming."

Together, they started down the moonlit road.

19

Aaron lay in his childhood bed and stared at the television. Usually he'd be deep into a marathon session of *Call of Duty* or *Halo* by now, the endless hours that were a constant source of friction with his father, but tonight the games seemed too demanding. *SportsCenter* was recapping playoff baseball and looking ahead to the weekend football matchups. He watched idly, head against the pillows, hoping for sleep. After the day he'd had, surely his body was exhausted enough for sleep.

His mind wasn't, though. As they'd promised in rescue swimmer school, the mind was a far more potent force than the body.

So that others might live.

The old sign was still taped to the inside of his door. It was yellowing and curling in at the edges now, the old masking tape going brittle. There had been at least a thousand occasions since he'd returned home when he intended to rip it off the door and throw it away.

His mother's memory kept him from doing that.

He'd done the meticulous lettering and then sketched a poor imitation of the rescue swimmer coat of arms beneath, but it had been his mother who found the tape, and the two of them had stood inside the narrow room together when the sign went up.

Just tear it down, he would think, but he'd never gone so far as actually touching the paper.

Funny, how much harder it was to discard your own dreams if someone else had once shared them with you. When someone else listened to your aspirational talk with sincerity and support, it became harder to pretend those aspirations no longer mattered.

On the nightstand, beneath a phone charger, two empty Corona bottles, a one-hitter, and some rolling papers, was a slim paperback book titled *The Rescue Swimmer Mindset.* The subtitle promised that the book would let you "unlock the psychological edge of the Coast Guard."

The book he'd taken so seriously at fourteen seemed absurd a decade later, with all of its platitudes about the mental edge that separated winners and losers, the things a boy could believe and a man shouldn't. Yet he kept it here on the bedside table like a Bible.

His mother had given him the book the week after he—*they*—had hung the sign on the door. On the inside cover, in her elementary teacher's penmanship, was the inscription:

> To Aaron,
> May you always bring light to dark waters,
>   Love,
>   Mom
>   June 24, 2012

The book, unlike the sign, he'd never considered throwing out. Not even on the worst, drunkest night since his return to Torrance had he considered harming the book.

He picked it up now, less out of intention than emptiness. He was used to reaching to the nightstand for his phone, finding distraction there, but his phone was still in his father's truck, which was still parked down at the Chill. The truck he'd refused to go get in the dark, like a frightened child, which was surely what his father was thinking of him now.

He flipped through it, skimming, trying to find amusement in the portions he'd once read with such earnestness, thinking he'd been given some incredible gift.

May you always bring light to dark waters.

Well, it had been a gift, beloved and cherished. But it was not a gift in the sense that he'd imagined back then, when he'd seen it as the Holy Grail, an advantage given to him. It was simply a book, words on pages; anyone could hold it.

It had felt so personal to him once, though. So damned personal.

He remembered some of the numbers cited in the book. At the time of the writing, there were 1,800 billionaires and 1,800 players on NFL rosters and about 1,800 students in the Harvard Business School each year, and yet less than a thousand people had passed the Coast Guard's helicopter rescue swimmer school . . . ever.

How remarkable that had seemed to him once. How enticing.

He stopped flipping when he reached the page where the author urged his reader to write down a goal. "By writing down your intentions, you now have something to look back on when times are difficult . . . It is important to answer this for yourself, it is the strongest evidence you will be able to provide yourself when you are in chaotic challenges that will make you question your decision."

Aaron laughed. Well, now, if ever there was a time of chaotic challenge, tonight seemed to qualify. He'd thought he was a murderer; it turned out he was just insane. A chaotic challenge indeed! Let's see what words of wisdom his fourteen-year-old, hyper-focused, ultra-confident self had left for such a moment!

He turned the page, and there in his all-caps lettering was a single sentence.

LISTEN TO THE WATER.

"Perfect," he said aloud. He needed real-world wisdom, and he'd found a teenager's attempt at Buddhist awareness. Listen to the water. It read like a line that had been cut from a *Kung Fu Panda* script.

Listen to the water. Sure. That had served him well today.

Holding the book brought his hand close to his face, and he could see a ragged red line there. The cut wasn't deep enough to require stitches, so they'd simply cleaned it and left it uncovered. It wasn't a scrape or a slice but an indentation, the mark of something thin and strong pressed deep enough into his hand to break the skin.

Fishing line. It was all around my hand, and when I moved, the body moved, and that was when I saw the skull clearly, when it slid out from under that black hood . . .

He flipped pages and switched the book from his right hand to his left so he no longer could see the wound.

This page contained more sage advice, counseling him to master the skill of "de-stressing."

Now, *that* was not such a bad idea. He set the book down, sat up in bed, and listened to the house. Silent. His father had to be asleep. It had been a long day for Steve Ellsworth.

Aaron cracked the window, letting a cool, damp breeze fill the room, and pulled a baggie with a nugget of pot from the drawer in the nightstand. He broke it, separated it, and rolled a small but potent joint. He felt the first pang of desire for something stronger, something like he and Riggins had hit last night. The synthetic shit with a name like a kid's sugared breakfast cereal but a kick like a mule on steroids.

Peaceful Passages. You promised.

Holding the joint put the line of sliced flesh along the back of his hand in front of his eyes again. Once more he switched from right hand to left, just to get it out of sight.

Chains and a padlock. And those hooks—they weren't for fishing. Unless someone thought there were tarpon in the Chilewaukee tailwaters, they wouldn't use a hook like that.

It was easy to hallucinate when you were underwater, though. Down in the dark depths, panicked and running out of oxygen, you could imagine anything.

But what about on the surface?

He could feel the weight of the bottle in his hand and see it slicing through the air and bursting on the stranger's face. The same stranger who'd walked out of the woods with his odd smile and chipper laugh just before the cop named Gillian Mathers would have arrested Aaron for murder.

The joint burned out, and it took him four tries to relight it. His fingers were trembling.

A chime came from under the bed. His iPad, forgotten on the floor, buried beneath a tangle of jeans and a gaming headset. He set the joint on the windowsill and picked up the iPad. A chat session was open, filled with messages. Riggins. Wondering where the hell he'd been, what had happened.

Bro—you out there? Or did your old man freak out and lock you down? the last one read.

Yes and no, Tyler. Yes and no.

He hesitated, then pecked out a response.

What in the hell did we get into last night? I had a strange day.

A strange day. Bit of an understatement, that.

Riggins responded immediately.

It could've been worse. Where are you? I need to talk. My lawyer says it would be a big help if your old man would throw a kind word my way. Like . . . a HUGE help.

The request made Aaron angry, although the previous night it wouldn't have. The night before, the idea would have seemed fair and reasonable.

A lot of things had seemed more reasonable last night.

He didn't answer, but Riggins didn't wait on him.

Let's get a beer. I've been calling your phone all day. Where the hell are you?

Home, Aaron answered, and again he hesitated. He wanted to ask Riggins some questions directly. Things that he didn't want to type, things he couldn't risk his father overhearing. Like some details about what exactly they'd smoked and whether Riggins had experienced any, ahem, unusual side effects.

You out? Aaron messaged.

Just cruising, yeah. You need a ride?

Yes. I need to get my phone, and my dad's truck. You sober enough to give me a ride?

He could almost hear the sneer in Riggins's voice when the next message came in.

Do you care?

Actually, yeah, Aaron typed.

He felt as if he could hear the sigh of disgust from Riggins when he wrote back, *Don't be a bitch. I'm fine. I'll head your way now.*

Aaron stood, stubbed the joint out between his thumb and forefinger, then tucked it in a drawer. He pulled on his jeans and a sweatshirt and his Wolverine work boots, going slowly with the right foot and leaving the laces looser. He grabbed a jacket from the post on the footboard and was about to leave the room when the iPad chimed again.

Riggins: *Where's your truck, anyhow?*

Aaron typed, *Down by the Chill. At the dam.*

Almost instantly: *Hell were you doing down there?*

Just come get me, Aaron replied, and this time he closed the iPad's cover.

He hadn't even made it down the stairs when his father's bedroom door opened and he came out and stood in the hallway. He was wearing sweatpants but no shirt, his wide chest pale beneath a tangle of gray hair. Although he still looked big enough and fit enough in his uniform, Aaron couldn't help but notice how he was aging now. Faster each year since Mom died, it seemed, the grief taking a physical toll.

Think you're not a part of that toll, too? a voice in his head chided him.

"You need some more Tylenol?" his father asked, wary, as he studied Aaron's wardrobe, which definitely suggested he was headed somewhere farther than the kitchen counter.

"I'm going to run down and get your truck."

"We don't need to worry about that now. It'll hold until morning."

"I'd like to get it now."

A pause. "All right. Let me get dressed."

"I've got a ride, actually."

That earned an undisguised grimace. Aaron knew what he was thinking: that everything Aaron had said on the ride back from the hospital had been bullshit and he'd needed only a few hours to fall back into his old ways. That he couldn't even make it through one night—twelve hours—of pretense.

"Riggins is coming to get me, and he's sober," Aaron said, keeping his voice level and his eyes on his father's. "If it turns out he isn't when he gets here, I won't get in the car with him. I promise. But I want to ride down there with him and clean up my mess."

"It's a truck in a parking lot. Not much mess."

"I want to tell him why I'm going to be gone soon," Aaron said. "And where." Then, as a thought came to him that was both hopeful and pointless, he added, "Maybe see if I can talk him into going to the same place. I doubt it, but . . . he doesn't have anybody else in his life who will even try. He deserves to have somebody try to help him. He doesn't have anyone like you."

His father stood silently in the shadowed hall. Behind him, the TV flickered in the bedroom. ESPN, but muted. Father and son had taken the same approach: retreat, put on sports. Sit up sleepless and silent. And separate.

There'd been a lot of those nights once Mom was gone.

"You have two choices," Aaron said, suddenly exhausted. "Trust me or don't. I can't blame you if you don't. But I also promise you I wasn't lying about Peaceful Passages, and I'm not going out to drink. I'm going to get your truck, and my phone, and tell my friend what I'm doing from here on out and what I think he should be doing."

The truth. Every word. He just left out the part about the questions as to whether Riggins might have had any intense side effects, any hallucinations so vivid that you questioned reality.

"There and back?" his father said so softly, Aaron could barely hear the words. "There and back, that's all?"

"That's all."

"So you'll be in home in an hour."

Aaron nodded.

"Please," his father said. "Please be home in an hour."

"I will be. Thank you."

He got the keys for the truck and went outside, using one crutch for balance, and sat on the old porch swing. A frigid wind blew across the yard. Dry, though. The rain had finally stopped.

He sat on the swing, easing it back and forth and trying to pretend he didn't see his father standing in the window, staring out at him. The creaking complaints of the rusted chain made him think of the chains he'd seen wrapped around the thin ankle bones of the corpse, and so he brought the swing to a stop. Then he sat motionless, waiting for headlights and trying not to remember things he could not possibly have seen.

DOWNSTREAM

20

The nightmare woke Deshawn just before midnight.

He lurched up on the couch, gasping and reaching, his hand outstretched and fingers spread wide, head turning, a Heisman Trophy pose, as if he were about to avoid a tackler.

The apartment was dark and silent. Almost silent. There was his heartbeat, so heavy in his ears it seemed audible throughout the room.

And there was the drip.

Plink, plink, plink.

The bathroom faucet had been dripping for weeks now. Probably a dried-out O-ring. A ninety-nine-cent fix. He kept meaning to hit the hardware store, but when he thought of it, he was usually at work. In the tunnels the sound of the drip was constant. Groundwater seeped and trickled, and when the Mole wasn't boring through the bedrock, you could hear the individual drips falling like composed music, a soundtrack to the experience of being so far belowground.

Deshawn would hear the water music down there and think of his faucet with the slow leak and tell himself to go to the hardware store on the way home. Then the Mole would rev back up to its shuddering roar or a muck car would clatter away or Matty Silvers would tell the dirty joke about the paratrooper, and the tunnel would be alive again, it would be work again, and you could no longer hear those soft, insignificant drips. When the Mole fired up and the crew got to work, it was back to real life, and in real life there were things you forgot.

That damned faucet in the bathroom was one of them.

Plink, plink, plink.

He sat up and took a deep breath and rubbed his eyes. His palms came away damp with cold sweat. He tried to remember the details of the nightmare and couldn't. How did that happen? You could dream something so real that it made your heart race and sweat spring from your pores—so real that you woke with a raised hand and a turned head as if expecting a blow . . . and then the dream was gone. How could that happen so fast?

The nightmare had involved the sound of the drip. He was sure of that. The real sound had snuck into his unconscious mind and caused havoc, but now the details of the havoc were gone and couldn't be recovered.

He stood up.

Just go to bed, he told himself, but the bedroom was dark, and for some reason he didn't want to walk into it. He went toward the only light instead, which came from the window that looked out onto the street. The Chinese restaurant across the way never went fully dark; the neon stayed bright at all hours, but that didn't bother him. In fact, right now it was a comfort. He stood at the window staring down at the street. Trash pickup was tomorrow, so the sidewalk was lined with overflowing cans. Two doors down from the Chinese restaurant was an empty storefront that had once been a dry cleaner's. A few kids sat on the stoop in front of it and passed a joint back and forth, the golden flicks of the lighter and the glow of the joint the only illumination where they sat just out of reach of the streetlight.

Deshawn watched them, then looked back at his dark bedroom and knew that he would not sleep again soon. Whatever had scared him awake was gone, but its effects were not, and he did not want to be alone.

I'll call Gillian, he thought, but then he remembered the time. If he called her at this hour, he would only scare her.

Besides, what would he tell her? That he was seeing ghosts in the tunnels? He'd never admit that. And he wouldn't tell her of the way the old memories were plaguing him—memories he hadn't thought of in years, memories he believed he'd boxed away.

Boxed, yes. But burned? No. You still have her sketchbook.

His mouth was dry and there was a cold, coppery taste at the back of his throat. He crossed from the window and into the bedroom slowly, as if afraid of making noise in his own empty apartment. As if something might awaken.

The gun safe was under his bed. There wasn't a gun in it, but still the steel box felt dangerous to him. He slipped it out from under the bed, placed it on the nightstand, and sat on his knees on the floor while he punched in the code: 1-8-0-4.

The light went from red to green. He spun the dial. There was a metallic snap, and then the safe was open. He pulled the heavy lid back, and where thieves might've expected to see Glocks or Rugers, there was a stack of letters, all with the TORRANCE, NY, postmark, and all with a handwritten return address of Galesburg, New York. As if Deshawn could return the letters with a line and sinker, and some postal worker would reach up from the depths, unclip it, and carry it away. *Sure, Kelly. You're not crazy. No, certainly not.*

I just want you to understand, she would say, trying to mask the unsettling desperation in her tone. *It's so important for our baby that you understand this place.*

Deshawn had understood plenty about the place by then. He understood that in the way you might've understood Jonestown or Ruby Ridge if you'd wandered through.

His hand was trembling when he pulled the first letter free from the gun safe, and he hated himself for that. He tossed the letter onto the bed, then clicked on the bedside lamp. Read the old lines, the last she'd ever written to him.

Deshawn, honey, there are so many important things I want to write, but I know it is asking too much to tell you too many of them. I understand what you believe, and what you don't want to believe, and that's fine. I will never blame you. How could I?

But if you never believe me, please, please promise me that you'll let my baby girl—OUR baby girl—believe me. Let her remember the lessons she was taught here. My mother's lessons. My grandfather's lessons. All that came before us. Please do not seal her away from those memories, from those stories. Those truths. She must understand her role in a larger eco-system. All things seem small to you in Galesburg, but they're not. Deshawn, they're so much bigger than you can imagine. And she is so special. Our beautiful baby girl is so, so special. She will embrace her legacy.

You'll have all the years ahead with her, all the moments. I envy you, of course. How could I not? But I don't blame you. Just promise me you'll never let her forget the lessons. The legacy. Promise me that you'll leave her with my mother until the time is right for you to take her.

He pushed the letter across the bed as if it were a living thing, a snake slithering out from beneath the covers and across the shadows.

The letter was the last one Kelly had sent before she'd driven off a ridge and tumbled two hundred feet to her death in the water below. Drunk driving, the police said; went off the road, they said; and before they told him where she'd landed, he knew. The Dead Waters, of course. There was no other option. She might have been drunk, but it was no accident. She'd needed the liquid courage, that was all.

His daughter's mother, dead of suicide. Or sacrifice, as she would have called it. Gone off to take up residency in a town that no longer existed. She thought there were people down there. Spirits, maybe. But active. Whatever was down there was definitely active, and she belonged with them.

Deshawn could join them, too. Whenever he was ready. No rush. They'd be waiting.

These were the things he'd heard and tried to forget. The things he had never even considered speaking of with his daughter. It was too difficult a conversation to imagine.

But weren't the most dangerous things the ones left unsaid?

Promise me that you'll leave her with my mother until the time is right for you to take her.

He had, too. Pathetic coward, sorry excuse of a man, let alone a father, he had left his daughter with Molly Mathers in that house in the woods. Made a lot of rationalizations about how it was the only home Gillian knew, how it would be only more traumatic for her if he brought her to the city, to a strange new world. Made a lot of promises that it would be only a few months before that happened. He'd let Molly help her get around the curve of her grief, that was all, and then he'd do the right thing and claim his daughter.

Never did he let himself consider the truth head-on: he was frightened of his daughter. He was frightened of the whole family.

So months turned into years, and the years would have kept going if not for the *right time* that Kelly had promised in her last letter. The right time coming when Molly Mathers kissed Gillian goodbye and went for a walk to the lake and never came home.

Before she vanished, she made two phone calls. One to the local sheriff, requesting someone come to check on her granddaughter's safety, and one to Deshawn. He was underground at the time, and so she left a message. It was time, she said, for him to take Gillian away. She told him that he was a good man, that she'd seen that in him despite all of the reasons she had to think otherwise, and that she knew he would be a good father. *Gillian will be fine,* she said. *She's a stoic little girl. Take care of my baby, Deshawn. Take good care of her, and don't blame her for things beyond her control. Don't fear her. You don't need to come back to this place again, and you don't need to speak of it. She'll remember when the time is right. Just love her. That's all you need to do.*

By the time he played that message, there had been a second one from the sheriff's office. That one was the more important message in some ways, but he didn't remember it well. Molly's, though, stuck with him. Lingered.

Don't fear her.

The woman had known him so well. Understood him better than he'd understood himself somehow. That chilled him and shamed him.

Then there was the promise: *She'll remember when the time is right.*

When the time was right for what?

He rose abruptly and hurried out of the room. Left the safe open and the letter on his bed. He'd intended to read the others and then move on to his daughter's old sketchbook, but now he thought that was a very bad idea.

Just sit and relax. Sit back on the couch and relax and sleep.

There was no way that was happening, though. Not tonight.

He'd lived alone for most of his life and yet he was bothered by the empty apartment now. Good news, though: he was in New York City. The city, as they said, never slept.

Ben's Porch would be open. That beloved old bar never seemed to close. The West Coast baseball game would still be on, probably, and while Deshawn didn't care about either team, he could pretend. He could have a beer or two and watch the game and listen to the drunks arguing. He could get away from the damnable sound of that slow, steady drip.

Plink, plink, plink.

Why hadn't he fixed that faucet? The sound was so loud. How had he possibly ignored it this long?

Tomorrow, he told himself as he pulled on his jacket and grabbed his keys and wallet. *Tomorrow I'll pick up an O-ring and a gasket. Pick up a whole damn faucet, maybe, and just gut the works.*

Of course, it wasn't his responsibility. It wasn't his building. He could call the super and ask him to do his job. Save his money, make the landlord spend it. That was the idea of the system, wasn't it? Deshawn didn't own the problem; he just rented it.

Plink, plink, plink.

The leak wasn't speeding up, but it seemed so much louder than he remembered. How was that possible?

Because it's midnight and you had a nightmare and then you opened a box that you shouldn't have. You let the past in, and you know better than to do that.

He stepped into the hall, closed the door, and locked it. Jogged down the stairs and pushed through the front door and into the chilled night air. The waiting garbage was pungent. Across the street, the kids with the joint laughed. Down the street, cars exchanged horn fire at an inter-section. Up the street, the old-fashioned neon sign at Ben's Porch prom-ised a Corona and a refuge.

The pleasant noise of life drove away the silly bad feelings that could develop from small sounds in darkness. The city blew those small sounds out of his mind like a street sweeper, and whatever faint memory remained from the nightmare was long gone before he reached Ben's.

21

Tyler Riggins drove a Dodge Ram diesel on a lift kit so tall that even Aaron could feel ridiculous swinging his six-foot-three-inch frame into the cab. He'd seen Riggins pick up girls who basically had to climb the tires to get inside the truck, because while Riggins had invested on the lift kit and the tires, he'd neglected to add running boards.

When he pulled into the drive with the big motor growling, Aaron crossed the yard on his one crutch, trying to make the effort look painless, because he knew his father was watching. In reality, his foot ached and burned and all he wanted was a hit of something to knock the pain on its ass. Knock *him* on his ass. He wanted to sleep for days.

He tossed his crutch into the bed of the truck while he held on to the door handle, then opened the door and hoisted himself upright, lurching into the high passenger seat.

Riggins stared at him over the top of a cigarette.

"The hell happened to you?"

"Stepped on a bottle."

Riggins began to laugh. He was a big, freckle-faced, redheaded slab of a kid and he should have been fat—once had been, in fact, before he found the weight room. Riggins was obsessive with lifting, but his body only thickened, never leaned up. In high school Aaron had never hung out with Riggins. Once he returned to town, though, most of Torrance High's best and brightest were long gone to other places, and he came across Riggins in the gym and at the bar and a friendship formed out of the things they shared: alcohol and anger, mostly.

"Stepped on a friggin' bottle," Riggins said, choking on his laughter and cigarette smoke. "Oh, shit. You've had a day, bro. Started in jail, ended on crutches?"

His cigarette ash fell onto his jeans and he laughed and swept it away. The cab vibrated with honky-tonk guitar and the twanging voice of Shooter Jennings singing "D.R.U.N.K."

"Drive out of here," Aaron said. "My dad's watching. You said you need him to think you're something other than an asshole, right?"

Riggins was still laughing when he dropped the truck into gear. Black smoke belched into the night, the floorboards shook, and then they were off.

"How pissed is your dad, anyhow?"

"Scale of one to ten, probably a twelve," Aaron said, but that assessment was taken from the morning, after the eviction from his own house. Just now, though, his father hadn't looked angry. He'd looked afraid.

"He's not happy," Aaron muttered, "but neither am I."

"Well, shit happens. We picked the wrong night and the wrong street, that's all."

They'd sat in his truck, drunk and high, with music blaring, parked outside one of the only bars in town that was guaranteed to have police presence. Wrong night and wrong street. Sure.

"What'd we have last night?" Aaron asked.

Riggins shot him a startled look, his face lit by the dashboard lights, his freckles gleaming.

"We smoked a couple of joints and had a couple of beers, man. Maybe six beers each. Well, no more than eight, anyhow. What'd you do, black out or something?"

"No. But you're sure it was just weed?"

"What'd you think, I bought some fentanyl-laced shit or something? Come on."

Aaron was almost disappointed. He'd wanted to hear about a pill or a rock or even a syringe, the type of drugs he'd sworn never to try.

Wanted to hear any excuse for what had scrambled his brains so badly today.

"What happened?" Riggins said. He turned down the volume on Shooter.

The pain was rising from Aaron's foot, climbing his spine, and poking at the base of his skull. Maybe this had been a mistake. Maybe he should've taken another Tylenol and turned off the lights and gone to bed.

"It was weird, man," he said.

"Explain."

"I can't. It was just . . . I guess I didn't remember last night all that well."

"Bullshit, Ellsworth. What's going on?"

Aaron didn't answer right away. The road rolled along, dead fields and leafless trees fading into the high black hills. Everything looked bone white in the headlights; everything would look gray in the day. Winter in the Catskills was often a two-tone color scheme.

It was too early for winter, though. The trees were leafless only because of the unremitting rains, which had stripped the hills of their autumn colors.

"Aaron? You look like hell, man. Talk to me. What's going on?"

"I had a . . . premonition, I think. That's probably what it was. Or at least it's the way I should look at it."

"A premo . . ." Riggins slowed the truck, staring at him. "What *did* you take last night?"

"Weed and beer, evidently. And then a ride to jail. And then a ride home with my dad. Then I went swimming."

"Swimming?"

Aaron nodded. "Out in the tailwaters, the way I always used to when I was kid. Start with the current, then swim back against it. I always made it, back then. No matter the weather. I didn't today, and then I cut my foot halfway to the bone, and then I . . . I think that I had a premonition." This sounded right. He hadn't considered the idea before, but now he liked it. A premonition sounded almost plausible, much like his excuse at the hospital about going into shock. This one was better, though. This one felt more plausible and less desperate.

"What'd you see?" Riggins asked. "Anything we can lay a bet on down at the Iroquois casino?"

Aaron ignored the sarcasm. "I saw that I'm going to hurt someone. If I keep going like I have been, I am going to hurt someone. I might not mean to do it, but I'll do it just the same."

"Oh, you're not gonna hurt anybody. Unless they ask for it, at least. You're not the type to start a fight. Seen you end a couple, but you don't start 'em."

"It won't be a fight," Aaron said. "I'm not sure what it'll be. But I know it's going to happen. Today I thought that it already had."

"Today you woke up in jail. It's not a great feeling. You'll get over it."

Aaron should've known that Riggins wouldn't understand. The night road rolled on, and at length Aaron spoke again.

"I'm going to be out of town for a bit."

"What do you mean, out of town?"

"Going somewhere to dry out. It's past time."

"Oh, you've gotta be kidding me. You're not talking some Amy Winehouse bullshit, are you? Aaron . . ."

"It's past time," Aaron repeated.

Riggins didn't speak until they reached a stop sign. Then, with the big Dodge idling, he looked over with disappointment.

"That's your sheriff daddy talking," he said. "That's him, not you."

"Maybe," Aaron said. "Either way, I'm gonna listen."

Riggins groaned and turned away, shaking his head as he hammered the accelerator. They pulled on down the road, on toward the Chill, and Aaron thought about what he'd just said and remembered what he'd written in the old Coast Guard psychology book, that gift from his mother, and suddenly his throat was tight and his eyes stung.

Listen to the water, he'd written, and while that was a child's fantasy of heroism, maybe it hadn't been terrible advice, either. He'd been riding toward trouble for too long, and today he'd awoken to that. He'd needed to go to the water for that to happen.

I miss my mom, he thought, a child's thought if ever there was one, and yet deeply honest. Oh, how he missed his mother.

"You're no addict," Riggins grumbled at his side. "Not even close. You *choose to have fun,* that's all. It was a bad night, a fluke. Don't go taking yourself so seriously or letting your old man convince you to."

They were closing in on the Chill now, the fields no longer visible, the woods crowding the road, which wound uphill on narrow S curves.

"I might not be an addict," Aaron said, "but after what I saw today, I definitely don't need any—"

"*Damn!*" Riggins shouted, swerving at the same time, and Aaron saw the flash of a white SUV's hood, and for an instant he was certain that they were going to strike it head-on and he was going to die while his father sat awake watching the clock.

Then the big Dodge was fishtailing to a stop, ribbons of rubber left on the asphalt behind them.

"*Son of a bitch!* I thought that fucker was on the road, coming at us!" Riggins shouted.

Only then did Aaron look in the side-view mirror and see that the SUV was actually parked on the shoulder. Or what was supposed to be the shoulder. The trees were packed in close.

"I did, too," Aaron said. "If you hadn't been doing Mach Five through the curves, though, it might not . . ."

He stopped talking, twisted in his seat, and stared through the rear window.

"That's his car," he said. His voice was quiet in the cab, buried beneath Shooter Jennings's wailing, and Riggins was already pulling away.

"Whose car?" Riggins asked indifferently.

Aaron didn't answer. He kept facing backward, looking at the white SUV. A Honda Pilot. He remembered it well. He and his father had stared at that car while they waited in the rain for the police to come down and take Aaron to jail.

"Go back," he said.

"What?"

"Back up, all right? I want to get a clear look."

"Another premonition? Maybe you *do* need rehab."

"Just let me have a look, damn it."

Riggins sighed, stopped the Dodge, and threw it in reverse. He backed up too fast, and one of the rear tires lost the pavement and plowed a furrow through the mud, spinning damp brown leaves into the air. Then they chunked back onto the road with a jarring bounce and Riggins brought them to a stop beside the Honda. Aaron put his window down and stared down at the Honda from the elevated position of the truck.

"Gimme your phone."

"What's the matter with you, man?"

Aaron just extended his hand. Riggins sighed and slapped his phone into Aaron's palm. Aaron clicked on the flashlight app and shined the light down. The Honda was empty, but an iPad and a leather-bound folder rested on the passenger seat. The same things Mick Fleming had carried.

He looked away from the car and out into the woods. White birches and dark oaks cast spindly shadows that were then swallowed up by the crowded pines that grew thick along the steep banks. Somewhere below, the tailwaters rushed downstream, out of sight but audible.

He felt a prickle along the back of his neck, a cold, mocking fear, as if something out there in the darkness were watching him with amusement.

"The hell is he doing out here at midnight?" he whispered.

"*Who?*" Riggins bellowed.

Some instinct told Aaron that the sound was too loud and that they shouldn't linger. His interest in the car was gone; all he wanted now was out of here. Get the truck and get home. Forget that he'd seen this.

Because Riggins saw it, too. How's that premonition theory working out?

He snapped a picture. The flash popped brightly. He leaned out the window, feeling vulnerable the farther he extended himself into the night, and took another, making sure to get the license plate in this one.

"What the hell are you doing?" Riggins demanded.

Aaron couldn't begin to explain it. The clean feeling of accepting his own mental breakdown had been good, in a terrible way. But here he sat with Riggins, both of them seeing the Honda Pilot parked in the lonely woods above the Dead Waters in the middle of the night.

Something was wrong, and it wasn't just with Aaron's mind.

"Not important, Riggs," he muttered. "Just get me back to my truck so I can get home."

"Talk to me, Aaron."

"Let's go."

"Screw that, man. Tell me what's going on. You made me drive back here so you can take a photo of a—"

"Let's go!" Aaron shouted.

Riggins's eyes widened, but not with anger. It was as if he'd seen something in Aaron that unnerved him. It was an expression not that different from the one Aaron had seen on his father's face when the man named Mick Fleming came walking out of the woods and told them that none of Aaron's memories were real.

Same car. Same man. What's he doing in the woods at midnight?

While Riggins drove to the dam, Aaron emailed the photos to himself. He wasn't sure what he intended to do with them, but he was glad to have them. Something felt wrong out here. With Mick Fleming and with the Chill. With the night itself, the skies finally clearing, but the earth still soaked from days of pounding rain, the trees emptied far too early, winter rushing in where it didn't belong.

When Riggins pulled into the parking lot, Aaron suddenly didn't want to get out of the truck. Not down here at the Chill, in this place where once he'd honed skill and built confidence, and where now he no longer trusted himself.

Or maybe it was the place itself that he no longer trusted.

"Okay, boss, there's your damn truck," Riggins said. "Listen, go home and sleep it off, okay? Don't do any dumb bullshit your dad's been in your ear about. Today got off to a bad start, and it only got worse for you. But don't take that too seriously."

Again Aaron saw the bottle burst above Mick Fleming's eye socket; again he saw the current tug the bleeding and unconscious man into the water and sweep him downstream.

"Right," he said. "I won't take it too seriously."

"Gimme a call in the morning, then. We'll hit the gym, okay? Nothing else. Clean all-American workout. You can be a good boy."

"Right," Aaron said again. "Thanks for the ride."

When he climbed out of the truck, he almost fell. He'd taken only two limping steps toward his father's Silverado before Riggins was peeling out in the Dodge, the back tires spitting mud and gravel. Too late, Aaron realized he'd left his crutch in the bed of the truck. He hollered at Riggins to wait, but Riggins didn't hear him over the sounds of the engine and Shooter Jennings.

"I'm gettin' D-R-U-N-K!"

Aaron stood in the gravel lot and watched his friend drive away and then turned and stared up at the massive shadow of the dam that held back the Chilewaukee Reservoir. The roar from the adjacent spillway was ceaseless as water thundered down.

A roar so loud he could scarcely hear the voice in the woods.

It was faint but audible, and it came from downstream. A man's voice, conversational, but the conversation seemed one-sided, because there was only the one voice.

Aaron took a few limping steps downstream, straining to hear the words. They cut in and out like a phone with a bad connection.

Of course, I understand . . .

Mountains pillaged, cities fed . . .

Do they heed the warning? No. Not back then and not today. In fact, Mrs. Mathers, it's probably worse today . . .

Alarms must be sounded. I agree . . .

Get their attention? It's not so easy as the . . .

Explain that. Tell me what you mean.

That's not an alarm. That's . . .

The spillway roar washed the next words away. Aaron hobbled forward again. On all of his night swims down here, he'd never felt so alone. The height of the dam and the cacophonous sound of the spillway and the black night itself shrunk the world to the sound of the big water and of the faint voice.

He stumbled over a slab of bluestone and almost fell, kept upright with an effort, and then came around a copse of young birches and saw Mick Fleming.

Fleming had his back turned, but Aaron was sure that it was him. He was standing in the water. Almost *on* the water, it seemed, but a thin slat of moonlight ran directly in front of him, and because of this Aaron could see that he was actually standing on something just beneath the surface. The water rushed around his knees but the current seemed to have no effect on his balance. What in the hell was he standing on? The water out there was deep, and yet Fleming stood in the middle of it with the assured balance of a man on a sidewalk.

"*That's much more than an alarm,*" he said clearly. "*It's a sacrifice.*"

When Fleming said *sacrifice*, Aaron moved backward, a stabbing pain in his foot, but the pain was useful now because it cleared his head. He was not imagining this man in the water, but the man in the water was imagining someone else, and Aaron needed to get the hell away from him—fast.

He gave up on backing away and turned to face the Silverado. He had the keys in his hand, and he hit the unlock button and the headlights flashed, bright in the darkness, and he felt exposed and frightened and so he began to run, ignoring the pain, sure that Fleming would be coming for him now. When his hand fell on the door handle, he half expected to feel Fleming's hand—or, worse, a hand that didn't belong to any living man at all—fall on his own shoulder.

No one touched him, though, and then the driver's door was open and he was heaving himself up into the seat and only when the door was slammed shut and locked did he chance a look out the window.

He was alone. Mick Fleming was out of sight, shielded once more by those young, thin birches that weaved like skeletal fingers in the night.

Aaron gunned the engine to life and spun tires pulling out of the lot. When he made it to the top of the drive where the road ran above the dam, he didn't bother to stop, just pulled out and banged a right turn. This route would take longer, but it also would not take him past Mick Fleming's car in the woods.

He was willing to endure the extra miles to avoid that.

The dashboard clock glowed green: 12:37.

Aaron would make it home within the hour as he'd promised his father.

He did not know if he would tell his father what he'd seen down here, though. After this afternoon, how could he?

The memory of Fleming's words chased him along the dark winding road.

That's much more than an alarm. It's a sacrifice.

Aaron wrapped both hands tightly around the wheel, pressed the accelerator, and sped away from the Chill.

22

Steve stayed awake until Aaron returned. When his truck pulled into the drive and the front door opened, he almost got out of bed to check on his son, to thank him for honoring the one-hour deadline . . . and maybe smell his breath and check his pupils.

He couldn't do that, though. Steve was anything but subtle when it came to studying his son for inebriation, and despite all of the day's madness there had been a tenuous trust building between them. If not trust, at least an open dialogue. Steve didn't want to risk that.

Instead, he left the bedroom door shut and thanked the Lord that his son had made it back home whole. Or mostly whole, at least. Aaron thumped into the house and up the stairs like Long John Silver entering the Admiral Benbow Inn. It sounded as if he'd given up on using the crutch already, but he was home.

Steve filed the missing crutch in well behind the hallucinated murder and the morning arrest and the alcohol and drug abuse, and then he slept, comforted by this simple knowledge: his son was home.

Once, that had not seemed like so much. Tonight it was more than enough.

Gratitude, like expectation, moved on a sliding scale.

He woke when the rain began again.

It was just after six and the sky was beginning to fill with light, although fresh clouds were building as if determined to thwart the effort. Steve lay in bed and tried to recall the last morning without rain.

Nine days ago? Ten?

He shut off his alarm before it sounded, then rose and dressed cautiously, determined not to make any noise to wake Aaron. The boy needed sleep. He'd surely not gotten any in jail, and the physical and mental battering he'd taken the previous day had to have been exhausting.

He's also not a boy, Steve chastised himself. Aaron was twenty-three years old. A man by any legal measure, as he was about to discover in the Torrance County courthouse.

And yesterday he'd seemed like a man, too. First at the dam, telling the story of the killing and owning up to it. Then, after the shock of his hallucination wore off, he'd bounced back like a man, continuing to own his disaster, albeit on different terms, promising to enter Peaceful Passages.

That couldn't have been easy.

And it wouldn't be easy today when Steve drove him there.

Steve didn't really know that much about the process. The paperwork said that there was a patient intake meeting, which probably meant some discussion with a therapist for Aaron and some discussion with a financial planner for Steve, but once that was done, did they check Aaron right in and keep him?

He slipped out of the bedroom and crossed to the kitchen, the old wood floors creaking beneath his weight. Upstairs, Aaron's door was closed and all was quiet. Steve snuck a look out at the driveway and was pleased to see that his truck was still there, meaning Aaron hadn't left again in the night. Then he was embarrassed for checking. No trust.

They would fix that, though. They were going to fix it. Something redemptive had happened at the Chill yesterday. They'd both believed the worst was ahead, but then Mick Fleming had wandered out of the woods, and as unsettling as that moment had been, Steve now believed that it was a good thing. Whatever had happened down there in the water and the rain had affected his son deeply. Perhaps that was a blessing.

He turned on the electric fireplace in the dining room, which threw faux firelight and real heat. Lily and Aaron hated the thing, always preferring the woodstove, but that required work, not a remote, and Steve's mornings were generally rushed.

Today, though, he supposed he was not rushed. He'd take his time talking to Aaron and figuring out the plan. Take a day off work, his first personal day since Lily's funeral, and focus on his family.

He stared at the flickering orange light and then picked the remote back up and turned the electric fireplace off. He walked outside, where a light but steady rain was falling, and he gathered some pieces of split hickory and cherrywood from the pile beside the shed, then brought it inside and filled the woodstove. By the time he'd lit a fire with newspaper and cardboard and gotten the cherrywood to catch, filling the house with its rich scent and putting out a deeper warmth than anything electricity could replicate, he was pleased with the extra effort.

Maybe Aaron would notice. Maybe he'd appreciate it.

His door was still closed. That was fine, though. Let him sleep as long as he could. He'd earned the rest.

Earned it? You think he earned a damn thing yesterday? Remember the jail pickup in the morning? Remember the lunacy he spouted off in the afternoon?

Steve tried to push the negative thoughts from his mind. Today he would be patient. Today he would not shout and he would not sheriff.

It was his wife who'd turned the title into a verb. *Don't sheriff me, Steve.* The memory made him smile.

He prepared his breakfast of Cinnamon Toast Crunch, another subject of Lily's amusement. *Do you think the voters would have second thoughts if they knew their sheriff ate a kid's cereal each morning? Want to try an egg, or at least maybe some Wheaties?*

Another memory, another smile. With the good memories and the warm fire, it had the feeling of a positive day. The first in a while.

Before adding milk to his cereal, he called his chief deputy, Sarah Burroughs. She was already at the office. No surprise. Sarah worked harder than anyone in the department. Steve had scarcely begun to explain his need for the day off when Aaron's door opened.

"I'll call you back," Steve said. "But don't expect to see me today, all right? If you need anything, call."

He'd just hung up when Aaron came into view. He was dressed in workout pants and a sleeveless shirt, and Steve saw the bruises and cuts lining his arms. He was pale and hollow-eyed, but he looked at the woodstove and smiled.

"I'm surprised you remember how to use it."

Steve made a scoffing sound. "I'm not *that* reliant on the remote."

"No?"

"No."

"So the smoke backing up isn't because you forgot the flue damper?"

Steve got out of his chair and hurried into the dining room and saw that tendrils of smoke were leaking out of the closed stove door.

"Son of a—"

"I got it, I got it." Aaron turned the thumbscrew that opened the damper on the flue. On the other side of the little window in the stove door, there was nothing but a faint glow of embers. The lack of airflow had choked out Steve's fire. You had to have all the forces balanced or that would happen. It required more attention than the remote.

"We'll probably need to restart that," Steve said, kneeling and opening the door with the lighter in hand.

As soon as he opened the door, the trapped smoke gusted out, and both of them coughed. Steve looked up at Aaron to apologize and saw his son smiling and suddenly he was smiling, too.

"Okay," he said. "Maybe I've been using the electric one more than I should."

As if on cue, the smoke detector in the kitchen began to shriek.

They both started laughing then.

"You get that," Aaron called over the wailing alarm, "and I'll handle this!"

Steve went into the kitchen, stretched up on his toes, and hit the reset button on the detector. The kitchen was filled with smoke now. *Well, I wanted him to notice my effort,* Steve thought, and then he got to laughing again as he crossed the room and pushed open the kitchen window to let the smoke bleed out. He tried to remember the last time he'd laughed with his son.

By the time he'd finished fanning the worst of the smoke out the window with a dish towel, Aaron had a fresh fire going in the stove, one that would last. He was stretched out in front of it, soaking in the warmth, his long, lanky frame unfurled across the floor. There was something about the posture that made Steve think of the way Aaron had looked at thirteen and fourteen, stretched out on the living room floor playing video games, seeming to add another inch of height with each passing week. On one of those nights he'd refused to move when Lily was vacuuming. She'd gone into the garage and gotten Steve's Shop-Vac, put it on reverse, and blasted air into Aaron's ears, chasing him out of the room like he was a puppy.

"What?" Aaron said now, looking back at Steve, catching his smile.

"I was thinking of the Shop-Vac."

That was enough. Aaron's lips twitched into a grin. "I still have hearing damage," he said. This was the old interplay between him and Lily over the incident, and so Steve offered her old retort.

"Went right through your ears like there was nothing there to stop it."

Silly old lines between mother and son, but the wrong line for this morning. Aaron managed to keep his smile but they both knew the moment had broken. No reference to his brains—or lack thereof—was funny right now.

Maybe it's time to get to it, then. Tell him you took the day off and ask him if he wants to call the rehab clinic first or if we just drive down there together . . .

"Hey," Aaron said, breaking the silence that had built, "do you have a number for that police officer, Mathers?"

"Huh?" Steve stared at him through the smoky air.

"I wanted to thank her. And apologize." Aaron kept his eyes on the stove. "I figured an email or a text . . . I don't need to talk to her, but I'd like to send her a note."

"I appreciate that, but I don't think you need to. She was—"

"I'd like to," Aaron said, and then, with a trace of churlishness: "It's not about you." He seemed to regret the last statement, because he looked back and added quickly, "It's something she should hear from me, that's all. You know?"

Be proud, Steve told himself. *This is the kind of ownership you want him to take, the kind of maturity you've been waiting to see.*

But for some reason he still didn't like the idea. Worse, for some reason he didn't trust Aaron's words. He thought he'd seen a glimmer of the old evasiveness.

He couldn't think of a good reason to disagree, though, so he simply nodded and said, "They're all first initial, last name over there, and then the agency. DEP.NYC.gov."

"NYC?"

Steve nodded absently. "It's our lake, but it's their water. She's technically with the city."

"Okay. First initial would be what?"

"*G.* Her name is Gillian."

"Gillian Mathers."

"Yeah."

"She from around here?"

There it was again, the forced-casual voice and lack of eye contact that was usually offered alongside some bullshit story about what he and Tyler Riggins had been up to the night before. But why would he be lying?

"No. Well . . ."

Aaron looked up. "Well?"

"When she was a kid. Her mother died, and then her grandmother, and her father finally came up and took her back to the city. I don't think she ever came back to Torrance until she was assigned here."

"The family has roots here, though?"

"Yeah. A long time."

"Really?"

Aaron sounded surprised, and Steve thought he understood it. Gillian had her father's skin, not her mother's. There weren't many black families in Torrance County who had a long history in the town. Weren't many in the Catskills, period. Between Albany and the city were a lot of white faces.

"Her mother's side," he said, and then, awkwardly, "The eyes are her mom's." He felt self-conscious, observing anything about another cop in the way he was now, but there was something about Gillian's blue eyes that reminded him of the way she'd stared at him when she was just a little girl waiting for answers about her grandmother. Answers he'd never been able to give. For a lot of years Steve had wondered why Molly Mathers decided to cut and run. Did she hate the girl's father for leaving, or hate the girl's mother for dying? Had she simply had enough of raising children and wanted out?

"Dad?"

"Sorry." Steve blinked himself back into the moment. "What'd you say?"

"I asked if her family had been here as long as ours?"

"Maybe longer." Steve was unnerved by Aaron's intensity. "What's it matter?"

Aaron's eyes went back to the stove. "Doesn't. I just thought the name was familiar, that's all."

"Oh. Well, my grandfather—your great-grandfather—he had some run-ins with them, I think." This memory drifted back to Steve like it was riding the smoke—vivid yet elusive, impossible to grab.

"Run-ins?"

"I think back with the dam construction," Steve said slowly. In truth, he did not remember the story. It was one his grandfather had never liked to talk about. "Maybe they lived out there. I honestly don't remember."

Aaron was watching him intently again, and Steve felt as if their roles had reversed and now he was the one who was being scrutinized for a lie.

"Let's have some breakfast," Steve said. "I might not be able to handle the fire, but I can still make cereal."

23

Mick was home before sunrise, but he waited in his car before entering the house. Come inside too early and Lori would have questions, such as why he'd said he was staying the night only to return at dawn. He had an answer for that one, at least, though he didn't relish the idea of sharing it.

For others, though?

No answers. Not even close.

This time the memories weren't all lost to fog. He remembered the bluestone wall that had emerged out of the moonlight, remembered each careful footstep out across it, remembered the boy with the pail and the man named Anders Wallace. He remembered starting down the road.

The rest was gone.

Well, not entirely. Because this time it seemed he'd taken notes.

He turned the dome light on, flipped open the leather cover of his notepad, and stared at the neat rows of notations in his unmistakable handwriting. They led off with an equation. It wasn't one he'd calculated by hand since college. He recognized it, though, understood all of the components: force, pressure, area, acceleration of gravity. All of the forces that were always at work on a dam, with one interesting addition: an uplift pressure calculation.

All of the work was waiting to be done, all of the numbers needing to be filled in except for one: 20.17. He studied that for a moment. The number represented the height of water in the equation, but it didn't make sense, because there was much more than twenty feet of water behind the dam. Twenty meters? Still wrong. And why was there any consideration of uplift pressure? It was the only element that didn't seem to belong until he glanced beneath the equation and saw the measurements.

Intake Chambers 1, 2, and 3.
16 feet, 7 inches—6.40 miles
15 feet, 4 inches—7.31 miles
14 feet—6.94 miles

Then, neatly lettered below that:

Three hundred million gallons daily with a frictional loss of 3 feet per mile, and of sufficient size to deliver the full 500,000,000 gallons daily with an additional loss of about 15 per cent. The estimated time of completion is four and one-quarter years at a cost of $26,000,000.

Mick read it three times, as if eventually the words would make sense. They never would, though. He understood the ideas: they all referred to water delivery from a reservoir. However, it certainly did not describe what he'd been asked to observe at the Chilewaukee and, moreover, it didn't describe anything that could be coming from the Chilewaukee, which had never been tapped.

He closed the notepad, uneasy.

The estimated time of completion is four and one-quarter years at a cost of $26,000,000.

Four and one-quarter years? There had never been a day in his life when he'd have used that phrase.

It was like something out of the past. Just like Anders Wallace.

That was impossible, of course. Mick Fleming was a firstborn son of science, a man without patience for superstition or religion, for anything that couldn't be demonstrated with measurements and math. So it didn't matter that he remembered Anders; it mattered that his memories were impossible.

As the night sky outside of Albany bled with the soft rose light of dawn, Mick wondered about brain tumors. Swelling, maybe. It didn't take much. The brain was a fine-tuned system. It didn't feel that way to people, of course, but that was simply because the brain was so exquisitely balanced that it could fool you into thinking the math didn't matter.

It did, though. And somewhere in Mick's mind, a number was askew.

It troubled him that he didn't remember leaving the water. Or leaving the dam, for that matter. He'd seemed to fall back into his own body somewhere on the lonely predawn highway, northbound toward home, with no awareness of how this had all come to pass.

Also troubling: his shoes and pants showed no mud stains, no water stains. He vividly remembered stumbling and tumbling down the hill toward the tailwaters, but there was no visual evidence to corroborate the memory. It was as if he'd waded out along that bluestone wall in the moonlight and washed himself clean.

When? How?

That he did not know. All he could say was that he kept emerging on the other side of his memories, no worse for wear. He hadn't slept, but he wasn't tired. He'd stood in the frigid water, but he wasn't cold. If the sheriff's son was to be believed, then Mick had also taken a beer bottle off the side of his face but remained unmarked.

He decided what had to be done as the rose light brightened and the landscape seemed to widen with it, exposing the sprawling subdivision, all of the brick houses on wide lots of browned lawns glimmering with frost. He had to see a doctor, obviously. A neurologist, most likely. He would see the doctor before he spoke with Lori. When he told his wife the problem, he wanted to be able to reassure her that he was still mentally sound enough to call for a doctor before he shared any of the disturbing visions with her.

If he did share them. He still wasn't sure about that.

The doctor would be his second call. Not his first. His first call needed to be to his boss. There were not many certainties before Mick this morning, but he knew that he would not—could not—return to the Chilewaukee. He wondered if his elaborate break from reality had roots in something very real, something that had stalked him for years, the way depressives referred to the black dog that would appear without warning, darkening their moods.

Mick's trouble wasn't depression, though. It was frustration. How many times could a man offer warnings that went ignored before he began to lose patience? It had gone that way for years. Mick was Paul Revere, and yet they all regarded him as the Boy Who Cried Wolf. The threat was real, he sounded the alarm, and the world ignored him.

The black dog, he thought again. That was the right idea but the wrong symbol. No poet had ever set out to capture the rage of righteous work ignored, dismissed, or kicked down the road. No one had ever offered verse to the plight of the maintenance engineer.

Maintenance. Such a boring term, and yet so critical. Everyone craved invention and innovation, but it was maintenance that kept empires alive.

Mick Fleming, not a poet, had no words for the feeling. You didn't need poetry to express the risk of a flood, though. All you needed was a thundering cascade of water. What came next required no imagination. Houses flattened, schools submerged, rescue workers steering boats through intersections built for cars.

"They deserve it," he said aloud, and he didn't like the sound of his own voice.

Call the section chief and then the doctor.

Yes, that's what he would do.

He remained in the car for another hour, wondering vaguely why he wasn't cold, sitting there with the engine off, and then the garage door of his house rose and Lori's Honda CR-V—they were a brand-loyal couple, and Honda's engineering had always pleased Mick—backed out of the driveway. He watched as she put down the garage door and pulled away, off to work, safe in the knowledge that her husband was doing the same somewhere in the Catskills.

Telling her the truth would be hard. Easier with a doctor's opinion in hand, though. By evening it would all be easier.

Mick waited until Lori was out of sight and then pulled into the garage she'd just vacated. The house was a two-story, brick-and-vinyl-sided home with an attached garage and a swimming pool that Lori adored. A swimming pool in Albany was woefully impractical, but during the short summers she used it plenty. Mick didn't, but he'd enjoyed watching the concrete go in, and he had a fondness for the filtration system, the careful calibrating and balancing of chemicals.

He entered the house and made it halfway across the kitchen before he stopped and tilted his head. He stood like that for a moment, then walked back into the garage, closed the door behind him, and stood in the darkness, breathing the vanishing vapors of the Pilot's exhaust.

He counted off thirty seconds and then went back in the house, closed the door, and crossed the kitchen, walking out into the living room with its vaulted ceiling. The TV was on, morning news playing, as if Lori had wanted background noise, but Mick didn't glance at that. Instead he went straight to the thermostat.

Seventy-two degrees.

This was troubling, and not just because he'd asked Lori on countless occasions to drop it to 68 when she left the house.

The garage had no heat and was poorly insulated. The temperature in there had to run fifteen or twenty degrees lower than the house. And out on the street, where he'd sat in the dark for nearly two hours? Colder still.

Yet he'd felt no transition. Out of the cold and into the warmth, and he detected no difference. He hadn't been cold in the car; he was not warm in the house.

"I will need a doctor," he said, the second time he'd spoken aloud, and this time far more comforting, because he sounded like himself and the message was right.

The doctor was second, though. His responsibility to the public was first.

It was just past seven, and he knew that Ed Cochran wouldn't be in until eight. Ed was his direct supervisor, the man whose job it was to tend to every facet of the inspection and protection of the New York City watershed. Mick felt that waiting for Ed to get in would be a mistake, though. With the way his mind was wandering—*Wandering? You're walking into rivers, buddy . . . You call that* wandering?—he didn't trust himself to stay on task, which was somehow almost more frightening than all the rest of it. Mick had his faults and failings, but a lack of focus wasn't on the list and never had been.

So he called Ed even though he knew he wouldn't reach him, thinking that he should leave a message. Get the ball rolling.

He got the voicemail and he muted the TV so it was just the sound of his voice when he said, "Ed, it's Mick. Listen, boss, I'm going to need to talk to you about yesterday's inspection at the Chilewaukee. It was, um, a—"

The shower turned on upstairs.

For a long moment he stood there with the phone to his ear and his words forgotten, just listening to the sound. Hoping it could be anything else.

There was no doubting it, though. The high hissing water splattering off tile and glass was clear. The house was quiet and the shower was loud. They had excellent water pressure here. Mick had always been pleased with that.

He finally realized that dead air was filling his boss's voicemail, and so he cleared his throat and said, "Sorry, Ed, I got distracted. There was . . . uh, Lori just walked in. Anyhow, what I was saying . . ."

What *had* he been saying? And why was he still jabbering into the phone instead of going upstairs to see what in the hell had happened?

He looked at the stairs, still with the phone to his ear, and he did not want to walk up them. He wanted to walk right out the front door. Not walk, he wanted to run—wanted to *sprint*—out of his own home and tear down the street of the quiet subdivision, screaming until someone heard him and helped him.

"Just give me a call, please," he said woodenly, and then he disconnected. He put the phone into his pocket, each motion methodical, because he did not want to rush.

Oh, no. He did not want to rush up those stairs.

Above him the shower pounded away. In the wall behind the leather couch, he could hear the soft gurgling of the drainpipe whisking the water back out of the house.

He took a breath, ran his fingers through his limp, thinning hair, and then nodded as if agreeing with someone else in the room.

Yes, he thought, *I* do *need to look, don't I? I do need to check this out.*

He moved then, finally, and managed to bypass the front door, which seemed to beg for him, and turned left toward the stairs. He went up them one at a time, careful to keep his feet on the runner carpet so each step was muffled, soft.

With each step the sound of the shower grew louder. It no longer seemed possible that it was the shower, in fact. No shower had ever roared like this.

A burst pipe, maybe. A real gusher. Dumping water on the floor, maybe behind the tile and drywall, making an unholy mess. But a mess I can fix.

He reached the top of the stairs, rounded the corner, and entered the master bedroom. The door between bedroom and bathroom was open, and he could see steam on the mirror.

I should have told Lori last night, Mick thought numbly. *I should have told my wife the truth.*

Then he stepped inside the bathroom.

Empty. The big mirror over the double vanity was misted over with steam, and Lori's robe was draped over the hamper. One of the towels on the rack hung heavily, still damp.

But the room was empty. The jetted tub beside the glassed-in shower was dry and empty, and the shower itself was empty, although the water steamed and pounded down with force that exceeded even Mick Fleming's high standard for water pressure. It blasted out of the showerhead like a fire hose, as if it might loosen the grout between the tiles, chisel it out.

Just turn it off, Mick. It's water. That's all. Reach in there and turn it off.

He opened the door and a wave of steam flooded out. He had the dim thought that the water was very hot and yet he could not feel its warmth, but that was secondary to the goal of simply turning the faucet handle. One counterclockwise revolution and this would be done and then he could call Ed back and then the doctor, or maybe the doctor first, maybe that was the—

"Let it run."

He had his hand on the faucet when the voice came. He didn't let go of the faucet but he didn't turn it, either. Just looked behind him.

Anders Wallace was leaning against the vanity. He wasn't three feet away from Mick. His arms were folded over his fussy, old-fashioned jacket and vest, and his neatly trimmed white mustache bristled above a mouth that was twisted into an expression of disappointment. Of anger.

"There seems to be some confusion, Mr. Fleming."

"No," Mick said, his hand still on the faucet, the shower still blasting away, that hot, steaming water that felt like it had no temperature at all as it pounded on his arm and soaked his shirtsleeve. It felt neither hot nor cold. Felt simply *natural*, like his own skin.

"No?" Anders cocked his head and leaned forward, swinging his weight off the vanity. He put his right hand into his pants pocket, a casual gesture, but one that pulled his jacket back to expose the gun holstered on his hip.

Not a real man. So not a real gun.

Anders smiled coldly then, as if Mick had spoken the thought aloud.

"Some confusion," he said once more. "Yes, there seems to be. I thought I made this clear already, Mr. Fleming, but you're struggling to comprehend it. You are not alone. Do you understand that? You'll never be alone."

You'll never be alone. It was the statement you'd offer a lover or a child. Reassuring. Eternally reassuring. And, in Anders Wallace's voice, the single most terrifying sentence Mick had ever heard.

"You'll need to understand that," Anders Wallace said. "It will become easier in time. Soon it will feel natural. But you can't lose track of the idea, Mr. Fleming."

"I won't," Mick said.

"Your phone call would suggest otherwise, sir."

"I wasn't . . . that call was not about . . ."

He stammered to a stop. The thing that he didn't remember from the night suddenly felt close. The last thing and the most important one.

"It was not about our business," he said.

There it was. Their business. How had he forgotten it? No wonder Anders Wallace looked so disappointed, so angry. He'd stood up here and listened to Mick making a call to Ed Cochran as if he owed him that? He'd listened to Mick call Ed Cochran *boss*, no less? Anders had every right to his rage.

"I took the job," Mick said. "Working for Galesburg."

"Yes, Mr. Fleming. Yes, you did. I hope you also took it seriously."

"One hundred percent," Mick said.

"You must remember that always. Not just in fits and bursts. Always."

"I know," Mick said as the shower rattled off the glass door beside him and steam drifted in front of Anders Wallace's face but did nothing to diminish the intensity of that unblinking, blue-eyed stare.

"You know?" Anders echoed.

Mick nodded. He opened his lips to speak, then hesitated. This man—*not a man; he can't be a man, he's a phantom, a ghost*—was not one you wished to disappoint. And yet . . .

"There are things I don't remember," Mick said. His voice soft and weak, almost drowned out by the sound of the shower.

Anders didn't show anger. He just nodded almost sympathetically.

"That's to be expected," he said. "But confusion can't be allowed to flourish into something greater. Something more like doubt." He paused, and whatever hint of sympathy had been in his face faded like the steam. "This is a serious job for a serious man. A man can't succeed at important work if he doubts himself. In moments of pressure, focus must be maintained. That's the task, Mr. Fleming. Your people demand it. Your town demands it."

"Yes," Mick said, and he nodded slowly. This made sense to him. Concentration was critical. The greater the pressure, the sharper the focus. These were his gifts. For too long, they'd been unnoticed or undervalued. Anders, though . . . Anders was different. He understood so much and he missed nothing. Look at him here, with those piercing blue eyes. He missed absolutely nothing.

"It will be easier soon," Anders Wallace said, "because I travel with you now. You'll see, sir. Now, let's send a message to the man who thinks he is your boss."

Mick blinked. "I didn't think I was supposed to talk to him anymore."

"Quite the contrary, Mr. Fleming. You've been given an extraordinary opportunity because you have unique reach. Your value exceeds the Chilewaukee; don't you see that? We need a surface man with authority, as we made clear to you last night."

"I forgot," Mick murmured.

"Understood. It happens. It will happen less soon. That's why I'm here. To make sure you do your job."

"I'll do it."

"Excellent. Then let's craft our message, shall we? Wording will be critical. So will timing."

Mick didn't follow. His face must have shown this, because Anders nodded as if he'd spoken.

"It's a process, sir. What began in Galesburg will not end there. You'll be needed elsewhere before it's done. You'll be needed all the way downstream, don't you remember?"

Maybe he did. "In the city?" he ventured.

Anders Wallace's face split into a wide, horrible smile. His eyes lit.

"Yes," he said. "In the city."

PART THREE

24

Gillian was drinking coffee and reviewing the day's pending casework at the Owl & Turtle café in the heart of downtown Torrance—all three blocks of downtown Torrance—when her phone chimed with an email notification. She ignored it, keeping her attention on the file before her. Today's work was an anonymous complaint alleging that a local contractor wasn't building his septic leach fields up to watershed standard.

Despite her desire to be back in the city, Gillian had developed a fondness for Torrance. The bucolic village was an undeniably beautiful place to live, with its mountain-town charms. She loved her apartment in the Arlington Heights Inn, a three-story brick building that had been a boardinghouse long ago. The inn had been lovingly restored into town homes, and the combination of real history with modern amenities appealed to her. She knew the reason went deeper than dark wood trim and high arched windows, though; the apartment was also an intersection between two childhood homes. The wood trim and the windows made her think of the old farmhouse in the woods, while the walk-up apartment made her think of her father's building in Queens.

Most of the good memories were from Queens, but there had been good memories in the farmhouse, too. The wide-plank floors of the apartment at Arlington Heights conjured those up, making her remember the best moments she'd spent as a child in Torrance County.

And the apartment didn't have any bookcases that pulled back to reveal a disturbing relic of a schoolhouse, a dark chamber of madness in an otherwise sane house.

It did have a family just beneath her with a newborn baby who tended to shriek at two in the morning, though. So far she'd made it through the child's early months without banging on the floor and pleading for silence. So far.

The people of Torrance were mostly good and sometimes friendly. Friction between citizens and police existed almost everywhere, but it was on a different plane when it came to Catskill towns and the DEP. Generations after they'd first arrived to police the reservoir work camps and the soon-to-be-submerged villages, the DEP officers in the Catskills still battled against the perception of being an invading force.

In the days when the Catskill reservoirs were being constructed, the Board of Water Supply police, as they were known at the time, had moved in to keep rule on the thousands of workers who'd come to the mountain villages and to pacify the locals who were in the midst of being evicted from them. Not surprisingly, the BWS force was regarded as an antagonistic presence.

The legacy lingered. More than a century later Gillian still encountered bumper stickers that said *DEP get off my back!* Even Gillian's cruiser drew hostile attention. It was a Ford Explorer with a garish blue-and-green-on-white paint job, the letters *DEP* emblazoned on the side in a size more appropriate for an interstate billboard than an SUV. Beyond being ugly, it incited anger. The sheriff and the state police were viewed as protecting and serving the community; the DEP police were viewed as pokers, prodders, and pesterers. The friction had reached such a head that in 2014 the state removed the authority of the DEP police to make traffic stops, citing complaints about a culture of harassment and the need for a friendlier image in the Catskill communities. If Detective Sergeant Gillian Mathers saw a local barreling down Route 5 at one hundred miles per hour, she was invited to call the sheriff's department or the state police.

She was on her way back to the counter for a coffee refill when her phone chimed again. Another email. This time she checked it.

The messages were from a sender she didn't recognize, no name attached, just the email address, which was a collection of initials and numbers, standard fare for someone with a common name trying to find a Gmail account handle that wasn't already taken. She opened the first message and saw that it was a photograph of a car. A white Honda SUV parked in dark woods, skeletal tree limbs reaching out for it.

What in the hell was this?

She scrolled to the second message.

Dear Detective Mathers:

I know I should apologize to you for what happened yesterday. A few hours ago, I meant to. But then I saw something that I would like to talk with you about. I heard something, too. I know you're probably wishing that I would just talk to my dad and keep you out of this, but there are a few problems with that. Some of them you might understand, and some of them you might not. If you decide you need to make contact with him, I won't blame you. But I also want to request that you give me one chance to explain it to you first.

I will send a photo next. I took it last night, just after midnight, in the woods above the Chill. I believe I know whose car it is, but I can't run a license plate. You could do that.

I think you might be interested in what I heard last night. He said your name. Your last name, I mean. He was down there in the middle of the night in the water and he said your last name and talked about a sacrifice.

If you think I'm crazy, that's understandable. Maybe it's even right. But I do have the photograph. I think that's enough to ask a few questions. I hope you agree.

Sincerely,
Aaron J. Ellsworth

Gillian had been out of her seat on the way for more coffee, but now she sank slowly back into the chair and whispered, "Holy shit."

The coffee shop chatter swirled around her. Everyone relaxed and cheerful. Unaware of her.

He said your name. Your last name, I mean. He was down there in the middle of the night in the water and he said your last name and talked about a sacrifice.

She stared at the text, and a soft voice in her head chided her. *He's making some damn good guesses, isn't he?*

Gillian wanted to ignore this email. Wanted to forward it to Steve Ellsworth and wish him good luck with his son.

There was only one problem with that approach.

If Aaron told Steve the story first, then Gillian might never hear it. Steve wasn't the most extroverted guy in Torrance County, and when it came to personal problems, Gillian had the sense that his lips would seal even tighter.

She didn't need to hear the story, of course. She had absolutely no need to hear the crazy kid's crazy story.

How'd he guess about Haupring?

He hadn't. She'd put those words in his mouth.

She slid the phone into her pocket, gathered her paperwork and coffee, and left the café, walking out into the misting rain.

Even in the rain and against the nickel-colored sky, downtown Torrance was beautiful. Brick buildings and clean sidewalks and trees, all framed by the fog-shrouded mountains just beyond. The only thing missing right now was the color. This time of year, the landscape should have been electric. It was monochromatic and dull, though, as if the endless rains had washed autumn away and rolled out a bleak gray carpet in anticipation of winter's arrival.

She walked to her Explorer, slid behind the wheel, and started the engine but didn't put it into gear. Sat there and sipped her coffee and debated. Call Steve? Call Aaron? Ignore it all?

In the end she didn't take any of those options. Instead, she called the operations center at the Chilewaukee. Arthur Brady answered.

"Hiya, Sergeant," he said, cheerful enough. He was always pleasant. Of course, Arthur Brady also took his paycheck from watershed protection. Different gig, same mission, and thus a natural bond. People talked about town-and-gown divides in college communities, but in Torrance it was town and water.

"How you doing, Arthur?"

"Better than yesterday, at least."

"Yeah. That was . . . that was something, wasn't it?"

"I never heard such craziness. And poor Steve. He's been through plenty already, but that had to land a different kind of punch, you know?"

"Right." Gillian turned her coffee cup in her palm, soaking in the warmth. "Say, Arthur, you mind if I stop by the dam for a few minutes?"

"Of course not. What's up?"

"I'd like to see the surveillance footage."

Arthur was quiet. When he spoke again, his surprise was evident. "You don't think anything Aaron said actually happened, do you?"

"Do I think he murdered the man who walked up to chat with us? No, Arthur. But I've got to write a report regardless, and I want to do it right."

Brady sounded nonplussed. "It's a busy day. Flood stage and rising. We're closing in on twenty feet above pool level. This damned rain."

"I'll make it quick."

"Look, I didn't know what-all was going to happen," Arthur said. "I would've thrown the kid outta here if not for him being the sheriff's son."

"I'm not worried about that. It's my job to police the place; it's your job to handle the dam. I won't confuse the two."

"Okay. Good. I don't know what you think you're gonna see, though."

"I'm not expecting a thriller," Gillian said. "I just need to see the videos so I can say that I did my due diligence."

"I suppose you've got to. Although it's just foolishness at this point."

"That's what I'm here for," Gillian said, and Arthur chuckled. "I'll be out there in fifteen or twenty, if that's okay."

"Sure."

"Great. Thanks. Oh, you mind doing one more thing?"

"What's that?"

"Can you pull up the videos from last night, too? Midnight to one?"

"What's that about?"

"Hopefully nothing," she said, setting the coffee into the cupholder and shifting the transmission into drive. "But I've been asked to give it a look."

She headed out of town, into the hills, and into an intensifying rain.

25

They still hadn't spoken of Peaceful Passages.

Aaron declined breakfast, saying that he needed a good, hot shower first. Then he went back upstairs and the shower ran, and ran, and ran. There was no way the water heater could be keeping pace.

What's he doing up there? Steve wondered, picturing pills and needles, then feeling guilty. It was hard to shower with only one good leg. If he was lying up there unconscious, blood seeping out of his skull while Steve sat here sipping coffee . . .

"Aaron?" he called.

The water was shut off, and Steve's chest loosened.

"Yeah!" Aaron hollered back. "I'm coming down. Took me a while to figure out how to keep my foot dry!"

Clear words, reasonable excuse. Steve exhaled again.

"Just making sure," he shouted up, and then his phone rang. Sarah Burroughs, his chief deputy.

"Can't run this county without me, can you?" he said.

"Steve, I hate to do this to you, because I know you really need the day, but the guy from the dam at the Chill called. Arthur Brady, the operations guy?"

"Yeah? What'd old Arthur want?"

Already Steve had a bad feeling. Any reference to what had happened out there the previous day was troubling.

"You, and you alone. He wouldn't talk to me. Said he needed to speak to you. Said it was important, and about Aaron."

Steve sat with the phone to his ear and his untouched cereal in front of him and watched the fire his son had started in the woodstove.

"Steve?" Sarah nudged.

"Yeah. Okay, I'll give him a call. He leave his number?"

"Yes."

Steve wrote it down, thanked her, and told her to call him if there was anything serious in play.

"I hope it's quiet," she said. "Always do, but especially today. I know that you . . ." She hesitated, then settled for "Good luck today, Steve. That's all."

"Thanks, Sarah."

He hung up, then called Arthur, who answered immediately.

"Sarah said you had something to say about the mess down there yesterday," Steve began. "I'm happy to listen, but first I want you to know that I'm going to be getting Aaron the help he needs. Okay?"

"Okay, Sheriff. But I'd appreciate it if you could get out here. I've got to deal with the DEP detective and I don't know exactly what she's angling for. She wants to review surveillance videos."

Steve frowned. "Surveillance videos for *what*?"

"I got no idea, and that's why I want you here. If she's got ideas about charging Aaron for trespassing or false informing, whatever, it's going to be a mess I certainly don't need. I always let him swim down here. After yesterday, I'm thinking that could cost me my job."

"Nobody's firing you, Arthur."

"I sure as hell hope not! But I'd like to have you here."

Steve sighed. "When's she coming out?"

"Now! She didn't give me much warning at all. I don't see the need. We all saw that man yesterday and we all know that Aaron didn't—"

"I'm on my way," Steve said, cutting him off. He'd thought yesterday was done and today would be a fresh start. Apparently, Gillian Mathers had other ideas. He hung up, dumped his coffee into the sink, and shouted up to Aaron once more.

"Hey! I've gotta go out. Just for a quick run. You're not leaving, right? Because we need to . . . we've got to discuss things."

From behind the closed bathroom door: "I'll be here. Don't worry. I'm good."

He *sounded* good, too. He really did. Last night he'd come and gone in an hour, as promised. This morning he'd been the closest thing to his old self that Steve had seen in months, if not years. Extend the trust, then.

"Thank you!" Steve hollered. "I'll be back quick."

"Where you headed?"

Steve had his jacket in one hand, the doorknob in the other. He hesitated.

"Some quick BS with Sarah Burroughs," he shouted, and then he left to drive back to the Chilewaukee, having just lied to the son he was wondering if he could trust.

26

The misting rain had matured into another downpour by the time Gillian reached the dam and discovered that Steve Ellsworth was already there.

What was this? She wanted to watch the videos in privacy.

She pulled in beside the sheriff's car. Up above, a door opened in the gatehouse and Arthur Brady waved a hand, indicating that she should come up the steps.

She'd been in the gatehouse only once, and that was on a tour when she was first assigned to the Ashokan Precinct. It sat like a discarded medieval tower atop the dam, and just above the spillway. Beneath it were the gates that controlled the outflow of water into the stepped-stone chute of the spillway, which was a deluge today, thundering down the spillway and into the stilling basin, where the energy dissipated before carrying on down Cresap Creek and alongside the town of Torrance.

The gatehouse had seemed imposing and bleak to her then, and it did again today. The room was cold and filled with gauges and monitors and iron wheels. There were traces of new technology, but for the most part it felt like the machine room of an ancient ship. It was big and yet felt confining, like being inside a mausoleum. In one corner stood a pair of massive red lights, as big as traffic flashers, that would illuminate in the event of a breach and send the sound of sirens echoing down the flood-plain, giving residents in its path a precious few minutes of warning.

"Nice view," she said. The view wasn't actually so great. The windows were narrow and showed little of the surrounding mountains. Arthur

Brady spent a lot of hours staring out at gray water on one side and gray concrete on the other and waiting for trouble, lonely as a lighthouse keeper.

He also had cameras. There was a bank of monitors on the eastern wall showing livestreams from different angles. Security cameras had been installed around all of the New York City water system facilities following 9/11.

"I wasn't expecting to see you here, Sheriff," Gillian said.

Steve Ellsworth wasn't in uniform, but he wore a sheriff's department windbreaker over an untucked flannel shirt, his face shielded by a New York Giants baseball cap. He met Gillian's eyes reluctantly.

"Thanks for your help yesterday," he said.

"Of course." She started to add *Sorry about Aaron* but stopped herself, unsure of how to finish that thought without making them both more uncomfortable. "May I ask what brings you here today, though?"

"Arthur called."

Gillian shot a hard look at Arthur, who made an apologetic face.

"It's his jurisdiction and his son," he said.

"Actually, it's not his jurisdiction. As for it being his son . . ." She let her words trail off and waved her hand. The hell with it. "If we see anything unusual involving his son, I trust Steve to make the right decisions. Let's take a look at the night action first."

Steve frowned. "Night action?"

"Yeah. I got a tip that some folks came back around midnight."

Steve's broad chest filled and his jaw tightened. "He came back to get my truck. That's all. In and out in an hour. I can promise you that because I timed it."

Gillian held up a calming hand. "It's not even Aaron that I'm interested in. May I just watch?"

Arthur Brady was sitting on a stool below them, a remote control in his weathered hand. He looked from Gillian to Steve. He was rubbing his thumb over the side of his index finger in a nervous, fidgeting fashion.

"I never granted Aaron any access," he said. "I just want everybody to know, on camera it might look like I gave him a free pass, but I didn't. He wasn't listening, and—"

"We get it, Arthur. Play the videos of the parking lot, starting at midnight?"

Arthur sighed, pointed the remote at one of the monitors and initiated playback, then scrolled through time stamps until he reached 23:58 and pressed PLAY. The video feed of the parking lot showed Steve Ellsworth's pickup truck sitting alone.

"Go ahead and speed it up a little?" Arthur asked.

"Just slow enough that we won't miss anything."

He advanced the frames, and the time stamp changed but the frame did not: Steve's truck, an empty lot, darkness beyond.

At 12:18 a new truck entered the frame. This one was an oversized pickup on massive tires. The passenger door opened, a man climbed out, and the big truck drove away.

"That's Aaron," Steve confirmed. "Coming to get . . ."

His voice trailed off when Aaron began to move. Gillian leaned forward, curious. Aaron was limping downstream and his head was tilted forward and to the side, as if peering at something just off the frame.

He stopped walking. Stood frozen as the seconds ticked by. Suddenly leaned forward again as if he'd heard something he didn't want to miss . . . and then he began to shuffle backward. His right foot caught on a rock and he stumbled but regained his balance. When that happened, he broke from the cautious steps, pivoted to face the truck, and began to run. It was an uneven, halting stride that had to be painful, but he ran. Hard.

As if something were pursuing him.

Gillian inched closed to the monitor, staring at the corner of the screen, waiting to see what had spooked him, fully expecting that something was coming.

Nothing appeared. Aaron Ellsworth made it to the truck, fumbled the door open, and started the engine. Lights glowed harshly and then the Silverado was in motion as Aaron sped up the lane and out of sight.

It was 12:24 a.m. He'd stood staring into the darkness for a full five minutes before running.

Gillian glanced at Steve. His face was as gray as the hair that stuck out from beneath his Giants cap. She knew what he was thinking: they'd just had a live-action look at his son's hallucinations.

"I know he needs help," Steve said softly. "*He* knows he needs—"

The video was still playing, and Gillian was the only one facing it, because she'd taken her eyes off Steve, embarrassed for him. A flash of white appeared in the upper left-hand corner.

"Stop," Gillian said.

"I'm not going to stop, damn it. He's my son and I'll defend him until—"

"Stop the *video*!"

Steve and Arthur looked back at the monitor. Arthur pointed the remote, pressed a button, and brought the feed to a halt. The white blur took shape. It was at the far end of the camera's reach, but the outline of a white SUV was clear.

Gillian took a step closer. "Who's this?"

"I got no idea," Arthur said. "Let's see if they drive down."

He hit the remote again. The video moved, but the white SUV didn't. It remained in place, idling at the top of the hill, headlights angled down, searching, hunting, the exhaust smoke fogging the air like a wolf's breath on a winter night.

"Can you zoom in?" Gillian asked.

This took Arthur a minute. He played with the remote, testing different settings, and finally found the zoom. It was only slightly better than useless. The video was the uneven blend of light and dark taken by infrared cameras, and the clarity became worse with each click of the zoom. The front plate was illegible, but you could make out the big silver H across the grill.

Honda.

Gillian removed her cell phone, thinking she wanted to compare the vehicle Aaron had sent her with this one, but Steve Ellsworth was watching her and so she pulled up the camera application instead of her email and snapped a quick photo of the video monitor. For a reason she couldn't explain, she didn't want him to see the email from his son. Not just yet, at least.

"What's it mean to you?" Steve asked.

She looked into his ashen face, saw his wary eyes hunting for the truth.

"Nothing."

"Come on. You requested this, now you're taking pictures, and it's nothing to you?"

"It's strange," she said. "All of it was strange. Don't you think?"

Steve didn't answer. Arthur Brady cleared his throat.

"She's thinking it was the same car she saw before."

They both turned to him. He made an odd, patting-the-air gesture, as if to press down hackles that were rising.

"We were all right here! We all saw it! Hell, I can prove it if you want— I can go back—but we all know that car was the same one that Fleming drove down." He swiveled his chair to face Gillian, his eyes narrowing, smug. "Am I wrong?"

"It looks like his car," she admitted.

"It is," Arthur Brady said. "It's Mick Fleming's Honda."

"How are you sure?" Steve said.

"Damn thing was parked here all day."

"It could be another Honda Pilot," Steve said. "They made a few of them."

"Could be. But it isn't."

"What was he like after I left?" Gillian asked.

"Pardon?"

"Steve and Aaron left first. Then it was me and Fleming. Then he went up to talk to you, and I went . . ."

She didn't want to say where she'd gone. Didn't want to tell them how she'd paced the shoreline in the rain, staring into the Dead Waters and wondering . . .

I need to take a walk by the lake, her grandmother had said.

"He was odd," Arthur said, looking at his boots, his bald head bright under the lights.

"What do you mean, odd?" Gillian asked.

Arthur ran a hand over his face and sighed. "I've known that guy for years now. He makes quarterly inspections, right? He's an anal-retentive son of a bitch, and he *always* has problems to report. He hates this dam and wants maintenance money for it. He's just . . . he's an engineer. You know the type. Detailed, analytical. And he has never once left this place without concerns. Hell, he *showed up* with concerns! But yesterday he just left in kind of a fog." Arthur paused, nodded at the screen and said, "Or I *thought* he left, at least."

"So what do we do with him?" Gillian asked.

"What do *we* do? Lady, it was *you* that dragged us all down here!"

"Sergeant," Gillian said mildly. "It's 'Sergeant,' not 'lady,' and, yes, I asked you to see the videos. I didn't ask you to call the sheriff."

Brady looked back at the floor and let out a soft exhalation.

"When I found Aaron yesterday—when I called for you, Steve—he was lucid. He wasn't ranting and raving. He wasn't high. He was grim as the crypt keeper. I sat with him until you came along and he never said anything crazy. He was shaken, but he wasn't seeing dancing pink gorillas in the woods or anything, okay? He knew where he was, and it seemed like he knew exactly what he'd done."

For a long moment it was silent. Gillian looked at Steve Ellsworth, who wet his lips and shifted awkwardly.

"You're not trying to tell us that Fleming lied about the whole thing, are you? Because that's hard to swallow, Arthur."

"No shit, Sheriff." Arthur lifted a hand in apology. "Sorry. I don't mean to snap, and I don't even know exactly what I *do* mean to tell you. It's just . . ." He paused, then gave an embarrassed laugh. "I believed your son."

Steve Ellsworth rubbed the bridge of his nose. "Look, what in the hell are we all saying here? The man was a victim of my son's attack but lied about it?"

Neither Gillian nor Arthur answered.

"Okay," Steve said at length. "I'll ask Aaron what he was staring at. That's what you want out of me, right? To know what he saw." His face darkened, and then he added, "Or what he *thinks* he saw."

"No," Gillian said, and both men looked at her with surprise. She met Steve's stare. "No, you shouldn't ask him just yet. It should be me."

"How do you figure, Sergeant?"

Was there some snark to the way he said her rank? Gillian thought so, but she pushed on despite it. Or maybe because of it.

"I *figure* the Chilewaukee Reservoir is my department's jurisdiction and has been for most of a century, Sheriff."

He took her tone well. Studied her for a few seconds and nodded.

"Ask him your questions, then. But"—he waved his hand at the bank of security monitors—"I've got bigger problems than this, and so does Aaron."

"Fair enough," Gillian said. "I just want to talk to him. And maybe you can verify that Fleming actually went back to Albany. If that was his car that came and went out here last night . . . well, that would be good to know."

"Agreed," Arthur said.

The wind rose and drilled a line of raindrops off the window in a staccato clatter. They all turned reflexively. On the other side of the glass, the Chilewaukee's surface was pitted from the downpour, giving it the look of hammered metal.

"We really need a break from that," Arthur said softly. "Cresting twenty feet above pool level now."

"What's the record?" Steve asked.

"You're looking at it."

"You're *over* twenty?" Gillian asked. "By how much?"

Arthur studied a monitor. "Tenth of an inch, right now. Yesterday we got up around there and I increased outflow, but there's only so much of that we can do with the flooding problems downstream. People would rather have the floodwaters in the lake than in their backyards."

There was a pause while they listened to the pounding rain. Then Arthur repeated "We really need a break."

As if in response, thunder knocked in the west, an unwelcome visitor arriving with bad news. The rain wasn't stopping.

Not today.

DOWNSTREAM

27

The New York City Department of Environmental Protection head-quarters in Queens looked as if it had been designed to shout, *Boring municipal work; nothing to see here!* at passersby.

Ed Cochran couldn't have been happier with that. Let Midtown have the media companies, the Wall Street power brokers, and whatever was left of the old publishers. Let Midtown have the tourists, forever and ever, amen, let Midtown have the tourists.

He was happy in Queens.

The bland building was jammed up alongside—and below—the Horace Harding Expressway and the Long Island Expressway just beyond, and it stood adjacent to a preschool, of all things. Hundreds of thousands of people passed his office on the LIE every day and had no clue that the DEP was down here. That was absolutely perfect as far as Ed was concerned. His mother had been a state representative, and she'd always proclaimed to anyone who would listen that the real work got done in boring buildings.

His mother would have been a fan of his office.

He was in a good mood when he arrived that morning. A good mood despite the weather, which was the sort of chilled rain that shouldn't arrive until those weeks on the fringe of winter and snow, but in this climate, who the hell knew what you were going to get and when? Ed was in a good mood because last night he'd reviewed the progress report on Water Tunnel Number 3. The day that all of Water Tunnel 3 came online was the day he could finally begin shutting down stretches of Tunnels

1 and 2 and getting engineers down there to assess maintenance needs that existed mostly as unknowns. Once they'd put a submarine through a few miles of Water Tunnel 1, because it was too dangerous for a man. And then there'd been the spring of 2000, when they'd used the deep-sea divers to repair an original bronze valve. The leak in that sucker was scarcely bigger than the hole a .22-caliber bullet would've left, but water was geysering out at nearly a hundred miles an hour, and that, boys and girls, was bad for business. After prep in a decompression chamber, the divers had gone down in a diving bell lowered by a crane. It took ten days to repair that single leak in a bronze valve—plus the fifteen days of time in the decompression chamber. *The New Yorker* had covered that. For a little while, people cared. Then the news cycle moved on. People forgot.

There were other leaks, deeper leaks, leaks that even the submarine couldn't tell him about, or leaks that hadn't sprung but were close, with all that ancient metal working against torrents of water. Ask any engineer who'd win that battle, given enough time.

Ed had spent years worrying about running out of time, but today he thought they might avoid the calamities. As he entered his beautifully bland building, he was feeling as confident as he could.

Then he sat down behind his desk with a cup of coffee, opened his email, and found the message from Mick Fleming.

Re: Chilewaukee Dam Spillway—Urgent

Ed—

I left you a voicemail earlier. Knew you wouldn't be in yet but I was up because I haven't been able to sleep. I think the situation at the Chilewaukee could be dire. While the water is not yet threatening to crest the dam, that's only because of excessive and demanding use of the spillway. The spillway was not constructed for this level of water volume over sustained periods, and it has not been properly maintained nor outfitted with aeration, as noted in my previous site inspections, which are attached for your convenience.

During yesterday's site inspection, I observed bubbling along and below the face of the spillway that I fear may be indicative of cavitation. As you know, the only way we can be sure of this is to shut down the spillway. Instead, Mr. Brady is only increasing the water flow. My attempts to make the risk of this clear to him seemed unsuccessful. He is typically dismissive but yesterday was a new low. In his defense, further conversation was made difficult thanks to some hysteria surrounding the Sheriff of Torrance County, Steve Ellsworth, and his son, who I believe had some sort of drug-induced outburst near the dam. My attempts to communicate concern for those in the floodplain with Sheriff Ellsworth and with Sgt. Gillian Mathers, DEP police, were met with further dismissals. It appears no one immediately involved with the Chilewaukee is willing to grasp the stakes here or appreciate the risks.

It is my recommendation that we arrange a full site inspection with consulting engineers from Tabor, Bruce & Goy, as well as all concerned parties in Albany and NYC. The risk at the Chilewaukee is real, and with the existing forecasts calling for even more rainfall upstate, time is of the essence. I will be returning to the dam today in an attempt to speak further with Mr. Brady and his associates. It would be enormously appreciated if you can communicate to Mr. Brady the critical importance of following my recommendations regarding the spillway, and intake and outflow. Please relay to him that a failure to follow these recommendations will be regarded as breach of duty for which he may be held liable. If this seems like an overreaction, I assure you it is not. I've struggled with the people in Torrance County for long enough. Meanwhile, if you could please arrange for a full site inspection, I would urge that for tomorrow at 8 a.m. If anyone views that as inconvenient, please convey the absolute necessity.

I will be in touch shortly. If you need me, please text or leave a voicemail, because as you know reception in the area is abysmal.

Regards,
Mick

Why hadn't he called Ed's cell? Something this big, why in the hell would you leave a message and then send an email?

Because he's Mick, that's why.

There were a lot of things that Mick Fleming was not—socially skilled, for starters—but none of that mattered to Ed where dams were concerned. The cliché about having forgotten more than other people knew should have been written exclusively for Mick Fleming's knowledge of sluice gates and spillways. If Mick was worried, there was trouble.

Ed called him. The phone rang and went to voicemail. He called again. Same result. The frigging Catskills might've been settled for four centuries, but they could still eat a cell signal.

"Mick, call me. Soon as possible. You know what I'm going to sound like assembling everyone on notice like this when I haven't even spoken to my own engineer? Call me."

He hung up. The morning's good mood was long gone, and in its place was old dread. He got to his feet and turned to stare at the wall behind his desk, where a map of the New York City water supply hung.

His eyes drifted northwest, past a thousand quality sampling stations, past a holding reservoir that was home to the world's largest ultraviolet water treatment facility, past a hundred miles of tunnels. His eyes locked on the upper-left-hand corner of the map, where it all started, 125 miles away from where he sat now.

"Son of a bitch," he said aloud. Then he went back to his desk and got to work. As he made his first call, he was thinking, *Just be glad it's the Chilewaukee. Not Pepacton or Ashokan. Not Cannonsville. It's the Chilewaukee: surplus only, a risk to the region, maybe, but not the city. It can't reach out a long finger of disaster and touch New York.*

The only good news at the Chilewaukee was that Ed had the right man for the job up there.

28

Aaron was pouring a drink when Gillian Mathers called.

It was the one thing he'd promised himself he would not do. He'd promised his father the same, of course, and while that shamed him, weren't the most troubling lies the ones you told yourself?

Aaron hadn't meant to lie. Not this time. And yet forty-five minutes after his father left the house, he was pouring two fingers of twenty-one-year-old Glenrothes into a tumbler. Like an adolescent, he'd chosen the booze that was least likely to be noticed missing. The bottle had been a thank-you gift from some well-meaning county resident, or maybe one looking to make a clumsy bribe. Either way, it had been a swing and a miss, because Steve didn't like whiskey. What little drinking he did was limited to light beer. The whiskey was stored in a largely unused cabinet above the fridge.

Aaron was light with the pour, as if an ability to limit his lie in ounces preserved some dignity. He wanted something to dull the sharp edges of his memory, that was all. His father had not gone out for any quick chat. Aaron didn't believe that for a moment. Gillian Mathers had summoned him. She was sharing Aaron's email, sharing her concerns and sympathies, and breaking the tenuous trust that had been building between Aaron and his father.

Aaron wanted a little buffer in his bloodstream for that.

He didn't get it, though. He'd lifted the whiskey to his lips but hadn't had a sip yet, when his phone rang. A 212 area code, someone calling from the city. He was about to ignore it when he remembered his father's explanation of why Gillian Mathers had an *NYC* in her email address. *Technically, she's with the city.*

He answered it at the last second. "Hello?"

"This is Gillian Mathers."

"You ready to have me committed yet?" he asked.

"Not just yet, but I'll keep the idea in mind," she said dryly, and he was relieved, because people didn't joke around with anyone they thought was insane.

"I don't blame you." He pushed the untouched whiskey away. "I don't care how crazy it sounds: last night—"

"It looks like he was out here, yes," she said. "I'd like to talk about that. Can you drive with that foot, or do you need a ride?"

"I can drive. I did last night."

"I saw that." She paused. "Saw you run on it, too."

"You were out there?" he said, shocked.

"No. Surveillance cameras were."

Of course they were. Why hadn't he thought of that?

"Did you see Fleming on them, too?"

"Possibly. Saw his car, at least. Listen, if you can drive, I'd rather have this chat in person." She paused, then added, "And your dad's on his way back. I haven't shown him your email yet. You can disclose what you want to."

He was already on his feet. He dumped the Glenrothes into the sink and reached for the truck keys.

"Tell me where to meet you, and I'll be there."

"You know the Galesburg overlook?"

"Yes." The Galesburg overlook was a lonely perch looking upstream at the Dead Waters and the dam with a few picnic tables and a statue commemorating the town. It was a popular place with kids in the summer and photographers in the fall, but a strange choice for an interview in the rain. He didn't care, though. She was going to listen. That was enough.

"Meet me there in, what, fifteen minutes?" she asked.

"More like twenty. That's a long drive."

"I know it. But I also thought from there you might be able to point out the place where you went into the water." Another pause. "Where you saw the body."

She really is *listening,* he realized with a relieved thrill.

"I'll be there," he said. And then, almost too late but catching her just before she hung up, "Thank you."

"It was you or septic tanks," she said, and then she disconnected.

29

Gillian had been to the overlook only once since her return to Torrance County.

That had been three days after taking the job. She'd driven out to the wooded hills southeast of the lake with the intention of finding the old house. She knew it was still there.

Once, she'd timidly asked her father what had happened to the house. He said it was foreclosed, a word she didn't know but found in the dictionary.

He didn't like to talk about the house. He certainly didn't like to talk about the school. Once, he'd asked to see what she was drawing, and she'd felt safe showing him that. It was a sketch she'd done from memory of a photograph from the school: three men standing before three tunnels, each man dressed in high boots and suit coats. The tunnels seemed to narrow and darken behind them. It was one of her favorites, but she saw that it scared her dad. She didn't want to lose the sketchbook, so she said she wanted to draw a giraffe, which was his favorite animal. Would he like to see that?

He'd seemed relieved, and she gave him the giraffe picture, which was the first and only page she ever ripped out of the sketchbook. She hid the sketchbook then. Tucked it between the mattress and box spring and later climbed on a kitchen chair and slid it on top of the cupboard above the refrigerator.

When she was older, she tracked the property records on the house: foreclosure, sheriff's sale, another foreclosure, another sheriff's sale, the price point declining each time. She used Google Earth to look at the house, watching as the years went by and the forest moved in around the grounds, overwhelmed the vegetable garden, claimed the flower beds. She expected the house to collapse beneath the years of neglect in all those brutal upstate New York winters. Somehow it remained upright, though, protruding just above the tree line like a raised middle finger.

On the day she'd gone to find it, she was more than fifteen years removed from her last visit to the place, she was a cop, she was confident . . . and she backed out. Turned off and followed the winding lane up to the overlook, where the Galesburg memorial statue stood above the reservoir, a plain monument with a tidy, simplistic inscription. Today she followed the same route and read the inscription once more:

On September 21, 1940, what remained of the village of Galesburg was evacuated prior to the flooding of the valley for the construction of the Chilewaukee Reservoir. Galesburg was at that time one of the oldest settlements in the area, with documented history dating back to 1682, when Hiram Wallace and Isaac Mathers established farms in the area.

Families and memories of Galesburg live on in Torrance County to this day.

She wondered who had crafted that epitaph. So clean, so neat, claiming to tell you something but offering nothing that mattered. Sanitized.

Beyond the statue was a shelter house, so she could get out of the rain if not the wind. From the shelter, you could look to your right, northwest, and see the Dead Waters and the dam; you could look straight down and see a beautiful stretch of Cresap Creek carving its way through the valley below; or you could look left, southeast, and see the Mathers homestead. The house was scarcely visible through the trees, and on the day Gillian had chickened out and come here instead of the house, she had to strain to find it.

That had been August, and the trees were in full leaf. Today most of them were bare, picked clean by the unseasonable winds and rains, and she found the house quickly. The high roofline with its steep pitch to shed snow seemed to rise a bit higher now, as if it had grown over the years. The siding had been white when she lived there but now was faded to a filthy gray that matched the sky. The front porch railing was gone and it looked as if the porch itself might have collapsed.

She was considering going back to her car for binoculars when Aaron Ellsworth pulled in.

He walked toward her with a slight limp, but it wasn't nearly as bad as she'd expected. He was wearing boots and jeans and a black jacket open over a flannel shirt, and seeing him like this instead of down on the ground, raving about corpses and killings, she was reminded of just what a good-looking kid he was, tall and broad-shouldered but narrow waisted, the swimmer's V-tapered torso evident even under the jacket.

He wasn't really a kid, though. Was maybe five years younger than her.

"So . . . why here?" he said, hands in his pockets, head ducked against the wind and rain. He had long, tousled dark hair, in contrast with all of the photos of him in Steve's office. She wondered if he'd grown it out to ward off questions about his short-lived military service, trying hard not to look the part.

"I'm curious if it's all a joke to you," she said. She'd turned and leaned against the railing, which allowed her to face him and keep her old house at her back, the way she preferred.

His expression seemed to grow sad, as if he should have known better.

"You could've asked me that on the phone," he said. "And I wish you would have, because I don't have the energy to talk to anyone who thinks I'm full of shit. I dealt with enough of that yesterday. If I wanted more, I would—"

"Easy." She held up a hand. "I said I was *curious* if it was all a joke to you. Not that I thought it was."

"Why here?" he asked again, and she watched him closely.

"There are old stories about my family," she said. "I don't know how many you've heard."

"I don't remember hearing much of anything about your family. That's honest. Sorry if I missed out. I was too busy trying not to be known as the sheriff's son. What are you famous for?"

"Me? Nothing. My family was . . . eccentric, though. I figured your dad might have told you some of the old stories."

"He hasn't." Aaron took his hands out of his pockets and crossed the deck to stand beside her, only he was facing toward the water and she was still facing away from it.

"Have you heard about the schoolhouse?" she asked.

"No."

"You know what the Dead Waters are?"

"Yes. Those I know. You can still see some of the old buildings. I never liked it up there. When the light is right and the water is clear, you can see down and . . ." He trailed off and looked at her with fresh interest. "Hang on: they set it on fire, right? The school. I did hear that. That's one of the stories about the Dead Waters, at least. There were so many, but I never really paid attention. Every town has their dumb old stories, Halloween shit. That was never for me."

Their dumb old stories, Halloween shit. That dismissiveness angered her. It shouldn't have, because he was right, of course. Old stories and Halloween shit, childish campfire tales. But if you'd done any years in the Galesburg School, you couldn't be so blasé when referencing the old fire. In the Galesburg School, the fire was treated like Pearl Harbor.

Or the book of Genesis.

"There was a group of landowners who wouldn't sell," she said, trying to keep her tone neutral. The wind had shifted and was blowing the rain in underneath the overlook's roof. It was coming from Aaron's direction, and she was grateful for that, because it gave her an excuse not to face him. "Old families. Some went back to the 1600s. Every little town they flooded out had them: West Shokan, Cannonsville, wherever. But none of those towns had families that hung on quite so . . . resolutely. These families in Galesburg just *would not leave.* The city claimed eminent domain, and still they stayed. They'd been told the police were going to arrest them. I guess that would have been your great-grandfather, right?"

He nodded without much reaction. This was all new to him, and that struck her as incredible. How had his family never spoken of it?

Because it happened eighty years ago, Gillian, in a town that no longer exists.

"Anyhow, it had gotten dangerous for the workers up here. Attacks on the camps, sabotaged equipment, that sort of thing. There was a tunnel collapse that killed a bunch of people, most of them from the city, men who'd come up to check on the progress. There were rumors that the tunnel collapse was anything but an accident."

He was watching with interest but no personal stake.

She wanted to grab him and shake him and shout, *Why didn't your family talk about this? They were part of it, they were here to protect the townspeople, and they chose to protect the outsiders. How have you not heard that?* But of course he wouldn't have heard it. The Ellsworth family had survived it and drowned it, just like the town. Buried it down deep where it couldn't scare them or shame them.

But in the Galesburg School, such an approach didn't fly. In Galesburg, local history was paramount. The only risk was in forgetting it.

"You okay?" Aaron asked. Only then did Gillian realize she'd stopped talking and was staring past him, up the flooded valley and toward the dam.

"Yeah. Sorry." She swallowed, refocused. Plunged ahead. "This group of Galesburg residents called for another meeting with the state. The people who were in charge of settling the eminent domain deals came up here thinking this was finally the end. They'd been told the residents were prepared to negotiate. So they drove up with their surveys and their maps and their checkbooks, and the locals asked to hold the meeting in the school. There was a real school, a nice brick building, newer. But the locals wanted to meet in the old school. This dingy one-room place built back in who-knows-when."

Gillian knew when—it had been built in 1887 by Abram Wallace and Eli Mathers; the year and the names were answers to questions that had been on some of her first school exams—but she wasn't inclined to over-share.

"They got them all in there, five people from the state who thought they were going to close a deal, and ten people from Galesburg who knew better. And while they pored over the maps and deeds and dollar figures, someone dropped iron bars across the doors and windows and then lit the schoolhouse on fire."

She wiped rain off her cheek and turned back into the wind, forcing herself to look him in the eye when she said, "That was *my* great-grandfather."

"You're serious?"

"Yes. His name was Amos Mathers."

"Was his wife one of the ones who died?" Aaron asked, and she felt some of the dissonance melt.

"No. Why do you ask?"

"Because Fleming said your name last night." His voice was low.

"You're sure?"

"I'm sure. He was talking to somebody, but . . . no one was there. Or if someone was, I didn't see them." He paused, staring at the creek below them, and added, "I still don't know what he was standing on, either."

"What do you mean?"

"He was right out in the water. It was almost up to his knees, but it should have been over his head."

"What did he say about me?"

"Nothing *about* you. He acted like he was talking *to* you. Other people, too, but he said Mrs. Mathers at one point. I heard that clearly."

A tremble worked through Gillian's knees and thighs. She put her hand on the railing, trying to make it look casual and not show that she needed the support to stay on her feet.

"Okay. Well, I'm nobody's Mrs. Mathers, and I definitely wasn't standing in the water down there."

"Nobody was except for him."

Her mouth was dry. She ran her tongue over her teeth. "Hear any other names? Isaac, maybe? Anders?" She took a breath, then rushed out: "Or Molly or Kelly?"

"No." He paused, swallowed. "But he mentioned a sacrifice."

"You said that in the email."

He nodded. "He said, 'That is not an alarm; it is a sacrifice.' Something like that. I cleared out pretty fast then. I guess you saw it if you watched the security videos. When he said the word *sacrifice* it scared the hell out of me. It was the middle of the night, and he was standing out there in the water, carrying on a conversation with no one . . . Yeah, it frightened me."

"It looked like it did."

If he was ashamed by the idea that she'd watched him run away in the darkness, he didn't show it.

The rain picked up, clattering off the shelter house roof, and Aaron shifted closer to her to keep from getting drenched.

"So your grandfather—great-grandfather, whatever—he murdered *fifteen* people?"

"Five."

"The rest escaped?"

"No," Gillian said, and he stared at her, puzzled.

"Then how—"

"The other ten were suicides," she said. "They'd signed a document attesting to that. Notarized it, even. They were determined that it be formal."

Now he was finally interested, because he was horrified.

"*Ten* people were willing to die over that?"

"Eleven. My great-grandfather killed himself, too. He used a shotgun outside the school. Lit the place on fire with fifteen people inside, and then walked away from it, went down to Cresap Creek, and blew his brains out. They found the body downstream a day later."

"I can't believe there were so many," he said. "I mean, one crazy family, okay, but . . . ten? Eleven?"

"It was only four families. Last of the originals who'd settled here centuries ago."

The old knowledge was rising without hesitation now. And why not? She'd had to memorize all of this.

"I think it was like Waco or Jonestown," she said. "Grievances collided with faith that collided with insanity, and whatever was legitimate about the grievances or redemptive about the faith got swallowed up by the insanity. That's the way I *think* it happened, at least. I can only guess, obviously."

"All of that was to stop the lake from coming?" he said. "To keep their land?"

He said that as if the notion were insane. Dying over land? *Killing* over land? She felt like snapping at him, asking if he understood the first fucking thing about the history of this country—or *any* country, for that matter. Die for land, kill for land. Rinse and repeat. Grow an empire, destroy another. Everyone was righteous in their cause at the moment; it was not until you looked back with the sophisticated eye of a supposedly more civilized time that you found the old beliefs and the old actions to be absurd, barbaric. *Those savages would scalp people, burn them at the stake!* historians would say in shock, even while their own nations fired cruise missiles, carpet-bombed villages with napalm, and raced one another for development of nuclear and biological weapons. Some of the same people who were appalled by a scalping were proud of the invention of VX nerve gas.

She took a beat, took a breath, and kept her tone level when she spoke again.

"Initially, that was the idea. They thought they were providing a voice for the town. The rest of the townspeople took their money and left, so then they decided they were a voice for the land. By the end, yeah, it was awfully damn strange."

Aaron pushed back from the railing and straightened up. He was standing closer now and she was aware of his full height—he had to have eight inches on her five-seven.

"So your question is whether I'm crazy enough to have incorporated all this into my delusions or if I stumbled across you yesterday and decided that I'd, what, just screw with you for the fun of it because of your name?"

"I don't think that."

He stared at her steadily. "Then what *do* you think?"

She turned from him and pointed upstream. "Where did you find the body? The one with the hooks and the bag over her head."

"He was up—" He caught himself, looked back at her, and said, "Why'd you say *her* head?"

"It was a man?"

He frowned. "It could have been a woman. All I saw was a skeleton in the water. Trust me, that was plenty, too. I wasn't looking for identification after that."

"Right."

"Is somebody missing out here? Did some woman go—"

"Let's get back to the question of *where* you say you found the body."

He turned and studied the water. Shielded his eyes with one hand and pointed with the other.

"It's hard to see from here because of the trees, but it was in the Dead—in the stilling basin."

Gillian stared at a high rock bluff above the stilling basin. The Dead Waters.

"You said there was a hood over the head? Or it looked like there had been?"

"Yeah. It was starting to decay, and I could see the skull, but it wasn't like a hood on a sweatshirt or anything. It was more like a bag that had been pulled over his—or *her*—head."

Gillian couldn't stop looking at the bluff. She remembered picnic lunches and sunset viewings there with her grandmother. Molly Mathers had been very partial to that spot.

"I'd like to know if it's real," Aaron said quietly. "If there's nobody down there, okay, then I hallucinated my way through the whole day, and I'll have to deal with that. But if there *is* a body, then . . ."

"Then you've got new questions about Mick Fleming," she finished for him.

"I guess so."

"They're going to seem like very strange questions."

"They're going to seem utterly insane."

"Let me give you one more fun fact," Gillian said. "Mick Fleming's grandfather is the man who designed the dam."

"*What?*"

She nodded. He looked deeply troubled, but after a pause said, "I guess that doesn't mean much, but it feels weird, you know?"

She didn't answer. It might mean a lot more than he thought.

"I'm going to call for a diver," she said. "We'll give the basin a look."

"Thank you," he said, earnest. "Thank you for believing it's worth a try, at least."

"We'll see what we can find," she said, and then she bit the tip of her tongue to keep from saying what she felt: *I think you're right, and if you are, then my grandmother died in the water with a black silk bag over her head. She died thinking she was a hero, though. So that's something, right?*

Keep biting the tongue. Don't put all the memories into words.

The fewer the better, in fact.

30

Mick's phone rang repeatedly on his drive back through the rain and into the mountains, but he ignored every call. Most were from Ed Cochran, no doubt wanting to chat about Mick's email. Fine. He'd warned Ed that reception would be bad out here. He'd return the call in due time, but he wanted to force Ed's hand first and make sure that he contacted Arthur Brady. When Mick arrived at the Chilewaukee, he needed Brady to be in a cooperative mood.

There was much to handle. The longer he rode with Anders Wallace at his side, the more he understood. The Chilewaukee would not be an easy task, and it was only the first step.

To reach the city—the sacrifice that mattered—he would need to achieve much more.

Another call came in, from a number he didn't recognize, but the area code covered the part of the state that included Torrance County, and so he was curious enough that he almost answered. He decided not to, though. There was a structure for his day, a system of priority assignments, and he couldn't interrupt that for unknown callers.

The closer he got to Torrance County, the harder the rain fell. He turned his wipers to high and sent them into a slashing frenzy and still it was hard to see. Cars in both directions had their headlights on in the middle of the day. Pools of floodwater lined the roadside. In some areas the median looked like a creek. Fields had turned to ponds.

He'd seen such flooding in the area before, but only a few times, and always in the spring. That was the danger season, when snowmelt and spring rains collided to engorge the creeks and rivers and then the reservoirs. He was used to worrying the most about his dams in the months of April and May. For this to be happening in October was very strange.

"Not so strange," Anders said, as if Mick had spoken the thought aloud.

Maybe he had. It was hard to tell now. Anders came and went visually; sometimes he'd be there in the passenger seat, fastidious and formal, but others he'd be gone, and then his voice would return as if aware of each of Mick's thoughts.

Thoughts that were, right now, focused on the aged infrastructure that was creaking and groaning to process this round of flooding. Almost none of it was slated for winter repairs. The snowpack would melt off, the spring rains would come, and the infrastructure would be tested once more.

How long could you go like that before disaster struck? Why couldn't people think about risk with any level of long-term outlook or horizon view? They cared only about the immediate, cared only about the news of today. Tell them a dam might fail in the next five years and they shrugged.

They need a wakeup call, he thought, gripping and regripping the steering wheel as he sped south, his tires shedding plumes of water. *They need to hear the alarm.*

"Exactly," Anders said, floating into Mick's peripheral vision again. "And that means someone must *sound* the alarm."

Mick nodded. If a few sacrifices had to be made to prevent a larger catastrophe, so be it. The math on that was very simple. Greater than, less than, or equal to. When the figure in question was death toll, there was only one correct answer: less than. Always.

He wondered why he'd never been able to see the clarity of this before. No matter. He saw it now.

"Not only do you see it," Anders told him, "but you know your role in it."

"Yes," Mick said. "Yes, I certainly do."

31

The farther Steve got from the Chill, the easier it was to feel embarrassment over how seriously he'd treated the idea that Mick Fleming might have lied to them all.

Back at the gatehouse it hadn't felt that way, for some reason. In the gatehouse he'd been able to believe there was something deeply wrong with Mick Fleming. Maybe it was fatigue, or maybe it was shame and shock from watching Aaron on the security cameras, peering into the darkness and then running away as if to escape an unknown terror.

Whatever the reason, while he was in the gatehouse, Steve had allowed Gillian Mathers to drive the conversation toward foolishness. Ridiculousness.

DEP detective. Hardly the real deal.

The thought snuck into his mind like an intruder. This attitude had long been prevalent among police in upstate counties where the DEP had their own units, and Steve had long fought to eradicate it. The DEP force was capable and competent and needed to be treated as such.

Steve suddenly resented Gillian Mathers, though, blaming her for disrupting what had been a good morning.

That only worsened when he arrived home to find Aaron already gone. Then he stepped inside the house and saw the tumbler glass in the sink.

He approached it slowly, as if it were a coiled snake. The glass was empty. Steve picked it up and smelled it. The lingering pungency of whiskey hit him. He closed his eyes as if that could shut out the scent.

It wasn't even noon yet.

Enough, he thought. *This has gone far enough.* He took out his cell phone and called Aaron's. It went to voicemail. He started to leave a message but couldn't come up with the right words, and then he felt stupid for letting the seconds tick by in silence, so he disconnected, found the card Gillian Mathers had given him, and called her mobile number. She answered.

"I think I let you talk me into some bad ideas," he said. "Are you with Aaron? Or is he out drinking somewhere?"

"He's here, Sheriff. And he's not been drinking."

"Bullshit. He left a whiskey glass in my sink. What's he got to tell you about his little piece of dinner theater for the security cameras?"

She was quiet for a moment.

"He's sober," she said. "And he's been helpful."

"There's nothing he needs to provide help on," Steve snapped. "He needs to *get* help, and today that's what I intended to be working on. Now that's all shot to hell. Send him home, Sergeant. Nobody needs to waste time like this."

"I'm going to need him for a couple hours longer."

"*Hours?* What are you asking him to do, memorize Shakespeare?"

"I'm asking him to guide our diver to where he found the body yesterday."

"You're not serious. Mathers, this is getting out of hand. Before you put somebody at risk in the water, let's—"

"I don't think there's risk to diving down here. It's in the stilling basin. The current isn't strong down there. I want to know if he saw what he said he did. I'd think you'd support that."

"I don't need a diver to tell me there's nothing down there. I also don't need anyone to tell me Aaron didn't murder a man who's walking among us. I believed you felt the same, but it seems I was wrong."

"All due respect, Steve? It's my jurisdiction. It's my case."

"It's my county."

"*You* called *me.*"

"A mistake I won't make again."

"You all through, Sheriff?"

His inhalation seemed to draw more anger than air.

"I don't want any divers going in that water. I'm the county sheriff and I—"

"Don't have jurisdiction at the Chilewaukee Reservoir," Gillian Mathers barked. "I hope that's what you were going to say, because it's correct, and it is very damn important that you remember that today."

"That's right, the 'fauxlice' have jurisdiction down there. The Busy With Something folks. It's still my county, and that's still my son."

There was a silence before she said, "Are you hearing yourself right now?"

He almost hadn't been. What was he snarling out at her? *Fauxlice* was a nickname for the DEP officers, one that he chastised his deputies for using. But the other one, the Busy With Something folks, that didn't even make sense. That went back generations, to when the DEP police had been called the Board of Water Supply police. That nickname belonged to his grandfather's era. Steve had never had a problem with the DEP, and yet here he was, using those childish slurs on Gillian Mathers?

"I'm sorry," he said. "It's just . . . I had a plan for this day. The plan was to get my son some help. He *does* need that help."

Her voice softened and she said, "I understand that. I'm sending him back home as soon as I can. I need you to respect my case in the meantime. Please."

Steve didn't answer.

"Did you find out about Fleming?" Mathers asked.

"What?"

"You were going to check on him. See if he actually went back to Albany last night."

Who the hell cares? he wanted to say, but he held his tongue.

"Not yet. I'll make some calls. Just do me the favor of making sure Aaron gets home soon and making sure that he's sober. I've got my doubts."

"I'll make him blow if you want."

"Do that. I'm curious what he's showing. It's not going to be three zeros."

"I'll let you know," she said in a tone that was somehow both cooperative and defiant, a voice that promised she could be counted on to do what she said but not that she agreed that it needed to be done. "I'll check on Aaron, and you check on Fleming. That was the deal. Is it still?"

"Yeah," he managed. "You let me know what he blows, okay?"

"Ten-four, Sheriff," she said, and then she hung up.

He tossed the phone onto the counter with disgust. When he'd called her from the Chill, it had seemed like the right thing to do, removing himself from a situation over which he should not exert any power or influence. Now he regretted that and wanted the power and influence back. He'd taken her for compassionate; he'd not taken her for crazy. But here she was, summoning divers to check on a hallucination.

"Fauxlice," he muttered again. The DEP, baby: Doing Errands, Probably. Dumbass Endless Patrols. All sorts of names had sprung up over the years, and some of them were earned. The DEP officers were nothing but a hassle, and he'd invited them into his life. What in the hell had he been thinking?

"How'd you get that badge?" he said aloud, cutting off his own angry thoughts. It was a question his wife used to ask with biting sarcasm when he was acting foolish or childish. *How'd you get that badge? People elected you? On purpose? So I guess they haven't seen you act like this, then? Because I can't believe you'd be winning votes right now, Sheriff.*

She could always shame him straight, and while there'd been more than a few times when he resisted, he couldn't look back and say that she'd been wrong. Not when it came to his bitching and grousing, at least.

But that's our son, and so it is *different,* he thought, as if Lily could rise from the grave to agree or object.

He sighed, rinsed the whiskey glass out, and put it in the dishwasher. Then he picked up his phone and walked to the desk where his laptop waited. He'd call Albany and ask about Mick Fleming. He would do that much.

32

Aaron heard his father's voice on Gillian's cell phone, but then she walked away and spoke in hushed tones. He heard one word plain as day, though: *sober*. Gillian was defending him, telling his dad that he was sober.

He stood with his hands in his jacket pockets and his back to her and tried to pretend he was oblivious to it all. He *was* sober . . . but only by a few minutes. If her call hadn't come, he would have taken that first drink, and the first drink always had a way of shaking hands with the second.

He was sober now, though. Sober and cold and wet. He hadn't expected to stand out here in the rain again, but here he was, pointing directions to the divers.

"Center and down, then look left, and follow the timber?" one of the divers asked. He was already knee-deep in the water.

"Yeah. There's part of a tree down there. The limbs split into a Y, and the body is pinned between them. Be careful. There are hooks."

The diver nodded, lowered his mask, and inserted his mouthpiece. His partner gave a thumbs-up and then followed him into the water. They swam about fifteen feet and then descended, leaving a trail of bubbles that was hard to see because of the way the rain dimpled the surface.

Gillian Mathers returned to stand beside Aaron. He couldn't see her face because she had the hood of her rain jacket up. She looked smaller in the rain jacket, and the shadow of the hood made her dark skin deepen a few more shades. The blue eyes contrasted against her skin with a fierceness.

"That was my dad?" he asked.

"Yes."

"Thinks I'm drunk?"

"Was worried you might've had one or two."

He nodded. "I haven't, but I was close. Poured it down the sink when you called."

Gillian looked away, embarrassed. "He wants me to test you."

Aaron gave a soft laugh. He was going to be Breathalyzed even while the divers searched the bottom to check on his sanity?

"I don't have to," she said. "I can tell you're sober."

"No," he said. "If he wants to know, then do it."

She hesitated, then shrugged and walked back to her car. A minute later she returned with the Breathalyzer.

"It's just a field test," she said as she fitted a plastic tube into it. "Not even admissible in court anymore. Only official chemical tests or blood draws are—"

"I'm familiar with the process, trust me. Blow until the beep, right?"

She nodded almost apologetically.

He put the cool plastic tube between his front teeth, sealed his lips around it, and blew hard. She was still holding the device, which brought her in close to him. She kept those bright blue eyes on him, her dark hair framing her face, while she watched and waited on the truth.

About five seconds later the device beeped. He parted his lips and she pulled the device back and looked at the screen.

"Zeros," she said.

He nodded.

She rooted around in the pocket of her rain jacket and came out with her cell phone. Snapped a picture of the screen.

"Just to add some documentation for him," she said. "He means well."

"Yes," Aaron said. "He does."

One of the divers broke the surface in the stilling basin. He lifted his hand, waving to get their attention, and then spit his mouthpiece out.

"You've got a ten-zero down there all right," he shouted. "Tangled up in the tree. Heavy lines and hooks. There was something over the head. It's pretty well decayed now, but I don't think it was clothing. Looks like a bag or something, pulled over the head and tied off at the neck."

For a long moment Gillian Mathers didn't answer. She just stared out at the water as if she could see through it, down to the depths. As if she hadn't needed the diver at all.

"Okay," she said at last. "I'll call it in. Can you bring her up, or will you need help with her?"

"We can bring . . ." The diver hesitated. "It's a woman?"

"You don't think so?" Gillian asked.

"I couldn't tell. I mean, it's a skeleton. I don't know how you—"

"Sorry. Slip of the tongue. Can you bring that corpse up, or will you need assistance?"

Aaron glanced at her, wondering what this was all about. It was the second time she'd referenced a female corpse, and each time she'd become edgy.

"We can get it," the diver said. "Are you okay with us cutting those lines, or you want them untangled?"

"Cut them if you have to."

He made an *Okay* gesture with his thumb and index finger, then put the mouthpiece back in, roll-turned, and submerged again.

Gillian looked at Aaron. Neither of them spoke. It was as if words would break the moment, send the diver shooting back to the surface to shout that he was just kidding, there was no corpse, and Aaron Ellsworth *was* out of his ever-loving mind.

Bare limbs shivered in the wind, but the surface of the stilling basin earned its name, remaining placid as a pond. Just upstream, the roar of the water thundering down the spillway could be heard, and just below the basin it surged back through the creek bed, toward Torrance. The stilling basin slowed the energy but didn't stop it.

They stared at the water and nothing happened and Aaron was just about to speak when the skeleton hand broke the surface.

He almost screamed, because for an instant it seemed the skeleton was rising under its own power. Then the first diver appeared just beside the hand, and then his partner surfaced. From there they rose in a triangle—divers at each end, corpse at the point. The divers handled the corpse as gingerly as they could, but they were bringing old bones through resistant waters, and the skeleton shifted and slackened and slipped. The body collapsed in on itself as if insulted or ashamed.

As Aaron watched the divers haul the objecting bones out of the water he thought that Gillian Mathers had made a mistake, allowing them to handle this task. Then he wondered how it would have been better accomplished. With ropes? With a net? What dignity could be granted to a disintegrating body in the depths?

He wanted to look away, but instead he mimicked Gillian's stance, arms folded and eyes steady, as if this sight were a normal thing. He tried to channel the spirit of his father, his grandfather, his great-grandfather. Lawmen.

The corpse was pulled clear of the water. Remains of old boots flapped around the ankle bones, rubber soles held together by scraps of leather and metal grommets that glistened. Thin strips of blue-black fabric interspersed with tendrils of dead weeds weaved between ribs. At the top of the body, flopped against the right shoulder, the skull rested on the broken neck.

On the surface, the black hood that had covered the skull was clearly nothing but shreds of decaying cloth. The shreds clung damply against the sides of the skull, but the empty eye sockets and the full set of teeth were unobscured.

One of the divers put his hand gently on the back of the skull and lifted it so that the head aligned more naturally with the spine. It was a pointless effort but a tender one, and for some reason it was the thing that made Aaron look away.

He saw then that Gillian Mathers already had her back to the scene.

Her arms were still folded across her chest and her chin was still held high, oblivious to the driving rain, but she was facing away from the corpse and up toward the dam. Only when the divers had pulled the body ashore did she turn back.

"Bring her out of the rocks and then leave her alone," Gillian Mathers said.

Aaron could see nothing but bones and disintegrating cloth, and yet he knew that Gillian was sure of the identity of the remains, and he knew that it mattered to her. The divers seemed to recognize that as well, or perhaps they were just overwhelmed with moving the corpse, because they did not speak, and they did not rush. They carried it—*not it:* her—*the bones once made up a woman*—out of the water and out of the rocks and laid her slowly and gently onto the dead grass above the bank.

"Who was she?" Aaron asked.

"My grandmother," Gillian Mathers told him, and then she walked toward the body before he could respond.

33

Deshawn woke with a hangover, but it wasn't until nearly midmorning when the sad truth caught up to him—he was just now sobering up. What he'd believed was the hangover was in fact only the cloudburst ahead of the storm. When the foreman called his name, the sound made Deshawn's head throb.

"Ryan. Yo, Ryan?"

Deshawn was down on his hands and knees, attaching a security cable to a muck car, and when he looked over his shoulder at Caleb Stiles, he knew it was trouble. Caleb had been his foreman for the past decade. Caleb was a big man, a quiet man, and a hardworking man. He commanded respect and he didn't tolerate fools. All of these things made Deshawn certain that he was about to be ripped for his obviously hungover condition.

"Your daughter still working in Torrance County?" Caleb Stiles asked.

"Out of Ashokan Precinct," Deshawn said, an automatic response that changed nothing. He simply did not like to say that Gillian was in Torrance County. It didn't matter that she was grown now; responding to the question of whether his daughter was in Torrance County felt old and familiar and like an indictment of him as a father. *Yes, she's in Torrance and I am not, but I send checks. Twice a month, I send checks. Doesn't that count?*

"Right," Caleb said, unfazed. "Well, I guess they've got some kind of mess brewing up there."

Deshawn dropped the clamp. The steel hit the rail and echoed in the tunnel.

"What do you mean?"

"Not sure what the story is, but half the department's headed that way tomorrow morning. I was supposed to meet with Cochran over at the valve chamber, but he canceled. Said he's got to be up at the Chickewaukee."

"Chilewaukee."

Caleb shrugged. Beneath his hard hat his broad face was streaked with the gray dust of crushed stone, his beard powdered with it.

"Whatever. Some kind of spillway problem, I guess. Sounded serious, and I can't say I'm surprised. Shit, how old are those dams? And with the way it's been raining up there. Saw something on the news yesterday, it's like an all-time October record up there."

He hocked phlegm out of his throat and spat. His eyes drifted past Deshawn and toward the Mole.

"If shit's half as bad as Cochran seemed to think, your girl might be on evacuation duty by tomorrow."

"It's that serious?"

"Cochran's not a hysterical type."

Deshawn didn't know Cochran. He knew the name, but Cochran worked well above Deshawn's pay grade.

"I'll have to give Gillian a call," Deshawn said. "See what she's heard."

Caleb nodded without much interest, his attention locking down on the Mole, eyes narrowing as if he saw something he didn't like.

"'Scuse me, Deshawn." He stepped past, bellowed, "Yo! Matty! The hell you doing with that?" and then he was gone and behind him stood a man in thigh-high rubber boots with a vest and suit coat. His hair was combed back in a slicked pompadour and he had a tiny, cropped mustache. He was standing in the middle of the tunnel, not ten feet away, as if the only thing blocking him from Deshawn's vision all this time had been Caleb Stiles.

He was not real. Deshawn knew this. He was no more real than the figures he'd seen lounging on the high timber beams. Yet there he was, looking every bit as flesh-and-bone as Caleb had.

And familiar, too. Deshawn was somehow certain that he'd seen the man before. Maybe not met him, but he'd seen him.

"The whole system," the man said, "requires nothing but gravity. Gravity and pressure. That is all. Marvelous, don't you think?"

Deshawn didn't answer. Couldn't. He just stared.

"Provided for man, to be harnessed by man, for the sustenance of man," the phantom continued. "Some look at the challenge and think it is a matter of invention. But it is not. It's a matter of utilization, that's all. We have what we need. The successful engineer simply understands how to utilize it."

Behind him, Caleb and Matty Silvers were carrying on in loud conversation, and farther down the tunnel a car was clattering this way, its headlight carving through the darkness.

"When forces of nature are properly met by forces of man," the ghost continued, "the potential is nearly limitless."

The headlight of a railcar was brightening, making the man's silhouette stand out against it in stark relief.

"Do you know how much I'll be able to do with only gravity and pressure?"

The car was almost upon him now, slowing but not slowing fast enough, and though Deshawn knew the man wasn't real, he still felt like he had to warn him, grab him, save him. He was scared to touch him, though. He stood where he was, a tremble welling up in his legs and through his core.

"I'll quench a city's thirst," the man told him as the light brightened and the clatter rose. His staid bearing broke suddenly, and he gave a wan, almost rueful smile.

"Do you think they will remember me?" he asked Deshawn an instant before the car struck him.

Deshawn shouted. Couldn't help himself. He gave a yell of shock and fright that echoed through the tunnel.

The man was gone, and the railcar carrying the crew was easing to a stop some fifty feet behind where it had seemed to be. It was as if Deshawn had blinked and the distance increased, like the click of a zoom button.

Now he was back in reality, and everyone was staring at him.

"What happened?" Caleb Stiles shouted, rushing back. "We need medical? Deshawn! What in the hell happened?"

"Nothing," Deshawn mumbled. "I mean, sorry. I just . . ." He stared at Caleb, then looked over to where the rest of the crew was standing and watching him, and he tried desperately to come up with something—anything.

"I left my gear up there," he said, waving a hand in the direction of the railcar. "Thought they were gonna crush it."

"Gear?"

Yes, what gear? All of Deshawn's gear was either on his tool belt or in his pockets. The only thing that wasn't with him right now was his lunch.

"My lunch," he said. "I've got a sandwich . . . I set it down back there. Stupid thing to do."

Caleb's eyes widened. "You're screaming about your *lunch*? Holy shit, man, not down here you aren't!"

When a man screamed in the tunnels—and it happened, oh, it happened—it was because of something real. Real pain, real trouble, real fear. Hands caught in winches, legs smashed by sliding granite slabs, faces torn open by whipping chains. Deshawn had seen all of that and more.

No man had ever screamed in the tunnels for fear of a smashed sandwich.

"I didn't even think it was out loud," he said, and tried to laugh. "Thought I was in my own head."

"Well, you sure as shit got into *my* head! *Damn!*"

Caleb turned and stalked back down the tunnel. Deshawn didn't look any of the others in the eye. He just knelt and found the steel hook of the security cable and got back to work.

Somewhere behind him, he heard the soft plinking of water dripping into water. He thought idly of his sink faucet and tried to keep his mind there. Real problems, real things. Gaskets to fix, Gillian to call. The real duties of a man in the world. Stay focused on those things.

Do you know how much I'll be able to do with only gravity and pressure?

He slammed the steel hook into the eye at the base of the muck car and moved for the ratchet. He wanted to stay busy, wanted to make noise, wanted to drown out all the sounds he didn't wish to hear, and all the memories he didn't wish to have.

34

Steve was unable to find a direct number for Mick Fleming, so he called the main number given for dam safety and inspections and told the receptionist who he was and who he was looking for. Her tone went wary and she asked if he'd please hold and then the call was rerouted to a man who was not Mick Fleming but seemed unsurprised by Steve's call.

"What the hell is happening up there, Sheriff?"

Steve was sitting with the phone held between his shoulder and jaw with a notepad and pen in front of him, the laptop shoved to one side. He knew he should just use the speakerphone but had never been able to get in the habit. Better a stiff neck than a lack of privacy, he always figured.

"Mind giving your name before you start yelling?" he said mildly.

"Ed Cochran. I just got done reading Mick's report and it sounds like he wasn't very welcome in your county yesterday."

"Well, I apologize," Steve said, not liking the guy's tone but understanding it. If Fleming had been one of his deputies, he wouldn't have been thrilled by the report, either. "My son has had better days. We all have. But what I need to—"

"Your family issues aren't my concern, but the citizens in the floodplain should be a concern to *both* of us with the threat to that dam."

Steve straightened. He felt a pop in the base of his neck.

"What threat to the dam?"

"What *threat*? It's called *water*! Rain. Flooding. *Water!*"

"I grasp the concept. But who's calling it a threat?"

"The professional engineer whose job was interrupted and whose advice was ignored! He's identified the situation as urgent and I'm in the middle of gathering a full inspection team to be up there tomorrow morning. I expect your cooperation. This is critical infrastructure. *Old* and critical infrastructure. And the rain isn't cutting us any breaks, either."

Steve lifted his eyes from the blank notepad and looked out the window. Rain stringed from the overtopped gutters, and the puddles in the lawn looked like wading pools.

"No, it is not," he said. "But I'm curious about the communication gap here. I don't recall Mr. Fleming showing any concern."

"I'm looking at his report, Sheriff. Mick is the best structural engineer I've ever had. He is *very* concerned." Cochran's voice softened. "Look, I understand there was an issue with your son. I sympathize, but I'm also scared, quite frankly. I've never seen a report like this from Mick. I know you people have your issues with—"

"'You people'?"

"Torrance County. Don't get defensive, damn it. You've been there for long enough to know there's some resistance to *our* people in the area."

"Fine. I won't deny that. But I don't think there was any yesterday."

"I'm told otherwise."

"*Your* engineer assured *your* dam operator there wasn't anything to worry about," Steve said, heat flushing into his voice. "Arthur Brady told me—"

"Arthur Brady was uncooperative and dismissive is what I'm told."

"That doesn't sound like Arthur."

"I'm looking at the report. We are going to have to be a team on this today. There can't be any feuds or territorial bullshit. Not with something this serious. Mick is headed back down to assess for cavitation, and it is absolutely imperative that he have full support from Mr. Brady and his team today."

"Have you spoken to him?"

"Mick? Not yet. I've got the report, but I haven't had the chance to speak to him. Now, Sheriff Ellsworth, I've got lots of calls to make, and not much time. Can I count on your full cooperation at the Chilewaukee? That is the only question that matters to me right now."

"Full cooperation," Steve said. "You'll have it, sir. Torrance County will do whatever's needed."

"I hope so."

"Do you have another engineer, though?"

"Excuse me?"

"I'd like to talk to someone other than Fleming. Surely, you've got more inspectors."

"Yes, we do. But I don't appreciate the tone of that request. I can't send a better engineer than Mick Fleming, and when he gives a report, you need to take it seriously."

That's him, Dad. That's the man I killed.

"We're taking him seriously," Steve said. "I promise you that."

"I hope so."

"I'll see to it that he's satisfied. I'll see to that myself."

"Thank you." Cochran seemed mollified if not happy.

"Would you do me a favor, though?" Steve said.

"What's that?"

"I'd like to speak to his wife. I'd actually like my *son* to speak to his wife. What happened down here yesterday was chaotic, unacceptable, and embarrassing. My son's trying to do the right thing. I want to back that play, you understand? Surely, you understand that."

"Is it drugs?" Cochran asked in a soft voice. Steve didn't answer, more because he was beginning to feel guilty about the lie, but Cochran pushed ahead. "I'm sorry, Sheriff Ellsworth. I've got a niece who . . . it doesn't matter. The point is I get it. I'm sorry, too. I truly am. But I can't just give out Lori's number."

"Of course," Steve said, and he finally wrote a word down on his notepad: *Lori*. "I know you've got things to do. Keep my number handy, though, okay? I want to hear what's happening, what you need. I want to know that as soon as you do."

He gave Cochran his cell number and disconnected. Sat with the phone in his hand, staring at the pooling water in the yard. He thought of his grandfather on the front porch of the old house, eyeing the western sky and muttering about wind when everyone knew he was afraid of the rain.

I'm also scared, quite frankly, Mick Fleming's boss had said.

He could join the party. There were more than a few people who were scared. The trouble was that they were scared for different reasons.

Lori Fleming's LinkedIn page identified her as the community outreach director for the YMCA. She answered her phone on the first ring.

"This is Lori. How may I help you?"

Her voice was so warm and genuine that Steve almost hung up. Somehow his day had progressed to the point where he was frightened by warm, genuine people.

He introduced himself. Said he was the Torrance County sheriff and he needed to track Mick down and his deputy had left a sheet of possible numbers on the desk but no indication of what was what. It was a bad lie, but Steve wasn't embarrassed by his lack of practice at the art. Lori Fleming accepted it, laughing and reciting Mick's cell phone number.

"If he left Albany this morning, he may be at the dam already," Steve said. "What time did he head out?"

"Oh, he's been there. That's why I'm laughing, Sheriff—you're calling Albany looking for him, and he's still in your town."

"You're kidding," Steve said, hoping his voice sounded neutral. "Stayed the night after all, did he?"

The phone beeped in his ear. Someone else was calling, but Steve couldn't be distracted by that. Not now.

"Yes, he stayed," Lori Fleming told him. "I guess it's pretty serious down there, isn't it?"

For the first time, Steve was able to meet her tone honestly.

"I think it might be," he said. "I'm sorry for bothering you. I was so distracted yesterday, I must've just ignored him when he said he was staying."

"That's when I knew it had to be serious," she said. "Mick isn't the sort of man who stays the night if he isn't packed and prepared for it, you know? He's . . . well, he likes his routines. He doesn't like surprises much."

"I can appreciate that," Steve said. "We sheriffs usually aren't big fans of surprises, ourselves."

Her laugh came again, easy and warm. He thanked her once more and was moving his thumb to end the call when she caught him.

"Sheriff Ellsworth? Take care of him for me, all right?"

"I intend to," Steve said, and then he disconnected and checked to see what call he'd missed.

It was Arthur Brady, and he'd left a voicemail. Mick Fleming had just pulled in at the dam—right after the police divers had left.

The divers, Arthur informed him, had come up with a body, too. He'd watched them load it into the ambulance and take it away.

"Getting to be an exciting day down here, Sheriff."

Before he left, he put a note on the table for Aaron.

Home shortly, thanks for helping Mathers. Lots to discuss.

He hesitated there, wondering if he needed to put Peaceful Passages into ink or if it was understood. In the end he left it out. He needed to trust his son, who had just blown triple zeros after Steve's accusation, who had just helped police locate a body, and whose wild claims about Mick Fleming's nocturnal activity might not be so wild after all.

He didn't write anything about rehab, but he wanted to close the note with something more personal than *lots to discuss*. He wanted to write *I love you* because it was true, more crucially true than Aaron could ever know, or at least ever know until he had a son of his own. They'd never really been an *I love you* kind of duo, though, so he thought it might weird Aaron out, make him think that Steve was already taking his cues from a rehab therapist. In the end he just wrote, *Thank you, son,* because at least that implied some level of trust. He didn't mention rehab and he didn't mention the glass in the sink that smelled of whiskey. Those topics were better saved for conversation.

He put on his hat and uniform jacket and his gun belt. He'd taken the day off, but when he arrived back at the Chill, Steve Ellsworth was damn well going to look like the sheriff of Torrance County.

35

Aaron stood in the cold rain and waited in silence while the body was loaded into an ambulance for transport to the county morgue. He kept a respectful distance, but even so, the disintegrating condition of the corpse was obvious. Gillian Mathers put on rubber gloves and clipped the long, dangling fishing lines away from the body, then coiled them methodically, bagged them, and tagged them. She reached out with one gloved hand and touched the decaying fabric over the skull gingerly. She rubbed it between index finger and thumb as if the touch could tell her something. Then she stepped back, removed the gloves, and nodded to the ambulance driver. The doors swung shut, and the remains of her grandmother headed away.

The divers had already left, so when the ambulance was gone, it was just Gillian and Aaron again.

"I'll give you a ride back," she said.

"Huh?"

She looked at him. "Your car? Going to want that, right?"

"Oh. Yeah." He'd forgotten about his dad's truck, still parked up at the overlook. "Thanks."

"No problem." She started for her own car, the Ford Explorer with the brightly painted DEP logo. He fell in behind her, feeling that he should say something but unsure what.

"Your grandmother?" he blurted finally. "You're sure?"

"I'm sure." She opened the door without looking at him and had the engine going before he was even in his seat. Okay. Maybe Gillian Mathers was not interested in telling any more family stories.

"I'm sorry," Aaron said as she drove away, and it wasn't clear if he was expressing sympathy for her loss or for talking. Gillian didn't seem to care one way or the other. The gatehouse stood like a lonely sentry in the rain, with its medieval arched windows and stacked block walls. The parking lot below was now empty except for Arthur Brady's car.

It was ten minutes on winding roads from the dam to the overlook, but it felt like an hour with her silent tension weighing down the air. When she pulled up next to the Silverado, he said, "Thanks," and was acknowledged with another silent nod. He popped the door open and then she finally spoke.

"You got time to take a walk?"

"A walk?"

She nodded. Looking across the flooded creek and into the woods, not at him.

"I've got time," he said.

She looked at his foot. "*Can* you walk, though? It's not far but it's not easy."

In truth, his foot had been aching from just standing there watching the divers, but he shook his head. "I can walk fine."

She seemed to know he was lying but then shrugged, as if it didn't matter, and cut the engine.

They left the parking area and entered a trailhead not far from the shelter. She left the trail almost immediately, headed downhill. Aaron followed. She pushed through saplings and young pines, thin branches flinging water like windshield wipers.

They'd made it about a hundred yards up the slope when another trail became clear, and she followed this, walking sidehill on a narrow ridge. More of a ledge than a ridge, really. The rain was falling harder, drumming into puddles on the narrow trail and streaming down the slope. Aaron was breathing hard and his heart was thumping in his ears and his foot was hurting, really hurting now, but he limped along, fighting to keep pace.

The trail curled downhill, and they arrived at the banks of Cresap Creek once more. They were facing an ancient wooden footbridge that Aaron had never known existed. The creek was narrow here, and the bank on each side was rock, which forced the water higher, almost to the bridge. Gillian eyed it and said, "Been a few years since I crossed. Think it'll hold?"

"No idea."

"You're a good swimmer, at least."

Aaron looked into the walnut-colored water below, which was tinted dark from all the soil the flooding had inhaled.

"Right," he said. "There's that."

She started across the old bridge, stepping quickly but wisely, each foot coming down where the rotted planks seemed sturdiest. The bridge creaked but didn't break. Aaron had to have seventy pounds on her, maybe more, but he followed in her footsteps. The old wood held.

The bridge deposited them into what seemed like a pine forest, but they were young trees. Gillian walked through them and up another rise and then they were in a cleared stretch, one that had definitely been a road. Shell casings from hunters lay in the gravel, and a few rusted beer cans. Gillian walked farther up the hill. Aaron stopped and stood for a moment, catching his breath. His throbbing foot felt damp in his sock. Sweat or blood? Had he torn the stitches open?

She realized he was no longer keeping pace and turned back.

"Coming?"

The question was hopeful, not challenging, and although he'd intended to ask her what in the hell this was all about, he just nodded.

"Catching my breath," he said, and started up the hill.

Another hundred yards and the old road leveled out in a clearing that was on a plateau about halfway up the mountain. At the back corner of the lot stood a house.

It was an old Colonial-style structure with a high, steeply pitched roof, evenly distributed windows, and a long front porch that was collapsing, the rails filled with missing or twisted boards that gave it the look of a meth addict's smile.

"Where are we?" Aaron asked.

"Home," Gillian Mathers said. "I lived here until I was nine."

What to say to that? The place looked like it was auditioning for the next *Amityville Horror* reboot. Was he supposed to ask why she moved? *Was it the poltergeists or the black mold?*

She walked up to the porch. "If my grandmother saw the way it looked now, she'd spin in her—" She caught herself before the last word, gave a little chuckle, and shook her head. Her grandmother didn't yet have a grave to spin in. She was probably being shaken out onto a morgue table right now.

"It used to look better," she said.

She stepped carefully over the first broken step and then crossed the creaking porch. Aaron followed and grasped the railing for balance. It came free in his hand.

"Sorry," he said, and tried to set it back in place. It fell into the mud, taking two balusters with it. *Nice place you've got here.*

He limped up the steps and then across the sagging porch. Gillian tried the door, but it didn't budge. Either locked or swelled shut. When she stepped back and kicked it, there was real anger in her, as if the house were an enemy.

The door burst open with a splintering sound and wobbled inward, revealing the staircase directly in front. The interior of the home smelled of moisture and mold but the stairs looked sturdy enough. Gillian stepped inside, looked left, and seemed to bristle, like a bird dog on point.

Aaron pushed closer to her and looked over her shoulder. The room was a small library. Shelves with damp and dusty books lined the walls. In the center of the room a thin line of water leaked out of the wall. Or maybe seeped up from the floor. No sign of a leak overhead, and no sound of a drip. The only water sounds were outside. In here, despite all the damp smells, it was strangely quiet. The disrepair of the porch hadn't crept inside the house, and the walls stood straight and solid.

"Why's it empty?" he asked, but she ignored him and crossed the room. Gripped the molded lip of one of the built-in bookshelves and tugged. The shelf swung on a soundless hinge. It was cut perfectly into the wall, every joist plumb, and built out of good hardwood that didn't swell or contract with the seasons. Redwood or good seasoned fir, cut from the heart of the tree. Chosen with care.

"What's back there?"

"Welcome to the Galesburg School." Gillian's voice was empty.

He edged closer. Peered into the darkness. "This place was the school?"

"Not exactly. But it was *my* school, for a little while."

She unzipped her rain jacket, found an inside pocket, and withdrew a small tactical flashlight. When she thumbed it on, the hidden room lit up. He saw over her shoulder a single desk in the center of the room and felt a prickle. The desk was ancient, built from wood and iron and with a glass inkwell in the upper right-hand corner. The way it sat there alone in this room hidden behind a wall felt deeply disturbing.

"What do you mean, *your* school?"

"Just what I said." Gillian slipped into the room, and Aaron hesitated. He wasn't sure that he wanted to set foot in there. It was wrong. That was the only word for the place. *Wrong.* Everything from that hidden door to the old desk to the very *feel* of the room, with its chilled damp air and lack of windows and . . .

He saw the photos then.

They lined the wall. He stepped inside. Looked left, then right, and realized that, no, they didn't line a wall; they lined *all* of the walls. Each was framed, mostly black-and-white or that even older brownish-gray tint, sepia. Some hand-drawn sketches in the mix. All of them seemed to be of construction sites. He stepped closer, realizing as he moved farther into the room how the smell changed—not the odor of flooded basements or stagnant water but of fresh water, cool and clean and in motion.

He studied a row of old photographs. Dam construction in one. Maybe the Chill? No, too old for that. This photo had to be at least a hundred years old, the images almost washed-out. The one beside it showed men in a tunnel. The men wore high boots and overalls and leaned on shovels and picks. Just above that picture was another of workers in a tent, gathered around a central woodstove. One man held a banjo, another had a harmonica, and the rest were looking on.

Below each photograph, a thin silver plaque was fastened to the frame, identifying the pictures as being from the Curtis B. Haupring Collection.

36

Aaron's breath caught.

"Is this some . . ." His words drifted off.

"Kind of joke?" Gillian asked. "Same question I asked you up at the overlook. But you know better."

"Is it a family name? Is this guy part of your family?"

"No."

"Then who was he?"

"Said he was a documentarian. Archiving the old towns for history before they vanished from the face of the earth." She pointed at the photo of the men around the woodstove. "Workers in camp, Ashokan Reservoir, 1910. Winter. January, I think." She moved to the next, the one in the tunnels. "Excavation of the Garrison Tunnel, halfway between here and New York City. June 1911." She moved her finger to the one of the dam.

"Not the Chill, right?" Aaron said.

"Correct. That's Kensico going up."

"So he was taking pictures the whole time. Documenting the system. And yesterday someone thought it was, what, funny to use his name?"

The way she was holding the flashlight out in front of her, it was hard to read her eyes.

"That's one possibility," she said.

"Give me another."

"His grandson."

"Maybe."

"It's either a family member or someone pretending to be him."

She looked at him in silence.

"Can't be the same guy," Aaron said.

"No?"

"No. Because . . ."

"Because that would be madness, right? Absolute lunacy."

Aaron looked at the photograph closest to him. In it, a worker was driving a sledgehammer into a massive piece of stone. He was working in the shadows of a derrick that threw spiderweb patterns. It looked like a spillway somewhere. Maybe the Chill.

"Do his pictures matter?" He was thinking suddenly of the way he'd felt with the camera on him, unsettled by the strange silver light of the lens.

"I think so."

"You have to think so," Aaron said, voice rising. "You wouldn't have covered the walls with them otherwise."

"I didn't hang those pictures," she said. "Trust me."

"Then what in the hell are they doing here? What's *any* of this doing here?" He waved his hand around the room. In the shadows came a soft dripping sound. He couldn't see any water, though. Why couldn't he see the water?

Gillian lowered the light and paced away, toward the front of the room, where an old chalkboard stood. "You remember what I told you up at the overlook, about the families who stayed in Galesburg?"

"Families who killed themselves in Galesburg. And others."

She nodded without looking back. "My grandfather got most of the blame, and maybe he deserved it. But he wasn't the architect or the leader, whatever you want to call him. Remember when I said it was like Waco or Jonestown?"

"Yeah. Like a cult."

"Like that, yes. So the, um . . . spiritual leader, I guess you'd say, was a guy named Anders Wallace. His family was the first to settle in Torrance County. Four hundred years ago. Cleared land, built a cabin, and the Iroquois burned it down. The Wallaces built another. The Iroquois burned that one, too. The Wallace family stayed the winter in a tent. Or in a cave. At any rate, the cabin was ashes, the snow was flying, and the Wallace clan stuck it out. In the spring, they built another cabin. The Iroquois came down. The Wallaces fed them. This is at least what we—what *I*—was taught. And lo, duly impressed with the courage and generosity of these white folks, the Indians didn't kill them, and Galesburg began." She paused. "In retrospect, it would've been great if they had killed them."

She walked the room, shining the light from photo to photo. Ancient faces stared back.

"A hundred and twenty-five years go by, and then the French and Indian War starts, and the early Galesburg families sided against the British, and then another hundred years goes by, and now they've fought in the Revolution with the colonists, and in the Civil War with the Union almost a hundred years after that, and wars are really the only things that get them out of their valley. The nation moves west, but some Galesburg families stay." Pause. "The Mathers family stays. By then we were here. Another couple wars go by—you know, we did a hell of a lot of fighting when you think about it—and other than those who went to war, we stayed. Generation after generation. They kept winning the wars, but then along came the city and the Board of Water Supply. And this one they weren't gonna win."

She made a wide arc around the single teacher's desk that faced the single student desk. Started coming back toward him, her face dark behind the light.

"Around this time," she said, "a photographer arrives. From where, nobody knows. He was there to document it, as you say. He stayed with the Wallace family. My grandmother remembered him. Didn't like him. She couldn't remember why, only that she didn't—"

"Want her picture taken," Aaron said.

Gillian studied him. "You felt that, too?"

"I was half-naked, so I wasn't really eager for a photo regardless, but . . . yes. I did not want him to take my picture." He tried to force out a laugh. "I know, I sound like some sort of aborigine, right? Afraid the camera was going to steal my soul."

Gillian didn't laugh. She looked at him steadily and then moved the flashlight beam on to another photograph. This one showed what looked to be a collapsed derrick. A silhouette beneath might have been a corpse. It was hard to tell, but it looked like a man trapped beneath a few hundred pounds of lumber.

"There were all kinds of problems with construction at the Chilewaukee," Gillian said. "Equipment sabotage, shit like that. But they kept plugging along. Then things got worse. A handful of engineers came up. They went into the tunnels that were supposed to link the Chilewaukee into the Ashokan, into the city's supply. They didn't come back out. They were killed, along with some of the workers. A tunnel collapse was the official verdict, but not many people believed it had been accidental." She paused again. "Work got started again, though. This time, the engineer in charge was on site permanently. Jeremiah Fleming. He'd been going back and forth from the city, but as problems mounted up, he relocated. Most of the locals hated him. Anders Wallace, of all people, went out of his way to befriend him. After a few months, he actually moved in with the Wallace family."

"And with Haupring?"

She nodded. "By now, people in New York weren't feeling as good about Galesburg as they had been originally, but it didn't stop just because a few engineers got killed or a few bulldozers were blown up. They were building an empire, right? There was talk of adding National Guardsmen to the police force already here, like an occupying army. Before it came to that, though, the resisters in Galesburg said they'd play nice: 'Come on up, we'll sign the papers, and take your damned eminent domain money. We know when we're beaten.'"

"That was the night of the murders?"

"The sacrifices, if you were one of the weird families who preferred that idea."

"Where was Fleming?"

"Inside. Officially, he was considered one of the murder victims."

"Unofficially?"

"There was a lot of talk that Anders Wallace had gotten in his head. That Jeremiah Fleming had begun to hate his own creation up here."

"That he was one of the killers, you mean. Not one of the victims."

"Essentially. My grandmother remembered Haupring being there that night, too. She remembered him taking pictures of the old school. His body wasn't found there, though. By the time the meeting happened, my grandmother was home. Then morning came and she woke up to learn her father had burned the place and that he was missing. It took them a while to find his body."

Aaron tried to imagine that. Waking up and realizing that your father had never come home was a regular nightmare for a police officer's son. But the rest of it? The idea that your father was a mass murderer? Even his darkest childhood dreams hadn't reached that place.

"Is all of this why they decided to leave it a surplus reservoir? Why they backed off on the tunnels?"

"Not on its own. That was October of 1941. And what happened in December of 1941?"

He waited. She frowned. Prompted, "December 7, 1941?"

Aaron felt like he should know this one. "We dropped the bomb?"

"We dropped the— Are you serious? December 7, 1941, was *Pearl Harbor.*"

"Right. I was close."

"You were . . ." She shook her head again. "Sure. Close. End of war, beginning of war, whatever, you got the war. The war ended construction up here, and by the time it was done and they were ready to go back at it, they started looking elsewhere. The slope grade wasn't right, they said. The water flow wasn't right. Engineering mistakes had been made. The rock was different from what had been anticipated. On and on. Nobody talked about the murders as a reason, but . . . by then they were all done with Galesburg, too. The tunnels at the Chill were sealed, and the term *surplus reservoir* was deployed."

She put the flashlight beam on a photograph of water ripping through a spillway.

"That is Neversink. That one still boggles my mind. I mean, you've literally named your town Neversink and it ends up submerged? It's too strange to be true, but it is. Anyhow, all this is going along well, and the Chilewaukee by then was . . . not a real popular site. People in the city weren't feeling great about it, what with the way their best and brightest had a tendency to die up here, and the way our locals had a tendency of turning themselves into human torches. So in 1948 it's officially changed to a surplus reservoir, which means the tunnel system isn't completed, and the whole thing just . . . sits. They still claim the tunnels could now be finished in under a year if needed. They'd just haul Nora up here and blast away and—"

"Nora?"

"The Mole."

"I know I should've gotten Pearl Harbor, but Nora the Mole feels a little more obscure," Aaron said.

He saw her give a faint smile in the darkness.

"Fair enough. Nora is the name of a boring machine that is called the Mole by the people who work in the tunnels. Those guys are called sandhogs."

"*That* I've heard of."

"But not Pearl Harbor?"

"It's not that I never heard of it, I just—"

"Don't test well under pressure," she laughed, but he couldn't join her. He'd heard something similar to that phrase in helicopter rescue school. A question, a challenge, the instructor leaning down close and talking about pressure, talking about how all the talent in the world didn't mean you could handle pressure . . .

"Relax," she said, seeing his face. "I'm kidding. It's not a history exam. I'm telling a story, that's all."

"Then tell it," he said, and he sounded churlish and childish, and all of a sudden he wanted a drink or a joint. He wanted out. He didn't want to look at any more of those pictures, all the frozen faces staring back at him.

"There are people who believe the Wallace and Mathers families would've been really pleased when the tunnel work stopped," she said. "But that's not true. By the end they wanted the tunnels open. Because they thought they could do a lot more damage if they were part of the life system of New York City. That was the goal. Galesburg was supposed to be a bubble in the blood. Slip downstream and burst. They'd remember us then."

The statement came so flat and so chilling.

"You guys wanted to kill people in the city?"

"Not *we guys*; I wasn't even born yet. My mother wasn't even born yet." She looked away. "But . . . yes. I would say that's accurate. The idea of those fires was a pact. A sacrifice, like I said."

He thought of the way she'd touched the fabric on the hood of the skull. The skull she thought was her grandmother's.

"All of that's so old," he said. "You're talking seventy-five, eighty years ago. Why was your grandmother in the water?"

She lowered the light so it was pointing at the floor, giving most of the room back to darkness. Aaron heard water drip again then, but from where, he couldn't say.

"It was a drought season," Gillian Mathers said.

"Excuse me?"

"The dead can dig the tunnels," she said in an eerily toneless voice, "but they need the water to help. Otherwise, it's slow going. So if there's no water? Well, then they'll need more help."

Aaron's flesh prickled and crawled. "I don't—"

"So we have to sacrifice," she said. "We have to join the struggle. But it was always clear there wouldn't be many of us at work down there. With so few true believers left, and recruits hard to come by, we'd have to go slowly. That was the job. Procreate, educate . . . and sacrifice. Only when you were sure that there were more left to follow could you leave."

The single student desk glowed in the corner of the flashlight beam.

"Drought season is when they need the most help," she said. "That was the myth that I was taught, at least. When you joined them, you should go when the water was low. When their backs were weary."

"They raised you like this," Aaron said, his voice hollow. "Taught you this as a child?"

"My grandmother did. My father did not. I was saved from it." She spread her hands, the light traveling with her, bouncing off the photographs of all those ancient watching eyes. "From all of this. We had to keep the story alive, explain what had happened, and why. And then . . ." Her voice wavered, and she cleared her throat again before she said, ". . . we had to die. My mother went early. She went much younger. I never knew her, but I always wondered if she couldn't really bear to teach me the old stories anymore. If that's why she went before my grandmother did."

"How did your mother die?"

"Drove her car into the Dead Waters."

"Holy shit."

Silence.

"They were raising you to die?" he said finally. "Teaching you *that*?" She nodded slowly.

"That's the worst thing I've ever heard," he said.

"You know how many schools teach you what's worth dying for?" she answered with an oddly defensive tone. "We've got kids in some other country saying prayers right now, ready to strap bombs to their chests, believing it's both right and necessary. We've got kids in *this* country saying a different prayer, ready to pick up a gun and die, believing the same things. When you're inside of it, it doesn't feel so terrible. It's just . . . it's what you know. Every culture in the world has their sacrifice story. Their rituals, things worth dying for, worth killing for. We know a lot of them, but we don't remember just how many cultures this world had once. How many stories they told. Whatever the first European found up here in 1600-whatever, or whatever he brought with him, it merged into a culture that already had stories that were believed. Stories that were acted upon. These little villages in the deep, dark wood is where old European myths blended with Native stories, and then they grew cultures onto themselves."

"You're saying the story was right? It was true?"

"No. I'm saying . . ." She stopped, struggling for the words. "I don't know. I never intended to share any of this with anyone."

"But you're sharing it now."

"Yes. Because we just brought my grandmother's bones out of the water in what was once Galesburg, and because you're seeing dead men moving among the living and listening to conversations with people who were burned to death years ago. So, yes, I am sharing them now."

He turned and stared at the old photos. "The dead disappear in your story. They don't come back. Not like Mick Fleming did yesterday."

She was silent for a moment. Then she said, "They can when the math is right."

"Pardon?"

She looked embarrassed. "It's a crazy story told by crazy people. But they were waiting on a specific day. You know the Mayan calendar story?"

"Yeah. Supposedly it stopped in 2012. People thought that would be the end of the world. There was also a religious movement back in the 1840s, when people around here sold their farms and went up to Maiden Mountain to wait for the Rapture."

She nodded. "The Great Disappointment. People did that all over the country, actually. The Millerite movement. Maiden Mountain was just one of the places they gathered. Our myth about Galesburg is similar."

"What's the date?"

"It's not a date. It's the moment when an equation works." She pointed at the chalkboard, where a long equation was scribbled, barely visible beneath the coating of dust. "The rules change when those numbers work."

He stared at it. The equation was elaborate and he couldn't begin to parse its meaning.

"The number that matters most is right here," Gillian said, walking over and tapping the board with one fingernail.

20.17

"2017? Good news—that year has already come and gone," he said, trying to sound amused but failing. "Galesburg didn't predict any better than the Mayans or the Millerites."

She did not laugh.

"It's not a year," she said. "It's a water level."

"What?"

"Height above normal pool level. When it reaches 20.17, they're released. Sent downstream. Toward the city."

It was hard to find his voice. "The dead will rise?" he asked finally. "That's what you were taught."

She nodded. "The rules change then. And the dam goes."

"What do you mean, the dam goes?"

She finally turned from the chalkboard and faced him. "Bursts. Collapses. And then Galesburg is free, and headed for the city."

"Headed for the city to . . ."

"Destroy it," she said. "Galesburg wants their water back."

PART FOUR

PART FOUR

37

Steve passed the ambulance carrying the corpse away from the Chill. He knew from the radio chatter what its cargo was. By the time he got to the dam, though, the police were gone, and neither his Silverado nor Gillian Mathers's cruiser was in the parking lot.

The white Honda Pilot was.

Steve was staring at the car, thinking it was empty, when Mick Fleming climbed out, carrying his iPad and notebook just as he had yesterday, raincoat hanging open, collared shirt beneath, mechanical pencil tucked in the pocket.

Steve popped the driver's door. Stepped out into the rain. Fleming turned to face him. Smiled. Steve didn't like that smile. It was a huckster's grin, somebody who'd stacked the deck of a low-rent card game and thought he was slick, thought he was big-time.

It also didn't seem to suit the man Steve had heard described. The Mick Fleming depicted by Arthur Brady, by Ed Cochran, and by Fleming's own wife was a serious type, methodical, and worried. He wasn't a smiling-in-the-rain type. Not on this day, and not below this dam.

"Morning, Sheriff," Fleming said. "How's your boy feeling?"

"Son."

"Pardon?"

"He's my son, but he's no boy. Grown man. That's how the judge'll see it, too."

"The judge?" Fleming gave him a look of polite confusion, all while tucking his iPad and notebook inside the open raincoat to keep them dry. "I certainly don't intend to press charges." The smile returned. "And I'm still alive, so I'm not sure what charges I could press that would match his confession."

"Yeah," Steve said. "I get that. You said it yesterday, so I don't need to hear it again."

"Apologies. Sensitive subject, I'm sure."

"Not so much." Steve looked downstream. "I spoke to Ed Cochran."

"Oh? I bet he was in a foul mood."

"Yes. Wanna tell me why?"

"He didn't?"

"That's not what I asked."

There was a pause, and Fleming's lip curled in the faintest hint of that cardsharp's smile he'd seemingly developed overnight, and then he said, "I get it. We're unhappy today, aren't we, Sheriff? You got a negative report in the big city, and as much as you don't like the big city, you've got to worry about it. Your reputation is made up here, but it can be ruined down there. You control Torrance County only until Manhattan comes knocking. Then you're outgunned, aren't you?"

"Outgunned?"

"Big fish swimming into the small pond."

"You've got a whole different attitude today, Mr. Fleming."

"Well, it's been a long night, Sheriff. After that fiasco yesterday, with you and your boy—excuse me, your *son*—keeping me from doing the city's business."

The city's business. Everything about the man was different, from the smile to the taunting tone and even the phrasing.

"Let's talk about business," Steve said. "Let's talk about the dam."

"The dam."

Steve nodded at the spillway. "Big stone thing, holds the lake back."

"You weren't so glib yesterday, Sheriff."

"And you weren't so smug."

Fleming didn't say anything.

"I understand that you're concerned about the dam," Steve said. "I understand half the DEP is descending on us tomorrow morning because of your concerns. And somehow I missed a single word about those concerns. Arthur Brady seems to have missed them as well. Gillian Mathers, too. Everyone you spoke to in Torrance County lacks recollection of your concerns."

There was no trace of the smile now. Instead there was the cold sullenness of a quiet, smart boy who didn't like being called on to show his work. He had all the answers, and he thought that should be enough.

"You want to understand the trouble?" Mick Fleming asked. His voice was now closer to what Steve remembered from yesterday, higher and fussier.

"I think I ought to."

"You think you *can*."

"I'm not expecting to make the calculations, but I can grasp the concepts."

Fleming looked at him with amused distaste.

"All right," he said. "Cavitation. One word. What's your familiarity with it?"

"I brush twice a day. Sometimes even rinse with that stuff, Act, I think it is? The fluoride. I haven't been so good about that since my wife died, I have to admit."

"This is entertainment to you? We stand here in the rain and trade snarky remarks, is that it?"

"No," Steve said, good and tired of him now—so tired of him, in fact, that he was feeling an urge to throw a punch. He hadn't felt that since he was a young deputy wrestling a drunk man out of a house where a woman and two children with bloody noses and black eyes watched. One of them had called 911 for help, Steve wasn't sure who, because all they'd done was leave an open line while Daddy beat the shit out of the family.

Steve had been more tired on that day than any other in his career. He'd seen worse things, but you couldn't anticipate the moments that would break your spirit. He was tired now, too. Tired of Fleming, tired of this day, and so damned tired of the rain. It was running down his collar, chilling his spine.

He said, "No, I don't want to trade snark, but you seem intent on making me look like a fool, Mr. Fleming, so I'll play along with that, or you can offer me some fucking respect and we can go address the problem."

Mick Fleming looked away from Steve. Turned to his left, smiled, and nodded. "Oh, yes," he said. "I heard it."

Steve followed his eyes. Fleming was looking downstream, but no one was there. Just wind-ravaged trees and the swollen tailwaters.

"Mind telling me what you think you're—"

"Walk with me, Sheriff," Fleming said, moving toward the stone steps that led to the gatehouse. "I'll try to give you a grasp of what the situation is out here. I'll try to show you exactly what it is that you people have been ignoring and how it might have manifested into the worst loss of life your county has ever seen if I hadn't come down here."

Steve followed, glad they were going to the gatehouse. He didn't want to be alone in the woods with this little pissant. Fleming was a physically unimposing man and Steve was armed, but all the same Steve was uneasy about him.

They went up the steep concrete steps. At the top, the massive reservoir rested in the rain, millions of gallons of cold gray water filling it drop by drop. A thin mist rose from the surface like steam. There wasn't a boat in sight. Why would there be? On a day like today, even the die-hard fishermen stayed inside.

"Your people were here from the beginning, weren't they?" Mick Fleming said. Up here the roar from the water going over the spillway was so loud that he almost had to shout, and Steve wasn't sure he'd heard him right.

"Excuse me?"

Fleming was using his left arm to press the iPad and notebook against his side, protecting them with the raincoat. He used his right arm to gesture across his body, out at the Chilewaukee.

"Before it was built. Don't you all go back in Galesburg a long while?"

"Torrance," Steve said.

"What?"

"The town is Torrance. The county is Torrance. Galesburg is not a place anymore."

"You think it went away?" Fleming was looking at him intently, rain on his glasses, dripping down his forehead, pasting his thinning hair to his skull.

"It's not a matter of opinion," Steve said. "It's underwater, bud. Has been for sixty years." He thought about it. "Seventy-five, actually. Almost eighty. Point is, I'm from Torrance."

"I see." Fleming used his right hand again, pointing at the massive stone expanse of the spillway. "Remember the word I told you?"

"Cavitation."

"Very good. I'll keep this simple, because I don't have much time to waste, but cavitation involves bubbles."

"Bubbles."

"That's right. Millions of them. Billions of them. So small you might not notice them in all the chaos and churn, but what they represent, Sheriff, is big-league trouble. The system depends on balance. You've got a lot of elements at work here. Stone and water and air, mass and force and friction. When they're working together, it's an amazing thing. But it's also an illusion."

Fleming's half shout didn't have the cold caustic bite of his conversation in the parking lot. If anything, he seemed focused up here, a man devoted to his craft. He seemed, finally, like the man everyone had promised Steve he was.

"How's it an illusion?" Steve said.

"Because those forces don't truly work together. They only seem to. That's the great trick of engineering. We take opposing forces and balance them. Things in balance seem to have a nice, peaceful harmony. They seem *cooperative*. But that's the illusion. Those forces are always at war. They're always seeking an advantage. Day by day, minute by minute, drip by drip, forces of nature fight to dominate. And that, Sheriff Ellsworth, is why something as trivial as a tiny bubble in a big body of water can be a very dangerous thing."

Steve nodded. This much he understood far better than the patronizing engineer would ever know. Lily's blood clot had started in her thigh, slipped through veins that were slimmer than the finest ultralight fishing line, crept unseen up her torso, through her heart, along her neck, and into her brain.

Steve Ellsworth didn't need to be told about the importance of keeping a system in balance.

"The problem is down below," he said. "It's not about the rain at all."

"It's about both. There are problems down below, and the rain is adding problems from up above. That's how we get to disaster scenarios."

"So what do we need to do?" Steve said, his voice hoarse and loud and still nearly drowned out by the roar of water thundering over all that old stone. "How do we stop it?"

Mick Fleming's face sagged as if he was disappointed by the question.

"That's just the point," he said. "You don't stop it. You only delay it."

Steve sighed and wiped rain out of his eyes. "I grasp the big picture. But how do we *delay* it? Because when that big old bitch bursts, it's not going to be on my watch."

"No, it won't," Mick Fleming said, the first agreement he'd offered. He nodded at the gatehouse. "Let me show you how we make sure it's not on your watch."

Fleming walked to the door, tugged it open, and held it for Steve, squinting into the wind and rain. Steve crossed the steel-grated catwalk that let water drip into the crushed stone below, ducked through the door, and entered the gatehouse.

Arthur Brady sat in his chair in front of the old computer monitor and beside one of the far older, massive steel valves. The handle of the valve, which resembled a ship's wheel, was flaked with rust. Arthur was studying the rust.

"Hey, Arthur," Steve called as the door clanged shut behind him. "I brought company."

Twin realizations floated toward him then. The valve handle wasn't flaked with rust; it was flecked with blood. And Arthur wasn't slumped in his chair; he was dead in it.

Then the third realization: Steve had just made the last mistake of many an old lawman. He had turned his back on someone he didn't trust.

He got halfway turned around and got his hand on the butt of his duty pistol before the bullet came.

Then he was down on one knee, shot in the back but looking at a bloody hole in his chest. He kept trying to turn. He had to brace his left hand on the floor to do it, but he got around and he saw Mick Fleming. The engineer's iPad and notebook were on the floor at his feet. The third thing he'd been clutching inside that raincoat—the thing Steve hadn't considered until too late—was in his hand.

A revolver, short-barreled, smaller caliber. Probably a .38. Cheap pawnshop trade. Saturday night special. Rusty junk with no range.

Still, a killing piece.

The wind rose. Rain hammered the old glass of the arched windows where the gatehouse kept watch on the Chilewaukee Reservoir. Blood dripped out of Steve's chest and onto the floor. He watched the red drops while he fumbled with his gun. He thought, *Aaron was right. My son was right. My son saw it coming.* He finally cleared his gun and lifted it to kill Mick Fleming. Then he lost track of Mick Fleming and saw his grandfather instead, saw the old man standing on the front porch of the family farmhouse, watching the rain clouds massing in the west, and Steve thought, *Yes, he saw it coming, too.*

His grandfather turned to him with a sad smile, and then came a thunderclap, and day went to night.

38

Mick intended to put both bodies in the water, but Anders Wallace stopped him.

"Poor choice," he said.

Mick stared at him. "I can't just leave them here."

"But into the water, sir? Considering all you've learned, you still find that wise?"

Mick thought about it. Looked at Anders, and then looked out at the Chilewaukee. Saw his own face reflected in the rain-washed windowpane.

"They don't belong there?"

"It would be a risk, don't you think?"

"Yes," Mick said, but he wasn't sure why.

"Think of it this way," Anders said, as if reading Mick's confusion. "You don't understand much about Galesburg, but you know it presents options. Are these men"—he nodded at the two corpses—"the type of men you want to have options? After what happened here?"

Anders posed the questions as if they were remedial problems, but they were far too complex for Mick. He was embarrassed by that. All his life, he'd solved the hardest problems, and yet this one was beyond him.

"They're dead," he said, his voice soft, almost wheedling. It echoed in the empty room with all its stone and metal, and he hated the sound.

"In another life, weren't *you* dead?" Anders asked, leaning against one of the massive iron pipes.

Yes, Mick supposed he had been. But here he was. He understood at least vaguely how that had come to pass, so Anders must, too.

"You're in charge of that," Mick said. "You must be."

Anders gave a rueful laugh. Turned and looked out the arched window at the nickel-colored water beyond. He was utterly unbothered by the blood at his feet, but he seemed perpetually distracted by the rain.

"I'd love for that to be true," he said. "But I'm afraid it's not."

"You must be," Mick repeated, and this time he didn't mind the echo of his high, insistent voice. He was right about this—sure of it. The only way his existence here made any sense was if Anders was in charge of the situation. How it all worked, Mick couldn't say, but it seemed clear that there was a boss to the situation. The man who transcended space and time and place, the one who could appear in Mick's home in Albany or at his side in Torrance County, the one who could lead him underwater or aboveground—he was surely the boss.

He must be.

"Do you remember what you were explaining to the sheriff about cavitation?" Anders asked him. "About bubbles?"

Mick looked down at the sheriff. His eyes were open but they saw nothing. Blood dripped in twin rivulets off his hips, forming crimson stains on his jeans that looked like holsters.

"Yes, I remember that."

"Millions of them, you said. Some make it downstream; others burst on the spillway surface. Some ride the current; some die in the current. You want ironclad rules, Mr. Fleming, but you of all people should know they don't exist."

"Why not?"

"Answer that yourself."

"I can't."

"Try." Anders waited expectantly. Mick turned away, and then he was looking at the sheriff's dead eyes again but seeing the bubbles in the water below the dam. He tried to focus on that problem. To consider the individual bubble, swept along in a strong current among so many others, stone beneath, rain above, limbs and weeds and stumps scattered all about.

"There are too many factors to control," he said. "Each scenario is different. You can't control them all."

"Very good. And so we control what we can, to stay in balance. Am I right?"

Mick nodded again.

"Then I'd hesitate to add these gents to that water, personally," Anders said. "Because we know some strange things happen there. Some we can control. Others? Maybe not. You were always en route to Galesburg. You've been part of the equation for a long, long time. It was a matter of timing. We had to be patient. The water had to rise. But we knew you'd arrive."

"You couldn't have known that."

Anders smiled.

"I came here for work," Mick said.

"Of course you did. The dam is yours, after all."

"That was my grandfather who designed it. He's dead."

Still, Anders didn't speak. Just smiled.

"You couldn't have known I'd be here," Mick said again.

"Perhaps not. But you did come, didn't you? The water rose, and there you were. Drawn back to this special place. Sacred place."

Mick didn't say anything. Anders nodded at the corpses and nudged the sheriff's boot with his foot.

"I'd keep them out of Galesburg today," Anders said. "Just to remove an unknown. We don't like those, do we?"

"I never have," Mick agreed.

"This way, then." Anders moved toward a catwalk that looked out over the lower floor of the gatehouse, the manual control room for the big gates themselves.

Mick followed, dragging the sheriff's body over the cold stone floor. Blood trailed behind. Fluorescent overhead lighting jittered and flickered. The light's ballast was failing. It would need to be replaced or the place would go dark. That annoyed Mick; how long had Arthur Brady ignored that flickering light? The ballasts had a purpose. They burned out slowly for a reason: to give you time. It was just like the noxious smell of eggs that came from a gas leak. The smell wasn't natural. It was added to the gas, added by humans to save humans. And every year you read about another family who'd died of carbon monoxide poisoning or blown up their home, ignorant of a gas leak, because they'd ignored the smell.

You could only do so much to help humanity. At some point you had to shake them awake.

Yes, Mick thought as he dragged the dead sheriff through the Chilewaukee Dam gatehouse, Anders Wallace was right: you could control only so much.

At the end of the catwalk, iron ladders led down to dark pits. These were access chambers, designed to give workers a view of the massive outlet gates that controlled the flow through the spillway. The outlet pipes were nearly three feet in diameter, and they were protected above and below by steel grates that let water pass through but trapped larger debris.

Here the corpses could wait in the water, but they couldn't move downstream. They would never reach the Dead Waters. Never see Galesburg.

Mick shoved the sheriff's head and shoulders between the railing and the floor, then grabbed him by the boots and pushed. It was awkward, because the sheriff's corpse seemed determined not to cooperate, bending and folding rather than sliding, but Mick finally shoved him through.

There was the whisper of fabric on stone, then a splash and a muffled pop, like the breaking of rotten wood. The sheriff was gone, and darkness hid him.

Mick went back for Arthur Brady. It went faster this time. Arthur was lighter, and his body slipped between the railing and the floor easier. Push, shove, splash.

Bodies gone, blood on the floor.

Mick went in search of a mop.

39

Gillian and Aaron made the walk back from her old house in near silence. The only times either of them spoke it was to offer soft words of guidance: *careful*; *steep here*; *watch that branch*. Gillian was fine with that. She had no desire to talk after opening the floodgates for Aaron back in the terrible schoolhouse room of the home she'd once known as largely a good place—or at least a *home* place. Even in bad times, children trusted home. It was the den that kept you safe from the world. Never mind if it was filled with wolves.

The wolves hadn't been all bad, though. Her grandmother had been lovely in so many ways, kind in so many ways . . . and a complete believer in the terrible story she was teaching.

As Aaron Ellsworth held back a whiplike branch so Gillian could step under it, she thought of her father.

What did he know? He knew something. He hated the school. Wouldn't talk about it. And the first time you drew anything from the schoolhouse, the look on his face . . .

Those were the memories, at least. But memory was a shifting thing, fluid and deceptive, and it had a way of carrying facts from one place to another so subtly that you didn't recognize the redistribution until too late. One summer the sandbar had been over there, and the next summer you were running aground on it over here. That was memory. You navigated with it, but it was shifting all the while.

When she thought of her dad's face, though—of how he'd looked when he saw her sketches—she was sure that he'd known about the Galesburg School.

Then why didn't he speak of it?

"No answer?" Aaron Ellsworth said.

"Huh?" She turned to him.

"I said, how long will it take them to identify the body? Like, positive identification. Dental records or whatever."

She hadn't even heard the question. Looking at him now, she saw that he needed a rest probably more than he needed an answer. He was leaning against a tree, breathing hard and trying to take all of the weight off his bad foot. What had she been thinking, dragging him all the way out here with that injury?

I had to tell someone. Had to share it with someone.

"I'm not sure," she said. "This is the first time I've had charge of a scene with an unidentified body. Or a body, period."

"We can talk to my dad about it," he said between breaths. "Maybe he can help. You know, expedite it."

"Maybe."

His broad chest rose and fell as he fought for air, but his eyes were keenly focused on hers.

"You don't want me to tell him."

"I don't care. He'll find out soon enough. Everyone will."

"Not her identity. I'm talking about all the rest of it. You're not ready to tell people about that yet, are you?"

"I don't know."

"If you believe in it, though, then shouldn't you . . ."

"What? What should I do?"

"I don't know. Are you kidding me? How would anyone know? But you've got to do *something*, right?"

Yes, Gillian thought, remembering the blackboard in the schoolhouse, the sound of the chalk, the way the white dust rose and hung in the air when her grandmother's hand picked up speed. *I have to leave.*

That's what I have to do. Because my family was evil, and the water in Galesburg is not the kind that washes your sins away. It's the kind that preserves them. And it doesn't lose track of its debts. Being here is a bad idea.

Yet she was here. She'd come back, when there was absolutely no reason to do so, and every incentive to avoid the place. On the day that the reservoir crested twenty feet, she was on hand.

Just as promised.

"Maybe," she said, and turned from him again. She pushed through another thicket, thorns tearing at her jacket, branches whipping back. She didn't pause to hold them as he had for her. She was doing all she could to avoid running. Each step farther from the house helped, but she didn't feel she was taking them fast enough.

"He'll listen," Aaron said behind her.

"Yeah?" She kept walking. Below them, Cresap Creek churned toward Torrance, the water dark with soil. *Turbid*, that was the official term.

"I'm serious," Aaron called, falling farther behind. "He'll remember the old stories. Some of them, at least. He'll take them seriously. I know that."

She slowed, then half turned so she could see his face. "Why?"

"Because his family did. His grandmother, his grandfather. I remember that. My mom would just shake her head, because she never liked the . . ."

Halloween shit, Gillian thought, remembering the phrase he'd used at the overlook.

"Never liked superstitious people," he said. "But I know that his grandparents believed in that sort of thing."

That sort of thing. Murder and blood sacrifice, old debts and new ghosts.

"Your father doesn't seem like he's got that kind of patience."

"I think you'll be surprised."

She didn't answer. Telling Aaron Ellsworth had been hard enough; telling Steve Ellsworth was almost implausible. And yet . . .

You've got to do something.

She moved on, thinking that he had the right idea but the wrong man. They needed to speak to someone's father, certainly. It just wasn't his.

40

When Caleb Stiles asked if Deshawn could pull overtime, it felt inevitable. On this day, when all Deshawn wanted was to get out of the tunnels and back to the waiting city above, back to a place where he had cell phone reception to reach his daughter and where no visions plagued him, the tunnels didn't seem inclined to give him up so easily.

He suspected there was another reason, too. Caleb was curious after that meltdown with the oncoming railcar, when Deshawn had screamed and then told his foreman that it had been out of concern over a sandwich.

Deshawn wouldn't have been the first sandhog to crack from claustrophobia, although after all these years that would be rare. Still, he'd shown something today that had unnerved Caleb, and he didn't blame the man for testing him.

"Second shift's two men down this week," Caleb explained. "They need help, and it needs to be a veteran." He watched Deshawn like a psychiatrist eyeing a patient. "You know, someone experienced. Steady. Someone like you."

"Whole shift?" Deshawn said.

Caleb nodded.

Eight more hours. It was barely legal, but it was also hardly unheard-of. They were over budget and behind deadline—by years and millions, or decades and billions, depending on whose original estimate you trusted.

"Sure," Deshawn said. "Double money? I'll take that any day."

Caleb watched him for a beat longer before saying, "That's what I was counting on. Thanks."

"No problem."

Caleb turned and walked down the tunnel and Deshawn lifted a water bottle to his dry, chapped lips. His head still ached from the sleepless night and too much drinking. The relentless pounding of steel blades into granite seemed to be boring through his ears.

Eight more hours. Screw it. What could go wrong in eight more hours?

He walked back toward the Mole, and when he passed the crew of men in filthy overalls who stood on high wooden timbers and watched him from above, he didn't look up. They weren't real, let alone worthy of attention.

Stay down here and stay focused. One more shift.

41

In the last minutes of his life, Arthur Brady had proven obdurate, but before he'd died he'd also demonstrated the process for opening and closing the spillway gates, and for deactivating the siren system and the security monitors. If he'd continued to do his job without complaint, if he'd simply followed orders, he might still be alive.

Arthur had been edgy with him from the first, but it was only when Mick requested the second gate be raised that he voiced any reluctance.

"If it's the spillway you're worried about, then this will do more harm than good. We should be closing gates, not opening them."

"I was told you'd spoken to Mr. Cochran. I was told you understood your role here and would not question my authority."

"I'm not questioning your authority," Brady had said, "I'm questioning your idea. If it's cavitation and that stone face is peeling off, we'll make it worse increasing the flow. We should be shutting her down completely."

"In a record flood? With the reservoir this high?"

Brady had faced him defiantly. "*Yes*. Because the dam can hold on."

"Not for long."

"Longer than if the spillway is cutting her knees out from under her!"

Mick had regarded Brady with a measure of surprise and admiration right then. The old dam operator understood the structure better than Mick would've guessed. Mick remembered the way Brady had compared the sound of the spillway to a sick human. *More from the chest*, he'd said. *It ain't a head cold anymore.*

"Mr. Brady," Mick had said, "this situation requires my focus, and my expertise. I can't engage in debate over the matter."

"You're gonna have to. Because she can hold it. For a few days at least. We've got time. Not much, maybe, but—"

The gun had come out then, and they moved swiftly from talk of structural integrity to talk of sirens and surveillance cameras. Arthur Brady was more compliant with the weapon at his head.

Too little, too late, of course.

Mick had fired with the barrel of the revolver nearly pressed to Arthur Brady's forehead. Close range was critical. He knew he wasn't a marksman, and he needed to be sure.

He'd been sure.

He'd left Arthur in his chair, taken his keys, and gone outside to observe in person the changes along the spillway. He was in his car, alone in the rain, when the sheriff arrived.

Now, while Arthur's body floated alongside the sheriff's in the access chambers below, trapped by the steel grates that caught the debris like a giant strainer, Mick opened the spillway's third gate, bringing an additional thirty thousand gallons of water per second storming down the old stone face and downstream.

He was frowning while he did it, and not out of guilt.

The math didn't work.

The math was thrown off by $T = time$.

All of the terrible risks of cavitation were offset by the pace of the process. Cavitation could devastate a dam—it could create a full breach, yes—but not quickly. Even if the eroding spillway face was chewing a hole at the base of the Chilewaukee Dam, increasing the water flow and pressure would hasten the process only so much.

Arthur hadn't been wrong about that. His understanding of the structure's *chest cough* was on the money. Pneumonia killed you, but not quickly. Not by morning.

Mick needed the dam to be dead by morning.

He sat in the gatehouse in Arthur Brady's chair, swiveling between one arched window and the next, watching the reservoir at one end and the surging tailwaters below, and then he regarded Anders Wallace sadly.

"It won't work," he said.

"It will," Anders told him. Anders stood by the locked door at the stairs with his perfect posture, a bearing that wasn't rigid but elegant. A bearing of purpose and confidence.

"I don't think so. It will take too long. They'll have to hurry, yes, but they can. They'll kill me, they'll close the gates, and then they'll come with full awareness of the ticking clock. It would have been better if I'd never said a word. The way I left yesterday was the way to go about it. No one was going to trust Brady's word against mine. So long as I told them the structure was sound, they'd have believed me. You made me rush. That was the mistake."

As he sat here in the old gatehouse with its shining floors, mopped clean of blood, he knew that he wouldn't succeed. It had all been for naught. Oh, he'd draw attention to the Chilewaukee, certainly. Helicopters would circle, news cameras would run, politicians would make statements, but the dam would hold and thus the story would become that of a man gone mad. They'd miss the point.

"They'll still forget," he said. "The panic will be temporary. Then they'll get it fixed, and everyone downstream will say, 'See, there was never anything to worry about,' and no one will have learned a thing."

Anders gave a wan, almost sad smile. Then he stepped away from the door and walked to the far end of the room, where the iron ladders led down to the access chambers. The corpses of the two men Mick had killed bobbed just below.

"You fail to understand the math, sir," Anders said.

This accusation made Mick indignant. If there was one thing he absolutely understood, it was the math.

"It will take too long," he said. "I'm sure of that. It's about the issue of time, nothing else. This approach takes too much time."

"It is about the idea of time," Anders agreed, resting one hand on the top rung of the ladder. "But you don't have a full understanding of time." He beckoned. "Come here."

Mick sighed, but he rose and crossed the room and joined Anders at the top of the ladder.

"Go down," Anders said.

Mick stared into the darkness. The only sounds were the soft lapping of water that had leaked through decaying pipes or thin cracks in the stone, and the sloshing thumps of the dead men hitting the trash racks.

"Go down and see what you're failing to account for," Anders Wallace said, and his voice was less genial now. "Remember your equation?"

He remembered it, but he still hadn't made sense of it. There was the strange inclusion of the uplift pressure.

"Go on," Anders said firmly.

Mick wrapped his hand around the cool iron rung. He swung his foot out, felt in the darkness, and found the next. Stepped down, and down again. He paused when his head was level with the floor, and looked up. Anders stared back down at him, seeming taller now, an immense figure. Mick turned away and went down the ladder into darkness.

He was twenty rungs down when he heard the sound of metal on rock. He paused and listened. It was a rhythmic noise, a whipping rush of air followed by the ping of iron on rock. *Whoosh, ting, whoosh, ting, whoosh, ting.*

He descended another step, and then another, and now a pale light began to emerge. He could see the rough-hewn rock floor below, dimly illuminated in a flickering light.

See what you're failing to account for, Anders had said.

Mick's foot left the ladder and landed on the stone floor. He should have been standing in water now, but just like last night there was stone waiting for him instead.

The light was coming from his left, and so was the sound—*whoosh, ting, whoosh, ting*—and now he could hear another sound, this one a scraping, also rhythmic. The light flickered but the sounds were steady.

He released the ladder and stepped toward the sound and the light.

He was facing a crew of miners. A dozen of them, maybe. Their dress was of another era, like Anders's, and men and women worked side by side. Gray dust rose all around them, and they worked in the shifting light of a lantern. The men swung picks against a sheer rock wall—*whoosh, ting*—and the women scraped the rock fragments up in wide shovels and deposited them in a tall, rusted iron cart. They looked at Mick but did not pause.

A tall man seemed to be directing the work. He was swinging his pick unrelentingly, dust billowing back into his face. The woman beside him scraped the rock from the ground and dumped it into the cart.

They worked on, at a feverish but precise pace, and it made Mick think of the old story of John Henry versus the machine. The furious but fruitless endeavor of human strength pitted against mechanical power, a race against . . .

Time.

It is about the idea of time, Anders had said. *But you don't have a full understanding of time.*

Uplift pressure. A force that Mick hadn't understood. Unseen but powerful.

Mick watched them work, the iron picks spitting sparks when they struck granite, the shovels gathering each fallen fragment. They were as fine-tuned as any machine, an unbroken chain of efficiency until the tall man set down his pick. The others worked on, but he leaned on his pick, wiped his filthy face with his shirtsleeve, and stared at Mick.

There was something familiar about him.

"Do you understand now?" the tall man asked.

"Who are you?"

"You should know the name."

He did know it. Suddenly, the face was more than familiar. It was nearly his own. The man was Jeremiah Fleming.

Mick's grandfather. A man he'd never met in life.

Jeremiah Fleming smiled a wicked grin. "The man should be forgotten, but the work should be remembered. They'll know my work. They'll know *our* work."

Mick didn't answer.

"Do you understand now?" Jeremiah repeated. He leaned forward, his lanky, whip-strong body tensed, as if Mick's answer mattered a great deal.

"Yes," Mick said. "I think I do."

He meant it, too. He was beginning to understand it all—the world down here wasn't far off from the one he'd explained to the sheriff just before he'd killed him. Back then, he'd told the sheriff that the disaster brewing at the Chilewaukee wasn't a problem of rain alone, or of failing stone. It required both. Forces from above, and forces from below.

For years, Mick's interest had been on the surface, but other forces had been trapped below. They'd pushed on, fighting for an advantage, just as he'd described to the sheriff.

And they were relentless.

Whoosh, ting, whoosh, ting. Scrape, dump, scrape, dump.

They'd been working a long time for this moment. Tirelessly. Forgotten but undeterred.

"It won't take all that much help from me, will it?" Mick said. "You've got the head start. So now it won't take nearly as much pressure as it should. Which means not nearly as much time as I expected."

"I'm not sure," Jeremiah said. "You're the surface engineer." He wiped his face again, staring at Mick through the haze of rock dust. "But I'd say we're close, wouldn't you?"

"Yes."

"Very well. I've got to get back to work now. So do you. We will need you downstream. You understand that?"

"The process starts at the Chilewaukee," Mick said. "It doesn't end there. It doesn't end until it reaches the city. You'll need me to guide it downstream."

"Correct."

Jeremiah Fleming turned from Mick then, whipped the heavy pick backward, and drove it forward. Iron sparked off rock, a chunk of the wall fell free, and a shovel scraped in to claim it.

Mick walked back to the ladder and climbed out of the lantern light and back through darkness to the gatehouse above.

42

Aaron arrived home feeling both exhausted and jittery, as if he'd over-caffeinated to fight fatigue. He wanted to talk to his father. He knew that Steve would listen to Gillian's stories. His father always listened, even to the most deranged jailhouse phone calls. There was a reason he'd been elected time and again. When people spoke to Steve Ellsworth, they felt as if they'd been heard. Whatever the result might be, they didn't go away feeling voiceless.

The sheriff's cruiser was gone, though, and the house was empty, a note left on the table, three sentences, two scrawled hurriedly, the other printed with care, almost as if left by two different hands:

Home shortly, thanks for helping Mathers. Lots to discuss.

And beneath it:

Thank you, son.

Aaron started to toss the note into the trash but then stopped. Moving toward the garbage can required facing the sink, and he saw that the whiskey glass had been moved. He'd left it in the sink, but it was gone.

He understood the Breathalyzer demand now. He also thought he understood the different pacing of the writing on the note. *Thank you, son* had been added, written with care. Written after he'd passed the Breathalyzer. Maybe even after the corpse had been found and Aaron's story validated.

He put the note back down on the table rather than depositing it in the trash. Then he called his dad's cell phone. It went directly to voicemail. Aaron said, "Hey, it's me. Just wanted you to know that I'm home. I'll be here."

Ordinarily, that would've been enough. But ordinarily his father wouldn't have thanked him in a note, either, so Aaron felt a pull to offer something in reciprocity, some gesture of appreciation.

"Be safe," he said, but that sounded ominous or nervous, and so he added, "In this weather, I mean. Be safe in the rain, Dad."

He disconnected then. His throat was thick and he wasn't sure why. He looked at the note again. Why did those few words seem to matter so much?

Listen to the water, he'd written once in a book given to him by his mother. Not many words, but they'd mattered. Maybe because there were so few.

He left the note on the table and then went upstairs. He intended to inspect the wound on his foot, clean it, re-bandage it, and take an Advil. Instead he fell asleep with his boots on, waiting on his father's return.

43

Ed Cochran couldn't remember a more miserable day. Hours of rain, hours of angry phone calls.

Most of the time, he was the recipient of the anger. The lone exception was his brief, terse chat with the sheriff of Torrance County. The sheriff was cooperative beneath his crankiness. Concerned for someone other than himself.

That was a pleasant change from the rest of the calls. Every other elected official seemed worried about what they'd known and when they'd known it. The calls with the engineers were better—but unsettling. The engineers seemed both grim and smug, with *I told you so* sneers barely buried beneath the *Oh, shit* responses. The engineers knew Mick by reputation if not in person. If Mick Fleming was nervous, the others were scared. If Mick was scared? Well, then. That was a different situation.

Three different people told Ed that an evacuation should be considered based simply on Mick's concern. Then, just when he was about to agree with them, Mick called.

"Please tell me you're at the Chilewaukee," Ed said.

"I'm here." His voice was steady. None of the usual haughtiness, that sense of a barely suppressed sigh that was typical of Mick.

"Good. You're about to have company. I don't think we can wait until tomorrow," Ed said. "I'm freaking out more people with every call I make. I can't get a full team up there today, but I can get—"

"You've got time."

"You're sure?"

"If Arthur Brady does what he's told and operates the gates so I can see that spillway react to flow changes, then yes. He's become more cooperative. So has the sheriff."

"I talked to Sheriff Ellsworth," Ed said. "Made it clear that this thing can't be fixed with a bass boat and a winch."

Mick laughed. Ed smiled, but almost more out of curiosity than amusement. When was the last time he'd heard a genuine laugh out of Mick Fleming? Had he ever?

"The guy needed a little prod, didn't he?" Ed said.

"He certainly did. He went down in person to make sure Brady did what he was told. It's been easier since I've had direct contact. Knowing the locals is critical."

"Sure," Ed said. "Boots on the ground, brother. I get it. But I'm going to send you some help anyhow. Tabor, Bruce & Goy are sending some people up. I'll be right on their heels."

For a few seconds he thought he'd lost Fleming. Then the voice came back with a new, albeit more familiar, tension.

"That's a mistake."

"Excuse me?" Ed leaned forward, elbows on the desk. "I read your email, Mick. You told me this was *urgent*."

"I know what I said. I also said that *tomorrow* was the day for a full team."

"Got that, but this isn't a full team; this is the bare minimum I can send up there and keep my job. The friggin' politicians? They're *scared*, and if they're scared, then I'm in the crosshairs."

"Tomorrow," Mick Fleming said. His voice was bristling, almost enraged.

"Listen—" Ed began, but Mick cut him off.

"You'll ruin it. I'm not kidding, Ed. You'll ruin everything."

"What in the hell are you talking about? *You asked me to*—"

"I asked you to get people ready for tomorrow morning! And I *told* you that was because I needed time to get the locals on board. I told you this. I wrote it down. It was in fucking black-and-white for you."

Ed's eyes went wide. Was this *really* Mick Fleming? Mick Fleming, who never raised his voice, who couldn't make eye contact when he was disappointed? Mick Fleming was now reading his boss the riot act?

Nerves getting to him. That has to be it. The little prick would never be insubordinate if he wasn't scared.

"I don't think you understand the significance of a dam failure to all of us," Ed said slowly. "City and state. I won't even ask you to consider my role in the moment, but let me explain why I am sending—"

"Come yourself. Just you. None of the consultants. Not yet."

"They're the best in the country, Mick! And they want to see—"

"Please," Fleming said, his voice going weary and ragged. "There are two ways to address the situation at the Chilewaukee. One of them embarrasses all of us. The other is a quiet fix. We are not past the point of a very quiet fix. But the minute you roll consultants out here, it changes. Not the fix, but the level of public attention given to it. Do you follow me?"

Of course Ed followed him. You didn't get this job without grasping the idea of media timing. And, sure, the idea of showmanship. What was stunning to him was that Mick Fleming cared about either of those. Was aware of them, even.

"I think our guys at Tabor will be fine," Ed said.

"You've got wannabe heroes at Tabor," Mick told him. "Trust me. Worse, you've got wannabe heroes with Twitter accounts. They're going to leak details. The fucking dam won't leak but *they* will. And I don't need them yet!"

Ed could hardly muster a response. Mick Fleming was shouting and swearing at him about leaks to the press?

"Mick? An outside opinion might be—"

"Cavitation."

"What?"

"That's what we've got here. Cavitation on the spillway. Bad, yes, potentially fatal, yes, but not rapid-fire. We've got time. You know more about the mistakes at Oroville than I do. But if they'd handled it right, do you think they'd have gotten their asses burned in the media like they did?"

Oroville. Holy shit. The modern Johnstown, if it hadn't been headed off in time. Oroville had been evacuated, though, and that was what put Oroville in the news. Mick was right. If the fix had been made, would Fox and CNN and all the rest have known, much less given it attention? Probably not. The attention came with the evacuation order.

"What's the condition of the spillway face?" he asked.

"Deteriorating but not failing. Listen, Ed, you can come up here and see what I'm seeing. But don't call FEMA and the Red Cross out just yet, okay? This thing can either be all done in a week, a *quiet* week, or it can turn into a few panicked hours that will embarrass us for years. The process won't change, and the result won't change, but the way everyone views us will."

Us. How strange it felt to hear Fleming say that word. Fleming never showed an interest in the reputation of the agency.

"The dam is solid?" Ed asked.

"The dam is solid. The spillway is deteriorating, which I've noted in every report for the last—"

"I know, Mick."

A deep breath, then: "The spillway is in the preliminary stages of failure. But the dam will hold."

"It's still raining, Mick."

"Let it keep raining."

"Say that again?"

"We've got days before the reservoir tops the dam, even if the rain keeps coming. By then I'll have a fix." Mick paused, then said, "Or, screw it, Ed, do what you want to do. Order an evacuation, get the TV helicopters in the air, and then go on camera explaining why we've ignored a decade's worth of site inspections. Fix it in silence or in front of an audience. That's not my call. That's yours."

Fix it in silence or in front of an audience.

Ed said, "I'll head your way. I'll tell Tabor and the rest to stand down tonight. By morning, though, I need to be ready to have somebody go on camera and say this is a nonstory." He swallowed. "Or tell them we're ordering an evacuation."

"By tomorrow you won't need to make a statement."

"That confident, eh?"

"Yes. By tomorrow, it'll speak for itself. But it's your call. If you want to get out in front of this . . ."

"Not if there's time. I'll head your way, and I'll keep everyone else quiet until tomorrow."

"Perfect."

"You understand the trust I'm putting in you right now?"

"If you've got a better engineer, send him up here."

It was fascinating how different Mick Fleming could sound when you touched a nerve. But after nearly two decades of working with him, Ed knew there was no better engineer.

"It'll just be me," he said. "Where do you want me?"

"The gatehouse."

"You'll still be there?"

"I'm not leaving until it's done," Mick Fleming said.

Ed felt better, hearing that.

44

The Torrance County Coroner's Office completed a successful identification of the corpse that had been tugged free from the waters below the Chilewaukee Reservoir in under four hours.

That was possible when a detective could tell you who the subject was and what dentist she'd used.

Molly Mathers had never missed a dental checkup. That habit expedited identification.

That, Gillian thought, was a hell of an endorsement for dental hygiene. She sat in her car and laughed, imagining the commercials that could be made pushing this unique benefit. She should drop by the dentist's office, let him know how impressed she was. She laughed harder, sitting there in the cold car in the parking lot of her department headquarters in Kingston while the rain sheeted down. Eventually, she realized she was crying, too. Then the laughter stopped and it was just the tears.

And the rain.

She'd never been much of a crier. After all, what good did it do for you, as her grandmother had asked so many times? It was better to be stoic. Such a familiar word, always heard in her grandmother's voice.

Be stoic, dear. The Mathers women are known for that. We've always been stronger than our husbands, but don't tell anyone. They're sensitive little creatures.

Playful talk, teasing talk, in a warm, safe house. Warm and bright, until you were sent to school.

Then it was different, yes. But outside of that damned bookcase door it hadn't been so bad at all. Gillian's grandmother, the woman whose teeth she'd just had examined in a morgue, had been kind and smart and strong. Patient.

The coroner's office hadn't listed an official cause of death yet, but Gillian could. The death certificate should read: "Molly Mathers, Dead of Indoctrination, October 20, 2000."

All her life, her family had hammered those wild stories into her head. Legends older than any of them, legends older than the family's existence in the region, dark tales that had chased early settlers from Ireland and Scotland. She didn't know all of the lineage, but she had her guesses. Some stories of the Druids, which she'd first encountered in a college history course, felt familiar. Then there were the old curse myths, which made their way across the Atlantic with the Gypsies, a persecuted people over there who'd remained persecuted here. And, of course, there was the Native mythology. The American Indian tribes of upstate New York were not without their share of stories about death and demons, spirits and sacrifices. They would hunt and fish in what became the Galesburg area of the Catskills, but they didn't stay there for long. They took their bounty—and their folklore—from the place and left. They didn't settle there in the way the Europeans later did, families with names like Wallace and Mathers.

And none of that matters, Gillian told herself. *You know this because you were saved from that house. Because Dad finally came back for you and, unlike your poor grandmother, you didn't endure decades of it. You remember it, but it never had the chance to infect you.*

Hooks and lines and chains. A black silk bag over the head. A step into what had to feel like terrible, infinite space.

Gillian put her hands to her eyes again, but there were no tears this time. She just sat there with her head in her hands. She'd intended to go into work, talk this through with her superiors. She'd intended to be a cool, distanced pro. Stoic.

She didn't get out of the car, though. Instead, she dialed her father's number. Somewhere on the island of Manhattan, a place that seemed impossibly far away right now, Deshawn Ryan's phone rang and went to voicemail. Gillian spoke carefully. She didn't want to let her voice break, and she certainly didn't want him to hear any tears.

"Hi, Dad. It's me. Listen, um . . . so we had a case today, I guess it was my case really, or at least mine for now, I have the lead on it, and . . ." *Stop babbling. Get to the point. Say it, damn it. Ask him.*

"Dad, I need to talk to you about my family. The Mathers side. We've just floated along without ever discussing . . . well, anything. That has to stop. Because I just watched divers pull my grandmother's body out of the water, and she had hooks and lines and chain on her, and a bag to cover her eyes, and this didn't surprise me. But I don't know whether it surprises you. I don't know whether anything surprises you, or if everything does. It's time to talk about that. I need to know what you understood about that house and what they were teaching me. It scared you; I'm sure of that. I'd draw the wrong picture, and it would *terrify* you. I need to know why. Some strange shit is happening up here, and it's time to end the silence." She paused. "I don't know if it will help, but I do know that it's time to end the silence."

She ran a hand over her face and through her hair. Took a deep breath, gathering herself.

"I love you, Dad. You know that. I always have, always will. But we've got to talk about things someday. I think today is that day. Give me a call when you can. I love you."

She disconnected. Looked through the rain-washed windshield at the low brick building and thought of all the colleagues inside who would have questions. *It was* your *grandmother? I didn't even know you had family up here. How long was she missing? Why wasn't it reported? Why were there chains and hooks, and just what exactly was wrong with your family?*

She started the engine, backed out, and drove away.

45

Deshawn got a break before embarking on his double shift, but he stayed belowground. Sat with his back against the cool stone of the freshly cut stretch of tunnel, watched the Mole chisel through rock, and sipped a bottle of water. He was tired and sore but actually feeling more energized for the extra hours than he had been for the first shift. His hangover had faded, sweated out as the day wore on. It was also nice to see the rest of the crew turn over, to watch the men who'd seen him scream in the face of the oncoming car make their exit. The story would circulate, but for a few hours, at least, he'd be working among men who weren't exchanging whispers about him.

He'd grown tolerant of the ghosts, too. There were more of them now, and they stayed in view longer, and he supposed that should have increased the terror, but it didn't. He just kept his head down and passed below them or beside them, never reacting. So long as you avoided eye contact, they wouldn't speak.

All of these things were reassuring, but the real source of his renewed energy was from the knowledge that this would be his last shift as a sandhog.

He was sure of it now. He was beginning to break, and things like that didn't always happen slowly. Sometimes, particularly down in the tunnels, it happened fast. He'd hardly be the first sandhog to start seeing things down here; encounters with phantoms probably went back to the first dig on the Croton Aqueduct, nearly two centuries earlier. They weren't stories that would've been quoted in newspapers, but they were there. They'd been told at old taverns along the Hudson and in tent camps upstate. Anyone who'd spent enough time belowground had heard a ghost story or two.

There were no rules for how you treated a man who claimed to have had such an experience, and Deshawn had never heard of management needing to get involved, although surely that had happened. A few sandhogs had visited Bellevue over the years for psychiatric care. Surely one of them must have seen something down here. Maybe the very ghost that Deshawn had seen. Who knew? All he was certain of was that he wanted to leave on his own terms. Today would put a dent in his reputation, but it would be small and quickly forgotten.

He'd been muttering about retirement for long enough that few would be surprised. There'd be a party for him, but that would be at a bar at street level, not down here in the dim light and the dust with the whirring steel blades of the Mole. He'd do fine at the party, have a few beers and tell a few jokes and maybe even turn his screaming episode into one of the jokes. Take ownership of the story. Yes, that was a fine idea. He could—

"Mr. Ryan?"

The voice floated down from above him. That was trouble, because there was nothing above him. He was alone in the quiet cool of the tunnel while the others worked a good fifty yards ahead. The Mole had stopped, which always brought a sense of solitude.

"Mr. Ryan?"

Deshawn didn't look up. The voice from above was impossible. He knew that, and so he would not look. He kept his eyes on his water bottle while he unscrewed the lid and took a sip. Rinsed his mouth out and spit. He would not look up, and eventually the ghost would be gone, and Deshawn would go about his work again. His last shift of work.

"*Mr. Ryan.*" This time the voice had an added bite to it, and then something moved in Deshawn's peripheral vision. Still he didn't turn.

He didn't have to. The ghost came for him.

It was the man in the high rubber boots and the suit jacket with the vest. The same man who'd stood in front of the railcar, speaking to Deshawn about pressure and water, asking if he thought anyone would remember him. He crouched down, looking right into Deshawn's face.

"Mr. Ryan, I'm afraid we can't continue with this approach," the man said. "I understand you'd rather work alone and not have to acknowledge the rest of your crew, and that's usually fine, because we can be patient. You'll join us when you're ready. But it's not possible today. There's trouble."

The rest of your crew. What did that mean? The rest of the ghosts, the ones who watched him from the old timbers that didn't exist down here? The gaunt-faced, grimy, weary men who seemed to be waiting on something or someone?

Were they waiting on Deshawn? *You'll join us when you're ready.*

"You're not real," Deshawn whispered.

That earned a pitying smile. "You'll need to listen to me today," the man said. "You'll need to accept your circumstances."

Deshawn looked from the man to the Mole, remembering the time a decade ago when a sandhog named Darryl Duncan had a premonition of something falling. Darryl just stopped in his tracks, refused to walk forward. It was only thirty seconds later that a chain snapped and two tons of rock fell from the muck cart just in front of him.

I had a feeling, that's all, he'd said. He never talked of it again, and people didn't push too hard. A thing like that? Nobody wanted to question it. They just hoped whatever voice whispered in Darryl Duncan's ear that day would whisper in theirs, too, when the time was right.

So maybe this was good. Maybe Deshawn wasn't losing his mind down here but rather seeing something that could help. The Mole was stopped, it was cooling, but maybe there was something wrong with—

"Not down there," the man told him, shifting back into Deshawn's field of vision, shuffling in his crouched stance like a catcher moving to take a pitch outside. His pale face with its close-cropped mustache was right before Deshawn's eyes.

"Upstream," he said. "We're hearing there's real trouble there."

Deshawn looked in all directions. Left, right, and over the man's shoulder. When he was sure they were alone, nobody watching or listening, he whispered back.

"Who are you?"

"We're just like you," the man said. "You'd know some of us. The newer guard, maybe, but not the old guard. You'd remember some names, though."

"You mean . . . you died down here?" Deshawn looked past him again, but this time up to where the impassive men in antiquated clothes sat or stood on timber beams staring down at him, waiting.

"That's right."

"But . . . there are so many of you."

"And many more behind us. A man a mile, Mr. Ryan."

A man a mile. How many times had Deshawn heard that quote? It was the average death toll for sandhogs in the water tunnels. For each mile carved to quench New York, at least one man had died. And that was just the sandhogs. That didn't count the camps upstate, either. How many had been killed in the reservoir constructions? Deshawn doubted that anyone had an accurate tally. There were more than a dozen lakes involved and construction spanning more than a century. The aqueducts and reservoirs had been built largely by immigrants or people who ventured into the mountains just for the jobs, transient laborers whose deaths might never have made the official record.

"You're all trapped?" Deshawn said. His breath left a trail of steam in the cool air of the tunnel.

"Not exactly," the ghost answered. No steam chased his breath into the air. "It's a complex system, Mr. Ryan."

A complex system. That phrase had been uttered by every politician in the city or state over the past fifty years. Probably longer. And it was true. The Mole up there, a feat of engineering in its own right, was really such a small component of the whole.

The ghost was watching him intently, and Deshawn finally realized that he wasn't talking about the water. Or at least not in the way Deshawn was used to thinking about it. The complex system the ghost was referring to was a different thing entirely.

The dead worked on. That was what he meant.

A complex system indeed.

Deshawn didn't want to join them. He didn't want to die, but he damn sure didn't want to—

"Am I dead?" he asked, the thought jarring but not implausible. Maybe it was the only thing that made sense, in fact.

"Not yet," the pale man told him.

Down the tunnel, the Mole started up again. The sound of it was enormous, but Deshawn didn't even glance in that direction.

"I don't want to go with you," Deshawn told him. He glanced up at the men on the timbers. Some sitting, others standing. All of them staring down at Deshawn.

"I don't want you to go with me, either, Mr. Ryan. Where you're needed, I can't go. Not like you can."

"Where?" Deshawn whispered.

"You know where."

And he did, too. Somehow he'd always known. The past didn't forget, and it didn't forgive. Eventually the past came calling.

"The Chilewaukee," he said, his whisper scarcely audible against the roar of the Mole's chiseling blades.

"They need help in Galesburg. Someone who can still move aboveground. Someone like you."

"Why me?"

"Because you believe. We don't have many like you. People who remember and believe."

Deshawn parted his lips to deny that, but he couldn't. Again, the man was right. Deshawn had been scared of the place because he believed what he'd been told about it.

"I go to the lake? What then?"

"Not the lake. The tunnels."

Deshawn was confused. The tunnels at the Chilewaukee had never been finished. They'd been abandoned during World War II. Abandoned, Kelly Mathers had once told him, after the schoolhouse fire and the murders.

"There are no tunnels," Deshawn said. "They gave up on them. Generations ago."

The pale man leaned closer still. So close that Deshawn could feel his breath when he spoke again. It was cold air and came without any power, like a gust of winter wind seeping through an uninsulated wall.

"Not everyone gave up on them," he said. "You know that."

Up near the Mole, someone shouted Deshawn's name. Deshawn didn't look. The pale man was watching, and Deshawn didn't feel that it was safe to turn away.

"Yes," Deshawn said softly. "I know that. But what do I do?"

"You go to where the tunnels were supposed to emerge. Where the ruins wait for completion. You know the spot."

He did. His daughter's mother had taken him there once. There was a discharge chamber at the base of a mountain and just above a cold-water creek, built with the expectation of siphoning millions of gallons of water out of the tunnels and down that creek, into the Ashokan, and then into the city. The never-used chamber was dry except for the rainwater it trapped, and the stacked stone walls were cracked and crumbling, with ivy growing through the crevices. It had seemed like an eerie archaeological mystery by the time Deshawn saw it.

Kelly had taken him there. *My special place,* she called it. They brought a picnic lunch and a bottle of champagne. They skipped stones across flat pools of trapped water. The sun went down early, blocked by the peak of Maiden Mountain. On the other side of the mountain, out of sight, the Chill sat in all of its untapped majesty.

Deshawn hadn't liked the feel of that spot. The vines shifted in the breeze and made him think of snakes and the light faded too soon and the place seemed forgotten in not just a sad way but a dangerous way. As if it hadn't been abandoned by intent but by mistake.

"I don't understand," Deshawn whispered. "I can find the spot, but then what? It's useless. It's a forgotten and useless place."

The pale man looked troubled, as if he'd misjudged Deshawn.

"*They* can make use of it," he said. "You know that. You believe that."

Old stories drifting back. Kelly's voice in his ear. Deshawn closing his eyes because he couldn't close his ears, and he didn't want to see her face while she whispered her sincere beliefs in a ludicrous legend, a campfire story gone terribly wrong. Kelly thought she could pass through the mountain once she was back in Galesburg. Kelly thought almost anything at all was possible down there.

"You think I'll see them?" Deshawn asked, his throat dry, voice cracking.

"If you do, you've got to stop them. You know that. You've got to stop them from breaking through. If that group makes it downstream, we all have to work. Do you remember? We will have no choice, then. They'll carry a different force with them, and it won't be one we can resist. Not in that water. Not with them."

"Deshawn! Yo, Ryan! Wake up, brother!"

Footsteps coming. Reality closing in. Time running out. Deshawn asked, "Down here . . . are we safe? Is the city safe?"

"That's up to you," the pale man said, and then he straightened and stepped back. "But you'd best hurry, Mr. Ryan. I'm sure of that."

46

The rain stopped just before sunset.

It had fallen almost without pause since daybreak and had fallen every day for two weeks. Thirty minutes before the night claimed Torrance County, gray clouds lifted in the west, and a red-tinted band pushed up as if sent forth from the mountains themselves. As the clouds thinned, the band widened, the glow deepening, as if the sun were rising rather than setting. The wind swung from north to northwest, and its knife-edge gusts dulled into a mild, fresh breath scented with fallen leaves and clean water.

In town, people seemed hesitant to trust it. Umbrellas were closed but not left behind. Rain jackets were unzipped and hoods lowered, but the jackets remained on.

The gray clouds kept thinning, and the crimson glow kept spreading. In the first minutes after the rain stopped, the earth steamed, a fine mist rising from saturated ground. Then the strengthening wind blew it aside, the red sunlight brightened, and everything was left looking cleaner, as if freshly rinsed.

At the courthouse on the square in downtown Torrance, a weary judge named Gena Lane finished a day of custody dispute hearings and walked out of the building with her head down, hurrying toward her car. The sunset stopped her. Gena stood and admired it, then moved to one of the benches on the lawn beside the Revolutionary-era cannon, brushed water off the wood, and sat down to breathe in the beauty of her town for a few minutes before going home.

At the Hard Truth Brewery just two blocks away, a bar manager named Jenn Strawn stepped outside to take a selfie. She uploaded it to Instagram with the caption OMG THAT'S THE SUN, I FORGOT IT EXISTED, #HARDTRUTH, and then turned to go back inside. Two regulars stepped out, Mike and Christine, and they laughed over the photo with her and told her that it was actually supposed to warm up overnight, a welcome burst of Indian summer.

"Could be porch weather," Mike said.

Mike had always had a knack for reading the weather, having been a boat captain at one point, so soon Jenn was wiping down the iron tables on the patio and a busboy was bringing out chairs. If Hard Truth could get one last porch night in this season, it would be a gift.

One block west of the brewery, a barber named Eric Dullmeyer flipped his sign from OPEN to CLOSED, used his scissors to cut a cigar, and then stepped onto the sidewalk to smoke it. He waved at a woman named Chelsea who jogged by, dodging puddles.

"Can't waste this weather," she said, and he smiled and agreed and then watched her run past. He sighed. What a beautiful sight it was, watching Chelsea jog. She was too fast, though, and gone too soon.

Eric lit the cigar, still smiling.

On the divided highway just outside of town, Tyler Riggins cracked his window as he drove in pursuit of happy-hour drink prices and boneless buffalo wings. After feeling the warming air, he put the window all the way down and hung his over-muscled arm out of the truck. He cranked the stereo louder. Shooter Jennings howled with delight.

At the Buffalo Wild Wings, a DEP maintenance worker named Dave Green was already ahead of Tyler, halfway through a plate of wings and a Genesee Cream Ale. Dave saw the sun but he didn't care. The day had already been a gift for him. He'd expected to be at work, but that morning Arthur Brady called to tell him he didn't have to come in. There was some inspector down from Albany, and Arthur always wanted to deal with the inspections himself.

That was just fine. Dave wanted to deal with the chicken wings.

———

Two miles northwest, in the Pleasant Ridge subdivision in the hills outside of town, a trio of thirteen-year-old boys watching *Stranger Things* for the third time in two weeks, turned the TV off, and hauled their bikes out. There wasn't much time left before darkness and dinner, and they didn't want to waste any of it. Too many daylight hours had been washed out by rain lately.

———

At a house on an isolated ten-acre parcel northwest of them, a man named Jeff Stone eyed the dry skies from his bathroom window while he stood beside his shower, waiting for the water heater to warm up. He shut off the water, dressed again, and went outside to split firewood. It had been days since he'd had the chance without rain.

———

One mile northwest of Jeff Stone's house, Ed Cochran pulled into the parking lot below the Chilewaukee Reservoir dam, exhausted from the drive but grateful for the sudden cessation of the rain. From the time he left the city until the time he crossed the Torrance County line, the downpour hadn't stopped. Now, finally, a reprieve.

He pulled in beside a Ford Explorer with police lights and a sheriff's decal. This, Ed thought, was a good sign. The sheriff was here, which meant the situation at the dam was being taken seriously. Between that and the dry skies, he felt hopeful. All he needed was a little time to sort this out.

Ed paused beside his car and stared at the spillway. Water was surging over it, roaring down the old stone face, but he'd seen deteriorating spillways before, and he'd seen them fixed before. And this one was at the Chilewaukee, a surplus reservoir, not technically part of his city's sacred supply. All things told, the situation could be one hell of a lot worse.

He was halfway up the steps to the gatehouse when he heard the dam groan.

He stopped with his hand on the railing and cocked his head. There was a rumbling sound, like falling rocks, and he instinctively looked back toward the spillway.

The water flowed over it, and there was no sign of any loose rock.

Then the groan came again—came from somewhere just below his feet but deep, deep within the earth. It sounded like a heavy old door being pushed open against protesting hinges.

He took three more steps before the earth shuddered. The force was enough to make him grasp the railing again. The railing was shaking, too.

He was there, standing on the steps outside of the gatehouse, when the Chilewaukee Dam burst.

He was the first to die, and when the water took him, he was still clutching the railing.

47

Jeff Stone was the next to die. He was running his hydraulic log splitter when he heard a rumble, and at first he thought it was from the equipment. He stepped back and cocked his head and looked down at the trusty Champion splitter, which had never failed him before, and which brought twenty-seven tons of hydraulic power to its task. He assumed the sound was coming from the machinery. Then the rumble turned to a roar, and Jeff turned away from the splitter and faced the twelve *million* tons of hydraulic pressure headed his way from the Chilewaukee.

He heard the water long before he saw it, and he never moved. He was frozen in place, staring uphill, watching as the old-growth trees along either side of Cresap Creek swung back and forth and then vanished like so many blades of grass ahead of a mower. His first thought was of a tornado; his last thought, as the roar closed in with what seemed like the snarl of some living thing, was of a monster.

Then his house exploded, the massive trusses snapping like dry kindling, and Jeff was under the water.

The *Stranger Things* fanboys were still on their bikes when the water reached Pleasant Ridge. One of them heard the roar and thought of the Demogorgon, the fantastical creature who terrified Hawkins, Indiana, in the show. *I was not wrong,* he thought, listening to the rising growl and watching the trees and telephone poles snap. *It was real after all.*

Then Pleasant Ridge was gone.

Inside Buffalo Wild Wings, Dave Green paused with his Genesee at his lips and stayed on his barstool while others rushed to the window to see what was happening. There was shouting and screaming and he heard the word *tornado*.

"Not a tornado," Dave said. "That's the dam."

No one heard him.

He still had his beer in hand when he went.

One block away, Tyler Riggins was driving with the windows down and Shooter Jennings singing. Tyler saw the wall of debris coming straight down the county highway at him, like land scoured by a bulldozer and pushed ahead.

The sheared telephone pole that punctured first his windshield and then his chest was still dry.

The water came behind it.

There were two overpasses above the highway just outside of town. They caught much of the debris driven ahead of the water. The first overpass collapsed, but it tumbled into the second, and the pile of stone and the logjam of trees, utility poles, houses, and corpses served to form a temporary, impromptu dam.

The water didn't care, though. The water rushed alongside, beneath, and over the obstruction. The water churned on downhill, as gravity demanded it must.

Then the water came to Torrance.

Eric Dullmeyer was still outside his barbershop, relighting his cigar, when he heard the oncoming sound, low and forceful as a jet engine, and felt the ground tremble beneath his feet. He turned toward the noise with absolute confidence and certainty that he knew the source.

"Earthquake!" he shouted.

Then he saw the deluge.

For a moment it was incomprehensible; it simply didn't fit the landscape. This was a wave, a great arcing wave that belonged to an ocean, not a mountain. The top of the wave was above the three-story house with the high turrets that stood across from his shop. So much water, coming so fast.

He wondered if Chelsea could outrun it.

Then he disappeared into it.

———

At the Hard Truth Brewery, Jenn Strawn carried a tray of Hurricane Lagers to the three diners outside. When she heard the roar of water, she thought it must be another rainstorm blowing in. *Captain Mike is an idiot,* she thought; *this isn't porch weather at all.*

The four on the porch died first, but it wouldn't have mattered if they'd remained indoors: the brick building collapsed on the crowd inside.

———

Judge Gena Lane was still on the courthouse lawn, seated on the bench, facing the sunset. She turned to the north when the sound came. Her attention fixed on the roof of a barn, and the woman riding it like a raft. The roof still had its framing intact, the classic New England pitch of it evident even as it rode the water, but whatever walls had once supported it were long gone.

The woman was on a barn roof, but there was no barn, and she was floating down Main Street. It was real and impossible, both at the same time.

The woman was screaming. Gena could see that but not hear it. The roar of the flood was too loud.

Gena never rose. She just sat there and watched the woman on the floating roof screaming those silent screams. Watched in awe as the water swept toward her and then over her.

The Torrance town square was under water then, waves lapping against the courthouse roof.

48

The most remarkable part of the event, Mick Fleming decided as he panned the scene with binoculars stolen from Arthur Brady, was how much of the dam actually held.

He'd expected a total failure. He'd expected the thing to *burst*, for the lake to empty in a single ferocious surge.

But the breach, when it happened, didn't trigger a complete collapse.

Oh, it certainly looked like that at first—looked like it and felt like it and sounded like it. The destruction was both breathtakingly savage and remarkably small against the landscape. It was as if the mountains had released a single snarl and snap that barely hinted at the real power of nature, and now all that remained of the evidence was the curled lip of a sleeping dog.

Downstream, though, it would not feel that way. Downstream, no one would look up into the mountains and think it had been only a warning snarl. The Chilewaukee Reservoir had surged down the floodplain and into Torrance, emptied into the streets, into living rooms, into gasping mouths searching for a last breath that would never come.

They had no idea that it had been only a taste.

Mick was sitting on a high bluff behind the lake, well out of reach of the devastation. He could see the swath of downed trees and overturned soil, which made the valley look as if it had been freshly tilled. And, he supposed, that's exactly what had happened.

The shock was how much water remained behind the dam.

The force of the water didn't burst the dam but split it, pushing it to each side. The earthen portions squeezed against the mountain, seeming almost to *tighten* on those sides. Because so much of the structure held, the water kept storming out through the initial split, carving the dam open in a V-shaped wound, but gradually the V cut tapered to an end, and the dam held the rest back. It had been a catastrophic failure but not a total collapse.

Fascinating.

Granted, the creek bed below the lake was different now. It actually looked more like a sea than a creek, with whitecaps churning on coffee-colored water. Mick could only guess what the initial surge had looked like when it swept into Torrance. The waves might have been twenty feet high. Roads turned to rivers. Houses obliterated. It would look a good deal like Houston or New Orleans after their record floods, or the way much of the Midwest had looked for the better part of a spring, but it would have happened so much faster than any of those.

"Told you so," Mick said softly, and laughed. Then he turned his attention back to the lake.

He glassed over the water that was still held back by the dam and tried to calculate how much of the reservoir had been released downstream. It was impossible to make an accurate guess, but he put it at no more than fifty percent. The dam was 235 feet high, and the V-shaped gash in its face extended perhaps 100 feet down. Wider at the top, of course, which had allowed for the initial surge of staggering power.

So much more remained, though.

"This was enough," Mick said. "They didn't want more blood than they needed, is that the idea?"

Beside him, Anders Wallace shifted and leaned his forearms on his knees and said, "Just watch, sir. Just continue to watch."

So they did. It wasn't long before the Galesburg crew emerged.

They came up out of the wreckage where once the gatehouse had been. They climbed carefully to the top of what remained of the dam, using their picks and shovels to gain purchase on the treacherous slope. Just as they reached the crest, a helicopter flew in low.

The crew didn't seem distressed by the helicopter. The updraft whipped a woman's dress around her legs, and one of the men shielded his eyes and gave a curious glance, but there was no real concern. Mick's grandfather, the once-famous Jeremiah Fleming, never even looked at the sky. He was staring downstream. Studying the results of his labors. How many years had he been working toward this moment? Mick hoped he was pleased.

Jeremiah Fleming didn't look downstream for long. If he found the flood damage impressive, he didn't show it. He simply lifted his pick and walked across the rest of the dam. The others followed. They didn't attempt to leave the dam but merely started down the opposite side, heading toward what remained of the reservoir. Mick studied them with confusion.

"What's happening?"

Anders Wallace didn't answer.

"Why are they going back to the water? They're free to go now. Wasn't that the point? To release them?"

Anders Wallace said, "Perhaps not, sir."

As Mick watched the Galesburg crew walk down the side of the dam facing the reservoir, he saw the ancient concrete structures that they were heading toward: the intake chambers. Unused and largely forgotten now, the intake chambers were entrances to miles of meaningless tunnels. They were usually well beneath the surface, but the dam failure had lowered the water and redistributed it, draining it away from the intake chambers until their doors became visible. They'd been sealed with concrete decades ago and so they were now nothing more than indentations with high stone arches, cosmetic but not functional, a forgotten relic of antiquated ambitions.

Suddenly—and finally—Mick understood.

"They're going to open the tunnels."

Anders Wallace didn't confirm or deny. He didn't need to.

Mick panned his binoculars from the intake chambers to the wounded dam and back across the surface of the reservoir. Still plenty of water in there.

I had the goal wrong, he realized. *They don't want to stop the job. They want to finish it.*

Galesburg had been drowned and forgotten. There were grievances to address, and the responsible parties were not in Torrance.

They were in New York.

"I get it," he said, and he found himself smiling again. "Anders, I get it."

Anders Wallace didn't say a word. He just nodded. But he was smiling, too.

PART FIVE

49

Gillian was on her way back to Torrance from Kingston when her radio blazed to life with the reports.

There were many voices, some controlled, some hysterical, and their words flowed over and around one another, but one description remained.

The dam has failed. The dam has failed. The dam at the Chilewaukee has failed.

She pulled over. Sat with her head back against the headrest, staring at the fading crimson band of sunset, listening to reports come in.

All units were needed. Substantial loss of life expected. Catastrophic damage. Repeat, all units needed.

A truck with white flashers roared by, headed toward Torrance. A volunteer firefighter. She watched him speed toward the disaster scene and forced herself to reach for the gearshift. She had her hand wrapped around it but hadn't yet gotten it out of park when her phone rang. She registered the sound numbly, looking over and expecting to see DISPATCH.

It was her father.

She punched the button on the steering wheel to accept the call.

"I'm okay," she said. "I'm alive."

"What?" her father said.

"I was above it."

A pause. She could hear the sounds of the city around him. Voices and horns, a street vendor, someone shouting in Spanish, the blare of a siren.

"I was above the dam," she said. "I was driving back from Kingston, so I wasn't anywhere near the floodplain."

"What are you talking . . ." He let his words trail off, and when he spoke again his voice was as soft and reverent as if he were offering a prayer. "It broke? At the Chilewaukee?"

"Yes. Isn't that why you were calling?" She shook her head. "No. You're calling me back because of the message I left."

"Actually, neither. I'm calling to tell you I'm coming up there. I need to . . . I think I need to be up there. But . . . you say it already broke?"

Gillian frowned, staring at the steering wheel as if her father could see her. "*Already?*"

"I thought I was . . ." He stopped, cleared his throat, and then said, "It's been a strange day down here."

"Strange up here, too."

"Yeah."

"I need to go," she said. "I need to go help."

"Me too. Be safe, hon. I'll be there soon. We'll talk then."

"You don't need to be here, Dad. You shouldn't be."

"I think you're wrong about that," he said. "I'm on my way."

She didn't want him here, in the danger zone, but she didn't want to tell him not to come, either. Because he was right. For some reason she did not fully understand, he needed to be here.

"Did you know?" she asked. "Did you know that it was going to break?"

"No. But . . ." He hesitated, then repeated, "It has been a strange day."

"Right." She wet her lips. "They pulled grandma's body out of the water this morning."

"I got your message."

Another vehicle roared by her. This one was a civilian car, an SUV running with hazard lights flashing. It was towing a bass boat. At first she thought that was foolish, some guy forgetting to unhitch his trailer before he went tear-assing toward trouble, and then she realized it was no mistake. *It is going to be that bad, isn't it? We will need boats.*

"I really have to go," she said. "I've got to go do my job."

"Be safe," her father said. "I love you, Gillian."

"I love you, too," she said. Then she blurted the question she didn't dare consider, the crazy question: "Dad, is this my family's fault? Were all of the things I learned real?"

He didn't respond right away. Finally he said, "I'm not sure."

It was a better answer than if he'd issued a flat denial or told her not to talk like that, think like that. At least he was admitting that he could consider the truth in all those old stories. All those years of silence were rupturing.

Too bad the dam had gone first.

"Good luck, baby," he said. "I love you. I'll see you soon."

"Drive safe," Gillian said. "Love you, too."

She disconnected the call, turned the siren on, and pulled onto the road, headed for Torrance. Or whatever was left of it.

50

Aaron woke to the sound of rattling glass. He was still on his bed, boots still on. He was facing the nightstand, and an empty glass on it was rattling. No, more than the glass. The nightstand was, too. The whole house.

He swung his feet down. As soon as he was upright, the rattling and shaking stopped. But there was still a sound . . . some dull, distant roar, like a train.

He looked out the window. The rain had stopped. There was a pale pink glow from the last of the sun. The puddles in the yard sparkled. A peaceful scene.

Except for that sound.

"Dad?" he called.

No answer.

He left the bedroom and walked downstairs. Outside, the strange rumbling persisted. No trains ran through Torrance County except for an old tourist line in the summer, eight miles of a slow-chugging locomotive while a tour guide offered local history and bad puns over a loudspeaker. That train was shut down after Labor Day.

What the hell am I hearing, then?

He walked onto the porch. There he could pinpoint the source of the noise better. It was to his right, down in the valley. Down closer to . . .

"No," he said aloud.

The churning sound continued, as if to mock him. *Yes,* it said, *yes, yes, yes.*

The dam had broken.

He didn't want to believe it, but he knew better. It was the reason they lived here, no matter what excuses his father offered for being so far out of town. Steve Ellsworth, like his father and like his grandfather, had always wanted to live above the Chilewaukee Dam.

There was a police scanner on the kitchen counter. It was an old thing that had been in the house for as long as Aaron could remember, and while it couldn't pick up the more secure bands, it would pick up emergency alerts. He went back inside, pressed the power button, and let the radio scan.

It didn't take long to find confirmation. The dam had broken.

He listened with a sense of inevitability rather than surprise. It all felt right, somehow. His swim, the madness with Mick Fleming, the corpse in the Dead Waters that had turned out to be Gillian's grandmother—all of it seemed to fit naturally together with this news. All of it seemed part of a story that had been in motion long before Aaron came along. The rain belonged with the story, too. The idea that it was interconnected sounded impossible, but Aaron Ellsworth was long past the point of believing anything was impossible.

Each CB band was urging for help in the disaster zone from anyone who was physically able to assist.

Then go help.

It was that simple, and yet he was scared of what he'd see, what he'd be asked to do, and whether he could do it.

He called his father first. Straight to voicemail again. The sheriff's direct dispatch line was busy. Overloaded. For the first time he felt uneasy about his dad. So much of the day had passed without contact. But this wasn't the sort of situation where Steve Ellsworth would pause to take a phone call, either.

I'll go help, and I'll run into him down there. I'll run into him, and he'll see me doing the right thing. That will mean something to him on an awful day.

He grabbed his jacket from the peg on the kitchen wall, then hesitated and hung it back up. He didn't have his Coast Guard active duty status anymore, but he still had his equipment.

He went upstairs and opened his closet. His waterproof duffel bag lay on the floor. His old uniforms hung above it: dress uniform and the flight suit, one designed for formality, the other for function, for real work. He pulled the bag out. Unzipped it and checked the contents, thinking, *Be meticulous,* because that was part of the drill when you were an emergency operator. Rescue swimmers were gearheads. They took good care of their equipment, and they double-checked it. They didn't forget anything. A meticulous rescue swimmer saved lives. An adrenaline jockey who forgot to check his gear before rolling out might get people killed.

Inside the bag was all the equipment he'd once expected to use in the harsh oceans that pounded the coasts of Alaska or Maine. An abrasion-resistant dry suit, helmet, mask, fins, snorkel. A throw bag and throw rope. An emergency satellite beacon. Gloves. Chemical lights and a strobe light and a headlamp. A J-hook knife and a scabbard knife. Smoke flares. Waterproof radio. GPS.

He'd spent hours with this gear, in and out of the water. Cleaning it, lubricating it, checking every seam, every blade edge. Waiting for training to become reality, the only questions being when it would happen, and where.

Listen to the water.

He removed the radio, clipped that onto his belt, then zipped the bag and slung it over his shoulder. He was ready to leave, but something felt wrong. Off. He looked at the rescue swimmer's radio clipped to his belt. Looked at his jeans and flannel shirt. Then looked in the closet again.

You don't deserve it, he thought, *and it's probably a crime to put it on.*

Maybe it was, but the flight suit was the right thing for this moment, a Gore-Tex and Nomex blend of water and abrasion resistance. Only an idiot would go down to a cold-water flood zone wearing jeans and flannel.

He undressed quickly and pulled on the synthetic base layer that hung beside the flight suit. Then he pulled the lightweight olive-colored uniform on over it. He zipped it up, picked up his gear bag, and left the house.

51

The first official to arrive at the Chill was a dam operator named Phil Peden. He'd worked at the Ashokan Reservoir for a decade but had only been at the Chill for two years, working as second-in-command to Arthur Brady, and targeted as Arthur's eventual replacement.

He'd been alerted to the disaster by his cell phone. Not a call, but a long, blaring tone. It was an alert courtesy of a free weather app, and the dire message was delivered almost nonchalantly.

All residents in the floodplain of the Chilewaukee Reservoir in Torrance, NY, are to evacuate immediately.

Phil hadn't believed it.

Then his radio began to go off. Desperate calls, panicked voices. He ran to his truck with his phone still in hand, the bleating tone telling him there was trouble, and once outdoors he thought he could hear the trouble, the far-off sound of something mighty moving, like a beast in the woods.

What he didn't hear, though, bothered him more.

He should have been hearing sirens. Up and down the Cresap Creek valley, emergency sirens should sound if there was even the *threat* of a structural failure. The dam was equipped with sensors, the sensors were linked to the sirens, and all of this existed to give people time to flee. Phil had overseen the siren system test himself just two months before. The system worked. The sensors read stress load, and they triggered the alarms. Why hadn't they gone off?

By the time he was on the road, there were sirens, but still not the right ones. These belonged to police cars and ambulances, and they were all headed down the valley, toward town.

He drove in the opposite direction. He lived above the dam. He didn't know anyone who worked at the dam and lived below it. Phil had gone through too many emergency planning meetings to sleep untroubled in the valley below the Chill.

The meetings served him well now, though, because he remembered the winding route that led to the dam without taking him through the floodplain. It was usually an extra ten minutes but he made it in five, coming in with smoking tires on the eastern side of the reservoir, facing the dam.

Or what should have been the dam.

The worst damage was to the spillway, the very part of the structure that was designed to ensure its survival. The beautiful old stone was ripped open as if by some incredible lightning strike, a blackened tear, water streaming out like blood.

This, he realized, was nothing compared to what it would have looked like in the moment of the breach. The real wave was gone from here, running somewhere down the valley, through the town, and still going. Chasing gravity.

He stepped out. His eyes were fixated on the spillway and his mind was still on the problem of the sirens.

They would have gone off. They must have gone off.

"Can you call for a helicopter?"

The voice startled him, and he whirled to find himself facing a thin man in a DEP rain jacket.

"We're going to need a helicopter," the man said.

"Who are you?"

"Mick Fleming. I was . . ." He stopped, looked from Phil to the dam, and then waved an exhausted hand, as if that should explain it all. "I was here."

Fleming. The engineer. He was the point man for inspections. Phil had heard the name but hadn't met him, or at least didn't remember him if he had. He was a forgettable sort of man, though. Nondescript, easy to look past.

"You worked with Brady?" Fleming asked, and Phil nodded.

"Yeah."

"I think he's dead." Fleming stared at the place where once the gatehouse had stood. The place where Phil had reported for every working shift of his life in the past two years. The imposing stone tower was gone, obliterated. There was no sign that it had ever existed. "Did you know him well?"

Phil stared at him. It was a strange question, and the wrong time for it. The dam was collapsing before their eyes, and Fleming wanted to make small talk?

Shock, Phil thought, and that made sense, because he was feeling a good bit of shock, himself.

"Yes," he said, although that wasn't exactly true. Arthur kept to himself.

The answer seemed to mean something to Fleming, though. He nodded thoughtfully, as if considering a problem, then said, "I think it was the sheriff."

"What? What are you talking about?"

"There were no sirens. Didn't you notice that?"

"Yes. Of course, I noticed that, but . . ." His words had gotten out in front of his understanding, and he stammered to a stop. "What do you mean, the sheriff?"

"Someone disabled the sensors. The sirens. The two of them were in there together. You said you knew Brady well. You don't think he'd have done that?"

Phil could hardly process what was being said. Someone had *intentionally* disabled the alarm? He looked away from Fleming and out across the flooded valley, into the carnage.

"No," he said, his voice hoarse. "I don't think he would have done that."

"Then the sheriff, I suppose. He hadn't been much of a help. And yesterday there was the chaos with his son. I didn't understand that."

"I don't understand a damn thing you're saying!"

If Phil's shout bothered Fleming, the engineer didn't show it. He just nodded, unruffled, and said, "It's not the problem of the moment, is it? The structure is. What's left of it can be saved. We're going to need that helicopter. Can you do that for me? Can you call for a helicopter?"

Phil nodded. Against this ghastly tableau, Fleming's calm demeanor was a reassurance.

"I'll call for one."

"Thank you. I'll need to talk with them. To get a sense of how it all looks from above. Do you understand?"

"Yes," Phil said. He reached for his radio, brought it halfway to his lips, and then stopped. "Wait—what do I say about Arthur? And the sheriff?"

"You can say they're dead. The rest doesn't matter much right now, does it?"

"But . . . the sirens. You said that—"

"Don't you think," Mick Fleming said, sweeping a hand out to indicate the ugly brown sea that swept from the reservoir to the town, "it's a bit late to worry about the sirens? There will be a time for that, and there will be a man for the job. But it's not this time, and I'm not that man."

His voice hadn't risen in volume, but the tone had tightened as fast as a bolt hit with an air wrench, and his eyes were hot with anger.

Phil called it in.

52

Deshawn stood in his apartment, staring at the TV.

The images were all aerial; there were no camera crews on the ground in Torrance. Not yet. Every now and then the broadcast cut away to some-one's shaky cell phone video, but mostly they stuck to the helicopter shots.

Roads turned to rivers. Bass boats cruising through intersections. Houses submerged up to their chimneys. The domed roof of the court-house reaching up out of the water like something from Atlantis.

A church floated through a high school football field. It was tipped onto its side and beginning to sink, but the steeple was still above water, like a desperate hand reaching for help.

The sun was now down in Torrance, and the water looked black and menacing, its surface reflecting the harsh lights of the helicopter spot-lights or the colored flashers of emergency vehicles. Coast Guard and National Guard choppers circled. Stretchers were lowered on waver-ing ropes. Stretchers were hauled back up. Now and then you could see someone lift a hand, but it seemed like so often they were motionless.

The text crawl below the images said, *Too early to estimate death toll.*

Somewhere amid all that carnage was Deshawn's daughter.

But alive, he thought. *She is alive, and that's all that matters.*

He thought of that, and then of his daughter's question: *Is this my family's fault?*

Could it have been? For so long he'd have said no. Today, though . . . today he could not say that definitively. Couldn't say *anything* defini-tively. Reality as he'd known it was gone.

He was late to leave. After begging off his second shift, claiming illness and earning skepticism, he'd intended to head directly for Torrance. Then came the call with Gillian. He'd slowed down a bit after that.

He left the TV and walked into a small bedroom that was filled with artifacts of failed ideas for the space: a treadmill, a dart board, a desk, all jammed in there together, monuments to the unsuccessful ways he'd tried to fill the emptiness of what had once been his daughter's bedroom. He picked his way through the clutter, shoved an old recliner aside until he had enough space to open the closet door, and then squeezed inside. Found the pull chain, tugged it, and turned on the light. It was a bare bulb, painfully bright when you looked up. He squinted, stretched up on his toes, and fumbled on the highest shelf. His hand ran over an old computer, a set of speakers, and two stuffed animals. Past a stack of video game cartridges. All these relics of his daughter's youth.

He found the sketchbook tucked in the far corner, under an old comforter, where she thought she'd hidden it from him. It had been years since he'd looked at it. He'd wanted to throw it away—no, burn it—but something deep within him had been afraid to do that.

He pulled the old sketchbook down, easing back to a flat-footed stance, and flipped open the cover. Stared impassively at the renderings of ancient faces looking back at him. Flipped through page after page, twenty-five drawings in all, skipping only the one he feared the most and remembered the best. He studied all the others and finally found what he was looking for.

It was a sketch of a man standing in ankle-deep water in a tunnel. He wore high rubber boots that reached his thighs, and above those a suit jacket and a vest. He had a small, closely cropped mustache that covered little more than the hollow above his upper lip.

A few hours earlier, the same man had stood before Deshawn and spoken to him.

But who was he?

Deshawn took the sketchbook with him when he left the apartment.

It was time, as Gillian had said, to talk. He wasn't sure what answers he'd be able to offer her, but he could try. He could do that much.

He'd never owned a car. When he needed one, he rented. He didn't need one much. The subway was the only transportation he needed, and paying for parking in the city could cost half as much as rent. The subway didn't run to Torrance, though.

He summoned an Uber, searching for the pricier versions that promised bigger vehicles. He found one driver in a Cadillac Escalade. Far too fancy, but four-wheel drive would be necessary. The app quoted the fare from his street corner to Torrance as slightly less than he made in a week. He touched the ACCEPT button with his thumb.

Two minutes later a black Escalade arrived at the curb. He climbed into the back, and a young Latina woman turned and looked at him with an arched eyebrow.

"You serious, or did you screw up the destination?"

"I'm serious."

"That far upstate? It's expensive."

"That's fine."

"You hear what's going on up there? I don't even know how close I can get to the town."

"I've heard," Deshawn said. "Just get me as close as you can, as fast as you can."

53

The water overflowed the road just a mile downhill from Aaron's house. A half mile beyond that, it was so deep that he no longer trusted the truck. The road ahead had a current to it.

The road ahead was also three miles from the heart of town.

He got out of the truck and stood with his gear bag over his shoulder, unsure of what to do next. Wade in and walk as far as possible, then swim it? Possible, but also foolhardy. He wasn't going to help anyone if he ended up needing to be rescued himself.

He was pondering driving all the way around the dam to come at the town from a different direction, when another truck appeared behind him. This one was towing a boat.

The truck came as far as Aaron and then stopped. The window rolled down, and he looked in at a gray-haired couple staring grimly back at him.

"Glad to see you," the woman said. "What do you want us to do?"

Aaron realized that she was reacting to the uniform. She thought he had some authority. He started to explain but then decided the hell with it. Right now the problem was getting to town.

"What's the draft on that boat?" he asked.

"Maybe ten inches," she answered, and her husband nodded. He was a big man wearing a sweatshirt that featured a jumping bass with a lure in its lip.

"Just a johnboat," he said. "Use it for duck hunting and fishing. It's not much, but it's something. We figured we'd try to help. Is that okay by you?"

Again the implied authority. Aaron nodded. "It sure is. You want to drive ahead maybe twenty feet and see if it's deep enough to float her?"

They pulled forward. The water rose over their front tires. Plenty deep enough to get the boat off the trailer.

If that's what it's like here, Aaron thought, *then what does it look like in town?*

He waded over to the trailer hitch, unfastened the security straps between the boat and the truck, and then began paying out the winch. The johnboat slid down the trailer and floated cleanly in the center of the road. He caught it and held it in place while the couple climbed out of the truck and stood in the water, watching him.

"Let me shut off my truck and we'll go see what we can do," he said.

He tossed his gear bag into the boat, then killed the engine on his own truck, and returned. The older couple was already seated, the man holding on to the truck's bumper to keep the boat from being pulled away. Aaron climbed in beside them, which wasn't as easy as it should have been. He had to push off using only his left foot. His right foot pulsed with pain, and he hoped his waterproof boots would keep the filthy water away from the wound.

"You want to run it, or want me to?" the man asked, nodding at the tiller. The boat had a twenty-five-horsepower Mercury outboard and a Minn Kota electric trolling motor.

"You can," Aaron said. "It's your boat. And I'm glad you've got the trolling motor as a backup, because I have no idea what your prop is going to be chewing through out there."

"We'll find out," the man said, and started the outboard. "I'm Ned Kelly, and my wife is Carrie."

Aaron shook their hands. "Aaron Ellsworth."

He opened his gear bag, withdrew one of the flashlights, and moved to the bow, where he could navigate. The beam penetrated the darkness about a hundred feet ahead. It was all brown water and floating debris. Tree limbs, boards, a single plastic garbage can lid.

Ned Kelly twisted the throttle and the boat moved forward, past the truck, and on down the road. Aaron shined the light ahead, calling out obstacles. The little boat was nimble, and its low draft and stable bottom made it a good craft for rescue work.

They cruised along in a world that Aaron knew better than any other place on the planet but now hardly recognized. If they'd been driving, they'd have been going downhill at a steep pitch, but instead they floated level, which added to the disorientation. A garage door drifted by, and then a basketball. A Mets pennant chased two lawn chairs. Plastic storage bins floated like fishing bobbers. A shed roof with a weathervane rode alongside them briefly. Aaron called out the obstructions, but otherwise it was silent, the three of them staring at the damage in shock.

At the base of the hill was an intersection that now felt like just another bend in the river. The water was just below the stop signs, but you could still see them, and as they churned through, Aaron felt a ludicrous urge to tell Ned to stop, as if the rules of the road still mattered. Then his flashlight caught on the man in the water.

He was floating facedown, but his arms were outstretched, and for an instant Aaron thought that he might be swimming.

"We're coming!" he shouted. "Hey, we've got you!"

Then he realized.

Ned slowed the boat without saying a word and brought them in close. Aaron reached over the gunwale and grabbed the drowned man by his jacket and hauled him aboard. He was maybe thirty years old. Thin, with a neatly trimmed beard that had something white and slick trapped in it. A French fry. He'd died eating dinner.

Aaron wiped the dead man's face clean with the back of his glove and lowered him into the bottom of the boat.

"CPR?" Carrie asked. Her face looked as gray as her hair.

"Too late for that," her husband said, and Aaron only nodded. He shifted the body gently to the side, trying to be as respectful with the dead man as he would be with an injured one, and then he moved back to the front of the boat, and shined his light across the black waters ahead as Ned motored forward.

Something threw strangely shaped shadows at the edge of the flashlight's beam, and there was a sound like the creak of a rusty hinge. Aaron leaned forward, squinting. The light illuminated a child's playset with two slides and a set of swings in the middle. Ned steered past it without a word, but Aaron turned to watch it go by and caught Carrie's eye. She was crying without making a sound.

As they neared town, the debris field thickened, and Ned was soon having to carve elaborate S-curves around sunken cars, pieces of houses, and countless piles of unidentifiable, sodden garbage. The air stank of mud, like being in a freshly plowed field after a hard spring rain. The lights of town that should have greeted them were absent, replaced with red-and-blue flashers. Sirens wailed, and Aaron realized that he'd heard no siren at the house. The dam should have triggered a county-wide emergency siren system, but it hadn't gone off.

What exactly had gone wrong up there? Beyond the obvious, what in the hell had happened?

That's more than a warning, Mick Fleming had said in the darkness the previous night. *That's a sacrifice.*

The roof of a flooded-out car reflected Aaron's light. Ned steered past it. Overhead, a helicopter thumped through the air, painting them with a spotlight.

"Your people?" Ned asked, pointing at it.

"National Guard, I think," Aaron said, not bothering to explain that he had no crew, no people. He signaled to the circling chopper with the flashlight, letting them know that the three in the boat weren't in need of assistance. The chopper lifted and flew on.

They found five more corpses in the next block. These were all floating close together, their bodies thumping off one another in the soft, sloshing waves. Aaron looked back at Ned and Carrie, and he knew they were all thinking the same thing.

"We don't have space," she whispered. "Not that much."

"No, we don't." Aaron shook his head. "Let's save room for the living."

Ned twisted the throttle and they pulled away from the drifting corpses and rode on with their one lonely dead man, understanding now just how much company he had in the water.

Nobody said a word for a long time after that.

54

Less than a mile away from Aaron Ellsworth, Gillian Mathers was also in a boat, floating just below the window of her third-floor walk-up apartment.

The Arlington Heights Inn, her beloved boardinghouse turned town houses, had somehow taken the flood's best shot and stayed on its feet. The 105-year-old building was on the same block as the Hard Truth Brewery, and nothing remained of Hard Truth now save for a satellite dish that spun on the surface but remained inexplicably tethered by its cables. It floated like a marker buoy above the restaurant where Gillian had gathered on so many afternoons for a beer on the patio. The bar was gone now but the Arlington remained, shifting on its foundation but not collapsing.

Yet.

The structure was canting to the left, and every now and then a muffled boom would rumble up from below the water. On dry ground, the sound would be much louder—it was the sound of joists snapping.

On the third floor of the building, just down the hallway from her own apartment, a dozen people were gathered in the highest window they could find. Five children were among them.

A DEP service boat floated below, and Gillian was trying to run an aluminum extension ladder from the boat to the third-floor window. They'd called for a helicopter but none had arrived yet, and the sounds from underwater weren't encouraging. The Arlington Heights Inn had taken the punch, but it was swaying on the ropes, and if it went, it was going to bury a dozen people in a cascade of broken brick.

The top of the extension ladder scraped along the wall, shifting with the rocking boat. The sound of the aluminum rasping across the brick blended with human screams and a baby's sobbing.

Gillian had never been a big fan of ladders, and she sure as hell didn't like climbing one that was resting on a floating boat, but when she saw the face of an eight-year-old girl who lived just down the hall from her peering down, she volunteered to be the one who went up.

"You sure?" Brett Roget asked. He was one of three of them in the boat, all DEP police, colleagues who had sat in countless meetings discussing dam security and never imagined it would actually lead them here. The town was filled with boats, some with official badging—National Guard and Coast Guard, state police and county police, EMS, game wardens—and many without. Volunteers and professionals were hard to sort out. The rain had started to fall again, and now everyone was in rain gear, faces hooded or shielded by hats. The dark-water world was lit by flashing lights and scored by shouts.

And by the wailing of one baby in a room above Gillian, where a young girl looked out a window in terror.

"I'm sure," Gillian told Brett, and started up the ladder. Almost immediately another boat went by, and the resulting wake made the ladder sway and tremble. Gillian closed her eyes and swore under her breath, then opened them and looked with outrage at the offending craft, ready to shout at them to pay some attention. Who was roaring by that fast?

It was another DEP boat. The tactical team. More of her colleagues, headed somewhere in a hurry.

She was still staring after them when a flash of light burst just up the road. A single, bright glare. Somewhere up there, a man in the water was raging and raving, shouting threats to the heavens, bellowing at an unseen enemy. He seemed to be looking for a place to direct his rage, because who was there to be angry at for a flood?

Plenty of people, actually. The furious man just didn't know them by name yet.

"Gillian?" Brett called.

"Yeah. Going up."

Another flash. This time she saw the source: it was a camera. In the momentary illumination, she saw a man with a dark beard perched on a slab of broken limestone, shooting down at the enraged man in the water.

Haupring. She knew it, although she'd never seen him. He'd come back—or never left?—and now the old camera was flashing again, or maybe it was a new camera, or maybe it was his charcoal pencil. But he was there, documenting, and that was not good.

"*Gillian!* You doing this, or you want me to?" Brett shouted.

She tore her eyes away from where the photographer sat in shadow and looked up again. The young girl stared back down at her, wide-eyed, jaw trembling. An adult woman, probably her mother, had joined her. Two pale faces in the darkness, ghostlike orbs.

"She can't swim," the mother said. "And there's a baby."

"Nobody's going to have to swim," Gillian said, and she started climbing, willing herself not to look back in the direction of the photographer, not even when another flash popped.

The higher she got, the less stable the ladder felt. She knew Brett and Tim were doing their best to hold the boat steady, but that was an impossible ask in water that had a current. All of the water in Torrance had a current now; it was still flowing through the valley and the town, although the worst of the flood surge would have reached the Mohawk River. Then the Mohawk would swell and carry the flood on, dumping its excess into the Hudson. Could the Hudson hold all of the water without causing a cascading series of downstream disasters? She thought so, but who knew? Every time it had been discussed before it was a purely theoretical conversation, with mathematicians showing models and equations. There had been no swaying ladders on boats, no crying babies in attic windows, no children who couldn't swim.

She actually felt better when she reached the top of the ladder, because then she could grip the window frame. She was wearing a head-lamp, and as she looked through the window and into the attic, she could see everyone: three women, two men, and seven children. She recognized some of them but not all. A baby shrieked while a father whispered unsuccessful soothings. Gillian didn't know his name but she knew his face and she certainly recognized the sound of that cry: How many nights had she put a pillow over her face at two a.m. when that sound began from one floor below? And how foolish, almost impossible, it now seemed to think that such a thing had ever been an annoyance.

"Who wants to get out of here?" Gillian said in a voice she hoped suggested some confidence, or at least didn't indicate the terror she felt as the ladder shivered beneath her.

A chorus of voices responded. Some grateful, some frantic. Too many to respond to directly. Gillian took one hand off the ladder and pointed at the baby.

"Her first."

The father looked from Gillian to the baby with a strangely indignant expression.

"Trust me," Gillian said. "I'll take care of her."

"He's a boy," the father responded.

"Apologies. I've never been great with kids."

One of the women laughed at this exchange, a high nervous laugh over the absurdity of it all, and while it was near the edge of hysteria, Gillian still thought that laugh was the most beautiful sound she'd ever heard. Against the sirens and helicopter blades and the fearful shouts and drumming rain, a simple human laugh was an impossibly sweet sound.

Gillian smiled and extended her arms. "Trust me with him? Please?"

She could see the shock in the father's face now. He wasn't sure what to do. His town was underwater, the building he was in was collapsing, and the rescuer in the window couldn't get his kid's gender right. Which problem first? Maybe none. Maybe just stand here and hold tight. Gillian understood it, but she couldn't afford to wait. None of them could.

"Please," she said.

The father came to the window. He had the child in one of those cloth slings that parents used to find a free hand while navigating with an infant, and now he held on to the baby with his left arm while using his right to slip the sling over Gillian's head and down to her shoulder. She heard a joist creak and felt the ladder shift and wanted to scream at him to hurry, but she understood exactly what he was entrusting to her and how hard it must be. She kept quiet and still, using the window frame to keep balance while the ladder swayed below, as he fitted the sling around her with excruciating slowness.

"He will be fine," Gillian told him. "Trust me."

He looked at her, squinting against the headlamp glare, and she thought of all he must see behind her: the emergency lights, the destroyed buildings, floating garbage, floating corpses. And here she was in the foreground, asking for his child, saying, *Trust me.*

He did, though. Very slowly, he moved the infant from his chest to hers. The baby screamed, his breath warm against Gillian's neck. The father adjusted the sling, bringing the child in tighter. She'd never actually held a baby in one of the slings, but it seemed like a wonderful idea right now because it allowed her to keep one hand on the ladder.

The father kept his hand on the sling, as if unable to release his grasp.

"I've got him," Gillian said. "I'll keep him safe."

Finally he moved back. Gillian backed down toward the boat.

Please hold steady. Oh, please, please hold steady.

The boat bobbed and swayed but Brett had a tight hold on the ladder. A minute later Gillian was down, and he was taking the child from her.

"Can we get them all?" Gillian asked, looking around the boat. "It's mostly kids."

"How many?"

"Twelve in all, but like I said, a lot of kids. This is the only baby, but the others are young. Small."

"Still two trips, probably," Tim said from the wheel. "Kids first. We can't risk—"

Two pops came from the building, joists giving way underwater with a double clap like gunshots, and the ancient building sagged. They all turned to stare at it.

"Yes," Tim said then. "We can get them all."

———

They managed it. Gillian made two more trips to guide children down, and then the older kids and the parents came down, and somehow the ladder didn't slide free, and the old Arlington Heights Inn didn't give up. When they were all in the boat, it felt like an overpacked tourist craft, one of those things families took in the summer to see lighthouses or lobster buoys. Gillian sat on the gunwale, ass hanging partially off the boat, while Tim guided them away.

The National Guard had set up an evacuation point on the high ground of what had once been the hilltop in a cemetery, where flags waved above the veterans' section. Now the flagpoles seemed to mark an island instead of a hill, like territory claimed by explorers in a new world.

That was precisely what Torrance now felt like. A new world, so different from the old one that they seemed hard to bridge.

That's because it's not Torrance. Not anymore. Torrance is gone and Galesburg is back. Just like my grandmother always promised.

She shook her head and turned to face into the rain. There was no time for thoughts like that. Not tonight.

Not even if they were true.

55

New York City arrived at the Chilewaukee in helicopters and Humvees, and the state was already there to meet them, in the presence of one Mick Fleming, chief engineer, Albany's finest. Many of the new arrivals had just been reminded of Fleming's status by Ed Cochran that very day, when he'd made his calls to mobilize the next morning's emergency meeting while reassuring them that his best engineer was already at the scene.

Ed Cochran was nowhere to be found. While no one was saying it out loud yet, it seemed likely that he was a casualty. That created a power vacuum and certainly a knowledge vacuum. In a crisis, you hungered for an expert. Mick Fleming had escaped the flood, so an expert was on scene when the decision-makers began to arrive.

He was trying not to smile. Trying to look properly grim. Grief-stricken, yes, but not overwhelmed. He had a briefing to deliver and action plan to deploy, after all.

Mick had never enjoyed speaking in front of a group, but tonight he felt relaxed, confident. That confidence came from Anders Wallace, who floated around the group, unseen by any of them, but a reassuring force for Mick.

"It's bad, but if we don't act in a hurry, it will get much worse," Mick said. The group was huddled in the hastily cleared landing zone above the dam, their shocked faces illuminated by the flickering orange light of the flares that the National Guard had used to mark the spot for the helicopters. He recognized some of the faces from personal encounters and others from television—the mayor of New York City, a senator, and at least two state representatives. The former group was going to be more trouble than the latter, Mick thought, harder to sell swiftly on his plan because they had technical understanding. He had one advantage with them, though: trust. The better they knew Mick, the more likely they were to trust his judgment.

He had two primary adversaries who needed to become allies in a hurry. One was Sandy Clemmons, who had served as Ed Cochran's right hand for years and had drafted the state's emergency management plan for dam failures in the upstate reservoirs. She knew the system as well as anyone. Another potential problem was Ben Quirk, of the Army Corps of Engineers. The corps had no authority over the Chill, but they did have authority of many of the nation's dams and reservoirs, and Quirk knew his stuff.

"How will it get worse?" asked a woman whom Mick thought was in the statehouse. Allison something? Angela? He was so bad with faces. She'd come in on a helicopter that flew low over the valley, giving her an up-close look at Torrance. You could see fires burning down there now, not uncommon when floodwaters and high-voltage electricity played together.

"It could get worse," Mick said, "if we lose the whole dam. It could get a lot worse, and in a hurry."

"You think the rest will go," said Sandy Clemmons. It wasn't a question.

"Yes. All the destruction down in Torrance came from a partial breach. If the whole thing collapses, it's a different story." He made sure the people from the mayor's office were looking at him when he said, "Torrance took the punch for the rest of the state, do you see? But if the rest goes, we risk cascading failures. It will flood right on down the chain, maybe into the city water tunnels."

"It's got more than one hundred miles to go before it gets there," Sandy said, and Mick wanted to slap her.

"Yes, it does," he said. "And we'll lose a few dozen bridges, half the state's power grid, and countless lives along the way."

"We can open a lot of gates, though," Ben Quirk said, his eyes far away, as if imagining each step along the chain. "Stagger capacity, stagger outflow. Evacuation first, of course. It's the plan we already have, the one we just reviewed last year. If we follow the—"

"If we follow the plan, we risk losing half of New York City's water supply for weeks if not months," Mick snapped.

The mayor of New York City blanched.

"We create emergency plans for a reason," Quirk said.

"The plan," Mick said, "doesn't account for the reality. I think we all need to be very keenly aware of that tonight."

"What do you mean by that?" This came from the mayor himself, which delighted Mick to no end. The man needed votes. The man knew this. The man also knew that you could get a lot of votes with the right response to a crisis.

"The whole system is already at flood level," Mick said. "Which means every piece of infrastructure along the way is under pressure. We can send more floodwater down and hope that every piece of the infrastructure—much of which is nearly a century old, mind you—continues to hold, or we can acknowledge that what happened here suggests that's a really poor idea. The old infrastructure failed in Torrance. Do we really want to test it downstream?"

Mick gave them a moment to think. He felt in total command. Anders Wallace nodded encouragingly as he paced among the group, unseen by any of their eyes.

"If the tunnels go," Mick said, "then you're looking at a disaster that will make Torrance look trivial. You're looking at a disaster that will make Katrina look trivial. If the tunnels go, you've got a city without water. It's not a quick fix, either. There will be millions without water for a long time. Weeks, minimum. Months, probably."

The mayor looked dizzy but he was nodding, because he knew this was true. Only two years earlier he'd been presented with an array of disaster scenarios for New York City. Everything from terrorism to hurricanes had been discussed. Biological weapons and dirty bombs. Out of all the nightmares, one had the potential to shut the entire city down for the longest time: failure of the two water tunnels that fed the five boroughs. If Water Tunnel Number 2 alone was lost, all of Queens and Brooklyn would go dry for months. Half of the homes in the city would be uninhabitable. Hospitals would shut down, disease would spread, the economy would crater, and chaos would reign.

That was the power of water.

The city's survival rested in the remote reservoirs of the Catskills. What happened there in the next twenty-four hours dictated life or death downstream in numbers that most people wouldn't dare consider.

Tonight they had to be considered.

"If we make the wrong choice," Mick said, "we'll be cutting New York City's throat."

Quirk, from the Army Corps of Engineers, was looking at the dam, and Mick knew he was envisioning the way it had held after the breach and, no doubt, envisioning what might happen when it failed fully. Sandy Clemmons was also staring in that direction, but she would be thinking less of the dam itself and more of the system it impacted, imagining each carefully constructed link in the chain.

"If the infrastructure was as sound as we'd like to believe," Mick said, "then this never would have happened. We've got a legitimate disaster down there in Torrance, we've got a death toll that might be shocking by the time it's counted, and we've got an overburdened rescue effort and evacuation under way. Now remember that we got all of that from a *partial* failure affecting a *small upstate town*."

He watched that sink in.

"The emergency plan trusts an enormous amount of old equipment," he said. "At each stop downstream and all the way through the city, all the way underneath Manhattan, it trusts antiquated equipment. Some of which has never been inspected because it can't be reached."

They all knew it was true. They'd known it for years. He wanted to scream that at them—wanted to scream, *This is what you've fucking ig-*

nored, don't you see? How do you like it?—but he couldn't afford to lose them by showing anger.

"I think we have two choices," he said. "We can wait for morning, which means trusting the rest of that dam to hold and trusting that the Chilewaukee is the only weak link in the whole hundred-year-old chain, so that even if the rest of the dam goes, it won't set off cascading collapses from here all the way into the city. Or ..." He swiveled his head, making direct eye contact with as many of them as possible. "... we end the threat right here."

Overhead, the air shivered with yet another approaching helicopter. The governor, maybe. Hell, the president. Mick had no idea how many they'd send, but so long as he was the lead engineering voice, he didn't care. The problem would be more engineers. They would come, and they would disagree.

Maybe. Maybe not. Because the plan is good. The plan, if you do not know what the people of Galesburg have been up to, is actually very good.

"How do we end it here?" Sandy asked. Mick was pleased to see the trust in her face. She didn't want to depart from her treasured EMP— Sandy loved that emergency management plan—but she'd relied heavily on Mick's opinion while creating it, too.

"We open the tunnels," he said.

"I thought that's exactly what we were afraid of!" one of the mayor's deputies blurted, but Sandy's eyes showed that she understood. Sandy's eyes actually seemed to glimmer with the idea.

"You're thinking of the city tunnels," she told the deputy. "Mick is talking about the Chilewaukee's."

Bless her, she remembered the map. There weren't many people who remembered how far the work at the Chilewaukee had gone before it was abandoned.

"Yes," Mick said. "One domino doesn't necessarily touch the others. Not up here at the surplus reservoir."

"How much do you think they can hold?" Sandy asked.

"Fifty million gallons."

"You can't be sure of that."

"Yes, I can be. It's what they were designed to do. Those tunnels were supposed to move between fifteen and fifty million gallons of water per day out of this reservoir. So we can move fifty million gallons into them right now, and in just the right spot—away from the dam. That's the key here: reduce the pressure against the dam. Agree?"

There was a pause and then some nods.

"It'll give the dam a pressure release, certainly," Quirk said. "We'll give it a chance to take a breath, and that's all it needs."

"Won't it just be replaced?" Sandy asked. "We're redistributing the water, that's all. More of the lake drains down, but the same amount of pressure is on the dam."

"No," Mick said. "You've got to remember what's beneath."

Quirk was now nodding in a methodical drumbeat of agreement.

"It was one of the original problems with using the Chill as a supply reservoir," Quirk said. "The valley that makes up the lake bed is like a tilted bowl, and it tilts *away* from the dam, which means away from the tunnels, too. If this reservoir had been truly needed during a drought, it would've been a challenge. Things were never done right up here."

"Agreed," Mick said. "But we can capitalize on the old mistakes now. Open the tunnels, siphon off water that's currently pressing against the dam, and then create a temporary structure inside of the dam to help channel the flow. The combination of the water already lost downstream, the water we can siphon out through the tunnels, and that tilted lake bed will give us time to work."

"Foolish question, maybe," the mayor said, "but once those tunnels are opened up, where does the water go, exactly?"

Mick pointed into the mountains.

"Explain," the mayor said, and Mick was struck by how patient his voice was and how engaged he seemed to be, even while the new chopper was settling down just behind him. The man would do just fine in front of the cameras tonight, Mick thought. He might even say Mick's name as a means of reassuring his nervous constituency. Wouldn't that be something? Lori would be so proud.

Lori. He hadn't thought of her in hours. She seemed vague and distant, a woman imagined rather than a wife of a decade. She felt far less real than Anders Wallace, certainly, who was standing at Mick's side.

The mayor was waiting, and so Mick refocused and explained. He reminded them of what had originally been envisioned at the Chill, and of what had been abandoned. He explained that the tunnels here hadn't been completed but that they still remained beneath the mountains, open and dry.

"We turn that mountain into a temporary dam, essentially," he said. "I can assure you, that mountain isn't going anywhere."

But the water will. Because, boys and girls, work has never stopped in Galesburg.

"It will bleed the reservoir down," Quirk said thoughtfully. "It will definitely do that much. And that reduces pressure on what's left of the dam."

"Exactly," Mick said, wanting to play off Quirk's expertise. "As a pressure release, it's guaranteed. What I don't know is whether we can achieve it quickly enough. Just getting the grading equipment in here tonight is going to be a big ask, and then I'm not sure they can work fast enough."

He knew all of the ways in which this fear could be avoided, but he wanted Quirk to come up with the answer, not him. The plan needed to be a group endeavor.

"We don't need to grade it at all," Quirk said. "We'll blast it. Blast those old intake doors open, and then we've essentially got a holding basin under the mountain. The water will do the rest. We've got gravity on our side up here."

"It's the same thing we're spending hundreds of millions on at the Schoharie right now," said one of the men Mick didn't know, someone who'd come up with the mayor, a lean-faced Hispanic man with keen eyes who looked at everyone when they talked in the way a chess master watched the board. "The new release tunnels."

Mick was embarrassed that he hadn't thought to make the comparison himself. It was perfect.

"That's exactly right," Mick said. "We're in the process of boring a new release tunnel into the bottom of the Schoharie Reservoir to bleed it down so maintenance can be performed on the dam and the intake chambers. Thanks to the debacles that stopped this project back in the forties, the Chill already *has* a release tunnel. Three of them, in fact. They just need to be opened."

"And the tunnels don't connect to *anything*?" the mayor asked. "They just . . . dead-end down there?"

"Yes," Sandy Clemmons said, "they dead-end under the mountains, and they'll work like outlet valves, if we use them right."

"It's enough to give up on the EMP we have in place?" This question came from one of the mayor's deputies. Mick remembered her from a meeting last spring. She'd been concerned about the age of the city's functioning tunnels. He'd liked that about her.

"You can stick to the EMP," he said. "Make the downstream evacuations and shut down everything you need to shut down. Hold to the plan, but pray we don't need it." He took a deep breath, one that he hoped seemed just nervous enough, and said, "We can't fix that dam overnight. We can't even assess it in a night. But we can take some pressure off it. In fact, thanks to those old tunnels, we can take a *lot* of pressure off it."

The mayor studied Mick, then turned to Sandy Clemmons. "Is he right?"

"I think so," she said. "It certainly can't hurt, and it can be done fast."

Sandy looked down to where the intake chamber doors loomed white in the emergency spotlights.

"I think we're awfully lucky that it happened up here," the mayor said. "It almost feels like the place was built for this."

"Doesn't it?" Mick said.

56

Deshawn's Uber driver was forced to give up four miles outside of Torrance, where the roadblocks started.

Just beyond them, water ran over the asphalt like a glittering brook.

It had taken them the whole night to make it this far. Long ago, his driver had gone from dubious to determined. When the highway was closed to anyone except emergency personnel, she navigated the back roads. When the back roads were flooded, she reversed course and found new roads. She drove up into the mountains and then back down out of them. Off of pavement and onto one-lane gravel lanes and then back onto pavement.

They'd gotten to know each other by then. Her name was Rochelle, and she had a daughter named Gloria. Gloria was five and she wanted to build robots. Or, more accurately, to *be* a robot, but Rochelle had talked her through the challenges of that particular approach.

It had been a talkative start to the journey, but then Rochelle turned the radio on to see if there were updates from Torrance. There were: an emergency evacuation of survivors, the threat of a total dam failure, and an early estimated death toll of one thousand people.

Deshawn had asked Rochelle to turn the radio off and tell him more about her daughter then. He was happier listening to the stories of the Girl-Who-Would-Be-Robot than thinking about his own daughter, up there among the dead in the flood.

At one point he'd glanced at his phone, hoping for any word from Gillian, saw the Uber app, and realized that Rochelle had ended his fare payment long ago. She was still driving him, but not for money. She was still driving because he had a daughter lost somewhere out there in the night and she had Gloria back at home in bed.

Four miles outside of Torrance, though, even the indefatigable Rochelle had been forced to admit defeat. There were only so many roads into the town, and they were all closed now, either restricted to emergency personnel or flooded out.

"I think this is it," she said, sorrowful.

"You got me right to the doorstep. I'll go find her now."

"Hang on." She reached over to the passenger seat, picked up her purse, and turned it upside down. The contents cascaded over the seat.

"There are water bottles in the backseat," she said. "Four of them, I think. Give me those."

"I don't need—"

"I don't care if you don't need it; someone up there will."

She turned and met his eyes in the dim glow of the dashboard lights. He wasn't about to argue. He thanked her and passed the bottles forward. She put them into her purse, then she rummaged through the contents on the seat, dropping a few more items into the bag. Popped open the center console, withdrew a small cylinder, and added that.

"Four waters, two granola bars, two packs of gummy bears," she said. "Mom's reserves, right there. I've always got something. Oh, and one can of pepper spray." She shrugged. "Hope you won't need that, but I'm not putting you out in the dark without it."

"You keep that. I'm not going to—"

She pivoted back to him again, braids whipping across her face. Fixed him with that stare.

"Did you not hear me when I said I wasn't going to put you out in the dark without it?"

She waited as if daring him to object, and when he did not, she handed him the purse. It was a big black leather bag with a line of shimmering stones stitched into one side. She watched him sling it onto his shoulder, gave an appraising glance, and said, "Yeah, you might need the pepper spray."

They both laughed then. Quietly, but enough to matter. Enough to make the darkness ahead not seem quite so endless and lonely.

"Thank you," Deshawn said, and put out his hand. She took it and squeezed.

"Go find your baby," she said.

"I will. Thank you."

"Stop thanking me, dude. Just make *real* sure I get my five stars outta this one."

He smiled, released her hand, and opened the door. His boot splashed into shallow water. He took Rochelle's purse and walked past the roadblocks and ahead toward Torrance.

57

Even after the water began to recede, chaos reigned in Torrance. No chain of command was clear, and even the idea of authority seemed irrelevant. Civilians and National Guardsmen and paramedics and police blurred and blended on shared missions to evacuate able-bodied survivors, then find the wounded and the trapped.

There were many of them.

As the hours wore on, the water level continued to drop, the flood surge dissipating into the lowlands and then on down to the Mohawk River. More searches wound to a close. By dawn, Torrance was giving up more of its dead.

Aaron had worked through the night. He'd left the boat that he'd come in on and joined another, and then a third, and then he'd been on the ground, stacking sandbags and helping with stretchers. Between the hours of two a.m. and four a.m., he'd done little but move corpses to higher ground to be counted and disposed of.

In theory they'd be disposed of. Nobody seemed to have a plan for that just yet. Instead, the bodies were piled in a fashion not dissimilar to the sandbags.

He'd counted them at first. Sometime after the number reached double digits, though, he stopped that and tried to numb his brain to the task. He succeeded in losing track of the number, but in the end he'd have happily traded the number for the memories that replaced it. One girl's butterfly-shaped barrette came off in his hand. An elderly man's watch slipped up and over his frail wrist and sank into the depths as

Aaron and another volunteer tried to pull him loose from the wreckage that had pinned him. The vacant eyes of a waitress who had served Aaron and his family countless platters of pancakes at the Spoon Diner seemed to track him as he carried her, as if a cry for help was locked just out of reach within her.

He'd dimmed his headlamp whenever possible and tried to work in the shadows. It made no difference. The faces of the dead couldn't be avoided, and wouldn't be forgotten.

Not ever.

Already he knew this.

By dawn he'd been moved from corpse retrieval back to sandbag installation. He shifted from one to the other as if it were natural. The tasks presented themselves, and he accepted them and worked on without any thought of the day to come. Thoughts of his father were flickers on the periphery. He knew that somewhere the sheriff was at work. He knew that at some time they would encounter each other. Until then, there were lives to save and bodies to stack.

The first light of day was breaking on the postapocalyptic-looking town square, when he found himself face-to-face with Sarah Burroughs, his father's chief deputy. She was instructing a group of volunteers in the removal of a collapsing pile of sandbags, but when she saw Aaron, she stopped talking and stared. Then she said, "Was he home? Do you know? Tell me he was home."

It was then, in the pale predawn half-light on the flooded streets of his hometown, that Aaron learned his father was among the missing.

"No," he said. "He wasn't at home."

Neither of them spoke for a moment. Water burbled through the sandbags and ran around Aaron's knees. Someone shouted a question at Sarah but she didn't turn from Aaron.

"He hasn't checked in?" Aaron asked, and his voice seemed to be coming from some place far away. "No radio contact or calls or . . ."

She was shaking her head.

He looked up the road—or what had once been the road—and

squinted as if he might spot his dad out there on the fringes and point and say, *There he is, Sarah; he's right there, just busy. He's working.*

"He will make contact," she said finally. "I know that. It'll be easier in daylight. So many people are out of touch. Not missing, necessarily, just out of communication."

"Right," he said.

"Maybe he's with the group at the dam," Sarah said.

"What group?"

"The mayor of New York, the governor, and the Army, for starters. They're all working with the engineers to keep the rest of it from going. They might have grabbed him. They'd need someone from the county, right?"

She seemed to be talking herself into the idea, but Aaron's mind had snagged on a single phrase.

"'Keep the rest of it'? The dam's still there?"

She nodded. "It was only a partial breach. All of this"—she swept her hand out over the ravaged town—"could be just the first round."

"Who are the engineers?" he said.

"I have no idea. I just know that they're trying to keep the rest of it from going." She looked numbly across the town square. "They'd better be able to get it done, too. Because if we get another flood surge . . ."

She didn't finish the thought. Didn't need to.

Aaron said, "Can you find out if Mick Fleming is there?"

Sarah blinked at him. "Who?"

"Mick Fleming. He's the dam inspector. Could you find that out?"

"That's not my role," she said. "And it sure isn't yours."

"Please. It matters, Sarah. I promise you, it matters."

She looked at him warily but unclipped her radio. Keyed the mike and spoke.

"Two-Three-Two, I've got a quick question for you. Is there a Mick Fleming up there? He's an engineer, I'm told. Handles dam inspections."

Silence. Then a crackle and a male voice: "Affirmative. You need him? I can try, but it looks like he's running the show, so it better be important."

Sarah looked questioningly at Aaron. He shook his head and she put the radio back to her lips.

"No need to interrupt him," she said. "Just wanted to confirm. Thanks. Any word from Steve yet?"

Pause. Crackle. "Negative."

Aaron looked away from her and up at the road that had turned to river. In the north, the jagged crest of Maiden Mountain was beginning to show itself in the dawn sky. He spoke without turning back. "I need contact with Gillian Mathers of the DEP. She's a detective sergeant, I think."

"What's going on, Aaron?" Sarah asked.

He was still staring at the mountain.

"It's urgent," he said, "and it's not about me or even my dad. Mathers knows what it is about. She's got jurisdiction up there and she's got an active case. She will want to speak with me. I'm sure of it."

He finally looked back, and while he was expecting skepticism, he wasn't ready for the personal doubt in her eyes. He saw in her eyes the reality of his reputation, all the credibility he'd lost.

Credibility his father hadn't lost, though. Dead or alive.

"The sheriff," Aaron said, "would be demanding Gillian Mathers at the dam right now if he had access to a radio. I promise you that. Evidently, he doesn't have a radio. Right?"

Still, she hesitated.

"I've got no authority," Aaron said, "and no credibility, either. I get it. But he did, right? Sarah? Didn't my dad have that much with you?"

"He *does*," Sarah said. "And when I hear from him, I will—"

"Stop it," Aaron said, and his voice broke.

She looked away from him, took a breath, and said, "If Mathers has a radio, I'll tell her you want to see her at the dam. She'll know why?"

"She'll know," Aaron said. "Thank you, Sarah. My dad would thank you, too. For a lot of things. This would be just one of them."

"He's going to turn up," she said.

Aaron nodded. Then he waded into what had once been Main Street and headed out of town.

58

Gillian wasn't sure whether the cell phone towers had been destroyed or if they were simply overloaded. The reason didn't matter; the result was that she had no cell contact, only radio. She thought of her father often as the night wore on, but she had no way to reach him. The radio crackled to life constantly with news, but not much of it was from downstream. There was flooding in the towns below Torrance, but it was minor. The surge of water was settling into the Mohawk River now, bleeding south. The rain had stopped with the dam break as if they'd been coconspirators.

The worst was done, she thought as daylight seeped through the night sky. Torrance had taken a beating, yes—Torrance had taken the kind of catastrophic beating that would be remembered for generations—but it was done now. Search-and-rescue operations would turn into rebuilding and recovery. She had a vague sense of what the days ahead held: FEMA camps and Red Cross shelters, rising death tolls and rabid media reports. They would seek a reason for the disaster, and they would find it in the long-neglected dam, but they wouldn't ask the questions that mattered, because no one was left to do that except for Gillian.

No one will ask about Galesburg, she thought as she sipped a bottle of Gatorade that a volunteer had handed her. She was both dizzy and numb, a disorienting sensation. Maybe everyone was dizzy and numb now, though.

She remembered, suddenly, the baby she'd carried down the ladder. She thought of the child's hot breath on her neck and the way the ladder had swayed beneath them in the blackness and how those joists in the old building had snapped like shotgun blasts, and her legs began to tremble. She dropped the Gatorade and leaned against the remains of a brick wall that had once been a hair salon, trying to use the ruins to steady herself. The roof and most of the interior had been swept away, but one barber chair remained, a strange artifact of a town that was no more. She wondered who'd been in the chair when the water came. She wondered if she'd handled the victim's body.

As if in response to the thought, her radio buzzed with static and a woman's voice came across, asking for Gillian. It was Sarah Burroughs, the chief deputy of the sheriff's department. Someone else answered—it sounded like Brett—saying that he'd seen her but didn't know where she was. He asked what was needed.

"I need to locate *her*," Sarah Burroughs said, and Gillian finally spoke. "This is Sergeant Mathers."

"I've been asked to tell you that Aaron Ellsworth—that's the sheriff's son—wants to speak with you. Something about an active investigation. I don't know what he was talking about, but he claimed you would."

Gillian put one gloved hand out on the sheared brick wall. Gripped it tight, feeling the abrasive, torn stone, searching for solidity.

"Okay. Put him on."

"I don't have him. He walked off. Waded off. You know what it's about?"

Gillian hesitated. How many listening ears were there right now? What had Aaron told Sarah Burroughs?

"Maybe," she said. "But if he's gone, I can't verify that. What did he say?"

"That he was en route to the dam and needed to speak with you. Said it was urgent."

"Thank you," Gillian said, and then she lowered the radio and clipped it back onto her belt.

The worst of it might not be over after all.

She pushed away from the busted bricks and looked for the man who'd handed her the Gatorade. He was walking through the crowd, passing the bottles out, and heading back toward his truck, which waited in about three feet of water. It was one of the newer Jeep pickups, a Gladiator. A lot of shiny off-roading muscle. She doubted he'd ever had it off pavement before this morning, but it had done the job nicely.

She went after him and called out, badge held high. He was almost back to the truck before he turned and noticed her. A young guy, maybe just twenty, with a beard and a baseball cap.

"Thanks for the drink," Gillian said.

"Yeah. Sure."

"I'm gonna need to borrow your truck, too."

He looked from her face to her badge and nodded without hesitation.

"Whatever you need," he said, and then reached into his pocket and held out the keys.

She was surprised, caught off guard by the complete compliance, and then felt foolish for holding the badge out. He was ready to give the truck to anyone who said they needed it. Material possessions didn't mean much in Torrance this morning.

"Thank you," she said, taking the keys. "I'll try to take care of it."

He laughed. "My house is gone," he said. "I'm not too worried about the truck. But let me get the rest of the Gatorades out before you go. A lot of people down here need them, I think."

She helped him unload four more cases of Gatorade from the bed of the truck.

"Where'd you get all these?"

"The Citgo."

"It's open?" she asked, and he looked at her strangely.

"No. They were floating in the parking lot."

The Citgo was two miles out of town. She hadn't even considered that the water had swept that far with that much fury.

"Good work," she said hollowly.

"Sure. Good luck," he answered, and then he turned away and began to break the Gatorade bottles out of the case. She stared at his back and thought about saying something more, expressing sympathy for his house, but it was clear he wasn't waiting on that, and it wouldn't matter. This wasn't a day for words. It was a day for deeds.

She left him there, passing out his Gatorade bottles, and drove away in his truck. He didn't even look up when she passed.

She drove northwest out of town, the Gladiator's knobby off-road tires chunking and thumping over unseen obstacles underwater. At one point the spray from the water began to rise in twin plumes in front of her, and the engine howled in protest. *Too deep,* she thought. *It won't work. I'll just get it stuck.* The tires kept finding purchase, though, and the truck kept grinding ahead. She felt a rise under the driver's-side tires and realized that she was actually driving down the sidewalk now, and then she spotted a thin antenna protruding from the water just a few feet in front of her, the tip painted bright orange.

What the hell is that? she wondered, and then registered it just in time: it was a snow marker for a fire hydrant.

She spun the steering wheel hard to the right and hammered the gas. The truck banged down from the sidewalk back onto the road, water geysered in front of her, and the engine growled like an angry cat. She missed the hydrant by inches.

A block farther on, the engine growl lessened and she felt that the truck wasn't pushing so hard. A little past that, and it was evident that the water level was dropping quickly. She was headed uphill now, and she could actually see dry pavement for the first time. It wasn't going to make for easier going, though; the asphalt had been carved up and lay scattered in slabs, like broken ice across a pond in spring.

Up higher, though, out of the floodplain, the road shouldn't be damaged at all. It was just a matter of getting there. She was reviewing her options and thinking that she needed to turn west and see if she could claw her way to the ridgetop, where Maple Ridge Road would likely be high and dry, when she saw a solitary figure walking ahead of her, knee-deep in the water, a duffel bag slung over his shoulder. He was in uniform. One of the National Guardsmen, maybe, or military.

He turned and looked back at the oncoming truck then, and she saw that it was Aaron Ellsworth.

He looked at the truck only briefly and then turned away and continued his slow, steady slog. She lowered the window and shouted.

"Aaron! It's me! Gillian!"

He stared at her, squinting into the rising sun behind the truck, and then headed toward her with an unsteady stride, favoring his wounded foot.

He'll be lucky if they don't need to amputate it after a night in this filth, she thought, but if the pain bothered him, it didn't register on his face. Not much registered on his face, actually. He looked washed-out, numb.

Looked, probably, just like her.

He waded up to the door and pulled it open and the water promptly ran into the cab, an inch covering the floor of the passenger seat. He looked down at it and said, "Sorry. Nice truck, though."

"Not mine."

"Even better. Nothing parties like a rental." He tossed the duffel bag into the backseat and hauled himself up. His face was lined with scratches beneath two days of stubble and his eyes were red-rimmed and sunken against dark, puffy flesh.

"How long have you been at it?" she said.

"Since it happened, basically. I'm guessing the same is true for you?"

She nodded. He sighed, peeled a glove off one hand, and then ran the hand over his face. "They tell you I was looking for you?"

"Yes."

"You know why?"

"Not exactly. But I think we've both got an idea."

He glanced at her and then out over the submerged landscape. "Right," he said. "We've both got an idea. I want to see him, though. I don't like him being up there. It's bad to have him up there."

Gillian didn't follow. "Who?"

"Fleming. He's been up there all night. He's the man in charge is what I was told." He rubbed his face again, wiping at his eyes with his thumb, and he wasn't looking at her when he said, "You hear anything from my dad?"

"No."

"That's a problem. He'd have found a way."

"Easier to say than do. Cell towers down, everyone working, total chaos."

"He'd have found a way," Aaron repeated.

She didn't argue. They sat there with the engine muttering and wisps of steam rising from beneath the hood. He said, "Were you going to take Maple Ridge out there?"

"I was going to try. It may be closed, too."

"It won't be. If you can get us up there, we'll be able to get close to the dam."

She put the truck back in gear and cut the wheel but hadn't yet moved her foot to the gas pedal when he added, "Is this what your family expected? What was predicted, I mean."

She was grateful for the simple questioning look in his eyes. No trace of doubt or indictment. He just wanted to know.

"It's close," she said softly, "but the flood went in the wrong direction."

"What does that mean?"

"Torrance was never the target," Gillian said, and suddenly her mouth was dry. She reached for the Gatorade bottle, unscrewed the cap, and took a sip. She saw his eyes follow it thirstily and extended the bottle. He took it and drank deeply.

"What was the target, then?"

"The city," Gillian said. "New York. It was always about the city. There was no score to settle with Torrance. Torrance was just a neighboring village; it meant no harm. The debt that's owed was supposed to . . ." She stopped, unsettled by how easily the matter-of-fact madness returned to her tongue.

"Supposed to what?" Aaron prompted.

"The debt that's owed was supposed to be paid by the city," she finished. "The idea was to take down the whole system. Reservoir by reservoir, tunnel by tunnel, until New York was dry. But that didn't happen."

"Or maybe it's not done," he said.

"If there was any truth to the old stories," Gillian said, "then it played out here last night. It's done, and it went the wrong way. They took all that evil and sent it into their own backyard. Killed their own neighbors. That's what they did."

Her voice was rising, and she stopped talking altogether before she reached a full-throated scream.

"That's not what I mean," Aaron said. "I'm saying this isn't the end of the Chill, even. All of this came from a partial breach. Most of the lake is still up there." He nodded toward the mountains. "It's still up there, and so is he. Fleming."

59

Deshawn almost died in a pothole.

The water wasn't deep, maybe eight inches over the road, but the pothole that had cratered open during the flood surge was at least two feet deep and hidden beneath the swirling brown water. It jarred his hip and wrenched his knee and he almost went down. He thought that if he'd fallen right there and cracked his skull, he might've drowned. Wouldn't that be something: live your whole life in the tunnels, working with explosives and whirling blades, and then die on the surface in a pothole and eight inches of water.

He wrenched his foot free and waded ahead, off the pavement and into a field alongside the road. It was hard to believe anyone had ever made a go of farming in this place. Everything was on an incline; even the fields were spread out across hills—nothing flat about them. He took a bottle of water out of Rochelle's purse and drank while he took stock. The road ahead had a four-way stop, and there were signs indicating Torrance to the left and the Chilewaukee Reservoir straight ahead.

He used one of the gold spangles to locate the zipper on Rochelle's purse and dropped the granola bar wrapper and water bottle back inside. He was fumbling with the zipper, trying to close it, when the sound of an engine came from behind him.

It was an old white SUV, a Ford Bronco, like the one O.J. had made famous all those years ago. The body had rust damage and there was a crack on the windshield but the tall tires were new and it had no trouble motoring down the road, shedding the water in plumes on either side.

Deshawn lifted his hand and put out his thumb. The Bronco came to a stop and sent a spray of muddy water into Deshawn's face. He rubbed his eyes clear with his shirtsleeve and when he lowered his arm he saw the bearded face of a wild-eyed kid grinning at him from behind the wheel and, just below, a Confederate flag decal on the driver's-door panel. Below, a coiled rattlesnake warned Deshawn not to tread on him.

Oh, boy, Deshawn thought, but a ride was a ride, and the kid was the only passerby he'd seen yet. Beggars and choosers, he figured, so he gave a little smile and nod and said, "Thanks for stopping."

The kid kept that odd grin. He was wearing a sleeveless shirt even though it was cold out, and there was a strap across his chest that Deshawn had mistaken for his seat belt and now realized was a bandolier filled with brass cartridges.

"Nice purse, boy," the bearded kid said, and then he swung a rifle out of the passenger seat and brought it to bear on Deshawn's chest.

"Thank you," Deshawn said. "I like it, myself. A real nice lady gave it to me. It's got water in it. You need some water?"

The kid barked a laugh. "Only thing *nobody* needs today is fuckin' water."

"Mind pointing that thing somewhere else?" Deshawn said, taking care to keep his eyes on the kid's face. "No need for that."

"Hell there ain't! We're in martial law now, boy!"

"No," Deshawn said. "We're in search-and-rescue. It's a very different thing. The law's doing just fine. So why don't you—"

"Give me the fuckin' bag and get down on your knees," the kid said. The odd grin was gone and his eyes were empty and Deshawn remembered how uncomfortable his father had been all those years ago when they were lost on the back roads, the first and last time they ever went into the woods as a family. He thought that this kid had probably never been in the city and that if he went, he'd be just as scared as Deshawn's father had been of the tiny mountain towns. That was a problem: everyone scared of the other just because they didn't intersect. And when they did, well, they might intersect like this.

That worsened the problem.

Deshawn tried to focus on the kid's fear. The one thing they shared.

"We're all scared today," Deshawn said. "I know I am. I need to find my daughter. Can you help me? She's with the police."

"Bullshit."

"The truth."

"Ain't no police left to matter, don't you get it? This day's been a long time coming and I've been ready for it. You think *I* was *scared*? Shit. I been *planning* for this day. And there ain't nobody gonna rob me or fool me or run me off. It's dog eat dog now." He grinned. "However you wanna look at it, I was ready, and you don't look so ready, standing there with your purse."

"Let's relax here," Deshawn said. "Let's try to help each other out and—"

"I said *on your fucking knees!*" He screamed it this time, and when he screamed, the gun barrel shook.

Deshawn nodded and went down on his knees in the mud beside the road. His right hand was still inside Rochelle's purse. It was an oversized bag, and he was grateful for that, because the bag didn't jostle as he moved his fingers over the water bottles in search of the pepper spray. He found the canister, slid it into his palm, and felt for the discharge button with his index finger. Found that, too. Was there a safety of some sort, some pin that needed to be pulled or tab that needed to be broken off? Better not be.

"Throw your shit up in the back of the truck," the bearded kid said, "and then we'll decide what else you gotta do to earn your life." He leered and blew Deshawn a kiss.

"Yes, sir," Deshawn said, and then he used his left hand to remove the purse strap from his shoulder and toss the bag into the truck. The kid's eyes followed the purse's arc, as if he'd thought Deshawn might swing it at him instead—and that was good, because by the time his eyes came back to Deshawn, the pepper spray was ready to meet them.

Deshawn fired the pepper spray with his right hand while lunging forward and grabbing the rifle barrel with his left. The kid screamed and the gun went off, a single, staggeringly loud shot that blew chunks of asphalt out of the water and pebbled them against Deshawn's face. The kid was torn between desire and instinct then, brain and pain—he knew better than to let go of the rifle, but he was also desperate to reach for his burning eyes. In the end, he tried to do both, reaching for his eyes with his right hand while clutching the rifle with his left.

Deshawn dropped the pepper spray, got both hands on the rifle barrel, and ripped it forward, thirty years of sandhog muscle and an overload of adrenaline going into the single yank. Not only did he get the gun but the kid came with it, tumbling out of the Bronco. No self-respecting redneck badass wore a seat belt on the day of martial law, apparently. He fell howling into the mud, pawing at his eyes with both hands now, and Deshawn stepped aside to study the rifle. It was a bolt-action hunting rifle of unknown caliber to Deshawn, who'd never been around many long guns. He understood enough about the butt end of it, though, and he used that to hammer the kid's skull until he was facedown and moaning and no threat to get back up.

"Son," Deshawn told him, "if the day of martial law ever actually comes, you'd be wise to sit it out."

He used the rifle to spread the kid's feet apart, and then he stepped forward and drove one powerful kick of his steel-toed boot into the hillbilly fool's testicles. The kid howled again, his pitch a good bit higher this time, and then slid down the muddy embankment and into the ditch.

"If you need your gun or your truck," Deshawn called down to him, "they'll be with my purse."

He walked back to the road, tossed the rifle into the Bronco's backseat, and then fished Rochelle's purse off the floor and set it beside him on the passenger seat. By the time he'd gotten settled, the kid was up on his knees in the ditch, one hand rubbing his eyes, the other clutching his balls.

Deshawn tapped the horn in a cheerful farewell—*beep beep bu beep beep!*—and drove away.

60

Aaron sipped the last of Gillian's Gatorade and rested his exhausted body while she drove them down the dry pavement of Maple Ridge Road. He was feeling better than he had in hours, seeing how much of the county remained unmarked by the flood and appreciating the way the dry, sunlit sky appeared to offer a confirmation of hope, when Gillian's radio brought them the news that his father was dead.

They'd found Steve Ellsworth's body more than a mile below the dam, in the carnage of what had once been a quiet, tree-lined neighborhood named Pleasant Ridge.

He hadn't drowned there. Hadn't drowned anywhere.

He'd been shot twice.

The call hadn't gone out on a shared band. The dispatcher was seeking Gillian directly, because the FBI was on scene and had questions for her about the sheriff of Torrance County.

"They want to ask you about the last time you spoke with him," the dispatcher said. "They seem interested in what he was doing at the dam, and they're hearing rumors about the way the sirens and surveillance cameras were disabled."

Gillian brought the big Jeep truck to a stop on the side of the road. A gentle breeze fanned through the pines and carried their fragrance into the truck. They were high above the flooded valley now, with the sun full on their faces. Gillian held the radio to her lips but didn't speak. She was staring at Aaron.

The dispatcher came back and asked if Gillian copied. Still, she waited on Aaron.

"My father did not do anything to disrupt their cameras or alarms," he said. His voice was ragged. "My father would've taken a bullet before that. It sounds like he took two of them."

Gillian finally keyed the mike and spoke into it. Copied the information and said she was en route to the dam.

"Sheriff Ellsworth wouldn't have tampered with emergency systems," Gillian said then. "That's insane."

"Sergeant, I'm just telling you what I've heard. We've got the county sheriff shot to death on the same night as the dam broke. Rumors are flying, and the Bureau wants you here, not there. Do you copy that?"

"I copy," Gillian said. "It'll take me a little while, but I can get there."

"You need transport?"

"No. I'm en route," she said, and lowered the radio.

Aaron stared straight ahead. Up here on the ridge, in the pines and sun, everything he'd seen in Torrance felt imagined, a nightmare from which he'd woken. Somewhere below where they sat right now in the idling truck, his father's body had been found. Somewhere in the mud, floating amid the garbage.

"He must have been up at the dam," he said. He heard each word distinctly and listened to them as if they were coming from someone else. "He must have been there when it happened. He wouldn't have been in Pleasant Ridge. The water swept him down there."

Gunshots. Two gunshot wounds. Someone had murdered his father and left him to the flood.

Gillian Mathers put her hand on his leg but didn't say a word. He looked down at her hand, thought about covering it with his own, but didn't move. The warming breeze gusted and filled the truck with clean, pine-scented air. The sun was bright on the hood of the truck.

"I wonder if he got the message," Aaron said.

"What message?"

"I left him a voicemail. It was in the afternoon. Right before I fell asleep. Before the dam broke and it all went to hell. I wonder if he heard it."

If he had, would it have mattered? Probably not. There had been no grand exchange of sentiment. Aaron had told him to be safe, that was all. His father had scribbled a note before he left, had written, *Thank you, son,* and Aaron had called back and told him to be safe. Not a great loss if he hadn't heard that.

Thank you, son.

Be safe, Dad.

The sun glare on the hood was harsh on his eyes. He turned away. Looked into the pines.

Gillian said, "They're not going to blame him for the cameras and the sirens, Aaron. He was murdered, and they'll understand those things all fit together."

"Does it matter if they do blame him?"

"Yes," she said, and her sharp tone brought his face around to hers. Her raven-dark hair was hanging in still-damp tangles across her face, underneath the DEP baseball cap, and there was a streak of blood along her right cheek. Maybe hers, maybe not.

"It matters," she said.

He nodded. He supposed she was right. It did matter. His father had policed the county in the right way for too long to leave any rumors behind.

"Then let's set that much right," Aaron said. "You can help. I'd appreciate that. But I don't want to go to Kingston. I want—I *need*—to go back to the dam. I need to see Fleming."

"That's where we're headed," she said.

"You said you were en route."

She took her hand off his leg and put it on the gearshift. Immediately he missed the touch, the warmth.

"It's a circuitous route," she said, and then she put the truck back in gear. Before she moved her foot to the gas, she said, "I'm so sorry, Aaron," in a voice that trembled.

"Thank you," he said, and he might have offered more but he wasn't going to get the words out now, so he didn't try. She pressed down on the gas and the truck rumbled forward.

Aaron looked down the valley. Birches and pines and hemlocks weaved in the wind. You couldn't see the damage down below, but when the wind shifted, you could smell it. The stink of overturned earth, like a grave.

I was sober when I called, he thought, *and I worked all night, Dad. I helped people last night. Saved a few, maybe. Maybe not. But I was there, and I was helping. If anyone saw me, they didn't feel embarrassed for you. Not last night. For a few hours there, I had it all together.*

He wished Steve had seen that much. It wouldn't have fixed everything—wouldn't have fixed anything—but it would have meant something for him to see it.

"I'm glad you kept me at the dam yesterday," Aaron said.

Gillian glanced at him, surprised, or maybe confused.

"We found the body where I said it would be," he said. "So he knew that much was real. And you told him I was sober. He knew that, too."

She watched him without speaking.

"I'm glad for that," he said simply, and then he went quiet again. She turned away, and they rode along the sun-splashed ridgeline together in silence.

61

An interesting thing happened at the Chilewaukee Reservoir in the hours between midnight and dawn. As more people from more agencies began to arrive, more people and more agencies began to lay claim to Mick Fleming's plan to blast the old intake chambers and use the antiquated tunnels to relieve pressure on the dam. Mick was amused by this but pleased by the consensus.

Let it seem as if it had been a group consensus, and let it gather momentum. The old tunnels beneath the mountain loomed like manna from heaven, too good to be true, a temporary and safe place to deposit millions of gallons of water while utilizing the natural grade of the lake bed to draw down the water level and save what was left of the dam. Then they could build a temporary dam behind the original structure and add emergency spillways. It would all work. It would save the day.

Over and over, he heard references to the *original flaws* of the water-tunnel design. His grandfather's design. He'd wondered about those flaws himself in years past. The engineering of the Chilewaukee tunnels simply hadn't worked.

Not for New York City, at least.

Mick finally understood that it hadn't been designed for the city at all. Somewhere along the line, Jeremiah Fleming had begun to work for Galesburg.

He'd done a fine job, too.

By the time the sun came up and lit the lake, mist rising off the surface like sea smoke, a temporary sluice made with felled trees and riprap had been finished. It wasn't much, but it would use the grade of the lake bed to channel the water where it needed to go.

He was intrigued that not a single soul seemed to remember the far side of the mountain. Somewhere over there, decaying and collapsing in on itself for decades upon decades now, was the discharge chamber that had been built to receive the water from the tunnels and empty it into Gideon's Gorge, funneling the water toward the Ashokan, the largest of all the reservoirs in the New York system. The old discharge basin was out of sight and out of mind now because the tunnels had never been completed, but nevertheless, Mick thought it would be prudent to send a team down there to get a good look.

He was hardly going to suggest that, though.

All they needed now was the blasting. Fuse cord had been obtained, but explosives that satisfied the Army Corps team had not. They were inbound on a helicopter.

It was only a matter of time before the Chilewaukee's tunnels were finally unsealed.

While Ben Quirk and Sandy Clemmons negotiated with the blasting engineers, Mick was finally able to slip away. In the early hours, every time he turned around, there'd been someone with a fresh question. Now they were focused on their endeavor, racing against time, and nobody seemed to have anything new to ask. The moonshot had been decided, and the moonshot would work. He could feel their optimism in the air like an electric current. They were going to conquer the dam, the lake, the mountain.

They were quite sure of that.

When Mick looked at the spires of granite reflected on the surface of the lake, he thought they seemed amused by all the human labors. *Don't they remember?* the mountains asked the water and the water asked Mick, the three of them in a secret alliance of whispers and snickers.

Of course not, Mick thought. *Of course, they do not remember. You smacked them in the mouth just yesterday, and already they believe they're back in control. They haven't even gathered all of the dead yet, and somehow they believe they're in control.*

Human confidence was extraordinary.

He made his way up the hill and into the birches, where he could watch the work but have a moment of privacy. Anders Wallace trailed behind.

"I'm still not sure it will work as you hope," Mick said as they sat alone in the cool breeze and watched a dozer move earth below. A helicopter made slow passes over the lake, its rotor wash roiling the water and whipping the treetops.

"Rest easy," Anders said, looping his forearms across his knees. "Much has been done before tonight."

"Have they made it all the way through?"

"They've been hard at work for many years, sir. Many generations. They've had no distractions." He paused, then qualified, "No options, actually. They work. They toil."

Mick remembered the ceaseless labors he'd seen below the dam, the crack of picks off stone, the scrape of shovels.

"Are there enough of them?"

"Don't limit your thinking, sir," Anders said. "Remember that where you see one crew, it's not the sum total. Think of the system."

Mick did. The system was more than a century old and spanned more than a hundred miles. How many had died building it? How many were involved in whatever work had taken place since? Sealed away, forgotten, but still toiling.

"It's only a matter of connecting them?" he asked. "Not just the water, but the . . . workforce?"

He was uneasy saying *ghosts* around Anders, as if the term might offend. While the Galesburg crew was most certainly made up of ghosts, they were unique, and they were proud. He didn't wish to insult them.

"That's a good way of looking at it," Anders said.

"You needed someone like me, though. You couldn't have done it without me."

"We're indebted, yes. And grateful, of course. But you were always headed this way, sir. The Chilewaukee was special. You always knew that."

"I don't believe that's true."

"No? You worried about it. The neglect angered you. It was personal, wasn't it?"

"Not personal," Mick said. Had it not been, though? Had his inspections of the Chilewaukee not struck a more emotional—and perhaps darker—chord than those conducted anyplace else? He loved the look of the place but hated the lack of attention it received. Hated its lack of utility. "My grandfather designed it, sure, but I didn't think about him much. Why would I? I never knew him."

Anders watched with a smile.

"I never cared for this place," Mick said. "That's the truth."

"Yet you came back."

"Because I had to be here. For the job."

"I agree."

Mick felt uneasy with him, which was strange on a day when Anders had been such a comfort.

"I don't understand what you mean," he said.

"The past is never passive," Anders told him. "Not even when it's forgotten. Especially not then."

As the wind shifted branches overhead, the dappled sunlight found him and slipped through him. He was clearer in the darkness, his existence undeniable there. Under a full sun, though, Mick wasn't sure if he'd be able to see him at all.

"My grandfather designed it for you, didn't he?" Mick said. "Not for the city. Not in the end."

Anders smiled. "He came to see what was special about this place. In time, he came to understand that it was not the right spot for a concept such as *eminent domain*. No, Galesburg was never the right spot for that."

Mick turned from Anders and studied the mountain at their backs. Reached out and laid his hand on an outcropping of granite, felt the coarse rock under his palm.

"The city was always told that," Anders said. "Repeatedly and stridently, they were told. The point was made in as many ways as it could be."

For a moment, tethered to the mountain by the feel of the cold rock under his palm, Mick had a memory of the man he used to be. Just a flash. He saw his office, his house, his wife, his life. Saw his maps of the system, his data on each dam under his purview. He remembered his visits here, and the ominous feeling that would overtake him when he saw the name Chilewaukee on his calendar.

He jerked his hand away in pain. A sliver of sharpened stone, invisible until his flesh touched it, had opened his palm like a blade's edge. A thin line of blood shone in the sunlight. No more than a paper cut, but still, it felt like a message.

"Where are you from, Anders?"

"Galesburg, of course."

"How long ago?"

Anders Wallace smiled without any trace of humor. "You ask too many questions, sir."

Mick looked at him and then back down at the line of blood creeping across his palm. He closed his fist tightly on the blood, and he asked no more questions.

62

Deshawn came to a stop at a steep Y-shaped intersection. Go left and it would take him down toward the dam; go right and the road wound into the mountains. He wasn't sure if it led all the way to the other side or if it would get him badly lost, but fortunately the fool who'd tried to rob him had an outdated Garmin GPS unit in the old Bronco. Navigation was critical for the days of martial law, clearly. Deshawn sat in the idling truck, studied the Garmin, and decided to go right. It seemed the road climbed up into the mountains and then back down and tracked parallel to a course that led toward Ashokan. There was no indication of the old structure that Deshawn remembered, but he thought it had to be down there, or close. Somewhere down there was the crumbling rock basin where he'd once sat with a beautiful girl and skipped stones and sipped champagne and tried not to show how unsettled he was by the place.

He cut the wheel of the Bronco, hit the gas, and started up Maple Ridge Road, the floodplain receding behind him as he climbed, falling out of sight behind sharp S-curves and forested hills. Even the smell of the flood began to fade, the air growing cleaner as he gained elevation.

As he came around one of the sharp bends, he heard an engine and saw a flash of gunmetal gray. He was driving across the centerline to hold a higher speed through the curves, and he thought it might prove to be his last mistake, causing a head-on collision. He pounded the brakes, the tires smoked, and he came to a jarring stop not three feet from the grille of the oncoming car. It was a big pickup, one of the new

Jeep models, and he lifted his hand in embarrassed apology toward the other driver.

Only then did he realize he was looking at his daughter.

He put the Bronco into park with a trembling hand and opened the door and climbed out. Gillian was already out of the truck. There was someone else with her, a tall young man in uniform. Coast Guard? That made sense. They'd been performing water rescues all night.

"Dad? What are you doing here?"

"Looking for you," he said, but of course that was only partially true.

Gillian gathered her emotions with a laugh and a shake of her head. He remembered how she'd done that as a little girl. In youth basketball games, when a call went against her, she would always step back and make that little laugh and headshake. He remembered that well. Look at her now. A grown woman, a police officer. Just look at her.

He didn't want to have to tell her the truth. It might break her heart if she heard the truth about Deshawn's headful of ghosts.

"This is Aaron Ellsworth," she said. "He's the sheriff's son. He's been helping me try to . . . to sort it out."

"It sounds very bad in Torrance," Deshawn said, shaking the young man's hand. Aaron had big hands and a strong grip but his eyes were foggy, exhausted.

"It is," Aaron Ellsworth said tonelessly. "A lot of people died. My father was one of them."

Stunned, Deshawn managed to say, "I'm so sorry."

Aaron nodded with the polite detachment of a grief that hadn't fully landed yet. Gillian was surveying the Bronco, with its *Don't Tread on Me* logo and Confederate flag.

"Nice truck," she said. "Where exactly did you think you were headed?"

"It was an Uber situation," he said. "Five stars for one, and none for the other."

"Where were you going?"

Deshawn looked away from her and up the winding mountain pass. How much time left? Enough to explain? Probably not.

"There's a place I need to see," he said. "It won't make much sense to you, but I need to see it, and once I do, we can talk, and I can explain."

His daughter's dark eyes bored into his. "What place?"

"It doesn't matter. It won't make sense yet, but—"

"We're on our third day of things that don't make sense, Dad. You'd be surprised at the things we're ready to understand."

We. He looked from her to Ellsworth and saw the young man's eyes had lost their bleary, distracted quality. He was focused now.

"Did you know?" Ellsworth asked Deshawn.

"Did I know what?"

"That the dam was going to break. Was that something you were told by her mother, or grandmother, or somebody in that schoolroom?"

"No," Deshawn said, "I didn't know that. I was . . . I've been told someplace I need to go."

"By who?" Gillian asked. She had her hand on his arm, squeezing just below his elbow. "Dad? Who told you to head up here?"

What was he supposed to say to that? *A dead man sent me, dear, and I can't be delayed, not even by you.*

He didn't know what he could tell her, but he could show her, at least.

He walked back to the Bronco. Opened the passenger door and fumbled through Rochelle the Uber driver's purse and located Gillian's old sketchbook. He was curious if she'd even remember it.

His curiosity didn't last long—her face changed before he'd even put the book in her hands. Just the sight of it was enough.

"Why do you have that?" she said.

"I want to ask you a question about it," Deshawn said. "It's time. You said so yourself, on the phone. It's time to talk."

"I wasn't talking about those old pictures."

"Yes," he said. "You were. You just may not know it yet."

He opened the book. Flipped through the pages filled with her child's work. A skilled child, yes, but a child's hand all the same.

Gillian's lips were pressed into a flat line and she stared at the pictures in silence as they passed. All those old faces. Men in helmets or high boots, men with picks, men with dynamite. Men in tunnels.

Deshawn got to the one that had scared him the worst, the one he hadn't let himself look at even a few hours earlier, standing in his own apartment. He looked at it now.

The sketch was of a hard-faced man with a broad jaw, a pug nose, and close-set eyes. Dark slashes of eyebrows that nearly met in the middle. A squat, muscular build, with a wide neck. He wore dungarees and a black T-shirt and his hard hat was in his hand. That would prove to be a problem for him later. His lip curled at the left corner in the faintest hint of a cocky grin. He was resting his weight on the rung of a ladder. Behind him, an empty cage hovered above a shaded circle of blackness.

"You drew this," Deshawn said. "When you were a little girl, you drew it. You remember that?"

She was staring at the sketch as if it might come to life.

"Gill? Do you—"

"I remember it."

He nodded. Wet his lips. Said, "Do you know who it is?"

Silence. The wind worked over the mountain, ruffling the sketchbook as if trying to flip the page. Deshawn put his thumb down to keep the picture from turning over.

"Biddle?" Gillian said. Faint-voiced and questioning, uncertain. "Eddie Biddle? No, Teddy." She looked up at him. "Is that right?"

"Yes."

"How do you know that's right?"

"Because I knew him," Deshawn said. "We worked together in the tunnels, before you were born. Before I met your mother. And he died down there." He paused, remembering the way the blood had rained out of Teddy's face when the cable sheared through him. "How'd you come to draw him?"

"Because I was supposed to," she said, almost whispering. "It was homework. I was supposed to draw them and remember them."

"You drew it from a picture?"

She nodded. Aaron Ellsworth was staring at her with fascination, not looking at Deshawn or the sketch but only at Gillian.

"Haupring's pictures?" Ellsworth asked.

Gillian nodded again, and Deshawn said, "How do *you* know that name?"

"Because I've met him," Aaron said. "I saw him at the dam. Two days ago. Day before it burst."

"I saw him last night," Gillian said, still in the near whisper.

Deshawn felt light-headed in the way you did when you stood up too fast, putting the brain out of equilibrium with the body.

"Did he take your picture?" Deshawn asked. "Either of you?"

Gillian shook her head, and Ellsworth said, "No. Did he take yours?"

Deshawn shook his head.

"That's probably why we're standing here," Ellsworth said. "Isn't it? He didn't pick us."

There it was, voiced aloud for the first time in Deshawn's life. How funny—or sad—that it hadn't come from him. All these years of silence and denial, and now a stranger just came out and said it.

"Maybe," Deshawn muttered. "I don't know. I didn't want to believe anything like that—didn't want to *think* anything like that—but . . ."

"He came to document the story," Gillian said suddenly.

They both looked at her. She'd gotten her voice back, and her jaw was tightly set, the way she'd gotten as a girl when they argued. Stubborn. Stoic.

"Haupring documented the story," she said. "But he wouldn't tell it. *We* had to do that."

Deshawn remembered her mother saying words so similar to him, right before he'd fled from her for good.

"He's not . . . he wasn't a real man, was he?"

She hesitated. Seemed to turn the question over.

"He had different rules," she said carefully. "That's what he told the families when he came to Galesburg. That he was a different man, with different rules."

"He just showed up?" Aaron Ellsworth asked.

Gillian shook her head. With the DEP baseball cap on, she looked younger, so much like she had as a girl.

"They found him," she said. "Anders Wallace. Maybe my grandfather. There were rumors about him, legends that went back to the older reservoirs, back to Croton, all of the earliest camps. Always the same idea: he was documenting the construction."

"Your mother told me that his name mattered," Deshawn said. "It was like a game to them. He didn't really have a name, or at least he never offered one, so they gave him one. Is that right? Some kind of joke. Or it seemed like a joke to people who didn't understand him yet."

"It was an anagram," Gillian said, and gave a sad laugh that almost broke into a sob. "I had to unscramble it. That was homework, too. It was a hard one for me, because I didn't know the last word. I had to learn it first."

"What was it?" Aaron Ellsworth asked.

"Hubris," she said. "Curtis B. Haupring. The letters of his name spelled *capturing hubris*. That was the joke. Anders Wallace gave him the name, I think."

"What *is* he?" Deshawn said.

"He looked for people who had contempt," Gillian said. Her voice was steady but she seemed very distant. She reminded Deshawn of her grandmother, a woman he'd hardly known but remembered well. Molly Mathers had a unique bearing. Present but contained, with critical parts of her held at a distance. "Contempt and arrogance. For the past, for nature, for power."

She reached out and tapped the sketchbook.

"Is this the one who told you where you're supposed to go?" she asked. "Teddy Biddle?"

"No." He turned the pages and found the man with the high rubber boots. "It was this one. Just yesterday."

She studied the picture. "Downstream," she said. "Sure. Somewhere between Westchester and the city. He died in a pressure tunnel. I think it collapsed on him. He was a foreman."

"You remember him, too?" Deshawn said, amazed.

"I remember them all," she said simply. "I've tried to forget, but I can't. I remember them all."

"You said they have to work," Aaron Ellsworth said. "By *work*, you mean..."

"Down below," she said. "I don't know what the work is like. I was supposed to find out, though. At some point, some drought season, when they'd be tired and in need of help, I would have to—"

"Don't," Deshawn said, suddenly unable to bear it, hearing these words again, words that once her mother had spoken to him.

"It's time to say it," she said. "I would have to die. Sacrifice myself to help them. Galesburg was waiting for me. It was up to me to make sure they hadn't been forgotten up here, that people still believed, and then ... then I was supposed to join them in the Dead Waters. Just like my grandmother. Just like my mother."

"What's different up here?" Deshawn whispered. "In the Chill? It's different than downstream."

"That's the point," she said. "It was built to be different. Wallace and Fleming and the rest made sure of that. The Chill is where old mythologies met modern engineering."

"I don't understand that."

She took a breath. "Think I do?"

"You know the idea, at least."

"Yes. The idea is that people didn't listen, and then people would forget they hadn't listened, and when that happens, people will pay a price." She shifted uneasily, looking almost embarrassed by her words. "They were told not to take Galesburg. They didn't listen."

"Why not just destroy the dam to begin with?"

"You can't destroy a dam that doesn't exist. But you can build one designed to fail."

Beside her, Aaron Ellsworth said, "That's the equation. The one on the chalkboard in your old house."

"Yes. That's what we saw yesterday. Only it didn't work, not the way they'd intended it to."

The wind gusted again and this time the pages did turn over, and Deshawn closed the book. They all faced each other there on the lonely mountain road, waiting for someone to speak.

"I need to go," he said finally. "I'm not sure what's waiting on me down there, but I know that I have to go."

"Where?" Gillian asked.

"An old spot. Other side of the mountain. It's the place where once they were supposed to bring the water out of the tunnels."

"The discharge basin," she said.

"You've been there?"

She nodded. "It's bone-dry, mostly. Not now, of course. After all this rain, it may be close to full."

"Can you tell me how to get there?" he asked. "I think wasting time is a mistake. A risk."

"I can show you."

"No. It needs to be me. Alone. Just tell me—"

"Nobody's going anywhere alone," his daughter told him, and then she turned on her heel and walked back to her truck. "You can follow me."

63

It was only five miles to the old discharge chamber in Gideon's Gorge, but the road was steep and winding and the drive couldn't be made quickly on the best of days, let alone after the rains had left washout and debris scattered across the asphalt. Gillian drove the first few minutes in silence before Aaron Ellsworth finally broke it.

"Did you know your dad believed it before today?" he asked as she braked hard on a banked curve that was blanketed by soil runoff and damp leaves.

"Believed what, exactly?" she said.

"Any of it. He stood there talking about ghosts with you, and it was like you were hearing him for the first time."

The tires threw mud and leaves into the air and found firm footing again, and now they were angling down, out of the sun and into the shadowed valley.

"We never talked about it."

"*Never?* It was your mom, it was his wife, and—"

"They weren't married."

"Fine. Still, he never talked about any of it?"

Gillian navigated another curve and found a straightaway below. The sun spilled through the trees here, landing on the road in drops, as if passed through a strainer. She looked in the mirror and saw her father behind her, driving the old Bronco. She tried to think of a way to explain it that made sense. Why *hadn't* they ever spoken of Galesburg?

"He was scared of me," she said. "When he first came to get me and take me home, he was scared. Not just of being a parent and having the responsibility. That was part of it, I'm sure, but he was afraid of what I believed."

"Then I wouldn't expect him to show up here talking about the advice he was getting from dead men in the water tunnels."

Neither had Gillian.

"Maybe," she said, "I misread his silence."

"What does that mean?"

"I thought we needed the silence because he didn't want to hear what I'd been taught. But maybe it was really because he didn't want to admit what he believed."

She nodded as if in affirmation of her own theory. She remembered his face on that drive back to the city, and she remembered the day he'd seen her sketchbook.

"He was *truly* scared, and the only things that can truly scare someone are the things they're capable of believing. The nightmares that linger in your mind during the day linger because they feel possible."

She crested a hill and drove down the other side. To her left, sparkling water flowed down the rock face of the mountain. A freshwater spring, one that would be dry in the summer, but now was open. The Catskills were offering up all their wealth this autumn. She had a feeling the discharge basin would be underwater and wondered what her father would do then. What he was expecting to find down there. The real action was on the other side of the mountain, and they were driving away from it.

"He needs to be right," she said, "or we're not going to achieve much out here."

If Aaron had an answer, it was drowned out by the sound of another helicopter passing overhead, its blades thumping the air, carrying someone or something across Maiden Mountain and toward the dam. Gillian glanced up, curious if it was a TV chopper or something more official. It passed in a flicker, but for a moment she saw it clearly: military paint job, a large, squat helicopter. A cargo mover, probably. What was being delivered to the Chill?

Then the helicopter was gone and she lowered her eyes and followed the road on down the slope. There was a pullout at the bottom of the hill that had once been lined with gravel. The gravel had been washed away, and all that was left was mud. She pulled in, and her father brought the Bronco in beside her. Gillian cut the engine and looked at Aaron.

"Well," she said, "I guess we're about to find out."

"This is it?"

She pointed to a narrow footpath through the trees. It was steep and rocky. Everything here was lined with rock. They were in Gideon's Gorge, a narrow notch in the mountains that funneled groundwater into the south fork of Cresap Creek and on toward the Ashokan and the eight million New Yorkers beyond.

"It's up there," she said. "And it's nothing but forgotten stone in the ground. Unless, of course, my father is right."

"Then what will it be?"

She opened the door. "I have no idea," she said, and stepped out.

Her dad was already out of the Bronco. He was holding the rifle and facing the trail with an expression torn between apprehension and appreciation.

"This is it," he said. "I would've driven right past it. I thought you could see the stonework from the road."

"No," Gillian said. "You've got to walk a bit. It's not far. There's a waterfall, and then there's the basin. It's nothing but overgrown old stone."

He nodded, eyes far off, as if remembering the place.

"Since when do you have a gun?" Gillian asked.

He looked at the rifle as if he'd forgotten it. He was holding it awkwardly, which was no surprise; as far as Gillian knew, her father had never fired a gun.

"I acquired it on my way," he said.

"You think you're going to need it?"

He didn't answer. Instead, he gestured at the trail. "Nobody comes out here, then?"

"Maybe some hikers, but it's not part of a trail system. We still come out here because technically the city still owns the land. It's something we have to check, but it hardly receives regular patrols."

She studied his broad, dark face, looking for some reassurance that he knew what he was doing. He looked confused but determined to see it through. He didn't know why he was on the mission, maybe, but it seemed he was damn well going to complete it.

"Let's give it a look," he said, and started forward. Gillian followed, and Aaron fell in behind them, walking beneath the steep, jagged walls of the gorge. Hemlocks grew along it wherever they could find enough soil to take root, and ferns lined the bottom. Clean water dripped from rocks in all directions.

They'd walked only a dozen paces when Gillian's radio crackled to life. Dispatch, asking for her twenty. The FBI was waiting. The FBI had questions.

Gillian stopped walking and so did Aaron. Her father kept pushing ahead. She wasn't sure if he hadn't heard the call or just didn't care.

She took the radio off her belt, looking Aaron in the eyes.

"Thoughts?" she said.

"We're either on the wrong side of the mountain," Aaron said, "or he knows what he's doing. But I don't know how in the hell you're supposed to explain that to them."

She looked up the trail to where her father's stocky form was already disappearing into the hemlocks. He was walking fast and with purpose. And a gun.

She clicked off the power on her radio.

"Let's see what we find," she said, and they started down the trail again, taking their lead from a New York City sandhog who hadn't set foot in Torrance County in two decades as he hurried down the path that a dead man in a tunnel under Queens had instructed him to find.

The walk was short, a half mile at best. Slippery going, stepping across wet rocks and mud slicks, and alive with the sound of dripping water. The sound intensified as they walked, and Gillian knew they were nearing the waterfall now. Usually it was twin trickles chasing the sides of a boulder, but today it was pouring over, the twin falls turned into one. They used rocks to cross the brook that formed below it, and then the trail curled to the right and brought them out into a stretch of dark valley. In front of them, bluestone walls lined a long chamber of churning brown water. A rusted, decaying fence ran above the stone walls. A handful of beer bottles sat on the walls, and some sodden trash was pinned against the fence, but otherwise there was no indication anyone had been there in years. Gillian hadn't seen the spot since summer, and then the basin had been nearly dry, with just a few trapped puddles. Now it looked like an angry sea.

"How deep is it?" Aaron asked.

"I'm not sure. Last time I saw it, we could have walked the bottom. Now?" She tried to remember, estimating the height of the walls. "Maybe ten feet deep? Fifteen?"

Her father had walked ahead. He gripped one of the rusted fence rails in his hand and looked down at the water and then up at the dark wall of rock on the far side.

"This was where they were supposed to hole through?" he said, using a term Gillian had heard from him before. Holing through was a tunnel builder's term for breaking ground on one side or the other.

"Right," she said. "But they never came close. It was a dead project long before that."

"Then what the hell are we doing here?" Aaron said.

No one answered. They just stood there in the cool shadows on the valley side of the mountain, staring at the forgotten, purposeless basin and all of its trapped rainwater.

Gillian was just about to speak, when her father lifted his hand.

"Listen," Deshawn Ryan whispered. "You hear that?"

They listened. Gillian heard the stirrings of tree limbs in the breeze, but those were very soft, with the mountain blocking most of the air. Other than that, all she heard was water—the churning in the basin beneath them, the tumult of the waterfall behind them, and the quiet plinks of dripping water in the gorge all around them.

"It's like a . . . knocking," Aaron said, stepping farther out, head cocked.

"That's coming from up above," Gillian said. "It's the water dripping down the rock."

Aaron and her dad shook their heads in unison.

"Not that," Aaron said. "The sound's a little bit deeper."

She walked closer. Listened and waited. There it was, yes, a deeper sound. Something close to the slow, steady drips, but with more force.

"It's a pick," her father said. "Or a rock hammer. But it's damn sure not water. That's metal hitting stone." He swiveled his head, listened for a few more seconds, and then pointed into the roiling waters in the basin. "It's not coming from above us, either. It's coming up from below."

This time she heard it and agreed. The sound was muffled by the water, and if you removed that buffer, you'd have heard the metallic crack of the stone clearly.

While her dad and Aaron pressed closer to the discharge chamber, listening and seeking the source, Gillian turned the other way. She looked downstream, following the water as it flowed into the shallow creek bed. It vanished in the wooded and shadowed valley, but she knew where it was going: into the Ashokan Reservoir, and then into the city.

"They got it right," she said softly.

Both of them turned back to her then.

"What?" her father said.

"I don't know why it hit Torrance first," Gillian said. "Maybe a distraction, maybe added pain, maybe part of the original design. But the water and the crew are supposed to come this way."

No one spoke for a moment. The wind whispered, and beneath it a muffled *ting* and *crack* tremored up out of the water and through the ancient stone walls of the basin.

"So what do we do?" she asked at last.

Her father swallowed, looking a little ill. He leaned the rifle up against the fence, muzzle toward the sky, and then bent and began to untie his boots. "I think we'll have to take a look. I will, I mean."

"Take a look where?"

He pointed into the unsettled, coffee-colored surge of floodwater. There wasn't much current to it, but it was still deep.

"You learn to swim at some point that I'm unaware of?" she said.

"I can swim," he answered with an indignant tone that would have made her smile on another day, in another place.

"You can tread water, Dad. I don't think it's really ideal for going down there to have a look. I'll do it."

"No, you won't," Aaron said. "It's why I'm here."

She hesitated. His eyes were fierce and his jaw was set. He wanted to do it. And, quite frankly, she wanted him to.

Still, it was her duty. Not his.

"I'm in charge," she said. "Sorry."

"Come on. It's the one thing I was born to do. This is it. It's why I'm here with you two now. I was going to end up back in the water at some point."

"It's supposed to be me," her father said. "I came all this way because it's supposed to be me."

"Or maybe you were supposed to get us here," Aaron said. "I don't know. But I think the only thing we all agree on is that we probably don't want to waste much time here. Someone's got to go down there and see ... whatever the hell there is to see. And that person has to come back up. Agreed?"

No one spoke.

"Then you put the best person in the water," he said. "The person who was trained for it. I trained for this. We can all go in if you're so damned stubborn, but I'm going in regardless."

"Your foot?" Gillian asked.

"Foot's bad," he admitted. "But you know what's fun about flippers? They're an improvement on feet once you're in the water."

"You've got them?"

He unslung the duffel bag from his shoulder. "And a mask," he said. "So there you go. The guy with the right tools wins, right?"

She looked at her dad. Deshawn Ryan was clearly unhappy but not vocally resisting.

"I thought it would be dry," he said. "I didn't expect that." He gestured at the dark, deep pool.

"Okay," Gillian said. "Best one in the water goes in first. That's the right approach, and I've got the command here. But, Aaron? You go in *first*. That doesn't mean you're the only one going in."

"Fine," he said, but he was already focused on his bag, unzipping it and removing his gear.

"You take a look, and see if . . ."

See if what? What was she supposed to instruct him to look for? The swimming dead? Ghost laborers?

Yes, she realized with incredulity, *that's probably very close.*

". . . see what's down there," she finished. None of them were sure, and as she and her father watched Aaron gear up for the cold water, she knew that neither she nor her father wanted to fill his head with any ideas of what might await.

When he came back up, he could tell them.

If he came back up.

64

The cargo helicopter brought in enough explosives not only to crack open the seals on the intake tunnels but to knock out what was left of the dam and probably split the lake bed in two. Mick was forced to leave his solitude on the bluff and return to the group gathered at the dam, where he listened patiently while Ben Quirk expressed his dismay.

"We're trying to punch through ten feet of concrete plugs, not rattle the remains of that dam right into downtown Torrance!" Quirk shouted, watching the crates of explosives being unloaded.

The Army sergeant who'd arrived with the payload calmed him down, explaining that he hadn't been given a specific requisition, just told to arrive with options and quantity.

"I'm not telling you we've got to use it all," he said. "I was just ordered to bring you plenty."

"Well, you sure didn't disappoint me in that regard!"

The sergeant was unflappable. "Under-promise and over-deliver," he said. "You've got options now, sir."

Indeed they did. There were your big three classics—TNT, ANFO, and nitroglycerin—along with a handful of varieties with which Mick wasn't familiar. His blasting education was limited but he knew the process would be to drill holes into the stone, pack the holes with explosives, and use fuse cord and detonators to fire the charges. His concern wasn't so much with the process, but with—as Quirk had aptly pointed out—the resulting vibration. An over-blast this close to the wounded dam might have catastrophic results downstream in Torrance.

A problem, because the catastrophic results needed to happen downstream in New York City. For the Galesburg crew to successfully redirect the floodplain of the Chilewaukee, things had to be held in perfect balance. The tunnels must burst open; the dam must not.

There were at least five blasting engineers on-site now, and all of Mick's structural knowledge had already been shared with them. Nevertheless, Quirk looked to him now and said, "Mick, any thoughts?"

He hadn't been anticipating the question, or the way the whole group would turn to him. For an instant he felt the old nerves and an urge to explain in rushed, clipped speech that this was not his bailiwick, thank you very much. Then he saw Anders drifting just behind the crowd, pacing on one of the pallets that had been stacked near the cargo chopper, and he felt the calm come over him.

"Dam's holding and the rain has stopped," he said. "There's urgency but not the kind worth risking too much ground tremor. I'm not sure how far back they plugged those tunnels. Fifteen feet, maybe? Twenty? It won't be far. So if you have to handle it in a series, blast and dredge, blast and dredge, that's worthwhile risk aversion. We don't need to drop it all in one shot."

This was met with the approval of the demolition experts—further evidence that Mick Fleming's general authority at the Chilewaukee Reservoir seemed accepted.

A hint of a smile started to slip over his face then. He pinned his lips back down, but not before Quirk saw it.

"Mick?" he said, more curious than upset. It was, after all, not a day for smiles.

"It's a strange time to be grateful," Mick said solemnly, "but I can't help but think how much we owe them."

"Owe who?"

"The originals," Mick said, gesturing at the intake tunnel doors that loomed just above the waterline. "Everyone who labored to take those tunnels as far as they did. I'm sure they felt it was a waste by the end, you know? Sealed up and forgotten. Pointless. But today we need every inch they gave us."

Quirk nodded, looking over Mick's shoulder and out to the cracked stone seals that protected the tunnels.

"I hope," he said, "they gave us a few inches more than we know."

This time Mick had to turn away to hide the smile.

65

Water had represented only horror and failure for Aaron in recent days, from the rescue school washout to the disastrous swim at the tailwaters that had left him bleeding and confessing to murder, yet as soon as he slipped into the frigid pool below the bluestone gorge, he felt a measure of peace.

He was able to use the basin wall to step down rather than making the jump from above, leaving a simple drop into the water. He allowed himself to sink, testing the current, which was negligible. This was trapped floodwater, and while it gathered speed quickly downstream, he was at the headwaters, and it was stagnant here. It also carried sediment washed down from the mountains, though, and that made visibility terrible. He could see his hands out in front of his mask but not much beyond that.

He surfaced and turned back to Gillian and her father, who were watching anxiously from behind the rusted fence.

"All good," he called, making the universal A-OK gesture with his right hand.

Before either of them could answer, another muffled boom sounded from somewhere just beneath him. This one was the loudest yet, as if something massive had given way, and he felt a tremor in the water.

All three of them looked at the high, jagged rise of the gorge. From down here in the water, the slope looked even steeper, and he could no longer see the peaks of the mountains beyond. He felt a moment of claustrophobia rise within him even though he was free and mobile. There was something about being down here, surrounded by the slick rock walls of the basin, that gave him the sense of being trapped. It didn't feel like open water so much as a pool.

Like the pool where it all went wrong. Me and Johnny Brass Balls and the panic drill. The moment when I showed the world what I was all about.

No. He couldn't let that into his mind. This place was nothing like that. It was open downstream, and he could lie on his back and let the current take him anytime he wished. There was no one struggling in his arms, no one determined to pull him down.

Crack, BOOM.

More rock breaking off somewhere down below, the sound like a submerged thunderstorm.

"Okay," he said, "I'm gonna go have a look."

He slipped back under. It seemed important to hurry now. There were multiple forces at play, and they were accelerating. He felt this with a certainty, as if the water carried the message to him in its cold tugs and trembles.

He swam toward the front of the basin, clicking on a headlamp, which offered limited penetration in the hazy, dark water. He was able to swim easily, though, kicking primarily with his left foot, although the right didn't hurt as badly as he'd expected. Maybe the cold water was an unanticipated friend in this regard, numbing the pain.

He was swimming quickly, and when the wall rose up in front of him, it appeared so fast that he almost went headfirst into it. His left hand made contact first, and he used it to push back. Then he looked from side to side, studying the obstacle. The ancient wall was cracked but mostly intact. He gripped it and held on, looking and waiting. What, exactly, was he supposed to see?

When his lungs began to burn, he released the wall and surged upward. Broke the surface, hauled in a breath, and turned onto his back to see Gillian and Deshawn.

"Nothing yet," he said. "It's just the old wall. I'm not sure exactly what I'm looking—"

Another muffled boom, and this time he felt a funnel surge in the water that flapped his right foot and sent a bolt of pain through him. The pain was almost unnoticed, though, because the water motion helped him pinpoint the source of the sounds.

"Be careful," Deshawn Ryan hollered, but Aaron was already submerging again, swimming with a destination this time: down and to his right, the far corner of the basin's wall.

As he closed in, he could see a swirl of bubbles rising toward him.

Memories of the corpse in the submerged branches teased his mind, but here the water was empty; there were no tree limbs or skeleton hands reaching for him. Another boom concussed the water, more felt than heard, and he saw more bubbles rise in the smothered glow of his headlamp. He followed them, descending while they ascended, searching for where they bloomed to life.

He almost swam right past it. The source was nothing but a shadow in the dark water, and he was focused on a cornerstone of rock, thinking that he would start there and work along the wall. Then the shadow flashed on his left, and he looked back over his shoulder and saw the hole in the wall.

It was more of a hatch than a hole, really—a neat square of blackness in the flat stone facing. But it was an opening.

He floated, staring at it, and while he watched, another boom shuddered through the depths. A single flat stone separated from the rest and tumbled free, falling, sinking . . .

And joining a pile of broken companions already on the basin floor.

Fascinated, he swam closer. Wrapped his hand around the rock that lined the hatch like a window frame and pulled his face down, peering through to the other side. His headlamp illuminated a rough-hewn tunnel. It was filled with water, but the tunnel angled upward slightly, and he thought that at the top it looked dry, as if the water wasn't coming from inside the tunnel, but rather had washed into it from the basin.

BOOM. Crack.

A stone just above him split free and fell. He twisted sideways in time to dodge it by a fraction of an inch. Watched it sink and nestle beside the others.

How in the hell is that happening?

He turned back to the hatch, grasped the frame of rock again, and leaned farther in, pushing his head and shoulders through the hatch, into the tunnel. Nothing. Just dark water and stone and—

A woman's face appeared directly in front of his own.

She came out of nowhere and suddenly was an inch away from his mask. She was gaunt and pale, with her bloodless lips pressed into a thin line and her eyes locked on his. Aaron tried to scream but instead bit hard on the mouthpiece as he jerked backward. Something bright and silvery flickered above him, and he looked up to see the steel head of a pick wickering down through the water in a streamer of bubbles, coming for his skull.

As he lunged sideways he knew it was too late, and braced himself for the blow.

There was no contact. The pick pounded rock instead, the water shuddered, swaying him in its grasp, and the stone in his hand tore free from the wall and sank, pulling him down with it. As he dropped, his face swung back around to where the woman had stood.

She was gone. Nothing but dark water remained.

He opened his fingers and released the stone, then kicked hard for the surface. Broke through, gasping in a breath. Gillian was shouting questions from above and behind him, but they didn't register right away. He was still seeing the woman's grim, gaunt face, and then the sparkle of that sharpened steel pick slicing toward him.

He swam to the side of the wall, grasped a ledge with one hand, and hung there, breathing hard. Now he could hear their questions: "What happened? What did you see?" "Do you need to get out of the water? Are you hurt?" The questions swirled around him like a snow flurry. He didn't bother to address each one individually.

"They've broken through," he said. "They're knocking the wall down now. There's a tunnel on the other side. I'm not sure how far it goes."

For a moment, absolute silence.

Then Gillian, softly: "Who?"

"The ghosts," he said simply. He looked up at Deshawn. "I saw one. She was there and then she was gone. Is that normal? Is that how you've seen them?"

Gillian turned to her father, and Deshawn seemed to shrink from her gaze.

"That's how it started, yeah," he said. "They'd kind of flicker in and out. Corner of the eye, you know? Then they'd be there longer. Finally I could look at them directly. And now they . . . well, now they take their time. For the past few days they've just sort of . . . lingered. Most don't speak. I'm not sure if they can't or don't want to."

"You're the only one who sees them?"

Deshawn nodded again. "Feels that way. Every now and then I think some of the others might see one of the flickers at the edges, the way I used to at the beginning. But they deny it, of course. Their brains do that for them, I think. It's not a lie so much as a refusal."

Deshawn was gripping the fence so tightly that the muscles in his thick forearms pressed against the skin.

Aaron thought about this and nodded. "Can they hurt you?" he asked.

Deshawn Ryan paused, his dark eyes reflective. "If they can," he said finally, "they haven't done it yet."

This felt right as well. The pick slicing through the water toward him had been terrifying, but it struck only the wall, and he didn't think that was because he'd moved fast enough to avoid it. The woman's focus had been on the rock, not on Aaron. She'd seen him, but he hadn't mattered much to her.

The rock wall had mattered to her.

"What did she look like?" Gillian asked.

He tried to come up with the right words, but it was difficult to give the ephemeral sight of the woman in the water the sort of stark power she deserved. He found himself choosing an emotion instead of a physical description.

"Tired," he said. "She looked very tired."

This seemed to jar Gillian. She winced and put her own hands on the fence.

Below, another boom reverberated. Aaron could envision the slab of rock that it had knocked free and sent tumbling into the bottom of the basin.

"I think the tunnel is dry," he said. "I didn't get far, but I think up ahead it's dry. The water that's in there is collected from all of this. It doesn't have any current or any pressure."

Gillian didn't answer. She seemed preoccupied with Aaron's description of the woman in the depths.

"Well," Deshawn said, "what do we do?"

"The hole is real," Aaron said. "I don't care if anyone else sees ghosts down there or not, the hole is real, and that means it can be sealed."

Gillian said, "I can call people down here and tell them we . . . I don't know, that for some unknown reason we decided to wander out to the basin and discovered the start of a tunnel? Yeah, that's gonna sound normal, isn't it?"

"I don't care how it sounds," Aaron said, switching his grip on the wall from his right hand to his left to relieve his aching shoulder. "I can show them the damn thing. It's real. Just like your grandmother's body."

She winced.

"You can't see how far it goes?" she asked.

"I'm not sure," Aaron said. "It's so damn dark in there." He thought of the woman's pale, tight-lipped face again, of the sparkle of the metal pick coming toward his skull. Then he swallowed and said, "I'll go give it another look."

"I don't know about that," Deshawn said. Aaron had a sense that Deshawn would rather be the one to go below. Maybe not in the water, but at least in the tunnel. And maybe he should be. Aaron didn't know the rules of the strange, terrifying game. He didn't know what could puncture reality and what couldn't. All he knew was that the water was real, and you had to be skilled in it just to get through that hole, let alone to make it through until you reached dry ground.

If you reach dry ground. If you push too far and don't find it, you'll never make it back. You'll die in there. Your body will be floating down there on the other side of that wall, beneath the mountain. Floating alongside that woman with the pick.

"If it seems to be more than a crack in the wall," Gillian said, "I've got to do something about it. I don't care what story I have to tell, how crazy it sounds, or what it does to my life, I will need to get people down here to seal it off. Because if the tunnel actually goes through that mountain . . ."

She pointed, and they both followed the gesture with their eyes, staring into the dark mountains.

"If it goes through, then it's connected to the Chill," Aaron said. "Or it's very close. I can't answer that for you. But I *can* see how far it goes."

"You get stuck down there, and . . ." She didn't finish, and he was grateful for that.

He held her eyes while he nodded. "I understand. But we've got to know, right?"

"It should be me," Deshawn said. "It was supposed to be me."

Aaron shook his head. "You won't make it."

"Bullshit."

"I'm not sure *I* will," Aaron answered, "and I'm the best in the water."

The best in the water. How long had it been since he'd said that? Felt it? He'd meant he was the best of the three of them, the best of bad options, but when the words left his mouth, for just a second there it had felt like old times. He was *the best* in the water. He knew this because the water told him so. It worked with him, not against him. The water knew him.

"Try it," Gillian said decisively. She faced her father then. Braced him, almost, a defiant look, one that brooked no argument. "We need to know, and Aaron's got the best chance of finding out and coming back to the surface."

Alive, Aaron thought, *say* alive, *not just* back to the surface. *Because Mick Fleming came back to the surface, and I do not want to return like that.*

"All right," Deshawn said in a grudging whisper. "Go see what you can see. But, Aaron? If you're not alone down there, just pass by them, okay? Like you don't even see 'em. Just keep your head down, son, and do your job. If they come for you directly, it'll be a different story. But you'll know that. I think they'll make that clear."

Just keep your head down, son, and do your job.

The word *son* had been a colloquialism, maybe even inadvertently patronizing, but Aaron was glad to hear it. The instruction felt familiar to him. It was Deshawn's voice, but Aaron seemed to hear it in Steve Ellsworth's.

"I will," he said. He looked from Deshawn to Gillian. "I'll see where it goes, and then I'll come back quick."

"Sure," Gillian said, but her voice was distant. Below, more muffled thunder echoed in the water. "Good luck, okay?"

Aaron gave her the A-OK sign and slipped the mouthpiece in. Then he released the wall, dropped, and let the water take him again.

PART SIX

66

When he was gone and it was just the two of them, they didn't speak. They just stared at the flat surface of the water where once Aaron Ellsworth had been.

"I'm sorry," Deshawn said, breaking the silence just before another concussed crack shook up through the depths.

Gillian looked at him with confusion. "For what?"

"Ever leaving you in this place. And then letting you come *back*. I knew better, I knew I should open my mouth then, but ... but I didn't."

She pushed away from the fence. "We both knew I shouldn't come back," she said. "You telling me not to wouldn't have made a difference."

"I mean telling you *why* it was a bad idea."

"You didn't understand why. Not the way I did. And I still came back. I would have pretended it was all a lie, the same as you did. We might have commiserated about poor me, and maybe even poor mom, living in the house of madness, growing up with all those disturbing stories, but we wouldn't have talked about anything that might have been real, would we?"

"Maybe," Deshawn said.

She gave a dry laugh. "You think, Dad? You really think the two of us, stoic souls that we are, were going to sit down and say, 'Now, what if it was the truth all along, and there are ghosts trapped in those mountains, working to finish a water tunnel that they can't possibly dig ... '?"

"No," he said. "I don't guess we'd have said that."

She smiled faintly. Reached out and squeezed his arm. "It was a story you couldn't believe. Don't blame yourself for that. Until you came face-to-face with it, how could you believe what you heard about Galesburg?"

He nodded, suddenly looking as exhausted as she felt. Another boom came from below, a shiver in the earth. They turned back to the water, stared into it, and shared silent thoughts about Aaron Ellsworth, silent fears.

"Why can he see them?" Gillian said. "How? The two of you can."

"I'm not sure, but I know it's only going to happen down there. In the tunnels, or in the water, maybe. Somewhere belowground. Somewhere within the waterworks. I don't know why they show up, or how some see them and others don't. I don't know why they were silent for so long and then chose to speak. All I'm sure of is that it will only happen to you down there."

She felt a perverse jealousy. The tired woman Aaron had seen—was that her grandmother?

The farmhouse where she'd been raised would be gone now, she realized. It had sat in the heart of the floodplain. Maybe the foundation remained, like the old homes in the Dead Waters, but the rest would be gone. The old boards of the schoolhouse would need to be dredged up again. Or left to rot. She could smell the clean dampness of the room and hear the rasp of chalk on the chalkboard and feel the cut-glass edges of the inkwell against her fingertips. If she closed her eyes, she thought she could actually hear her grandmother's voice.

Sacrifice. Be part of something bigger than yourself, Gillian. Something that was here before you and will be here after you. The rest of them only saw the town of Galesburg, you know. They only see the city in New York now. They forget what it once was, they don't remember and don't care, and there's a danger to that. Especially because the past isn't passive. What we are doing, what we are bound to, is the crucial work of making others look back. Making them remember.

She opened her eyes. The voice ceased. For a moment there, it had seemed as real as if Molly Mathers had been whispering in Gillian's ear.

"You said one ghost gave you instructions," Gillian said. "But are there more than him?"

"Yes. Lots of them, but most don't speak to me. They just watch and wait. I don't think they're all the same, then. The ghosts up here and the ones down there might be very different."

He was right about this, but when Galesburg arrived downstream, the ghosts that waited there wouldn't have options. They would have to go to work then.

Galesburg, like gravity, pulled you down whether you liked it or not.

It was a very special place. Her ancestors had tried to warn everyone about that. It was not the sort of place you flooded out and dammed up. Maybe it wasn't even the sort of place you should build a house in. The Iroquois had stayed away for a reason. The Europeans hadn't listened.

Now, nobody even remembered. Nobody except Gillian. And if the stories she'd been told were true, then those ghosts beneath the city streets weren't active yet, but they would be soon. When the Galesburg crew arrived with all of its unique force, everyone would work.

All they had to do was make it downstream. They'd be picking up a man per mile along the way. Probably many more than that. There were so many unrecorded dead from the old reservoirs, the old pressure tunnels, the aqueducts. Galesburg would sweep them all up, and keep on going. The work would go quickly then.

The city wouldn't have a chance.

Below them, steel struck stone again, but this time the sound had a different tone—higher, cleaner. Drier. It drew both of them to look back at the far wall of the basin, where Aaron had found the hole. Water sloshed at the surface line. Gillian stepped closer, staring. Another crack—not a stifled boom now, a *crack*, clean as an axe splitting wood— and this time she saw a piece of stone shear from the wall just above the waterline and splash into it. A band of blackness showed where once the blue-gray rock had been.

"They're almost through," she whispered.

Her father stepped close to her. Both of them staring together.

CRACK, scrape, splash.

Another block of bluestone sinking. The hole from beneath the mountain widening.

The Galesburg residents were almost back.

"I need to see them," Gillian said. With each block that fell, with each widening of the gap, she felt the magnetic, electric tug toward the darkness beyond.

Gillian. Honey. Gillian.

The voice seemed to come from beyond the wall. Gillian stared at it, then back to her father.

"You hear that?"

"I heard it, but I don't agree," he said. "You don't want to see them. Trust me. If you never see anything like them, you'll be better off for it."

"No, I don't mean did you hear what I said; I mean do you hear . . ."

She let her voice trail off, because she could hear more whispers floating at her out of the darkness.

It was true. The stories were always true, and it was your job to learn them and believe them and teach them. Sacrifice. Volunteer. You've got to make the hard choice for yourself. Make it with confidence.

She took a few steps closer.

"Hear what?" her father said behind her.

"Nothing," she muttered. She felt dizzy, untethered, and wanted to sit down. She wasn't sure if the whispers were actually coming from the other side of the wall or from somewhere within her own exhausted brain.

All of it was playing out just as she'd been taught. Just as she'd been promised. Except that she wasn't down there to help them. That seemed good, of course, because the carnage of last night had been so terrible, and the carnage that lay ahead? The great city gone dry? It was hard to imagine.

And yet . . .

Sometimes a wake-up call is needed, Gillian. A reminder of the past. A voice from the land, the water, the rocks. The bones and the blood. Without us, without our service, they'll all forget. That's worse.

Was it so wrong? So crazy? They'd asked for so little. Just for the right to keep the land they'd fought for, land they'd cleared with their own hands and their own aching backs, land they'd then planted and harvested. Land where they'd dug deep wells for cool, clean water. All they'd asked was for the right to keep a pocket of sacred earth. They'd been denied that right in the interest of the greater good. The city wanted the water, and so the city would have it. End of story.

But not quite. Not in Galesburg. The city could take the land but not the knowledge. Not the memories and magic. And so what if Galesburg struck back? There was a greater good in play then, too. A reminder to a disinterested society. An alarm about the price of forgetting. It wasn't all vengeance. It was . . . balance.

"I don't know if it's good or bad that he's taking so long," her father said, and she was annoyed that he was intruding on her thoughts, her memories. He was looking at the water again, not at the widening gap in the wall. She didn't understand that. How could you possibly take your eyes off what was happening there?

Because he always did, she thought. *He always turned away from the magic of this place.*

"Gillian," he said, "how long do you think we should wait?"

"Before what?"

"I don't know. Calling for help. Anyone can see what's happening now. It doesn't require a story or even an explanation. The wall is coming down."

As if on cue:

CRACK, scrape, splash.

She watched the stone fall free. Was that the flicker of a pale figure in the blackness beyond? A flash of white?

"They're in there," she said. "I think I can see them."

"Then it's time for you to go. With or without Aaron. I don't think this is a good spot for you. Go for help. Leave me to wait on him."

She didn't answer.

CRACK, scrape, splash. Stone falling. Blackness widening.

"Call it in," he told her. "Get help down here."

Gillian reached for her belt. The radio was clipped on the left side. Her fingers drifted over it . . . and slid right.

CRACK, scrape, splash.

She drew her duty pistol. Her father said, "Babe, you can't kill them. They're already dead."

"Do you remember how I used to scare you?" she said.

"Gillian . . ."

"Do you? When I was little, you'd look at me, and you'd be *afraid* of me. Afraid of a child. Do you remember that?"

He hesitated. Behind her, another stone split free and sank. Finally he nodded.

"I do. And I'm sorry. I didn't understand this place, and I didn't believe what I'd heard, and I—"

"Was right."

"What?"

"You were right to be afraid," Gillian said, and pointed the gun at him.

He stared at her. His mouth was hanging open in a half smile, as if he'd been listening to a joke and was still waiting on the punch line. His teeth were white against his dark face, his eyes kind. They'd always been kind. Even when he was afraid of her.

"I'm sorry, Dad," she said.

67

The ghosts let Aaron pass.

There were more of them now, five men standing beside the woman who'd swung the pick at him, and he could see the shifting shapes of a half dozen more in the depths beyond, but he swam through the ever-widening hole in the wall and they did not move to stop him. They just watched. Pale faces, but not translucent, just a washed-out gray, bones pushing at their flesh, all of them gaunt, all of them tired.

And all of them working. As he swam toward them he saw the flurry of swinging picks and shovels, blades whipping through the water without any trace of the resistance he felt from it. They watched him as he went, but they didn't move to stop him. He had the sense that their level of urgency was equal to his own, just headed in the opposite direction.

He swam on through the tunnel, ghosts all around him, flickering faces and sparkling steel tools, and he remembered Deshawn's advice: just pass on by.

That was easy enough to do, because stopping would be suicide. When he'd passed through the wall he was moving with a strong stroke, had plenty of air in his lungs, and felt good about making it to the air on the other side.

There wasn't any, though. The water went on and on.

In the light of his headlamp, muted by the dark water and wavering in the shadows of his hands passing in front of the beam, he could see the tunnel floor angling up. This was what he'd been counting on: the tunnel would rise and take him out of the water.

As he chased it, though, the water remained. Higher and higher he rose, and still he was underwater.

Now his lungs were burning and his muscles were threatening to cramp.

Panic in the water, his instructors had said, *is a different breed of panic than what you've seen on dry land, boys. It's one hell of a lot different.*

They were right. He'd learned that the hardest way. But he wasn't going to panic again.

His heart pounded in his ears with the steadily increasing drive of a bass drum, faster with each beat. A racing heartbeat, a heartbeat that promised

PANIC.

No. There will be no panic, because you've got nothing to lose here, he told himself. *It's just you and the current, Ellsworth, and the current is your friend.*

But there was no current. It was dead still, more like pond water than a river, more like the pool where everything had gone wrong, the pool where he had

PANICKED.

His hand touched stone, and then one fin scraped over it, too. The tunnel was closing in on him. The water still all around, no friend at all, no current, a stagnant enemy, a tomb.

He bumped into a wall. Lifted his head and cracked it against the ceiling. Everything tight as a coffin, and waterlogged, too. He closed his eyes, feeling as if the sight of the walls was worse than swimming in blackness. His hand hit rock again, sending a bolt of pain through his wrist. He kept his eyes closed, though. Kicked. Rising through the water. No, rising *within* the water, joined to it. You didn't fight it; you joined it. Old lessons and muscle memory. *Find the flow state.* He would need that now, because there wasn't another option. There would be no surfacing and admitting defeat, not down here.

Heartbeat louder and faster in his ears, and now a buzz, the sounds combining like a big angry rock band getting ready to play in the back of his skull, tuning up, drums kicking and the amps giving feedback. Was that the whine of an electric guitar behind? A high shriek, like a scream, a scream of

PANIC!!!

He spit the mouth guard out. Water rushed in his lips even as he tried to seal them shut, but that wasn't bad, because it cleared his head. Cold, dank water on his tongue but not yet filling his throat. Not yet.

The angry heavy metal band was stomping onto the stage now. Drums thumping, guitars humming, all buzzing with the anticipation of the final stroke of the pick, that moment of cacophonous, raging noise that would mark the end for him.

Another sound somewhere in the mix. Something soft as a whisper, but rhythmic. Plinking drops, like rain on a car hood. The first fat drops that fell before a big storm. He thought that those didn't belong with the rest of the noise. The angry band he understood. He knew what they were waiting on: permission. All he had to do was give them the sign, and then the pick would strike on the guitar strings and the noise would start and Aaron would cease. Panic was permission to die.

His hamstrings began to tremble with the teasing threat of a cramp. That would be the end, too. A cramp would kill him for sure.

So stop. It's not panic if it's your choice. Go ahead and stop.

Kick, stroke, kick, stroke. Heartbeat drumming, brain humming. He realized that drowning wasn't going to be a quiet death. It was going to be loud, at least to him. Somewhere in the distance, that sound of rain. A mocking torment, because there was no rain down here in the depths, there was only rain at the—

Surface, he thought, and suddenly he felt hope. The raindrops were real, and they were calling to him from the surface. He could hear them. Just up ahead. Reach for it. So close now. Two more strokes. Maybe three. It wasn't impossible. Let the guitar hum and the bass drum thump a little longer. The band didn't need to play yet. Not just yet. One more stroke. And another. And one more . . .

He broke out of the water and into the rain.

He opened his eyes a half second after he opened his mouth for air. Black threads danced across his vision. Water filled his mouth. He gagged and spat, tilted his head back, and found air.

His vision cleared slowly, the black threads wiped clear by a gray fog that then dissipated. He was on his back, looking at a cracked rock ceiling. Water dripped down from it, falling in slow, patient drops.

Not rain, after all. Just groundwater, dripping from somewhere high on a mountain above him. Seeping through, finding its impossible way through all that rock.

He floated, breathed, and steadied. As oxygen fed his muscles, the cramps receded. Knots loosening, surrendering.

I made it, he realized with amazement, and then he laughed. The sound echoed in the chamber of dark stone, giving him an audience, an elated crowd.

He'd actually made it. How far, he couldn't say, but he knew that it had been the longest swim he'd ever made underwater.

He crawled out of the water and onto the dry rock. The tunnel wasn't as steep here, just a long, rough cylinder, with no light ahead.

He tugged his flippers off. Beneath them he wore thin but rugged neoprene booties, strong enough to keep the rock from piercing through. But when he stood, the pain in his right foot was so bad that the black threads laced through his field of vision once more.

He breathed and waited out the pain. Used his left hand to find the wall and support himself. When his vision had cleared and the pain had subsided, he straightened, keeping as much of his weight as possible on his left side.

Then he limped ahead.

68

There was a moment, just before she looped the handcuff over his right wrist, when Deshawn thought he could have taken the gun from his daughter. She lowered the gun to put the handcuff on him, and by picking his right wrist she was underestimating the strength of his left fist. All those years in the tunnels had sapped some of his speed but not his strength. One piston-fired jab into his daughter's face and he thought that he could break her nose and take her gun.

That was an impossible ask, though. Even in this moment, with her eyes vacant and a gun in her hand, he couldn't bring himself to take the idea of harming her seriously. He'd spent too many nights awake worrying about all the things circling out there in the world that might do her harm to become one of them himself.

"Gillian," he was saying, over and over again, like a man crying out to someone across a great distance, although she was only three feet away. "Gillian, baby, you need to walk away from here."

Nothing. It was as if a fuse had blown and her emotional circuits were down now.

So hit her. Take the gun. For her own sake.

Yes. He needed to save her, because she was no longer herself, and talk wasn't enough. She'd seemed to seal him out entirely, as if she wasn't simply ignoring him but wasn't hearing him. His daughter, struck deaf and dumb and terrifying, holding a gun on him and handcuffing him to a rusted fence.

Hit her, then. Hit her!

But he couldn't.

He went on talking, right until the end, right until she snapped the other cuff over an iron stanchion in the fence and stepped back, out of range of the left fist that might have saved him—might have saved both of them.

"Gillian! Leave me, but you need to walk away from here now! *Gillian!*"

Nothing. Her face, so young and unlined—so misleading about her level of worldly experience, of knowledge and of pain—was absolutely empty when he screamed her name.

She holstered her gun, turned, and studied the hole in the wall.

"Gillian," Deshawn implored, trying to rise to his knees and face her, which was impossible because of the handcuffs. "You've got to listen to me. You've got to remember who I am. Remember who *you* are. This is not your home. These are not your people. Don't let this place work on you. Gillian, don't let it win."

Was he lying to her, though? What did he know of this place? And they certainly were her people. There was no denying that.

"Baby," he whispered. "Gill. Look at me."

Another stone cracked and split free from the wall behind her, and her face finally changed. It lit up like the expression of a child who has heard the first test firework before the big Fourth of July show. The *May I have your attention, please* firecracker that promised the dark sky was soon going to be filled with light and sound.

The gap in the stone face had climbed well above the waterline now. It was about four feet above the water, and nearly ten feet wide. All Deshawn could see on the other side was darkness.

"What do you see?" he whispered.

Gillian was silent. The sun that had filtered into the valley when they arrived was gone now, concealed by gray clouds, and down here it was very dark. A breeze spun leaves into the water and fanned Gillian's hair back from her neck and shoulders. She stood at attention, muscles taut, head cocked, as if listening, ready for action.

"You shouldn't be here," Deshawn said.

She finally spoke then. Without turning, she said, "No, *you* should not be here."

Another stone broke free and splashed into the water below. Gillian nodded, as if that stone had carried some instruction, and then walked away from Deshawn and toward the wall.

"Gillian!"

She didn't even break stride.

He sagged against the fence post, his right wrist cuffed above his head, and watched her walk the length of the fence, all the way to where it joined the mountain in a slab of crumbling concrete. There she climbed onto it. The old steel slats shivered under her weight, but they held. She moved nimbly, two steps and then over, swinging her legs over the top with the grace of a gymnast, then dropping down onto the lip of stone on the other side.

There she paused. The hole in the wall was at least five feet out across the water, and a few feet lower than where she stood. A long, awkward reach. She peered into the darkness, nodded, paused, nodded again. Then she turned her body at an angle, facing the wall, and spread her feet wider on the ledge. Bobbed up and down, testing her balance.

"Gillian!" Deshawn screamed. "Don't!"

No reaction. She flexed up and down once more, then crouched, paused . . . and leaped.

The cry that was in his throat died when she landed. She cleared the distance and then improbably, miraculously, made the landing. Rocked up on her toes, then came back down, arms outstretched for balance. She was standing on a narrow lip of stone at the edge of the widening hole in the wall. Deshawn watched in horrified silence, trying to understand what she was going to do now. Hang on there until another piece of the wall was knocked out and into the water, taking her with it?

He was about to call out to her once more, aware that it was pointless but unable to stop himself, when she bent at the waist and brought her head down to the break in the wall. She held that pose for a moment, then reached inside the wall with her right hand, found a grip, and pulled herself through to the other side.

Then there was nothing left of her at all. It was just Deshawn on this side of the wall now, Gillian and Aaron both on the inside, somewhere under the mountain. He was alone.

That was the thought, at least. When he finally looked away, he saw that he wasn't alone at all. There was a man coming down the trail. He had dark hair and a dark beard and he was carrying some strange weapon that looked like the reaper's scythe. Deshawn could have believed it right then. Then the man stepped out of the hemlocks and into plain view and Deshawn realized that the object in his hands wasn't a weapon at all.

It was a camera on a tripod.

69

The first blasting charges were in place, and the detonators were ready.

The sun had gone again, and the sky above the Chilewaukee Reservoir looked as it had for so many days before: gunmetal gray and with thin white clouds riding a high, hard wind.

Dry, though. No more rain yet.

The mayor seemed pleased about this. Mick nodded in agreement, but it was long past the hour when rain would matter.

Ben Quirk was moving the onlookers back. Quirk and someone with the National Guard. More people kept arriving on the scene. The media was being held at bay, and there'd been a shouting match over allowing helicopters in the airspace above the dam when the blasting began. The crew of a dozen or so who had begun the work that night had swelled to well over one hundred. Mick, once the lone engineer on the scene, was now one of fifteen. Maybe twenty.

That was fine, too. The more the merrier. Let them all remember that they were present when the release tunnels at the Chill finally opened. Let them all tell that story to their children, to their grandchildren.

It was an honor, Mick knew, to be a part of it. He might be the only one who understood that now, but in time he thought there would be others. When the tragedy became the history and the history became the great teacher of the present, he suspected that there would be others who remembered their role in a different light.

"We are ready now," Quirk shouted beside him. "On your order, sir."

This was to the military man whose identity Mick had already forgotten in the swirl of new arrivals. He felt more and more like Anders Wallace: a floating presence, unseen and unheard. That was just fine. He'd had his moment of command.

They'd remember him.

The military man—he was a major who'd arrived in one of the morning helicopters—turned to his blasting team, all of them wearing helmets and face shields, and said, "Fire in the hole."

He said it softly. No John Wayne here—just a man of quiet, commanding presence.

"Fire in the hole!" one of the helmeted men echoed, and then he punched the detonator.

Some people in the crowd turned away. One man lifted his hand as if to shield himself. One woman gave a high, keening laugh.

Mick's gaze didn't leave the tunnels.

The concrete blew apart in a cloud of bone-colored fragments. The earth shuddered. Mick could feel it ride up from the soles of his feet and spread through his body like a pulse of voltage. On the bank just above the tunnel, the limbs of trees rattled, shaking their few remaining leaves. The surface of the big lake shivered under the reflected gray sky.

The dam held.

There was a collective exhalation. Some people spoke, someone prayed aloud, and the nervous woman laughed again—laughed against her terror as if it were all a great lark. Mick thought she was the most honest human specimen among them all.

He didn't turn to look at their faces. Even when someone slapped him on the back, he did not turn. He kept his eyes on the cloud of dissipating smoke and debris.

The old archways were gone, pulverized. The concrete plugs in the tunnels below were scrap heaps of stone fragments. The lake rushed in, eager, hungry.

The lake sloshed back, denied.

Two men in fatigues and helmets descended the slope on rappelling ropes. They studied the damage and spoke into radios.

"About eight feet," Quirk said. "Maybe ten."

It took Mick a moment to realize Quirk was speaking to him and was waiting for a response.

"Excellent," Mick said. "I think we're only one strike away, then."

Quirk spoke into the radio. The demolitions team went back to work, setting the next round of charges.

Overhead, the clouding sky spit a few experimental raindrops at the world below.

70

Aaron was making good time for a limping man, grasping the rock with his left hand and keeping his weight on his left leg, when the mountain shook and brought him to his knees.

He landed hard, kneecaps clacking off the stone, and then the shaking ended as swiftly as it had begun, and the world was still again.

What in the hell had that been?

He looked up the tunnel just as a piece of rock about five feet long and a foot wide separated from the ceiling and fell, smashing in front of him, showering him with needle-sharp fragments.

The claustrophobia gripped him then. He'd managed to walk without fear of the tunnel because the tunnel had fresh air; he was out of the water and he could breathe. But he had no idea where he was or whether he walked a path of escape or a path of ruin. Or simply in a circle, as doomed and damned as the ghosts he'd passed at the wall.

Maybe they're not so doomed. They're coming out, after all. They're breaking the wall down and they're coming out.

He looked up at the ceiling. Painted its undulating gray surface with his headlamp, looking for another possible rock fall. Again he thought of the water. If he was back in the water, it would at least slow the rock. If whatever was happening above him caused this tunnel to collapse, then he'd have a better chance in the water, swimming toward a known destination, than limping ahead in the dark.

Maybe that was the rest of the dam giving way, he thought. *Maybe it's all gone now.*

He thought of the tunnel filling with water, a torrent that would splatter him off the rocks and roll on past. After the night of rescue work, he'd seen just how completely water could disregard the will of man.

If the water was coming, though, he couldn't hear it.

There were only two choices: go back, which was his best shot at survival, or go forward, with no idea what lay ahead.

He stepped over the slab of rock that had fallen from the tunnel roof and limped ahead.

The tunnel itself seemed like an impossibility. Stone had been carved clean and hauled away. The ceiling was high above his head. Nine feet at least. Maybe ten. Water dripped from small creases and cracks, but the tunnel floor was smooth and mostly dry. He wondered how it would be explained if anyone other than him saw it. He doubted that anyone ever would.

Each step brought another throb of pain. His right foot was warm and wet and he knew the wound was open again. If he ever made it out of here and back into the world, that would matter. Down here, though, it didn't. Or couldn't.

He counted steps to confirm his forward progress. Counted heartbeats to confirm his existence. His headlamp seemed dimmer now. Less of the tunnel visible now than before. But did it matter? How much of an endless road did you need to see?

He paused when the ache in his foot became an ache behind his eyes. He leaned against the wall, breathed, and waited for the pain to subside.

Can they find me? he wondered. *If Gillian and her father go for help, will anyone be able to find me?*

He unclipped his radio. Turned it on and searched from band to band. Nothing. He had an EPIRB, an emergency position indicating radio beacon, that would put out a GPS ping for help. It worked well on the open ocean. Under a mountain, it didn't seem it would work at all. There was no rescue band down here, no 911, no distress signal. Down here, the situation was stripped of any options. He would stay alive and find his way out, or he would not.

It felt clean somehow. The lack of options offered a cold comfort—he was down to the most simple and essential of existences.

Aware that the pain wasn't going to subside, he began moving again. He'd forgotten what he had been counting—steps, heartbeats, or breaths?—and so he counted drips of water instead. Listened for them up ahead and kept tally of them. Each drip that was out of sight was a reminder that he had more steps to take into the darkness. There was still ground to cover, at least. There was that much promised to him.

When the thunder came, he dropped to his knees and covered his head, sure it was a cave-in, the mountain collapsing down on him.

No rock fell. He stayed there, huddled against an impact that never arrived, and then he heard the sound again, one just like actual thunder. Not the rumblings of rock but the crackle of an oncoming storm. The sound was clear, too. Not nearly as muffled as it should be this far below the earth.

Could it be that he wasn't really so far down?

He staggered upright. Found the wall with his left hand again while adjusting his dying headlamp with his right. Walked ahead. He was moving on an incline now. A slight but undeniable upward slope. Thunder again, and he was sure of it this time. He was walking uphill, and there was a storm coming to meet him.

When the tunnel ended, he was more shocked than he should have been. At the start, he'd expected to find this wall of rock, impenetrable. The longer he'd walked, though, the more convinced he'd become that if it ended at all, it would be in some grander way.

Instead, it concluded in a bland slab of gray stone.

The wall was concrete, not the rough natural rock of the tunnel. Man-made. When he came closer, his dimming light showed cracks laced through the concrete. They brought to mind a strange memory, an image of the cracked driveway of his childhood home. Basketball games with his father, the two of them using the cracks for locating shots in H-O-R-S-E. *Shoot from this one.* A sneaker toeing a split in the stone.

He ran his hand over the wall. Some of the cracks were deep enough that he could fit his hand into them. Not big enough to let him through, though.

No choice now but to go back.

He sagged against the wall. The whole painful journey felt pointless. He'd affected nothing.

You said you were going to take a look. That's all. Take a look and tell them what you found.

All right, then. Finishing the job meant going back to report his findings. He knew the way easily enough, because it was a straight shot, no diversions, no choices. No need for the headlamp, even, and it was dimming, so he should conserve power. He could make the walk back in blackness and save the light for a moment when he might actually need it.

He reached up and clicked it off. The world went dark—but not black.

There was still some light in the tunnel. Filtered slats of pale gray light, like dawn breaking through the trees.

He turned back to the concrete wall.

The cracks were letting light bleed through.

That was how close he had come to making it all the way across. There was open air between him and the surface. He couldn't sneak through the cracks, but if light could . . .

He unclipped his radio once again.

71

A narrow ledge of chilled, damp stone ran just inside the top of the wall. Gillian crawled across it on her hands and knees. She didn't have to go far, though. She could see them in the water just below.

She could finally see them.

They were underwater but they moved without regard for it. Slipped through the water the way most people passed through air. There were two dozen of them at least. Maybe thirty. All at work, a beautiful synchronized effort of smashing, chipping, and shoveling. They were pale and gaunt, yes, but as she watched them she thought that Aaron Ellsworth had been wrong. They weren't tired. They were focused. Complete concentration could be misunderstood by outsiders. Unless you understood the mission, unless you shared it, you might misinterpret righteous effort for suffering.

Somewhere on the other side of the wall, back in daylight, her father screamed her name. It barely registered, though. It was background noise, soft static. The only sounds that mattered were on this side of the wall. The crack of metal on stone, the rasp of shovel blades, the cascading rock fragments.

The proof of a promise.

She told me the truth. All of those awful stories were not so awful after all. My grandmother told me the truth, and I disregarded it, disregarded her. Dishonored her.

She looked up the tunnel and into the blackness. How far had they come? All the way from the Chill. All the way beneath the mountain.

Just as she'd been promised. They'd had to come without her, though. Her own promise unkept.

"I'm sorry," she said aloud. Her voice echoed, boomeranging the meaningless apology back to her.

They didn't want an apology. They wanted help.

So join them.

Of course. That choice was obvious, wasn't it? She'd denied them and betrayed them, yes, and she was late, yes, but it was never too late to help. They wouldn't deny her. Galesburg had always welcomed, never refused. Until people came to claim it—to steal it and destroy it—Galesburg had never refused anyone. Only then had they fought back.

Sin flows downhill, her grandmother would say, time and again. *The city's sins up here can't be forgotten, and they will flow downhill in time.*

Gillian remembered all of the ancient faces in old photographs, old sketches. She saw some of the faces in the water below her now. They paid her no mind, because they were hard at work. Just the way she should be. It was the only lesson that she couldn't afford to forget, and she'd forgotten it—no, *denied* it, even worse—for too long.

She was a Mathers. She was of Galesburg. She knew the burdens of that, and she knew how to accept them.

What about New York, though? What about Queens? Her other home. Home to enemies of Galesburg.

It hadn't been so bad in Queens. It had been *good* in Queens. The first place where Gillian had seen people who looked like her on a regular basis. The first place where Gillian had heard different stories of different faiths, no one feeling the deep need to protect her from other ideas, to remove her from the world. The city, her prophesied enemy, hadn't been so evil in the end. They'd been ignorant of what had happened up here—that much was true—but did they deserve to suffer for it? To die?

Gillian's old babysitter, Mrs. Baerga, still lived in the apartment below Gillian's father. She was nearing ninety now. She lived alone, still

swearing in Spanish at the Mets games and still cooking the most marvelous food. She was the only person alive with whom Gillian had ever
spoken of sacrifice. The only person she'd come close to telling about
Galesburg.

Sacrifice is about salvation, Mrs. Baerga had said. *Not vengeance.
Whoever told you that story used the wrong word.*

She was such a kind woman. She didn't walk well now, and she was
alone. Who would come to help her when the city went dry?

*It's bigger than her. Bigger than you, bigger than Galesburg. They have to
be reminded of their sins. Punished for them. Or they'll repeat the pattern.*

Down below, in the water, one of the pale faces turned skyward.
Looked up at the surface—looked directly at Gillian.

It was her grandmother.

She wore the same clothes she'd had on the day she went missing.
Hiking pants and a loose button-down shirt, the sleeves rolled above
thin forearms. She held a pick in her hands. Her lips, so often curled into
a smile that suggested a barely suppressed laugh, were now squeezed
into a thin line. Her eyes, no longer blue but a dark, expressionless gray,
were fixed on Gillian's.

Tired, Aaron Ellsworth had said, and maybe he had not been wrong.
She looked exhausted. How could she not be? All of these years, all of
this work, waiting on help.

Waiting on Gillian.

"I'm sorry," Gillian said again, and again her voice echoed, drawing
no response except for a shout from her father on the other side of the
wall.

Beneath the surface, as picks whirled and shovels spun, her grandmother stood stock-still in the chaos, staring up at her, just as she'd
stood in front of the chalkboard in the secret schoolhouse room, waiting. Waiting on Gillian to give the right answer, make the right choice.

It was true, her eyes seemed to say. *So what are you doing up there?
Where do you think you belong, dear?*

A pick hit the wall and then a rock broke free just below Gillian's right foot. She tried to shift and keep her balance, but her foot slipped, and then her hand reached for salvation but found nothing but blackness.

She was facing her grandmother when she fell into the water.

72

The photographer came on down the trail and didn't say a word. He hadn't changed a bit since the day Deshawn had spoken to him about the source of the city's water, since he'd been shown that photograph of the long, empty road through the silent valley. The day Teddy Biddle had posed for the camera.

Deshawn pushed back against the fence post as if he could retreat. The handcuff bit at his wrist. He looked at the basin wall.

No sign of his daughter.

The photographer set up his tripod just ten feet from Deshawn, looked in the viewfinder of the camera, and then stepped back and assessed the scene, his eyes working from top to bottom—the distant peaks, the gorge slope, the crumbling wall—and, finally, down to Deshawn.

He smiled then, his teeth startlingly white against the jet-black beard.

"Remarkable shot," he said. "Don't you think?"

Deshawn didn't answer. He thought that speaking to the man—*not a man; I don't know what he is, but* man *is not the word*—was very dangerous. Better to follow his own advice, then—the counsel he'd given to Aaron Ellsworth—and pass by with his head down.

Deshawn could no longer pass by, though.

The photographer lifted one hand, his long, thin fingers extended, and swept it through the air. "Just look at it," he said. "The landscape itself, so lonely and rugged. Traces of the old wilderness. But then pan down . . . and we have the wall. Ah, a human touch! Wilderness conquered. But there's a problem with the wall, isn't there? It seems to be crumbling." He squinted, cocked his head. "And that square of blackness is rather enchanting. Is it an entrance into the mountain, or an exit from within it? A matter of perspective, no?"

His eyes flicked away.

"Below the wall, we have the fence. Progress. Stone becomes iron here. But it seems there's a problem with the fence, too! It's decaying and abandoned. Forgotten." His eyes lowered again, locked on Deshawn's, and his face split into that bright smile once more. "Oh, and another problem with the fence: there's a man chained to it! You'd have to frame that right, because the symbolism is rather heavy-handed in the foreground, don't you think? And yet, the image is the reality. That's an artist's challenge, I assure you. Can you be starkly honest and still nuanced? I think you can."

He stopped smiling. "I think I have been."

Deshawn spoke then despite himself. Croaked out his question.

"How do you do it?"

"Do what, sir?"

"Capture them. Force them to stay down there. Is it the camera?"

The bearded man's eyes widened. "Is it *the camera*? You think I'm, what, stealing souls with a photograph?" A rich laugh echoed off the stone and water at Deshawn's back, creating a hideous chorus, each laugh chasing the other. "I don't mean to mock, particularly a man in your condition, but that's quite an amusing idea."

"It's the truth," Deshawn said. "I don't know how you do it, but you do. All these years, up and down the line, in tunnels and in reservoirs, in the work camps and in the construction sites. You've captured lots of them. How many?"

The bearded man seemed aggravated now. He stepped closer and knelt so his eyes were level with Deshawn's.

"They write the story," he said. "They always have. I just document it, sir. Someone must."

"It's more than that," Deshawn said.

"Perhaps. But there's a difference between an author and an archivist. Choices were made, I assure you of that. Choices must always be made, and I didn't get to make them for you. Not you, or any of the ones who came before you. I just happened to be in the right place at the right time. It's not so hard to find, really. A keen ear and a sharp eye. I watch and I listen."

"For what?" Deshawn said. His mouth was dry and his wrist ached and he knew that he should stop talking, he was sure of that, and yet he couldn't. He wanted to know.

"Contempt," the bearded man said. His good-humored voice was empty now.

"Contempt of what?"

Another wave of the hand, a gesture across mountains, woods, and water.

"All of it," he said. "All that they do not understand and yet claim dominion over. The absolute faith in their own power. That is the contempt I seek. I assure you, it has not been hard to find."

Deshawn couldn't stop looking into the man's eyes now. They seemed to have taken on a liquid motion. The man himself looked ageless, but the eyes looked ancient. Eternal.

"Have you always been here?" Deshawn whispered.

"Here? Of course not. I go where the work takes me. I hope the work is discovered and understood." He gave a disappointed sigh. "Being discovered isn't nearly as hard as being understood. My work is known. Cave paintings in Rome. Carvings in Tenochtitlán. Some stone reliefs near Athens that I understand are quite well regarded. All sadly misunderstood. But in time? We'll see."

Only two of the three places he'd named had had any meaning to Deshawn, but looking into the man's dark eyes, the message seemed clear. He stared, both entranced and horrified, as the pupils roiled and spun and seemed to sink, waterfall-like, into themselves.

"You destroyed those places," he said.

"No such thing. As I've told you, I make no decisions."

"New York," Deshawn whispered.

"Pardon?"

"You've come for New York."

The smile came again. "We'll see, won't we? They promise me a land of stories there. Eight million daily, or some such? We will see."

"It won't work," Deshawn said.

The undulating eyes widened. "No?"

"You can hurt it. You proved that last night. You can hurt it badly, maybe. But you can't break it. Not the whole thing."

The bearded man looked at Deshawn with real interest. Studying him.

"That's some real confidence," he said. "What if you're wrong?"

"I'm not," Deshawn whispered.

The bearded man nodded with detached amusement.

"Of course you're not," he said. He straightened and stepped back. "I'm afraid I'll have to cut this exchange short. You've been most engaging, but you're not the subject of the day. No matter how tempting the whole tableau appears."

He smiled and then returned his attention to the camera.

73

Gillian sank slowly and landed on her feet. After the initial shock, the water became a comfortable cold, pleasantly numbing. She expected to fall to her hands and knees, but the water helped hold her upright among the ghosts. The picks and shovels remained in motion. No one was going to give up their work for her. Not now.

She looked at them, waiting for recognition. For work. Many of the faces were familiar to her, but she wouldn't be to them. They'd been part of the crew for decades before she'd been born. They'd occupied photographs on the walls of the Galesburg School long after they'd died.

Something silver and bright flashed to her left, and she turned and saw an outstretched pick. She looked first at the curved steel head of the pick, which was chipped and nicked but still sharp and strong, and then looked up and saw who held it.

It was her mother.

Gillian had no memory of her. Only photographs and the stories her grandmother had told. Her dad hadn't told her any stories of the two of them. Only that her mother had been a kind woman but a confused one.

Now they stood together in the water, and Gillian was vaguely aware that she had no need to fight for breath, that she had no real sense of being underwater at all. All that mattered was the woman in front of her.

More motion to her right. Another pick offered. This one in her grandmother's hands.

Molly Mathers stood just beside Gillian, close enough to touch. She looked the same as she had on the day Gillian last saw her, only without the same emotion in her eyes, the sense of life. Looking into her eyes was like looking at Christmas lights in broad daylight when they seemed empty and foolish and sad, before darkness settled and restored their purpose.

Another silver flicker in the water, like a trout in the shallows. A hand on her wrist. Gillian turned to her left and saw that her mother had taken hold of her. The grip was as cold and strong as a handcuff.

You need to help them. It's your turn. The day you always knew was coming.

Her grandmother leaned close, pressing the pick into Gillian's hands. Her face was fine boned and elegant, the same as Gillian remembered hovering over her at bedtime each night, leaning down to leave a kiss on her forehead, the last touch of the day, usually the last sight of the day. Everything about her was familiar, and yet something was wrong.

Tired, Aaron Ellsworth had said. That was it. An overwhelming sense of fatigue. An exhaustion that knew no end.

She pressed the pick handle into Gillian's palm. Smooth wood, the finish worn down.

Help them, Gillian thought. *Fulfill your promise. Do your part.*

Gillian suddenly felt a throb rising through her skull, a tightening pressure that forced her eyes shut and trapped her breath. She thought that she would do anything to alleviate that pain. Absolutely anything.

Get air, then. You need air.

Or maybe she didn't. Maybe she needed to accept the pick and get to work. All she had to do was curl her fingers around the handle. The rest would take care of itself.

The caress of the worn wood in the dark felt just like the old desk under her palm in the schoolhouse. So familiar and so sacred. Like the idea of sacrifice.

Sacrifice is about salvation, Mrs. Baerga had said in her heavily accented English. *Not vengeance. Whoever told you that story used the wrong word. Lots of people would die for family, honey. But how many would die for a stranger?*

That question had never been asked in the Galesburg School. That question had troubled Gillian for years, because it was a good one. Now, down here in the water, with lungs burning and skull pounding, staring at her grandmother's phantom figure, Gillian wanted to ask it herself.

Why did you call it sacrifice when it was murder? Why was the only way to remind people of the pain suffered in Galesburg to inflict new pain on others? They're not bad people down there in the city. You just think they are because you never met them. Everyone is scared of the other until they actually meet. It changes then. I wish you knew how quickly it changes.

Her grandmother stared at her, eyes flat, lips sealed. There would be no answers coming down here. There would certainly be no questions.

That was the problem with Galesburg—there had never been any questions. Just the demand for obedience.

Gillian pushed the pick away. Stumbled backward, hit the wall. The throbbing in her skull was gathering pressure, threatening to burst. Her lungs begged for air. Her mother and grandmother approached with their picks outstretched, waiting, waiting ...

I didn't volunteer, she thought frantically. *I fell, that was all. I'm not here to help. I do not want to help.*

The wall shivered behind her. Someone stepped back from it. She looked up, looking for help, but saw the face and recognized it: Jeremiah Fleming. She'd sketched him so many times. He was smiling, but not at Gillian. He was smiling at the wall, which was still shivering—no, shaking now, a more violent sensation. The wall was shaking and the water was roiled by falling rocks.

It's coming down, she realized as her vision grayed and the throbbing in her skull pounded at her eyes and ears as if seeking an exit. The water whirled around her as the others stepped back, all of them smiling now, and Gillian turned and saw that the black hole was widening as the rocks fell unaided, the whole ancient structure separating and collapsing. Somewhere on the other side, her father waited. She couldn't reach him, but she knew that she wanted to be on the right side of the wall when she drowned. She didn't want to die here, not even with her family.

She pushed off the bottom and lunged toward the collapsing rock wall. A hand grasped at her arm but Gillian tore free, reached for one of the stones that had not yet fallen, and pulled herself upright and through the widening hole. A rock struck her leg, another hit her shoulder. Somewhere up ahead was daylight.

She fought toward it even though she knew that it was too late and that the surface was out of reach.

74

The rain had begun again. A thin, sheeting mist. The clouds screened out any trace of the sun, and the Chilewaukee lay in shadow as the demolitions team installed the second round of charges. Drill bits whirred, boring through the old concrete. Dust rose. Explosives were passed from hand to hand and packed into the new holes. Fuse cord linked the charges, tracing the stone face like tangled fishing lines.

Mick stood with Anders Wallace, indifferent to the soaking rain, watching patiently. There was no need to rush. After so long a process, the end would come in a hurry.

Ben Quirk had walked down to observe the charge placement. Now he walked back to Mick. His eyes were ringed with dark, swollen circles, but within them was a glimmer of hope. No, not just hope: confidence.

"It's going to work," he told Mick.

Mick nodded. Ben was right and wrong all at once. A beautiful contradiction that showed how little Ben understood of the world.

"I think so, too," Mick said, and then someone shouted over him.

"Hey! Quirk! You hearing this?"

Ben pivoted, looked back at the man who'd shouted to him, and said, "Hearing what?"

"Put on the emergency band! Listen!"

Quirk took his radio off his belt. Mick watched as he changed the band and turned the volume up.

"I'm right on the other side," a voice called through static, and Mick felt a chill. He knew the voice. Who was it? How did he know that voice?

"What's he mean, on the other side?" Quirk shouted.

"He says he's right on the other side of the fuckin' stone!"

For a moment, no sound but the rain and the static. Mick looked at Anders Wallace. Anders was staring at the intake chambers. He looked troubled. Mick had never seen him look troubled before. Angry, yes, but not like this. This was almost fear.

"Who's speaking?" Quirk said into the radio.

Yes, Mick thought, *who? Whose voice is that, and why does it fit? Why does it somehow make sense in this moment?*

Static. Crackle. Then: "Aaron Ellsworth. Sheriff Ellsworth's son."

"Whose son?"

"The sheriff of Torrance County. Who am I talking to?"

"The hell is happening?" Ben Quirk said in astonishment, looking at Mick as if Mick could explain. Mick just stared. He felt control slipping away from him, receding like the floodwaters had done hours earlier. A force of nature one moment, then gone the next.

Quirk shook his head, lifted the radio again, and spoke into it.

"You're talking to the Army Corps of Engineers, among one hell of a lot of others. What do you mean, you're *right on the other side*?"

Static. Crackle. "Just what I said. I'll set off a chemical light. Your guys on the stone face will see it. It might take them some searching, but I promise you, they'll see it."

Words were exchanged from the team on top of the ridge to the men on the ropes below. Nods and hand signals, and then the men on the ropes began sidestepping across the concrete face of the intake chambers, moving on the balls of their feet, staring into the fractured rock. They were just above the waterline. Another blast, and the steeply graded tunnels would fill with water. The reservoir would empty into them. Just one more blast was all it would take; Mick was sure of it.

The rope team passed slowly over the rock, then dropped even lower, their feet actually in the water now, and worked back the way they'd come. This time one of them stopped. He hung there, suspended, attached to the forest above by the ropes, attached to the rock by the tips of his feet. Half in the water, half out. After a long moment he moved one hand to his mouth. The next voice on the radio was his.

"Affirmative. I'm seeing it. He's not far back."

A tide of chaos rose. Voices from all directions. Mick was vaguely aware of Ben Quirk yelling at everyone to shut up. Then Quirk was lifting the radio again.

"Where the hell did you come from, Ellsworth?"

Static. Crackle. "The other side of the mountain. The old discharge basin."

Ben Quirk sank down onto his ass. He was still holding the radio to his mouth, but he hadn't spoken. He just stared at the intake chambers, where his demolitions crew waited.

"That can't be true," he said finally.

Static. Crackle. "It's true. The tunnels go all the way through. Send someone down there to look."

Quirk lowered the radio and turned slowly. Stared at Mick.

"That's not possible," he said. "Is it?"

Mick didn't answer. He looked for Anders Wallace. Anders had moved away. He was walking away from the tunnels, out toward the high side of the dam.

Mick followed.

75

When the wall began to crumble, Deshawn stared into the widening darkness, searching with less and less hope for any sign of his daughter. The hole in the mountain was exposed now, but Gillian was nowhere in sight.

The photographer had been leaning down, eye to the camera, but he stepped back abruptly and looked up at the sky.

Deshawn followed his gaze. The morning sun was gone and bleak clouds had filled in again, but he had no idea what had drawn the man's attention. The photographer studied the sky for a few seconds. He seemed dismayed.

"Well," he said. "That was unanticipated."

Deshawn knew better than to speak, he really did, and yet . . .

"What happened?" he said. He couldn't help himself.

The photographer looked at him.

"Nothing," he said. "And that is just the trouble."

Deshawn didn't understand, but now the man was removing the camera with its troubling, oddly bright silver lens from the tripod, gathering his gear with the mild disappointment of a photographer whose sunset had been ruined by unexpected clouds. A shame, yes, but hardly a crushing blow. There would be other days and other sunsets.

"Take care, sir," he said. "I'll see you down the road." The photographer pointed at the peaks around them. "Something to remember, Mr. Ryan? The mountains don't sleep. People think they do, but people are wrong, and it's a dangerous thing to forget. The mountains don't sleep;

they creep. Ask any geologist. Think about how much of our earth has moved over time and how far it has come."

He seemed to want a response, be it an argument or agreement. Deshawn said nothing.

"There's nothing stagnant in this world," the photographer said. "That's what you must remember. Everything is in motion. The molecules are either in balance or at war, do you see? This world promises us only one thing: motion. Action. The world is never passive. Never."

Deshawn nodded. He did not want to exchange any more words. He wanted only for the photographer to leave.

"We'll see each other again," the photographer said.

This time Deshawn shook his head.

The photographer laughed.

Then he vanished into the trees and the rain.

76

Gillian felt the rain on her face before she opened her eyes, and then the brightness surprised her, so she closed them again and returned to darkness.

That was when the water rushed in on her, pummeling her. It filled her nose and mouth and suddenly she was thrashing, fighting it, fighting her way back to the surface, fighting to get out of the darkness and into the blinding light.

When she made it, gasping and choking, her eyes opened again, and she saw that the light wasn't so blinding at all. It was the dim, leaden light of an overcast day. She was treading water, and stone walls surrounded her. Forested slopes climbed above them, chasing up to distant peaks and the gray sky above.

Reality crept back in stages. Memory followed it but kept at a safe distance, as if unsure of things, as if to rush on her would mean disaster.

Someone was shouting her name.

She turned toward the sound and saw her father up above. He was looking down from the rim of the chamber basin, on his knees beside the fence.

No, he was *handcuffed* to the fence. She saw it and felt that it was her fault but couldn't remember how or why.

She floated, staring up at her father. "What did I do?" she said.

When she spoke, he sagged against the fence post. There was sense of relief in him that she didn't understand. There was not much at all that she understood at that moment.

"Dad?" she cried. "What did I do?"

Her father shook his head. "It doesn't matter," he said. "Just get the hell out of there, Gillian!"

In the distance, sirens were wailing. Coming closer. Coming down the road. She remembered the road; she remembered the trail. She remembered that Aaron Ellsworth had gone into the water. Where was he now?

Overhead was the staccato thump of a helicopter. The chopper was coming in low. She watched it hover, its nose pointed toward the mountain, as if someone was inspecting the scene. She looked in the same direction. Most of the far wall was gone, the stones knocked free in an orderly fashion. A gaping chasm of darkness lay beyond. She thought she saw motion in there. Maybe light, too. And was there a voice? If the sirens and the helicopter were silenced, would she be able to hear a—

"Gillian! You need to get out of there!"

This voice she heard undeniably. Her father was calling for her.

She turned away from the hole in the wall, swam to the side of the basin, found a jutting piece of stone to grab ahold of, and began to climb.

When she reached the fence, the cold and the fatigue finally hit her. The fence loomed between Gillian and her father. It wasn't so high, but she wasn't in climbing condition. She could see him but couldn't get to him.

"I need a second," she stammered through chattering teeth. Her back muscles cramped and she leaned forward to avoid a spasm. Her father reached through the fence, his left hand outstretched.

"Gillian. I've got you."

She took his hand. The sirens were right behind the tree line now, and she knew that they wouldn't be alone for long. He squeezed her hand tightly. Too tightly, but it felt good even with the pain. He turned away from her. He seemed uneasy, scanning the trees, searching the shadows.

"It's just the two of us," he said. "He's gone."

"Who is?"

He didn't answer. She rose shakily.

"Sit down," he said. "Help's coming."

"I'm coming across first," she said.

She made it on the first try, falling into the grass on the other side of the fence.

"Give me the key," her father said.

She looked at him blankly.

"For the handcuffs. It's in your pocket. You need to unlock me. When they get here, they can't see this."

She found the key with trembling fingers, bent to the cuffs, and unlocked them. He pulled his wrist free while Gillian released the opposite cuff from the fence post.

There were voices in the woods now. The sound of footsteps and snapping branches. People coming in a hurry.

"I'll explain it to them," her father said, and she was impossibly grateful for that, because she knew so little of what had happened here. "You okay? You can handle this?"

She nodded. "I'm good, Dad. I'm . . ."

Stoic, she thought, the word floating in a memory. But she just repeated, "I'm good."

Then the police burst through the tree line. Three of them, weapons drawn. A man in a military uniform behind them. The cops looked at Deshawn and Gillian. She found her badge, held it up. The military man barely glanced at them. He was staring at the hole in the wall. The hole in the mountain.

"*Holy shit,*" he said in a whisper that was almost reverent. "Is this where he went in?"

"Yes," Deshawn Ryan told them. "We don't know what happened to him."

"He walked through," the man in uniform said. "All the way to the other side."

"Swam," Gillian said. The man looked at her for the first time.

"How'd you find it? How did you know?"

She didn't have an answer, and she felt trapped and exposed all at once, felt like a criminal, not a cop. Then her father answered for both of them.

"I was here once before," he said. "A long time ago. I thought the place seemed dangerous then. I thought it would be a problem in a flood." He paused. "I wanted to give it another look, that's all."

A nice white lie, Gillian thought. *The right choice for today. Don't mention the dead men in the tunnels who offered instruction. Police tend to frown on that sort of excuse.*

"Well, bud, we're awfully glad you did. We were about to pour a few hundred million gallons of water through here and right on downstream."

"You stopped it?" Gillian asked.

"I think so."

They'll move on, she thought. *They won't get trapped again. They'll have to go slower without the floodwater to help, but they will move on downstream. They won't have the right force any longer, but Galesburg, like gravity, is always working.*

77

Aaron sat with his back against the fractured concrete wall and watched the chemical light burn down to a neon dusk, like a dimming bar sign. The chemical light was a more sophisticated version of the things they handed out to people at rock concerts. You had to crack it to trigger the chemical reaction, and then it glowed.

He remembered the Fourth of July at the city park in downtown Torrance, the same park where he'd helped retrieve at least a dozen bodies from the floodwaters. The Fourth of July had been his father's favorite holiday—and the only day he'd always take off work. He'd stay in uniform, but it was a family day all the same.

There was a bandstand in the center of the park, and merchants set up alongside and sold food and trinkets, junk souvenirs and deep-fried treats. There had been one tent filled with multicolored chemical lights. When Aaron was young, he was fascinated by them, and something about that amused Steve Ellsworth. He'd buy a half dozen of them and parcel them out, laughing each time Aaron carefully cracked the plastic tubing in inch-long segments, making sure to soak out all of the light that was possible.

Water seeped along his neck, but he didn't move away. It was a reminder of how close he was to the Chill: the big lake was pressing against his back, separated by only a few feet of cracked concrete.

He stared down the tunnel and tried to imagine all of the water pouring through. What would it have done? Ripped through here, charged through the basin, down Cresap Creek, and then on to the Ashokan.

Then what?

He couldn't imagine, but someone had been imagining that very thing, though. A lot of people, actually, for a lot of years. How many were down there, he had no idea, but the tunnels had taken time.

Already he knew that he wasn't going to try to explain them. He'd listened over the radio as help arrived in the discharge basin and discovered the hole in the wall. Listened to Deshawn Ryan and Gillian Mathers offer their explanation: Deshawn had been there years ago, and he thought it might have proved dangerous after the flood.

Some guess, Aaron thought. One hell of a guess.

He didn't blame Deshawn for the lie, though. He didn't think it would go well to explain that dead men in tunnels under Queens Boulevard had sent him north, and that Aaron had gone into the water, swimming past men and women with gaunt gray faces and flickering steel picks who were knocking down the wall one block at a time.

An intuition was the better story. A nervous father's hunch. People would want to believe that one.

His radio crackled back to life. The National Guard was in the discharge basin now. They were sending a team in to get him.

"You're sure it's a straight shot?" the man on the radio asked. "Nobody's going to peel off and head down a dead end, get lost?"

"It felt like a straight shot to me," Aaron said. Maybe he'd passed other corridors in the dark. He didn't think so, though. It had been a long walk, and at times a steep one, but it had been straight enough.

"I can come back to meet them," he said. "They don't need to come in for me. My light's burning down anyhow. I can make it back."

The way back wouldn't be so hard. It would be slow and painful, but he had no doubt that it could be done.

"Negative, Ellsworth. Sit tight, and we'll have you out soon."

So he waited. Sat there with the chemical light dying at his feet. The contracting light made the room feel bigger. The molecules that provided the glow played well together, but only for so long. They burned bright for a while, but then something in their relationship fell apart, and the light died. He didn't know the science of it, how such a thing could produce such a bright glow and then fall out of balance and fade to darkness, but at least it went slowly. It was nice to know when something was leaving you. To have the chance to prepare for the absence.

Water dripped out of the cracks, traced the back of his head, slid down his neck, and plinked onto the stone floor. The big lake whispered to him from the other side of the wall. He liked listening to it. A soft and peaceful sound. Hard to believe that it was the same water that had ripped through his town like the devil's plow, shearing Torrance to the bone.

Could've been worse, though. All the dead, all the buildings destroyed … and it was just a taste.

When the tunnel swelled back to brightness, he thought it was his chemical light catching some final flare. Then he realized it was coming toward him.

The rescue team was here. It seemed too fast, after the walk Aaron had made. He wondered how they'd done with the swim.

Then they came into view, and he realized they were carrying scuba tanks.

He started to smile then. Couldn't help himself. He was grinning like a fool when they gathered around him, but they started smiling back, and he saw that they thought he was just glad to see them, that was all. He realized then that he *was* glad to see them. Awfully damn glad.

"Ready to get out of here, Ellsworth?" the point man said. There were three others behind him.

"Yeah. More than ready." He struggled upright, lurching to his left, keeping his balance on his left leg.

"We understand you're injured," the point man said. Behind him, the others were already unfolding a rescue sling.

"My foot," Aaron said. "But it's not bad. I made it in; I can make it out."

"All due respect, Officer? We're not going to let you do any more walking or swimming. Not today."

Officer? Aaron looked at him, confused, then down at his uniform. Saw the Coast Guard insignia illuminated in the dying green-yellow light.

"Oh," he said. "The uniform isn't real. Well, it's real, but it's not . . . I didn't earn it."

He was trying hard to make sense, because it mattered a great deal, but the point man seemed disinterested.

"I'm pretty sure you earned it today," he said.

He guided Aaron down and into the sling. Aaron wanted to object, wanted to come out the way he'd come in, but the pain was strong now, and they lifted him easily. He complied, because he knew that it was a dangerous and frustrating task to save someone who was determined to fight you.

"We'll have to do a bit of underwater work at the end," the point man told him. "I guess you know that, but it'll be different this time. Just trust us, okay?"

"Yes, sir," Aaron said. "Thank you."

They were about to haul him out when he saw the chemical light resting on the stone floor. Not much left to the glow now, just a glimmer of decaying golden light on the dark stone, but still he reached out and snagged it as they carried him by.

He wasn't sure if it could hold the light for the remainder of the trip, but he didn't want to leave it behind, either. He held it to his chest, closed his eyes, and let himself be rescued.

78

Anders Wallace walked up the slope of the dam and out across the top of it to the edge above the spillway, to the crumbling earth that was all that remained of the place where the gatehouse had once stood. Mick followed, and when Anders sat, he sat beside him.

For a long time they didn't move. It was as if no one had seen Mick go. He could hear the distant voices and chaos back near the intake chambers, and sirens wailed and helicopters thrashed the sky, but up here on the bluff with the tailwaters far below, Mick felt detached from all of it.

"I didn't think we could be interrupted," he said at length. "Not before it was finished."

"That was unforeseen," Anders Wallace agreed in a distant voice. He hadn't looked directly at Mick since Aaron Ellsworth made his radio call and illuminated the cracks in the stone.

Mick was frustrated. He wanted an explanation. Wanted to know how the Galesburg crew's tunnels, so long in the making, had been interrupted by such an inconsequential man.

"How could they be stopped?" he asked.

"No one was stopped."

"It feels like it."

"There will be another day," Anders Wallace said. "Another place. We move downstream. It's that simple, sir. A steady process. A patient one. There's no other choice, after all. Not when you're committed." He rose and looked out across the lake and then back to the tailwaters, to the overturned earth and severed trees, the ripped slabs of stone and twisted iron scattered in pools of trapped floodwater.

"Time to move on," he said.

Mick felt a pulse of dread laced with shame. He had failed. He'd promised them good work, and he hadn't been able to see it through. They seemed like a dangerous crew to disappoint.

"Tell them I tried," he said. "Tell them it was almost done and that I made the right choices. I couldn't anticipate the things that I couldn't see. That's the only trouble. It's the things you don't see that cause the worst problems."

"You can explain it when we're downstream."

Anders stepped out onto the lip of the ruptured dam. Loose soil crumbled and fell beneath him. Fell far, far down and scattered in the carnage below.

"I don't want to follow you," Mick said. "I tried my best, but I'm not going to follow you now."

For the first time since they'd come up here, Anders turned to face him. "Actually, Mr. Fleming . . . you have to. Time on the surface is fleeting, sir. You'll have to serve below now."

79

A dozen people saw him jump. By evening, when the social media surge had carried it along to the point that the network news shows decided they might as well join in, several million more had watched.

In the hour after the Ashokan Reservoir had been saved from catastrophic flooding that might have rippled on down the chain and all the way to the city, eliminating fresh water from millions, Mick Fleming, chief engineer in charge of dam safety, walked to the top of the wounded dam, faced the lake, and turned to look out across the valley, at what was left of the village of Torrance.

Then he'd stepped right off. Stepped, some people observed as they scrutinized the horrific footage, as if he'd expected a staircase was waiting for his foot rather than thin air. It was a casual motion, almost nonchalant. Head down, hands in his pockets, two steps out and then the last, walking with apparent confidence.

He didn't make a sound when he fell. No scream, no cry for help. Down he went, eighty feet, until he met an upturned slab of stone that had once been the facing of the old Chilewaukee spillway.

The rain was falling hard, and by the time the first rescuer arrived, most of Mick Fleming's remains had been rinsed off the rock and into the floodwaters.

A few days of speculation followed before the FBI confirmed that they were investigating the actions taken by Fleming in the hours before the breaching of the dam, as well as ballistic evidence connecting his personal handgun to the murders of Arthur Brady, the dam operator, and Sheriff Steve Ellsworth.

The strange step into open air began to make a bit more sense then.

There would be an investigation and there would be investment, officials from all corners promised. Federal, state, and city organizations united in a task force. Vulnerabilities at other reservoirs, dams, and supply tunnels were being inspected and addressed. Money flowed. Blame was scattered and conspiracy theories abounded, but all parties agreed on one thing: the disaster at the Chilewaukee would not be repeated.

To the families of the 712 souls who had died in Torrance, this was a cold comfort.

80

They broke ground on the new Arlington Heights Inn on the last week of January, and it was snowing, but no one minded.

Everyone appreciated the snow that winter. After two months of demolition and destruction, after two months of a daily tableau of heartbreak and horror, gutted foundations and crushed roofs and downed trees and everywhere the stink of the flood, the blanket of white snow was most welcome in Torrance. The Catskill winter painted over the town's past, buried the carnage, and left a clean, bright landscape in its place.

Gillian and Aaron went down for the groundbreaking together. The Christmas lights were still up throughout the areas of town that had survived or had already been rebuilt. No one seemed to want to take them down.

The glitter of the lights and the clean snow and the brisk northerly wind made it feel like a less solemn affair, a more festive one. There was the first hesitant, experimental sense of fresh life in the air. The applause that went up when the first shovel overturned dirt felt genuine.

No one turned to look at the 712 candles that burned on the courthouse square. Not that night.

Gillian signed her pledge to return to the building—most of the survivors were returning to the Arlington—and then she went back to the Ellsworth house with Aaron. She'd stayed there nearly every night since the flood. Her own home was gone—both of them, if you counted the old house in what had once been Galesburg, swept away—but still she'd turned down all offers of reassignment to another precinct or a return to the city.

It was the wrong time to leave, she said, and she was the right person to stay. The DEP needed people who understood the town, its people, its losses. Its resilience. They needed people who were of the place.

They needed Gillian Mathers.

Aaron had been working with the county all winter. There was no shortage of work for the road department, which had been tasked with much of the cleanup and rebuilding efforts. He made friends fast. People remembered him, and people knew the family name. That was important. It was good to know your neighbors. The night of the groundbreaking, Aaron was referenced by one of the speakers. No surprise there. After all, it was Aaron who'd stopped a cascading disaster that would have taken the troubles of Torrance and swept them all the way down to Manhattan. It was Aaron who'd made it through the tunnel.

The tunnel itself wasn't addressed at the groundbreaking. Not by the speakers, at least. There were plenty of theories, but the official inquest wasn't complete, and no official answers had been provided. Most people thought the shock of the dam breach had something to do with that split in the earth and the crumbling wall. Others suspected terrorism. They wondered if Mick Fleming had really been the lone-wolf actor that he was made out to be. Like Lee Harvey Oswald, he was too dead to answer questions, and that felt convenient, didn't it?

The commission would provide answers soon, everyone hoped. The commission, Gillian knew from her own numerous interviews, also seemed intent on *not* providing the public with a few troubling details about their emergency inspections up and down the Catskill aqueduct. Repairs were being performed, reservoirs had fresh funding, and Water Tunnel Number 3 was racing toward an accelerated completion date. When that was done, the old tunnels could be taken off-line for complete overhaul.

Gillian hadn't heard anyone speak of Galesburg. It seemed anyone who remembered the tragedies that had come before the Chilewaukee—fires, murders, a pact—did not connect it to the tragedies of Torrance.

That was the sane choice, of course. Galesburg was long gone.

The owner of the Hard Truth Brewery—also rebuilding, with tentative plans to start in the spring—jokingly asked Aaron when he'd run for sheriff. Aaron smiled it off politely. Gillian could tell that he appreciated the need for humor in the night, and she knew that he was also not comfortable with the joke. Not yet, at least.

They made the drive out of town together, her left hand on the steering wheel, her right hand on his thigh. They didn't speak, but that was all right. They were good in silence together. Maybe better, in fact. Until the hard nights came, and then it was important to break the silence.

It was so very important to do that.

Out of town and up into the hills, the snow was blowing harder, dancing through the headlights, a whirl of energy. There were already fifteen inches down and more on the mountains. It would be a good snowpack this year, with plenty of runoff in the spring. The repaired dam would welcome the water. The Chilewaukee would fill again, and there was talk of officially connecting it to the city's system after all these years. The fractured tunnel beneath the mountain could be viewed as either a threat or an opportunity. It would need to be done slowly, done right . . . but the water was there for the taking.

When that happened, Gillian thought it was important that she and Aaron remain in Torrance County. She wasn't sure what would come—how could you be? Nothing was promised—but she knew that it would be good to have a few souls left in town who'd seen things the others hadn't. A few who remembered the old stories.

She called her father that night. Told him about the groundbreaking, and the fresh clean snow, and the lights. Asked how he was holding up. Urged him again to retire. Move north, maybe, to be closer to her. Move south, soak up the sun.

He'd think about it, he said. He always said that.

They talked often, and they talked deeply, more openly than ever before. The only thing they didn't speak of were the ghosts in the tunnels.

She remembered her grandmother's teachings, though. One day, they'd walked up the hillside behind the house and her grandmother had pointed out all of the puddles, trapped water waiting in pockets of stone.

"Individually useless," Molly Mathers said. "They have no force, do they? They just sit there."

Then Molly had turned on the hose and poured water down from the hilltop. They watched as the puddles were claimed, joined up in the torrent, and swept downhill, carving a new channel through the earth.

"They have to help, then," Molly said. "They have no choice. Do you understand, dear? The puddles aren't good or bad. They're just waiting. And when the right amount of force is applied, they join it. They accelerate it."

Gillian had stared at the deepening furrow in the soil. Then she looked back up at her grandmother.

"But you turned on the hose," she said. "Without you, they'd stay where they were. Maybe even evaporate if you waited long enough."

"That's the point, dear. That is precisely the point."

Gillian remembered that conversation often now. Her father had told her that the ghosts in his tunnels meant no harm. She could believe that was true, but they were waiting on something, weren't they? And when it came for them, would they have a choice in the matter?

Maybe they would now. Galesburg had intended to explode downstream driven by trapped fury, a burst of pent-up energy. Instead it had been reduced to a trickle, a slow leak.

But still moving. They are still on the move.

She did not speak of this, though.

On the night of the groundbreaking, she told her father that she loved him, and then she hung up and sat with Aaron in the flickering light of the woodstove and watched the snow fall. The moon was out and the wooded, blanketed hills looked like a landscape painting, one that could have been done this year or a hundred years ago. Two hundred. You could imagine a truck out there in the snow, or a sleigh, or a horse. A lonely band of pioneers huddled against the winter wind. An Iroquois hunting party. You could look out at those hills in the moonlight and imagine absolutely any of them appearing in the distance. From the right vantage point in the Catskills, the place could look as if it had never changed at all.

Acknowledgments

Emily Bestler brought unflagging enthusiasm and tremendous editorial insight to this project from the first conversations to the final revisions, and I couldn't be more grateful. It's been a pleasure and a privilege, Emily.

The team at Emily Bestler Books and Atria is fantastic. Thanks to Libby McGuire, Lara Jones, David Brown, Milena Brown, Paige Lytle, Al Madocs, and everyone else who has worked so hard on behalf of the book and shown such enthusiasm and energy for it. That means more than you guys know.

Richard Pine is an authentic writer's champion. Thanks for believing, encouraging, and seeing it through, Richard, and thanks also to the rest of the gang at InkWell Management, and to Angela Cheng Caplan.

If you picked up this book, odds are that Nicole Dewey and Erin Mitchell had something to do with it. Many thanks.

Scott Carson owes a special debt of gratitude to his wife, who supported and then tolerated Scott's existence, and to his dog, who was always up for a hike, no matter the weather or time of day. These are the things that allow a book to be written, and so they should get the credit for anything good that comes of the book.

As for the cat's contributions . . . well, he shows up at the desk every day, and he's never feared a critic. There are good lessons there.

WELBECK

PUBLISHING GROUP

Love books? Join the club.

Sign-up and choose your preferred genres to receive tailored news, deals, extracts, author interviews and more about your next favourite read.

From heart-racing thrillers to award-winning historical fiction, through to must-read music tomes, beautiful picture books and delightful gift ideas, Welbeck is proud to publish titles that suit every taste.

bit.ly/welbeckpublishing